BLOOD OF ANGELS
The Books of Joy – Volume Two

Alexis Brooks de Vita

BLOOD OF ANGELS
The Books of Joy – Volume Two

DOUBLE DRAGON

A DOUBLE DRAGON PAPERBACK

ISBN 978-1-78695-488-6

Double Dragon
is an imprint of
Fiction4All

This Edition Published 2020
Fiction4All
www.fiction4all.com

Cover art by Deron Douglas
www.derondouglas.ca

DEDICATION

For my Children

CONTENTS

CHAPTER ONE
SOME OF THE PEOPLE COULD FLY:
THE WINGED DAUGHTER, BORN 1740

Some of the people could fly.

I could fly. But my mother could not. The gift was known to skip a generation.

So I stayed in the slaver's stone tower with my mother and helped her kill her other babies.

She said it would be wrong to let them live and be sold across the waters into chaos. When I killed them, she said they would fly free.

I dreamed of freedom. What was it?

To be a girl who left my mother's snug hut to fetch fresh water in a gourd on my head? A girl who swept the earth smooth between the huts on my father's compound dreaming that, when I married, I might be first wife someday. A girl who stood in the sun to pound *fufu* for my mother's dinner, her middle baby tied sleeping on my back. I saw such girls when I was allowed out of the stone tower where my mother walked in her chains. I heard of such girls when my mother held me and her tears ran into the parts between my tight braids and cooled my itching scalp.

My mother had once been such a girl. I would never be.

I was a girl whose head no one patted in the marketplace when our captor left me coins and let me out of the tower for market days. I walked between the mats of spread fish and the brown piles of cassava and yam, and people turned from me as I passed. When I stopped to buy, they took the bright money my father had given me and held it up to see it shine in the sun that danced in off the sea.

I walked alone.

I slept on damp stones with the smell of my mother's bitter sweat to warm me, instead of a cooking fire.

We never had fire. We ate our food raw or dried, just as I brought it up the stone steps from the market. For my mother had no fire pit in which to cook, and she had no stones worn smooth and charred black by many meals, and she had no coals left banked and waiting.

But when our captor came in the night, he brought fire. He held it high and stuck it on our wall, so I had to shut my eyes not to see my mother.

What good did it do me?

For I must run for seawater in the morning and watch her wash the cuts his beard had made on her cheeks and the places where she said he'd left her unclean. Then I dumped the bloodied water with my mother's scanty refuse in the sea.

Down the stone steps to bang on the splintered door and yell for a red-eyed guard to let me out.

Across the sinking sand to the lapping, stinging water.

And back into the dank dark where one window let in light, but not enough air.

Each morning, my mother wept as she cupped her hands in the half-gourd of cluttered brine I'd brought her and splashed it quickly on her burning places. She hissed with pain.

Her tears ran. She said she thought she would have finished crying by the time I was so big that I

10

could tend her, instead of a guard. But she had little left besides her tears.

And me.

And the beauty scars of the tribe that had rejected her and would never shelter me. For my very color was shame, like the brand burned onto people led to the big ships. My mother and I were never to act out of fear and flee.

My mother was sold to protect her village from invasion. Had the daughters and brides of the village's elders been seized instead-for slavers honored no traditions-then shame would have fallen on the ancient name of her people, forever. To my mother's way of thinking, in our banishment lay our dignity and our belonging to those who had sold my mother away.

"We must wait and bear our anguish until our captor's own sense of honor makes him send us home. For it is he, not we, who act without dignity." She stared out the window, head high, beauty scars shot with light from the sun.

"Mother, how can it be right to chain a woman who does not mean to flee? He gives you no chance to show him your honor."

My mother and I knew nothing, really, of our captor and his people. She thought all women lived as did the women in her village. And my mother felt she lived with dignity in her sorrow, for her shame preserved the honor of her people for as long as the world would live.

I was the one who felt no such thing.

"Why am I of less value than other girls?" I had not asked to be born the bleached color of the sand that led to the slavers' ships and their distant shores.

Where were the people who asked this sacrifice of us, to weep with us and thank us for their freedom?

My mother's honorable shame was bitter to me.

I walked alone. I had one dream. I had one hope.

I knew I lived only because my mother had no older child to do what I did, to sneak from the beach to the bushes back from the shore, pick the thorns and scavenge splinters from the fishermen's boats to drive into her newborns' soft little heads.

As long as I could remember, I had gathered the thorns and splinters in the months when my mother's belly grew round and the skin across it rolled with a live baby's kicks like thunder and cracked with pale brown scars like lightning, waiting to burst with life and death.

I gathered thorns in the months when the weight of the captor's body left my mother pressed into the stones in the morning, her head pillowed on the bones of my hip as she wept and begged her old gods in her old tongue for mercies they would never grant.

Or maybe they did grant them in their strange way.

For sometimes the little sand-colored babies were born dead, limp and wet with blood and slime into my hands, too little to keep them from sliding between my mother's spread legs across the wet stone floor.

She rolled her dark eyes open and smiled as the thin warm limbs and faces of her babies turned a color like bad fruit.

She never smiled when she made me jab the live ones in their heads. She would nurse them and

12

watch the greedy mouths suck. "You must do it for me, daughter. My hands. My soul. I cannot."

It was true. Her hands trembled as she held the live ones. "Only to empty the breast," she assured me. "To fill his stomach for his journey. Then you must send him on his way."

The women in the marketplace bore their newborns on their backs with pride and stopped haggling and gossiping just so everyone might wait and watch them nurse. Those women with circles of gold, bronze, and copper round their ankles to make music of their footsteps.

The music of my mother's footstep was the drag of her chain. A black band clutched each ankle and ate into her swollen feet. The chain between them made her shuffle as her babies fell from her body and she paced, raising her ritual cry to ancestors who would not hear her, did not care.

She prayed while I laid her babies in my half-gourd and started down the steps. I heard her as I waited at the barred door for the guard, the rush of ocean keeping time to her stumbling chants.

I buried her babies, tiny soft skulls first, in the cool sands. I thought of her useless prayers. I thought of flight and freedom and buried their wings last. "Go to the gods."

Someday I would soar in the sky like birds. Someday, when my mother or her captor died. And when I soared, I would think of these babies and fly for them, too.

"Weak," our captor said. It was a word I knew well. My mother, still bleeding from her births, hung her head out of the circle of his torchlight. "Too weak to sell, old dear. No use as a breeder. I don't know how you ever survived in the bush. Chin up now, you needn't cry. I don't need the money from your pickaninnies. Have no fear." His hands glowed pale and red in firelight as he reached for her.

Sometimes my mother lay on the stones where our captor left her and said her urgent morning prayers. I could not truly understand, for I never learned my mother's ancient tongue.

But I have often trembled and wept from her fury. Her rage has sent me running for the barred door and the sand and the stinging sea. When no one was near to see me, I have lifted my arms and cried to know what curse the gods unleashed on the world when they set these slavers loose in ships with sails.

"When will it end? Where will it leave my mother and me, when it ends at last?" And the question I cannot say. What chaos spewed them out?

When I asked this of my mother, she scolded. "Never think such a thing! To think is to bring to you! Think of-think of-" her eyes went dull "-birds in an empty sky that does not smell of salt." Her faraway village.

Is that how things come to pass? One thinks them into being? Then might I not think my mother and myself free?

Free.

I would rip off the rags of the slaver's shirt that hid my bent wings. I would stretch them and leap into the air and fly.

But what would bring our captor to the sense of honor that would make him set us free? I had no faith that he had a sense of honor.

But maybe if he had a second wife. Then *she*. . .

My dream of freedom took the shape of a woman like the captor who would come and see his first wife living as his prisoner. Might she not demand right behavior? Might she not demand that he set us free?

One morning, I rose from a new grave already lost in the sand to pray to the spreading sea. "A woman for the captor like himself. Let her come and see his dishonor and our shame. Let her demand change." And I went into the tower with my new faith and demanded of my mother that she pray in the tongue that the gods heard.

She was afraid. "Daughter, we do not know these people. We cannot know what such a woman would do."

"What do all women do? They spit on the ground in the marketplace at the mention of you and how we live. No fire. No home. Like animals!" I wiped my angry tears. "A second wife would refuse to be part of such a family. She would demand that he take off your chains." I pointed to make her cringe.

Such fear. Her brows twisted above her pleading, wet eyes.

She feared me as much as she feared our captor, in that moment when she knew I had called to her old gods in his unclean tongue. Without honor. Without shame.

Born of such a man, I acted as he did. Defied what was right and dared what was wrong. Refused our honorable banishment and wrapped a foreign tongue around sacred words.

Maybe it was my prayer.

Or maybe it was simply that the sea and the land, the villages and the gods that rule them hate lost people. They hate us, and they hold us in contempt.

For the sea licked the bleached bones of the babies sacrificed to my mother's village and its honor, and the sea heard my prayer. And the sea brought the captor a second wife, a woman from his own land.

With her, it brought my mother's death. And then the sea took me away.

I looked out of the tower with my mother when the pale woman came. My mother's black body gleamed with more than its usual sweat. The patterned scars on her cheeks lifted and moved as she talked. "She is coming. He said I am to keep you from her. Daughter, you knew him. You knew all along! He fears she will demand that he set me free."

She rested her hands on the stone ledge of the window and panted from the work of walking. She stared out.

This time, it was I who said, "Mother, I am afraid."

"You must not fear. You must watch with me. When you see her, go to her. Kneel before him and call him father. She must hear you call him father."

My mother had taken my wild thoughts and built upon them a hope of justice. Her hopes were just. What had she done to deserve chains? My mother's treatment was not as men were known to have treated women since time began.

And yet. . . .

My mother saw little from her tower window. She had not seen what I had seen upon the beaches. Long lines of women, men, even children, dragging down the sand to more towers and to waiting ships. Why would gods who watched such sights reach down from the sky or up from the sea to succor my mother and me?

What could I know of prayers, the ignorant child of a slaver? I watched with my mother at the window and waited for the woman who would speak for her. I dreaded what might come.

The sun rose and burned us through the bars. We shielded our eyes and watched through the stinging sweat of our hands.

The sun was high.

And at last, a woman wrapped tightly in layers of strange cloth that clutched her bosom and swept the sand behind her came walking. The captor walked beside her with his long gun. They came beneath my mother's window.

We stared at her and at each other. We hesitated to speak.

How could one be sure that this being was not a man? Her heavy tread bounced her into the air. The sand itself could not soften the blows of her step.

I faced my mother, hard and hot like the bars, like her chains. "He has lied to you. He has brought no one here but his brother." I waited to see her give in and give up my own mad dream of freedom.

Instead, she wiped her eyes and leaned her head against the bars to get a closer look at the strange creature.

Just at that moment, the person beside the captor raised its face and peered at the burning sun. Sunlight fell on and through its thin skin on a face that had never grown hair.

My mother's sweating hand pulled me toward her. Her eyes were lit with hope. "It is a woman! Go to her!"

I stared and made no move.

"Go to her." My own mother fell to her knees and begged.

What could I do? My mother held herself in honor and understood no one's scorn. But if I did not serve her, how could she serve herself? Who was she, and who would I be, if I did not act honorably toward her?

I walked down the stone steps.

The guard smiled at me. "Come to see the lady? Well, why not?" He pulled open the door and waved me on.

People lined the sands to stare at the strange woman and bow, as if to greet a great king. I followed the wave of bending backs and found my mother's enemies.

I caught up with them just before they entered the open gates of the fort. I rushed to grab the captor's hand. I fell on my knees in the scraping sand before him.

He looked down at me as if from the burning sky. His dry lips parted and said not a word.

"Please, father." My words burned in my throat. "Mother sends me with empty hands but with her

18

blessings to serve your second wife." My voice shook. I looked at the woman.

Up close, she was a skeleton covered with a thin layer of boiled skin. This was clearly why she kept her dying body wrapped so tightly in those cloths. Wisps of something thin grew from her head and flew in the air about her as she turned to see where I now pointed.

Back up at my mother.

In her tower window, my mother raised a hand and waved.

The slaver watched her.

His new wife raised a piece of cloth to where she had lost her lips and much of her nose. She made a sound like birds crying out over the sea. It seemed she could not breathe.

She turned and her eyes flamed red as she looked at the man. She gave up her struggle for words and looked again at my mother.

And at last she looked at me. Now her eyes were wide, white rimmed, and washed of that sudden color. She shook.

Fear drove me from my knees. I ran to pull my mother from the tower window. I only knew she was not safe. I did not know just how unsafe she was.

There was an explosion behind me. My mother's waving arm fell. I watched her, too, fall back from the window.

There were shouts. "Mad!" The captor. I understood nothing else.

Now there were explosions all around. Grunts as men ran and the clank of their long guns. My heart beat in my ears.

The guard stared open-mouthed before his open prison door. Blinded by the sun, I slipped past him and stumbled all the way up to the tower. I crawled on my knees to feel for my mother.

She sat, dazed, on the stone floor. Propped against the wall, her head rolled. Her eyes stared wide and sightless. She struggled to rise. One of her arms poured blood from shoulder to wrist.

I pushed her to the floor. "Lie down," I whispered. "Close your eyes. Be dead for them when they come for you."

I heard the sound of many men in heavy shoes scuff the stone steps. Harsh words I did not know. The captor's men ran in to fill the little cell, stepping on my hands and on my mother. They pulled her to her feet. She cried out from the pain in her shot arm.

The red-faced men carried my mother between them down the stone steps. She screamed and cried out for mercy all the way.

I followed.

When she reached the sand, someone knelt at my mother's feet to unlock the black bands on her ankles. The cuffs and chains were yanked away, their rattling muffled in the sand.

We all heard my mother's screams as the metal that had eaten into her ankles came free.

She wobbled, forced to stand. The men let her go. I rushed to ease her fall against my body. We sank together on our hands and knees.

"Run!" someone shouted.

The people who had lined the beach to watch the captor and his second wife all shouted, "Run!" My mother struggled to her feet, pushing against the sand that drank her flowing blood. Before she was up, she was already running headlong down the beach.

Was this to be our freedom? I started after her and ran beside her, shoving her up straight as she stumbled.

She ran into the sun as the people shouted. She pumped her one good arm, as though she thought she had grown a wing.

Had she forgotten that she could not fly? I thought of her babies with their useless wings, buried in the sand beneath our running feet. Would their spirits rise to meet my mother? Would we turn from the sea and start toward the inland villages?

And when we got there, would we at last be accepted with honor, to live in peace?

I smiled as the people from the marketplace and the fishing boats along the shore added their voices to the cry. "Run!" My foreign-tongued prayer had been answered. The gods had heard us, their lost people.

A crack, like a large stone breaking.

My mother pitched forward into the sand. Her arms flopped beside her. She lay flat and still.

I fell onto her back to cover the spreading bright circle of blood. It seeped through the belly of the shirt I wore to hide my wings.

Hands pulled me from my mother. Men surrounded me with long guns.

My mother was still in the sand when I last saw her.

Our captor spoke to his new woman as I was dragged before him. I hung between the hands of the men until they dropped me at his feet.

I watched my father reload his long gun.

"I already told you, my dear," he said to the skeleton woman. "Not that it is your business to concern yourself with such matters. But as I said, this woman was clearly mad. Some of them are. That means they are of no use and cannot be sold. The surest test is simply to set them free. If they run in the direction of their old villages, why then one can rest assured that they are as sane as the savage mind can be, and they are well worth keeping. But where was this one headed? You saw her. Running nowhere, toward wasteland, as mad as a hatter. Mad ones are a waste of food and water, both here and on board ship. No captain will buy them. There is nothing for it but to rid oneself of them, as I have done. It's business. That's all. No need being sentimental about such things."

He finished reloading his gun and braced it against one hip. The woman stared at me.

People murmured and shielded their eyes to look into the sun where my mother lay. I watched the captor.

He looked down at me. "I taught her little bastard English myself, you know. I would never have expected her to get up to such devilish tricks. There's simply no trusting them. They are a superstitious and underhanded lot."

The woman made a sound into the cloth at her mouth. A sob? Or had my mother just sobbed a last breath, out there alone on the sand? I tried but could not bring myself to turn toward my fallen mother. My eyes were fixed, mindless, on my captor.

He turned from me. "Well, there you have it, old thing. I regret that this is your introduction to the Gold Coast. But you can't say I haven't warned your father. Most excellent man, and all that, your father, but he won't hear reason, will he? This godforsaken shore is no place for a lady. Now, come along, old girl, or these blasted mosquitoes shall be the death of us."

He touched her bent elbow. His hand wavered toward her cheek but dropped away as she turned from me at last to start through the fortress gates.

He let her go ahead. Then he doubled back to strike me in the face with the butt of his reloaded gun.

And that is why I never saw my mother, nor the sand on which she died above her babies' bones, again.

For when I came to, I was on board a ship that had already set sail. The shore, my siblings' graves, and my fallen mother had all been left long and far behind.

CHAPTER TWO
MY MOTHER CAME RUNNING ACROSS OCEANS:
DAUGHTER, BORN 1753

My mother came running across the great lapping waters to America.

She did not wish to come. But her father had shot her mother and sold her to the ship's captain who brought him his new wife. My mother woke up in the captain's cabin. The ship rocked on the sea, headed to the land of her worst fears.

She could speak English. So she understood when the captain found her awake, tied and trembling in a corner of his cabin, and told her he might not sell her in America, if she did not want him to. She could be his cabin boy if she would tell none of his sailors that she was a woman.

He stripped away her old shirt and discovered that she was not only a woman. She had wings.

The captain had heard that Africa had such people, but he had never seen one. He sat in awe on his hard cot and made my mother run and flutter about his cabin, trying to fly for the first time in her life. He held her and stretched her wings out with his hands and stroked them. He rested his cheeks against them. It hurt where his sharp whiskers and jagged gold earrings snagged among the tiny gray feathers.

Despite her wings, she could not fly. They were crippled from her years in her mother's prison.

She used to weep at night after the captain had fallen asleep, as she struggled to make her weak wings lift her to the ceiling of his cabin. But she could not cry out, as the captain never remembered before he fell asleep to remove the bit of rope he tied between her teeth to silence her womanly screams.

She wept herself to sleep around the gag and woke with it in her dry mouth in the morning. She could not remove it. Her wrists were bound to keep her from fighting off the captain. In the mornings he found her battered and bruised against a far wall, her face wet with tears, sweat, and the ocean's damp. He laughed as he unbound her. "Lass, let me see if I can help."

Soon they would come to the new world, where he might sell her away. Did she wish him to keep her? He had told his crew that she was his new cabin boy, the last having broken out with plague boils and been jettisoned.

Would she keep the secret of her sex? Be his cabin boy by day and his woman in the night? What if he taught her to fly?

My mother felt she had little choice. The new world was rumored to be the chaos where the gods had consigned souls to wander in hopelessness, forever. Who wanted to go there?

These were the stories my mother told me as I sat in the evening by our cabin's rag door, keeping watch for her lover and for the overseer who stalked her. "What did you decide?" I loved to ask even though I knew the answer.

"Nothing." Her teeth sparkled with banked firelight through the gathering dark. "You decided everything for me."

25

It was true. My mother discovered the fluttering little bulge of belly that she knew too well meant a baby was on the way. And she leapt one sunny day into the waiting sea.

No way out. Better death than the new world.

But my mother was young. She had seen much of death and very little of living. As soon as she touched the lapping tips of the placid sea, she no longer wanted to die.

If she was not brave, she must be forgiven. She panicked. And her crippled wings broke through her shirt and stretched to catch the sea breeze like sails. She rose above the waves.

And there she ran, skimming the water and beating her fragile wings as the sailors shouted and pointed overboard.

Sharks kept such ships company, awaiting keelhauled sailors and jettisoned cargo. A shark was drawn to my mother's frantic thrashing. It swam up beneath her and raised its smooth snout. Its dagger teeth snapped at her flashing feet.

My mother could neither fly away nor let herself sink, to be devoured. So she ran alongside the ship, sobbing as the shark's teeth drew fresh blood that whet its appetite.

As she ran, crying and flapping her wings through her broken shirt, the captain lowered himself in a little boat. He harpooned the shark and gathered my mother in beside him. She clutched her torn blouse and watched the bloody water fall away beneath her as she floated skyward in the captain's strong arms.

His men cheered him as his boat was lifted back up the ship's side. But they cursed as the shark sank in its pool of dark blood to the predators that lurked below. Why had the captain not taken men with him to rope the body and haul it in? His love for his cabin boy had cost them all fresh meat.

What the captain feared was that his men might see the puffy breasts and pregnant curving belly under my mother's rent blouse. Already, they knew of her wings. And they knew too much. For, now that the sailors knew the captain sheltered a magical creature on board, they began to plot mutiny.

Abomination was written all over this gold-skinned flying child. The sailors wanted my mother tied to the ship's prow, as an offering to the offended sea for their safe passage.

The captain discovered and hung three mutineers. Their decaying bodies bumped and rubbed the flesh from each other as they dangled from the mast, their stench a cloud that drifted back about the ship and eddied in its billowing sails.

Still, the captain left my mother tied in the hold, where his men wanted her.

He came to her at night where she sat, bound among roped bundles of elephant tusks, fragrant ripping sacks of cacao, crumbling cakes of salt, and crates whose cracks let out the faint gleam of Asian silks.

He brought her food, water, and the rope gag. For had she not broken her promises of compliance and secrecy by trying to escape him before all his men?

When he kept watch, he untied her and led her by the hand up on deck.

The captain's watch was in the smallest hours of night. He and my mother were alone. He taught her to grasp the pegs that stuck out from the mast, climb up it a ways like a monkey, and throw herself into his open arms.

He said he was a man of his word, and he was teaching her to fly. "Birth the brat when we make land, and fly back to me. I'll not leave port until you come."

One night he had her leap down to him all the way from the crow's nest.

My mother stood between the star-shredded pitch of the sky and the black sea that licked the ship's sides, far below. She looked down at the captain's hopeful face, his thick arms spread wide, three hammered rings in his left ear winking golden light as they danced beside his head.

Had she cared for him? Would he miss her, mourn her? She had no one else to leave behind but me, and I was going with her.

My mother closed her eyes and spread her arms to fall and die.

As she fell, she thought for a moment that she had slipped between the bars of her mother's prison tower window and would soon strike hot wet sand. She raised her head so as not to break her neck and lie there, helpless.

And as she lifted her head, she stopped hurtling toward the deck and rose, dipped just a bit, and rose again.

She opened her eyes and saw spread everywhere beneath her the starlit tips of the ocean's waves. She turned her head, looking for the ship, and felt herself glide toward it.

There stood the captain on the rocking deck, his mouth curved with joy and awe.

He reached into the air for her as she hovered near and crushed her wings against her back in a tight embrace.

"You did it, lass!" He pinned her to him so tightly that he felt me kick out. He backed away and swiped at her belly, as if to swat me. "Away with you, gamin!" He laughed in fine high humor.

"Aye, soon enough and we shall be shut of the brat, shan't we, lassie?" He pulled her to him again. "Ah, but you *can* fly. The plans I have for the two of us, darling. We'll be rich as lords. For I'll sell you at every port, I will."

That night, my mother said he let her refuse the gag.

His eyes shone with greed, lust-or was it affection? -even in the dark of the hold. My mother wondered yet again if she cared for him. He assured her that she did. Is this how it was when women cared for their men?

When they docked in the new world, my mother was sold. She, her lover, and I have laughed many evenings over how anxiously the captain must have waited in the harbor for a sold captive to come flying back to him. My mother eventually heard that winter squalls drove his ship into its mid-Atlantic grave.

Perhaps revenge is the justice of those who have despaired of justice.

Before I was born, my mother plotted to kill me.

She gathered the chopped roots of the cotton plants she hoed for her captors and boiled a potion that would force me, too small to live, from her body.

She never drank it.

When I was born, she pulled lit twigs from her cooking fire to drive through the soft patch where no skull bones covered the top of my brain. Each time, she flung her burning splinters to the dust of her shack's floor and wept. She could not do it.

So I lived. And she loved me.

For captive people, love is a knife in the heart when it is one's own, and a knife in the hand when it is anyone else's.

My mother loved me. So that love was a knife in her captors' hands, for she could neither leave me nor kill me.

My mother was loved by one of the plantation's studs.

His love for her ripped at his heart. She would not look at him or answer when he spoke. That is, until her captors noticed that I had grown big enough to work beside her in the fields, and yet her belly lay flat and barren.

The overseer who had spoken up to stud her was relieved of that duty. One after another, the plantation's studs were sent to her shack. But all this is a story my mother never told me.

Her lover did.

It took four full seasons of planting, weeding, harvest, and hoeing, until the man who loved her was finally sent to her.

He came through her rag door as the sun burned low in the dry fields behind him. She watched him come in and turned away as he greeted her. Instead, she cooked her day's ration of corn mush and fed it to me in the gathering darkness.

As she rocked me to sleep, the man who loved her sat just inside her doorway and told his village stories. "Now, it be folks ain't heard what happen to. . . ."

His stories were sometimes of heroes but mostly of animals who talked and walked on two legs, who plotted and outsmarted all their enemies and hunters. They made my mother smile.

When she laid me on my pallet, and he crept to touch her empty hands, she filled his ripped and loving heart with dismay. For she said, "Are you hungry?"

Their wings were a secret that their hands discovered in the tenderness of their first night's full embrace.

By morning, they had pledged themselves to each other.

They had one season. Planting. My mother boiled and drank the cottonroot brew that flushed a woman's womb. By the end of planting season, the Irish overseer announced to my mother's English captors that the studs had been no more successful at breeding her than he had been. "So might I have her back?"

Permission was granted without a backward look at my stunned mother.

My mother's sworn husband was sent to stud other women.

Slaving kept the lovers apart all day. They glimpsed each other's bent backs at the end of a budding row of cotton, or one saw the other's dim figure lift a dipper from its bucket against sunlight, water sparkling in a glorious spill.

All that spring, I crouched at my mother's feet, picking weeds from cottonroot unearthed by her hoe. And suddenly she would straighten. The hoe thumped the dirt as she raised both hands to cup her eyes. She would make as if to speak. A gasp. Her hands would drop. She would bend to feel like a blind woman for the wooden handle of the hoe. And I would know she had caught a rare sight of her husband.

I cannot blame studs when they do not wake in the night to go back to their wives. These are exhausted men, sent around the quarters to service their neighbors. They fall asleep in friendly arms and wake little rested for the next day's labor in the field.

My mother and her husband sometimes went months with only enough time together to share their supper rations. My mother was different that way, sharing her food with a man on his way to lie down with another woman. As gloaming darkens the quarters, I have heard many a woman scream, "Go fill your gut where you gone spend the night, nigger!" Who can blame her?

Love in captivity is hateful.

Love leads to broken minds, fights to the death between rivals, and suicide for some left sleeping alone on a pallet.

No love means no desperate promises whispered in the night, no broken vows, less despair. Fewer losses. Nothing but babies and abundance all around.

Captors and overseers got in the habit of studding couples who could barely stomach the sight of each other.

Women played all kinds of tricks to get the men they loved assigned to stud them. Spread word that they hated the very men they adored. These same women had to play more tricks than that to get those men to stay with them, once assigned.

Pregnancy meant a woman's husband would soon be assigned to another woman. No pregnancy meant her husband would soon be assigned to another woman.

My mother sent me with her bitter cottonroot brew and her wild herbs gathered in a midnight flight to the woods, to women lucky or clever enough to be studded by men they loved. Women snatched the gourds of brew and gulped it hot or shoved the herbs whole and raw into their mouths, fingers to their lips for my silence.

But some women's wombs could not be cleansed by any herb growing on the face of the earth. Their babies stayed. And their men were sent to other women.

I never heard of another man who risked floggings to sneak home to his wife at sunset, so she would know he was faithful, as my mother's husband did. His risks fueled her love with pride.

Her other pride was her garden. My mother grew clumps of forest weeds and tame flowers on all sides of our shack, right up to the rag door.

When her husband was home, I sat in our doorway after our shared rations to fan in a breeze that smelled of my mother's flowers, cooling the lovers who hid in the dark. Waiting for me to fall asleep, mother's husband told us his old stories.

Like my mother, my favorites were of animals.

He would name an animal. "That one was weak. He learned to think, think." He squinted and tapped his forehead. Or, "That one, he was a bully. Like a bossman. Strong and stupid." He pretended to crack a whip over his head into the smoke that drove mosquitoes from the shack.

His stories sent me to sleep smiling. Someday, I would be like the clever weak animals that made the strong ones destroy themselves.

Bossmen, overseers and drivers, were very strong. All the people dreaded them. When my parents were alive, the master and mistress of the plantation kept one overseer and one driver at all times.

People joked in the field that overseers were hired for their woman-lust. "Be she old or barren, overseer sniff her out and bring her to bear." A snort and a chuckle. It was true that overseers considered studding part of their pay. Sneaky ones sold their babies for pocket change in town, until the master found them out and fired them.

Not so, drivers. People said drivers were hired only if they couldn't see as far as they could spit.

Some old man in the field would gulp his dipper of water and wipe at his mouth. He would shake his head as if in grief. "Yes, childrens. Tell you I was there and seen it all myself. Master lined up all the toughs from the jail what come looking for a labor. Told them, 'Spit over yonder at the bossman. Show me what you made of,'" jerking his head toward the overseer. "First man what got his spit dead in the overseer eye and ain't said sorry done got the job. Master thought he found him one mean driver, so crazy he spit on his boss and ain't say sorry."

Now the old man telling the story broke his straight face and guffawed. "Truth was the fool wasn't nothing but blind in one eye and couldn't see out the other one."

It was true. Let an overseer wink at a woman he had his eye on, to say nothing of pointing his whip at anybody who fell behind, and those drivers, mostly jailbirds out of the British Isles scared to death of being sent back, would take off like they were shot from a gun.

They'd be all across the fields, slashing the backs of hardworking people and cotton stalks alike, stirring up so much dirt that nobody could see a thing to chop it, weed it, or pick it. Rumor in the quarters had it that drivers destroyed more property than boll weevils.

By sundown, people pulled themselves out of the bloody mud fresh made by new drivers and crawled on home. Drivers who didn't drift on, run, or get fired, sooner or later turned up rotten in the woods. A nod in the field the next day was congratulations to the hand that had done the killing, men with a work tool or bare hands, women with poison.

The children's heroes in the quarters were its known murderers. My mother's husband wanted to murder an overseer.

The overseer who changed our lives was set on having my mother to himself. First he asked our captor for her.

"That one doesn't bear," my mother heard her captor say. "Get yourself one of these pretty little plump young things." The captor slapped the overseer's back and walked away.

The overseer took to sneaking up to our shack at night to peek past the rag door and try to catch my mother alone. Her lover, her pledged husband, lingered later and later. If the overseer kicked him out of a feigned sleep, he claimed he was resting up for the night's work ahead. The overseer reported him to the captor for shirking his studding duties.

"I hide here in the dark, wait and kill that bossman," my mother's husband finally decided.

"Why?" my mother snapped at him. "So you can be stripped and beaten in the face until you spill your guts in the grass? What happens to winged ones when they are found out? They spend the rest of their lives dragging chains through the fields."

"They fly away, and they are free."

"Not if they are chained first. And not if they have a child who cannot fly." She touched the tight muscles of his arm. "Leave. Go when and where you must. Live. I love you."

She took to flying with me to the edge of the woods at night.

I was grown and gangly now. Carrying me strained her arms and back. But if I had run between the snagging cotton plants, the overseer's dogs would have scented me and brought me down.

Mother and I would sleep, cramped and clinging to each other, in a tree's high branches, safe from the dogs and the poor immigrant patrollers who hunted Africans for sport. As night's black grayed, we would wake and fly back to our shack to curl up, maybe with mother's husband if he had escaped studding duty. We could rest until the shout called us to the fields.

But one morning my mother did not return me to our shack. As the stars faded, she took me to the dreaded big house. She left me at its back door with a cook's helper.

The woman made me nervous, cutting her eyes at me and sucking her teeth as she rolled her dough. "Call everybody you see in this house master, if it be a man, and mistress, otherwise. Bend your knees like this when you see one of them. That be called a courtesy. You try it. Look at you. Nothing but a field hand, I don't care how light-skinned you is, all that long hair down your back like you think you quality. Put this rag on them kinks and act like you know your place. Step out of line in this house, and you and your ma'am in trouble."

She bound my braid around my head with a filthy cleaning rag and had me walk around the room's big wooden table, bending my knees and calling the air before my face master and mistress.

I was shivering with fear as I walked the stone hallway to the mistress's bedroom. I think I sensed even then that I would waste my life away between these walls, measuring grief.

The mistress had three rooms downstairs.

The cook's helper explained, as we walked through the dark, that the mistress had been in frail health since the birth of her second son. She had spent years taking all her meals in bed upstairs. The stairs shot pains through her hips. But finally the stonewalled cavern that was the original house, once used to host balls for the mistress as a city-bred bride, had been split into three downstairs chambers for her use. One room was the mistress's bedroom. The other was her sitting room, no longer used, for the walk to it tired her. The third room was where the women slept who served her.

A heavy door was shoved open. I was shown into the mistress's lamp-lit bedroom. The cook's helper dropped a quick courtesy against the flickering shadows and disappeared.

My eyes adjusted to the darkness. The stonewalled chamber was crowded with massive woodworks and finely woven cloths. Glittering metalwork held up lamps and candles, some lit, like offerings to the pale body that reclined on a finely carved sofa. The cushions below the failing woman grew sewn flowers that breathed more life than she did.

I had never seen a being so drained of color. She did not seem real. I retreated from her toward the door. Her eyes followed me.

Her mouth opened, a black cavern without lips to frame the small square teeth. "Your mother sends word that you will be an excellent companion for my son. He has outgrown his nurse. She has long been unwell, and we must sell her away while she is still able to earn her keep. We have waited too long already."

Her gentle voice drew me in to the words that beat me back. My mother? My mother had delivered me up to our captors?

But what had I done to lose the slim freedom of life in the fields? Why had she not warned me? Given me another chance?

The mistress's soft voice was relentless. "My son has need of constant care. Your mother says your English and your attentive nature will make you a helpful companion. Speak."

"Yes, mistress."

"Lovely. Perhaps too lovely. What are you called?"

"Daughter, mistress."

The pale gaze softened upon me. "Daughter? No given name? Such heathenish cruelty. How can Heaven call you?" She stirred among the threads of her flowers. "Names must edify. I will name you Magdalen. Do you know why, child?"

"No, mistress."

"To remind you, the daughter of a blackened Eve, not to indulge the vice of women of your race and station. Immodesty." I looked down at the threadbare man's workshirt I wore, a gift from my mother's lover so that I was better dressed than most of the naked children in the fields. Only childbearing women, and women who worked in the big house, received the shreds of actual dresses. Did the mistress think I, whom she called a child, had borne a child of my own and earned a gown I refused to wear?

I looked up to see that her candlelit eyes were fixed on me. "Magdalen was the lowest of women, but she became pure. So must you. Each time your name is called, Magdalen, remember to resist the dark woman's inclination to prey on the souls of wight men. My sons must meet me in Heaven. I have so little time. I have tried. I fear I have failed." Her eyes shifted away. "Does God know it is through no fault of mine?"

My mouth opened. I struggled. I spoke. "Beg pardon, mistress. You say the woman pursues the man, mistress?" Could she not know how we lived, just across the fields in the shacks?

She raised her head with great effort at dignity. It must have been an old habit. It cost her. Her jaw trembled with effort, perhaps with pain. Her breathing rattled between gritted teeth. "Surely, Magdalen, you of all people have seen the children of mixed blood running about. You yourself are unquestionably of mixed blood. I do not know who fathered you." She let her shaking neck drop her heavy head toward the fine bones of her chest. She blinked as if stunned. She murmured as if to herself, "We will not discuss such things. Ladies do not question gentlemen."

Her eyes trembled, coated with shivering water. "But, oh, there are such goings-on. Magdalen-I must call you so. Yes. I see that now-who could have known, when they sent me from my home?"

"Mistress." Most of what she said was lost on me. But there had been a moment of clarity. And now her very weakness, her fear and her tender voice, all touched me. Hope flared.

I saw a way out of my mother's dilemma, out of my banishment to this house. "Mistress, even now there are women trying to escape these men you mention. My own mother-"

A hand rose, thin and bright as the white of a candle flame. "Darkness is the sign of evil. Woman is the origin of sin. The two together make abomination. Dark women are sin incarnate. We are surrounded by evil in this place."

Did confusion twist the fragile skin framing her brow and mouth? "Were it not for male appetite, there would be no sin. No reasonable being is drawn to the dark. These women's arts must be great. Evil sits on them like a benediction. How otherwise could they overcome our men's repugnance for the dark?" She looked up at me as if in appeal. I moved to touch her, help her. Her words again pushed me back. "Who would choose darkness? Who would choose death? Oh, God, what have I done, raising my sons in this wilderness?" Her head rolled from side to side against her chaise.

I stared to the point of rudeness. I could make nothing of her ranting except that she did not intend to save my mother from the overseer's attentions.

Or could it be she was ignorant of the world she and her husband, our captors, bred just outside her stone bedroom?

"Mistress, if the women in the quarters thought it were safe, they could refuse the overseers, and maybe even your own menfolk. Mistress, begging your pardon, but the women fear the most savage beatings, and even being sold away from their husbands and children, if they refuse. Mistress?"

She had rolled to the floor and now began to drag herself toward my feet.

"Mistress, may I help you?" I fell to my knees and fought down my repugnance to reach for her. She frightened me.

She yanked her head up with such force I scrabbled back from her on all fours. She clawed a frail hand and swiped it at my face, out of reach. She tangled her hooked fingers in the threads of my work-shirt and yanked. "Filthy, wretched, lying creatures. Abominations in the sight of godly men. Sirens of Hell, away from my sons! Away!"

I yanked back at the shreds of my clothing.

She wailed. I could make no more sense of what she said.

I heard heavy footfalls on stone and men's shouts. I crawled from her, but she came on.

Men opened the door. I was dragged up from the floor in the arms of the mistress's younger son, Mr. Dennis.

I had seen him a few times as I grew up, entering particular shacks at the far end of the quarters or cantering on a horse, on his way to the main road. Up close behind my ear, he talked to me as I'd heard hands gentling the workhorses. "Steady. Steady, now."

The master, a shriveled man with round bits of glass glittering on the sides of his nose, ran for the mistress, who clawed at my dangling ankles.

Mr. Jared, the eldest son, entered last.

In those days, before he was disfigured, Mr. Jared was not horrid to see. He looked like frog legs left roasting too long on a banked fire. Shrunken, disfigured, and stringy.

"What has caused all this distress, my dear?" The owner encircled the mistress with his arms, shutting her away from everyone in the room.

Her garbled voice made keening sounds but no sense.

Mr. Jared said into the stutters of silence, "Is this the girl that is to be my nurse? Get your hands off her, Dennis. I am to be master here someday, and I shall begin by mastering my own affairs. You were not to interfere by interviewing or choosing without my knowledge, mother."

"Jared!" the master shouted. His voice, so loud in his distressed wife's ear, brought on fresh cries from where her head pressed low against his chest.

Mr. Jared may not have heard his father's call for he had already led me, weeping myself now, from the room.

That day, I learned that my nursing duties consisted of bringing Mr. Jared anything that struck his fancy, while keeping fresh water, strengthening tonics, and brandy at hand. That night, I came to believe that Mr. Jared's ma'ammy, if she had ever been his ma'ammy, must have been strangled or stabbed to death in the throes of his strange passions. I had never seen the woman, and I saw no one leave at the end of a trader's rope.

When Mr. Jared finally slept, I sneaked from his room and the big house and ran through the cutting cotton stalks toward my mother's shack.

All day and night, I had been heartsick. Now I felt nothing but the urgency of asking my mother why she had done this to me.

The first measure of grief is numbness.

My mother was not in our shack. I turned to the woods.

But the overseer's dogs were already barking. I saw them race like lunging shadows through the cotton fields, toward me. I was not even into the woods by the time they brought me down, their frenzied bites burning my legs.

The overseer carried me to the kitchen behind the big house and locked me in it. I found a basin of standing water to wash my wounds and then spent a sleepless night banging on the door and calling out for my mother.

Just after the dawn shout called people to work, a sad-eyed old field hand took me out to be tied to a post and whipped before the other hands. As he tied my wrists, he mumbled, "Why don't these here now young people never learn?"

He called me a runaway. Panic rose in me.

The overseer came coiling his whip from his elbow to his hand, stumbling with sleepiness and tugging at his filthy trousers. I looked wildly around.

My mother was with the gathered hands and screamed when she saw me. I twisted in my ropes and called to her. She ran toward me. The overseer, who had plagued us with wanting her, caught her with his whip around her ankles and snatched her feet out from under her.

Mother's lover fought his way out of the crowd and fell on the overseer with blows to his head.

The driver came running from his shack but could not beat him off. Not until the owner and Mr. Dennis joined the fight, firing off guns, did the other enslaved men lend a hand to restrain my mother's lover.

The overseer, limp and bloody, was pulled away through the grass.

My mother, her husband, and I had our arms yanked behind us and our faces shoved into the moist earth at the foot of the whipping post. We were pulled to our feet and pushed into a tool shed. It was locked on us.

In the dark, I said at last, "Mother, why did you send me away?"

"To protect you. Hush. Husband, what will become of us now?"

"You know what, woman."

"If you love me, take one of these tools and kill me. There must be something here you can use. I am afraid, and I am sick to my soul of being afraid."

"Eat your words, woman. You ain't hear me praying to my father gods back in the old country?"

"Praying?" My mother screamed the word at her lover. "Have you no better way to end our lives together?"

Her lover's voice murmured on in the darkness. I heard her strike him. I heard them scuffle. I heard someone sob.

I felt my mother's fingers grip my wrists. "Listen, daughter. This is what you must do. Beg to get out and get us water. But do not waste your time with water. Gather these plants I will describe to you, as much as you can carry in your shirt, and bring them back here to me."

She described to me what the plants looked like and smelled like, and where they were to be found in her garden around our shack. When I thought I could remember them, I banged on the shed door.

A worried voice said, "What you all getting up to in there?"

"My parents are dying of thirst. For mercy's sake, let me out to get them water."

"I call somebody fetch it."

"Have pity. It is my own mother. Let me out to serve her myself."

"You run way, I be whipped till dead. You done went wild, girl."

"You know I am not going to run away and leave my parents to die without me." Were we

45

really going to die? Even as I said it, I could not believe it.

"Tell you true, only one going die. That man in there. Woman going get gave to the overseer. Keep him quiet."

My mother leapt to her feet in the dark and began snatching tools from the walls. They gleamed in sunlight through the shed's splintery chinks as they clattered down around us.

Her lover stopped in mid-prayer to wrestle her away from the wall.

"I told you, kill me!" she shouted at him.

The door rattled open. "Hurry, gal," the guard urged me. I ran for my parents' shack.

I tore handfuls of leaves and bright flowers from their prickly stems. My hands stung and bled. When the folds of my shirt seemed full, I ran panting back to the shed. The guard watched for me, frowning. He shoved me inside.

I fell at my mother's feet. I heard her hands rustle among the aromatic pile that spilled before me.

"This and this," I heard her mutter, sniffing. "No, this is no good. This is. And this is. Husband, you eat these. I will eat these. Forgive me. I have always loved you."

He said, "Maybe you me fly in the world come now."

I slapped my hands into the space where the pile had vanished. Only wilted tendrils remained. "But where is mine? Mother? Have you forgotten me?"

"Hush," my mother said again.

Then I heard nothing else but the wet crunching of green and flowery things. I groped my hand into someone's pile of herbs. Someone shoved my hand away and held both my hands still while mother and her lover helped each other shovel the leaves and petals into their own mouths.

I listened and could not believe what I heard. It seemed as if I were not quite in the shed because we were gobbling down our supper in our shack before the overseer came creeping to spy, as was his nightly wont, on my mother and her lover. The sound of breaking leaves in closed mouths went on until, gasping, my mother pulled me to her.

I smelled the sharp green scent of her mouth.

Her lover's thick arms fumbled around us both. His arms shook. I had never known him to feel and smell afraid. He breathed loudly, his mouth open.

The heat in the shed was suffocating. I think it put us to sleep.

I woke when my mother jumped. Her body jerked. It would not stop. Her legs and arms flailed and struck me. I hung on to her, hugging her.

Her lover, on her other side, held on. I heard him croon words I could not understand. Words from his village, from his childhood, comforting because faraway.

My mother retched and gagged. She tried to scratch at her throat. Her fingers swept by my face and clawed my cheeks in passing.

I did not know that I screamed until her lover's damp hand closed my mouth.

We held her and each other. At last, she lay still. I curled up against her warm body. Hot horrible smells flowed from her.

47

I closed my eyes. I thought of our flights to the tree to hide from the overseer. I rested, knowing that, when it was light in the shed, we would all awaken together and fly home.

The tremble in her lover's arms grew stronger. The fingers of one of his hands dug into my arm and hurt badly. I kept my eyes shut and wished he would stop shaking.

I was not aware when he did stop.

When the shed door was opened again, weak daylight startled me. I blinked and looked at the two people beside me on the ground.

They were cool in the shed's heat. Their limbs were stiff. Their eyes stared at something beyond me. The stench of their refuse drifted against the wide fresh air.

"Mother? Father?" I began to work myself out of their arms.

The overseer sent the old guard running for our owner.

Red-faced, our owner covered his mouth with his square of cloth and sent the guard running for Mr. Jared.

I must have been a sight worse than any I have ever seen, plastered with the waste lost in my parents' death throes. But Mr. Jared neither flinched nor shied away from me. He looked at me, standing and blinking above my parents' corpses. He smiled.

"Well, father, there you have it," Mr. Jared said. "One of mother's vaunted miracles. Trial by fire, or some such superstition. The miscreants have died at my nurse's feet. I trust she has proven her loyalty. Enough is enough. Send her to the kitchen for a scrub with soap and some decent clothes. I want her returned to my room by suppertime."

He began to hobble away. He turned back. "By the way, father. Magdalen is not to be punished again. No matter what she does. I will see to her. I have no taste for whip-scars and dog bites."

I thought of Mr. Jared's tiny knife slices, what he had called "love cuts," that already decorated my abdomen. Mr. Jared clicked his tongue. "Now, just look at her face. All scratched up."

That night, as I rose to leave Mr. Jared's bed and make my way to the pallet at its foot, he caught my wrist. "You killed them, didn't you, Magdalen? Your parents. My God, but you're magnificent. How did you do it?"

His breath was sour and filled the room. I stared. I could not see him in the dark.

My parents' bodies lay in a pit at the edge of the woods and would be eaten by scavenging beasts by morning. "Master, why do you ask me if I killed my mother and her husband?"

"Never call me master again. It puts a distance between us." He pulled me closer. "I ask because, my dear, if you have nerve enough to kill your own parents, you surely have nerve enough to kill mine. What do you say? Can you do it? How on earth did you do it?"

I was silent.

"All right, Magdalen. There must be something you want. I can guess. As soon as my parents are dead, I promise that you are free. Answer me, Magdalen."

"I have no use for freedom any more. What I want is here."

"Here? What is it you want?" He was oddly alert. Waiting too intently.

"I want my parents buried where their bodies will be safe until they are ready to rise and fly."

"I'll have real graves dug for them," he said, "right outside the kitchen, where you'll prepare my meals."

I moved through the tinted light to the pallet at the foot of Mr. Jared's bed. I had never slept before as the sun rose. But that day, I slept until the sun was high.

CHAPTER THREE
THE MEASURE OF GRIEF:
DAUGHTER BECOMES MOTHER
MAGDALEN

When I woke and dressed in my borrowed gown, too loose and too short, Mr. Jared was gone. I went down the long stairway to the back room that let out on the pathway past the kitchen. No one stopped me or asked me questions.

I found my parents' graves already mounded in the little unused garden plot next to the kitchen. I spent the day planting and watering what was left of my mother's herbs in the new garden I planted to decorate her grave.

When Mr. Jared slept that night, I crept from my pallet and went again to my parents' graves. I dug the earth from where I thought their faces should be and found feet.

Shredded feet with the bones showing through. Had I been deceived?

I set my candle in its heavy candlestick at the other end of the mounds. I twisted it into the soft soil. I began to dig again.

I thought I heard footsteps. I heard dogs bark. But whoever came to observe me chose not to disturb me.

I vomited into the soft soil when I uncovered my parents' faces. Terror and beasts had already changed them for the worse. But now they would always be safe.

I covered my parents' faces again and scouted around for smooth large stones to mark the heads of their graves.

When I returned to Mr. Jared's room, he called out, "Magdalen, where have you been? Do you know you can't move around this house freely? You will be stopped and whipped before I can help you."

"Did I wake you, Mr. Jared? I went to my parents' graves."

"In the night?" He moved toward me. "Do you fear nothing, Magdalen? You frighten me. Maybe I am unwise to trust you." He reached for me, so eager his hands shook and sweated against my skin.

He was right. He was wrong to trust me.

And he was wrong when he said I feared nothing. I feared my new and only feeling.

Rage. I could name it, but it was strange to me. It was quiet and bitter. It tolerated no rest. It was now all I had. Perhaps numbness had been better. But it had given way.

I lay down promising myself my captors would eat the dust of their own graves the day my parents rose and flew.

The second measure of grief is rage.

I went about each day in an absolute freedom I had never known. No one questioned me. I spent my time at my parents' grave-garden, nursing poisons and healing herbs from the soil.

I cannot say I missed my parents. They never left me. In my mind, I was almost always in the shed. "Husband, kill me."

My mother's pleas to her lover surrounded me, echoed in me. Rarely, I emerged from the sound of my parents eating their deaths to see the sun's glare on the dirt and struggling plants of their grave-garden.

I could not miss them.

But I did miss the rhythms of the quarters.

I had never thought of the people's sounds before. But in my exile to the big house, I missed the clap of hands and the clack of hollowed sticks as courting lovers flirted, laughed, and danced at night on the edge of the forest, the beat of feet on the earth in a quickening rhythm like hearts love-excited. I missed waking from exhaustion and sunstroke to full-throated chatter at the crackle of a neighbor's fire, the thrum of crickets and cries of pleasure from the shacks and woods nearby.

The wail of a baby and a low-voiced lullaby. The shout of an angry stud staggering home to an ugly surprise, the sight of the woman he truly loved on their pallet with a stud or a lover, in his place.

The shriek of a driver beaten to death amid the trees.

I nursed my mother's poisonous herbs and wondered, *Why should I reserve such a gift for my enemies?*

As I watered them, I bent to kiss the prickly leaves that caught at my lips and thought how sweet it would be to fly from this life, find my mother and her husband, and live with them in a world as bright as a dream. Would my mother be disappointed, if I took her way out? Did I owe her revenge, now that Mr. Jared offered it to me?

If my mother had not allowed her lover to commit murder, would she disapprove if I did? I agonized over this. Should I use her herbs to seek vengeance or peace?

53

I knew so little about what was right and what was wrong. To look around me, neither held sway.

But then one night my parents' grave was desecrated. After that, I could not repent of my plans.

I woke up crying out in the middle of the night, sweat drenching my pallet.

What had I dreamed? Of my mother's face before me, contorted by death throes, her lover close behind, pulling her into the safety of his arms. I shook.

Mr. Jared sat up in his bed. "Magdalen. What has gotten into you now? You have more vapors than a wight woman."

"My parents. I have to go to their graves. Someone is taking them away from me."

I got to my feet and was at the door by the time Mr. Jared shouted, "They are dead, Magdalen! No one can take them from you. They are already gone."

When I shoved open the back door and ran down the little cobblestone path to the outdoor kitchen, I saw the dark shapes of two men bent over my parents' grave-garden. They each lifted limp skeletal bodies from the soft dirt.

I snatched up a fallen shovel. I raised it as high as I could above my head. The man who held what might have been my mother shot up one arm to block my blow just as the shovel fell on him.

My mother's remains slipped from his other arm. She lay crumpled in the hole at his feet.

The shovel knocked away the man's arm and bounced against his head. He fell atop my mother. His bright blood bathed her.

I backed away.

The other desecrator had tossed my father to the ground and run. I thought I recognized the driver's lank hair, slapping his back as darkness took him in.

I heard Mr. Jared's limp behind me. Mr. Dennis came around me with a lantern. The circle of light grew.

It was the overseer who lay feeding his blood to my mother's remains.

I knelt and tried to roll him off of her. Mr. Dennis set his lamp at my mother's feet and hefted the overseer's unconscious body away. He dragged the man as far as the footpath that went past the garden. Then he tried to bring himself to reach for my parents' bodies.

His mistake was that he looked at them. They were rotten with decay. Mr. Dennis looked away and retched.

But they smelled of clean earth. I slipped my hands beneath their backs, their most solid parts, and coaxed their bodies back into the broken soil. They slid in and lay twisted.

And I realized that they were really gone. These bodies dug up in the middle of the night were only mindless, helpless flesh strung to exposed bone. Mr. Jared was right.

My parents' sunken eyes were closed. I scooped dirt over their faces with both hands. I felt an awkward hand on my back. "There, now," Mr. Jared said behind my ear.

"We'll find out what this was all about, Maggie," said Mr. Dennis. "You know it's against the law to strike a wight man. But come on back in the house. Can't you control this girl, Jared?" They were still arguing as I dreamed my way back into the shed and the sound of my parents' crunching.

I slept until Mr. Jared woke me the next day. I sat up on my pallet and squinted through a dull ache in my head. Mr. Jared said the driver and overseer were gone, but it had been his mother who put them up to removing my parents' remains.

"She found it unsettling to have two field hands buried so close to the house." He returned to the previous night's patting of my back. An odd smile twisted his face. Any questions I might have asked died.

Desecrating my mother's grave after humiliating her, terrifying her? I wanted swift revenge, with lots of suffering.

My chance soon came. A sickness went around the plantation and began to take lives. By now, Mr. Jared had hired the next overseer, a desperate English vagabond named Mr. Peter. There was no new driver. The fewer people Mr. Jared had to trust, he said, the better.

Rumor had it that Mr. Peter had escaped chain gangs all over the conquered lands being swallowed into the colonies. Mr. Peter brought his own pistols. He was a wiry man with a mean eye. People in the quarters said he brought disease.

Hands died for weeks after Mr. Peter arrived. The burying pit at the side of the plantation reached capacity. It was going to overflow with bodies. The smell fouled the air, even inside the big house.

I steadily boiled herbs grown in my garden. Those who drank my teas night and day and stayed far from Mr. Peter lived. Those who were unable to do those things died.

Mr. Jared and Mr. Dennis drank my teas like nursing babies. They got their father to drink them.

Their mother refused. She said she was too weak to take strong medicines. Mr. Jared chuckled and said she did not trust me. I said nothing. She was right not to trust me. I wished my mother had never trusted her and sent me here.

The mistress was the first in the big house to fall ill. It got to where the women assigned to clean her and care for her could no longer stand to enter her sick room.

I was pleased. Maybe the sickness would kill her for me. I continued to keep her husband and sons well with my teas. But one at a time, I daydreamed, they would all die in pain, as my mother had.

Those who worked in the house became afraid to go out of it. When the cook and her helpers became ill, none of the more experienced maids would take their place and cross the path to the kitchen. I offered.

After sitting up nights with his wife, fearful she might die with no loved ones nearby, our owner took sick.

I warned Mr. Jared that my herbs were running low. He told me to search out wild herbs in the woods. I said I feared the woods.

It was true. I could not bear to so much as look past the woods' edge.

Mr. Jared refused to believe me and let me take a maid. "And if someone gossips, Magdalen? And uncovers our plans to poison my parents?" So I left alone, a woven basket clutched in both hands and a heavy shawl around me to fight off the late autumn's chill.

Mr. Dennis slipped out of the back door and followed me.

As I gathered my herbs, quickly snatching them at the woods' edge, he turned away but stayed near. His kindness, if it was kindness, shamed me.

I gathered healing and soothing herbs, as well, and they nestled beside the poisons. Hurrying to the big house's back door, I hated my indecision.

I left the house to cook three meals a day in the outdoor kitchen and fetch them to the back door. Maids waited there to take the steaming platters and tureens.

I knew little about cooking then. The meals were drab but hot, at best. I spent whole days in the kitchen, simmering soups and teas for the dying master and mistress.

My nights were spent huddled against the wall closest to my parents' grave, asking them to forgive me for letting Mr. Peter and his disease snatch their revenge from me.

I accused myself of cowardice.

Mr. Dennis roused me from my prayers one night, pounding on the kitchen door. "Why is this door locked? Maggie, come quickly. Bring something for my mother's pain. She's dying."

I scooped dark brown tea, bitter from long steeping, from two separate kettles into two separate clay jars and followed him. Let my over-thinking mind torture me as it might. I would decide later which tea, poison or purifier, to give her.

When I bumped my way past the maids and into the mistress's bedroom, our owner rose from the flowered chaise and took my clay jars from me. "Go look at her, gal," he said. His knees gave way and dropped him back onto the chaise.

"Why have you chosen me, master?" The stench in the room was of decay and deep pain. "Surely a doctor should be called."

Mr. Dennis bellowed, "Leeches and laxatives! They've been called, you worthless chit, and if you won't do what you can for her, I'll take you out and horsewhip you myself!"

I looked around, wild-eyed. Mr. Jared was not there to restrain his brother. Hands shoved me forward. I found myself close to a face that had always unnerved me.

Razor-sharp lines cut more deeply into the mistress's papery skin than ever. Veins that should have rested invisibly below the surface now protruded at her eyelids and temples. Again, as I had when I met her, I pitied her. She opened her eyes. Her gaze shivered before it fixed on me. "Help me."

Her breath reeked. A weightless hand seized my arm above the elbow. "My son says you can. I know you can take away the pain. Magdalen, that is all I ask."

"Mistress, you do not understand what you ask of me. A doctor should be called."

Her eyelids closed. Lifted. Through the haze of ache and dim candlelight, she seemed to see me more clearly than she ever had before. "I know what you will do, Magdalen. Daughter. I know who put you up to this. I love my sons. I am grateful. I can bear this no longer." Her words slurred. Her eyes closed. "I can't breathe," she whispered. "Can't go. Let go."

I worked her fingers from my arm and went to where my owner sat with my clay jars. He stared up at me, pale eyes bulging with fatigue, with unasked questions. I stared down at him.

How could this be? I could no longer remember which jar was which.

She was dying, anyway. If I relieved her pain, it would prolong her agony. If I poisoned her, it would free her of suffering. Had she a part in my mother's suffering, anyway?

Everything had been reversed.

I reached for both clay jars. I took them to the bed and sat on its edge. The pressure, as I eased myself down, made the mistress wince. "Mistress, there has been a mistake. Your husband took the jars from me and confused them. I brought two kinds of herbs, mistress, and I no longer know which is which."

Her eyelids struggled but could not open.

I put one jar on the floor and lifted the lid of the other. Steam escaped it and warmed my face as I sniffed.

I was angry with myself. I might drive myself insane with my tangle of thought and feeling. Or I might free myself with the cleansing torrent of my grief.

I sniffed again and closed my eyes. I heard my mother, frantically chewing in the dark.

This was the one. This was my mother's poison.

I lifted the mistress's head from her pillow. I trickled the steaming liquid down her throat. When she fluttered a thin veined hand, I let her head down.

"Thank you, Maggie," Mr. Dennis said.

"Mr. Dennis, it will not help her."

"But look, masters," a maid said behind us at the door. "At least, she sleep."

"She look peaceable, masters," another woman said.

"Wish I go that quiet when I go," someone whispered.

The mistress's face tightened. I leaned over her, to block her from the others' view. Color rushed to her face. Breath escaped her. When she went limp, I rose and backed toward the door. "I am sorry, masters."

Mr. Dennis stopped my retreat and held my arms.

His father said from the chaise, "Look how well your mother seems, Dennis. Gal, fetch me some of whatever it was you gave her. I'm a tired man. I will sleep and wake, or sleep in peace. Makes no more difference to me, after tonight."

Mr. Dennis released me. I took his father the jar of poison. He slurped as he drank it down. "Whoa, father," Mr. Dennis said. "You may take too much. How much should he take, Maggie?"

His father waved him away. "Go away, all. Leave me and your mother in peace." He lifted his feet to lie down.

I went back to the outdoor kitchen with my jars, one empty and one full, and slept profoundly.

The next day, the fouled chaise on which the master had died and the mistress's mattress were both burned. I waited to be hauled out of the

61

outdoor kitchen and shot or whipped to death. Mr. Peter, the new overseer, helped Dennis and Jared carry their parents' bodies from the house, shrouded in sheets. They were buried along the willow path at the side of the house.

Their coffins arrived too late. They were stored in the maids' room next to the mistress's abandoned bedchamber. The maids returned to their lovers and children and the hated studs in the shacks.

No one came for me for several days. One night, Mr. Jared tapped at the kitchen door, bearing a lantern. "Did you forget your first duty is to be my companion, Magdalen? Come back to the house." He turned and hobbled ahead of me up the path and the curving stairs, his free hand on the banister.

No more was said about his parents' deaths. No questions. In the early spring, I nursed rose tendrils and grape vines up a trellis at the mouth of the willow path, so that I might sit in fragrant shade and contemplate Jared's parents' gravestones.

The cuts on my belly healed in jagged scars as a baby inside pushed against the tight skin. When I gave birth, I rose from my mother's grave to see and feel my daughter.

I had not meant to give birth. Had I known that my fatigue and sickness meant life instead of death, I would have drunk cottonroot. As it was, I took it too late and brought on an early delivery. My body ripped and tore. The quarters' midwife staunched my blood and told me I would never give birth again.

The tiny newborn lived.

I soon became grateful that I had a child of my own. I became a mother. I became my own mother, and wished to be a better mother even than she had been to me.

Could I do anything to make this a world that would not drive my daughter, too, to anguish and thoughts of death?

My daughter, Angel, was born with my mother's little wings budding on her shoulder blades. I wished her life to be so sweet that she might fly for pleasure, never fear or need.

Her birth gave my life sweetness. I would not wait for my parents to rise. I had to live right now for Angel.

Jared gave Angel his mother's stone bedroom, deep in the dark of downstairs. He gave me the maids' parlor next door. He sent for me to come to his room upstairs, when now and then he still wished to take his peculiar pleasures. Angel could not hear my cries from upstairs.

Angel was not allowed to dine with her father, nor to be tutored. But she was treated like a lady of quality. She ate at a table in my back room with a lace placemat, linen napkin, and silverware. A crystal goblet held her sweet milk.

Mr. Dennis took great pleasure in Angel's refined manners and golden beauty. When he was at the plantation, which became increasingly rare, he moved his own fine china dinnerware into my stone parlor, to take his meals with Angel.

Mr. Dennis loved to thrill her with stories of the places and people he had seen in Asia and Europe. He brought her a casket of his mother's jewelry, to show her the finery that pampered ladies wore if they were careful to give themselves only to wealthy men. He agreed with me that Angel must marry a freeman or any well-to-do man who did not live in the Americas, so that she could never be stolen and enslaved.

For all his hearty laughter and simplicity, Mr. Dennis was a man of secrets. I often wondered why he was protective of Angel when his brother was not.

Mr. Jared grew suspicious of my concern for Angel's future as her adolescent delicacy matured into womanly grace. He began to barge into her little dinner parties with Mr. Dennis. "So, brother, what is property like this worth in today's market? A virgin. Octoroon. Very high yellow."

I would blanch and still the trembling of my hands by clasping them. Mr. Jared made himself a terrible threat to Angel's safety. But why?

Hadn't he arranged for me to kill his own mother, who was perhaps innocent of my mother's death? Surely he realized that I would never sit by quietly if he harmed my daughter?

For the first time in a decade and a half, I recalled the mistress's dying words. "I know who put you up to this. I love my sons." Did she know that Mr. Jared had put me up to killing her? Had Jared made her a target for my grieving rage?

I began to wonder who had ordered that my father be killed and that my mother be given to the overseer. Who had stationed the guard at the shed door with the heartbreaking news that the overseer would have my mother? How much power had Mr. Jared's parents allowed him while they lived? Had he used it against me, used me to speed his inheritance of the plantation?

Or was I simply entangled in the captive woman's endless thinking?

I could juggle the confusion no longer. I asked the overseer, Mr. Peter, to take Mr. Jared to the woods and strand him with a wounded animal, preferably something hard to kill, such as a bear. Mr. Peter wanted and feared me, in those days.

I persuaded Mr. Jared to leave the comfort of the big house and accompany the overseer on his hunt by assuring him that the liver of a freshly-killed bear was the world's best strengthener. Only, it was necessary to be sure the bear had been killed cleanly and quickly, without time to suffer. Otherwise the liver would be flooded with weakening gall.

It would have been easier and swifter to poison my detested captor. But ever since the death of his parents, Mr. Jared would take no food or drink that seemed to have herbs in it.

Not even from my hand. Or, should I say, particularly not from my hand.

Mr. Peter did his best. But Mr. Jared survived.

Mr. Peter brought most of Mr. Jared back home in his arms. The bear dragged forest mulch and pinecones under its belly, lashed to a travois, Jared's severed leg tied at the travois's peak. The horses who pulled it came lathering in, their eyes rolling as they searched for the beast whose scent followed them and frightened them, foam and blood splattered along their flanks.

I followed Mr. Peter as he carried Mr. Jared to bed. I waited at the doorway. As Mr. Peter came out into the hall, I said, "You failed."

"Miss Magdalen, that man in there can't live."

"I have to show his brother that I've done my best to tend him, Mr. Peter. Of course he will live."

When Mr. Jared returned to consciousness, he seized my wrist in his old familiar gesture and assured me that his brother had just tried to have him killed, so that he might inherit Jared's property.

Whispering, teeth chattering, Mr. Jared confided, "I've long suspected Dennis of trying to get you to poison me, so he can inherit. I know he's told you about enslaved children who inherit. But it isn't true. It's a trick." Rising a little as he held my arm and I backed away, Mr. Jared asked if I didn't know I was being used. Once free of Jared, Mr. Dennis would never keep his promises to me.

Pretending to die and hiding from Mr. Dennis until I could poison him, as I had done the master and mistress, was Jared's idea.

Mr. Peter carried Jared to the stone chamber that had been the maids' room. Mr. Peter and I chipped free stones sunken into the heavy earth. We helped Jared hide in the gap in the wall. We carried down caskets of the mistress's jewelry and bags of the master's gold coins and bank notes. We dumped them in one of the empty coffins and slid it into Jared's lair. He stared at us with reddened eyes as we worked the stones back into place.

Mr. Peter even helped me load the other coffin with a small rucksack of dirt and bones from the burying pit and carry it upstairs to Mr. Jared's bedroom. If any of the field hands witnessed our midnight work, they said nothing.

Angel wept the next morning as we carried the coffin back downstairs and out to the willow path, the only mourner at her father's funeral.

Mr. Dennis was gone, either to the woods or to some gambling den. The trickery was for Angel and the hands. Surely they would spread tales to Mr. Dennis about Jared's death.

When Mr. Dennis returned, he pulled the unmarked stone from the site of his brother's grave and returned it to my parents' grave-garden. He said nothing at all about his brother.

Jared became my private worry. I would not risk discussing him, even with Mr. Peter. I promised myself that, if Mr. Peter mentioned Jared, I would say that he had suffocated in the wall, and I had burned his corpse in the stone parlor's fireplace. Then Jared's death would have been his own fault.

But Mr. Peter never said a word about Jared to me.

I fretted day and night over how to rid myself of Mr. Jared. If I didn't move his stones to feed him every night, he might call out and draw Angel or Mr. Dennis to his hiding place. I knew no poisons that wouldn't look green or red in his food or drink. And even if he did die behind the wall, what if I could not dispose of his stinking corpse because Mr. Dennis was on one of his unpredictable visits home?

A torch tossed into Jared's coffin of stolen treasures might burn him alive in his hideaway. But the fire would endanger Angel, whose room bordered Jared's hideaway.

Jared began to crawl from his wall to frighten Angel in the night.

Early one morning, when I was in the outdoor kitchen, Angel screamed for me. Instead, Mr. Dennis heard and came.

So she confided to her uncle the nightmare visits her father had been paying and her fear that Jared was not truly dead but maddened.

Mr. Jared huddled behind Angel's wall and listened as she betrayed him. A doctor in a tall black hat came that very day to speak to Angel. When he left, Mr. Dennis tied Angel to her bed and locked her door, to prevent her harming herself or anyone else, in her lunacy. I tore apart the big house searching for the key, as she screamed.

For Jared had crawled from his hideaway through the wall that joined their rooms.

I tried to get through the stone passageway, but I was much taller than Jared and could not make myself fit. I banged on the door. I screamed for Mr. Dennis, who had left again for town. Someone ran for Mr. Peter and his gun.

I clawed at my daughter's locked door and heard her muffled gagging as she died. Then there were no more sounds.

Mr. Peter found me there when he ran in, sweaty, sunburned, and frantic, from the fields. He had people come and take me away before he shot the padlock from Angel's door.

I never saw Angel's bloody body, except in mirrors. I heard that she was placed in a coffin and buried by the willow path. Mr. Dennis erected a small monument for her. An angel with wings, to guard my daughter's sleep.

I covered all the mirrors so I might not see her image.

In the following years, while I tried to turn the plantation into a tomb from which Angel might someday rise and fly back to me, I knew neither numbness nor rage.

For the third and most enduring measure of grief is despair.

Despair lasts. It swallows up passion and numb, dumb rest. It aches, blinds, drains. Despair devours the years.

But clawing at the slippery sides of despair's pit, one catches sight of its limit.

If Angel could rise, as I used to wish my parents would rise, I could reach that fourth and final place where the measure of human grief at last spends itself in peace.

I might make peace with my unjust world.

CHAPTER FOUR
THE LAST TIME I FELT ANYTHING:
MAMMY WATER'S MIDDLE PASSAGE,
BORN 1756

The last time I felt anything, it was despair.

I stood between stones in a high tower and looked out over the sea between civilization and the chaos the gods created it to hold back. For the people had always ended where the sea began. My heart beat in rhythm with the lapping sea where lay my destiny.

Someday soon I would be forced to walk that sand to a great canoe made to cross the sea and the chaos beyond. I might follow the soul that had already escaped me to the world of my blessed ancestors.

Would my mother be there?

Would my fiance await me?

My beauty brought me here, fed on all my mother's prayers for a child and grown lovely from her desire. Everyone said so.

My parents had no one. And then they had me, cursed with a beauty that made the dead envious.

My mother used to lift my head so I would not see myself in the clay bowls of water she brought to her hut to bathe me. Nor did she let me look into puddles or streams as I crossed them, lest vanity make me vulnerable. But could she tell all the spirits and lost souls, other people's ancestors wandering the chaos between the worlds, to look away?

"Marry her quickly," everyone said. "Let some man's family distract the jealous ones."

My young man smiled, weak with love, when I knelt to accept his engagement gifts. Thoughts of a young man, lean and tall, who walked toward me, bent and reached for me, his sweet breath on my face.

My mother's happy tears wet on her cheeks as I rose, betrothed, into her arms.

My mother sat on the bank, watched and sang to me as I bathed and called, "You must not wade to the opposite side. Your destiny might lose you if you cross too much water. A new evil destiny might find you."

And when I laughed at her superstitions, "Spirits trick you."

For evil beckoned to me from the other bank. I gazed at its human shape, curious. But it was not human.

And my mother's song tore into screams.

I turned toward her and saw her, screaming, dissolve in flames.

And then the golden rage of flames and the people running, my neighbors lit by fire from the child soldiers who chased us, who shot us, who roped us and dragged us here to the sea. Somewhere in this tower was my betrothed.

But where was my mother?

I felt panic. Despair.

And then I felt no more.

Nothing for my mother's shriek that still splits my skull. And nothing for the quick shock fallen to damp stones beneath an inhuman's knees in this tower, and nothing for that endless moment when a stranger's demand breaks my last refuge, and my blood and his sperm burn in me and spill out of me, and life as I know it is over.

For I am now unclean. Worse than dead.

We sit, frightened people from many nations in chains and cry like babies, spitting, with brands burned onto our faces, lost from everyone and everything we have ever known, our homelands, our age groups, our ancestors, our gods. Where are our protectors? Lost somewhere between my dry hilly home and this flat glittering sand.

We call out and pray. I wept and offered my dead gods my tears, cupped in the salt of blood and semen in my hands, but now I am through with weeping.

For despair is a mouth that swallows the mind and now I have no words as I limp down from the tower pulled by the chain at the collar round my neck and drag my swollen leg through the stinging sand. Will my swollen leg burst like an antelope bladder filled with too much water?

Splinters of light and I am forced to see the purpled blood in the mat of hair beneath my belly's beauty scars and the jagged bloody tracks down my thighs and everything burns when I move but I am no longer sure why and I cannot close my eyes.

All around me, bronze skin puckers around whip-scars and sews itself together with black scabs.

And there, just there bent like an old man among the people chained squatting in the sand is my betrothed. He raises his head and follows me with his eyes.

But a singing chain that binds us yanks me up a flattened tree against the side of a great canoe whose white wings uncurl above our heads, rise and flap and gather in the wild wind. Prickles of pain as splinters snatch at my swollen feet, every stab a sign that my ancestors reach for me, to save me, to keep me here, where I belong.

I hover in sunlight.

Below I hear hoarse bellows, death cries like slaughtered game as the chain tightens, pulls, and I tumble into darkness and lie still. My stomach squeezes bitter juices through my throat, stinging. I grip damp splinters beneath my face and pull and crawl toward the yanking of my chain.

I huddle in stink against shuddering bodies, iron wearing our flesh against our bones. I drop my head and dream of my long legs in a stream, watch the water part for the carved bronze muscles of my thighs. I lift the rushing turquoise in my hands and let it run down my smooth face and between the tattooed nipples of my breasts. I adore my curved body, thrown back up to me in rippling lights from the stream.

For beauty is my body in the daylight and in the falling night that purples the world around me, and under the rising sun again as it blushes the new world pink. And I am at peace, alone in creation.

And then I wake in the soft caress of sweat against splintered wood and the wet heat of bodies piled against mine, smells of hot breath and suffering. We are all sick. We are all dying in this black pit together.

The canoe screams as its belly rips up toward sky. Brown of bodies tangled in melted wastes and

73

rats that raise their heads to the light that makes us hide our eyes. For some have died in our chains and begun to rot and steam.

Our chains pull, pinch gorged limbs and we rise, dead and alive as one, mouths glued shut. I hang on my chain as we drag free of the canoe's belly to stand in sunlight, and the women search blinded and blinking for their babies, unchained and tossed to the rocking waters and birds pick at the bright blood that leaps from the living who squirm between them and their dead prey. Someone begins a thick song, a chant that rises and wraps itself around the mourning.

I am that lament my dead mother never stops singing. My neck melts beneath my head, and my chin hits my bent knees.

And I watch my mother burn and walk from the water into the flames that claim her. I hold her and burn with her as I too wait to die, standing at the edge of burning streams where I understand at last that this has always been. I live burning in this stream of understanding, dreaming of a canoe bound for chaos, and this chaos will always be.

My body empties as I sleep. And I cease waking.

For now I can rest.

I open my eyes.

To velvet midnight skin against my face and arms like a forged metal rod that crush me to a beating heart. Soft words. "Poor Beauty. Wake. Come back to your Sami."

I raise my hands to touch the warm dark skin of my betrothed in this, the best dream of all.

I have dreamed him into being.

CHAPTER FIVE
THE WOLF AND THE TREE:
ANGEL GIRL, BORN 1769

My Mammy Water sleep. Big sleep go on for days and days. Sleep take her across big water. She go home to Africa, a magic place. See things. Come back. Wake up.

Tell the peoples what she see.

She see big things across them water. But she ain't see me right here.

Girl. Ain't nobody know about me but my baba.

Mammy Water belly big and bust and out come me. She sleep ain't know nothing. My baba pick me up, all small and blood. Hold me up to the night. Say, "Sky. Ancestors. Give this Girl a safe place."

Light cut the sky and hit the earth. My baba follow that light through rain. Dark night. My baba find my tree, burnt out inside. Put me there on leaves and pine. Put my Wolf with me.

Not like them other people. Slave. Us run the woods, my Wolf and me. Us run free.

My baba bring us food. Teach us to track and hunt. Teach me to talk and hide. Teach me my Mammy Water.

Come light, my baba sneak away. "Stay here, Girl. Stay in your tree. Stay safe here with your Wolf. Don't follow me."

I hide in trees and watch my baba go.

Till one night. Me, my Wolf, us climb out our tree. Quiet. Hush. There go baba. Light cut the sky, but he don't see. Like Mammy Water, he don't see me.

Us follow baba home to my Mammy.

Hut. Dark and still. Me, my Wolf, us watch and wait.

Till baba gone out in the night. Me my Wolf sneak in.

Mammy Water. Bone woman. Dark like night. Still. Sleep. Big sleep? Her gone home again to Africa?

I touch her hand. "Mammy. Mammy Water. Wake. Your Girl come home to you."

She wake. See Wolf.

Howl.

Wolf try to run. Peoples run. Bring fire. Peoples all around us. Me, my Wolf growl. Circle. Jump.

Big stick like fire. Wolf on the ground. Blood. Wolf in my arms, all blood.

"What the devil is all this?"

"Mr. Peter, it some kind of girl. Some kind of wild child. Us found her here in Mammy Water's hut. That dog thing there done try to kill somebody."

I howl like Wolf. For Wolf.

My baba come. "Oh, lord. No, Girl. Don't cry. Mr. Peter, let me explain."

Mr. Peter grab me.

"Mr. Peter, let me come with you to the big house. Let me explain to Miss Magdalen, sir."

Big house all dead trees like bones. A woman say, "Sami, what is all this? Who is this child? What's happened that she's covered with blood?"

"Miss Magdalen, is my Girl. I can explain."

"Miss Magdalen, it's the strangest thing I ever seen. Some kind of wild dog in African Sami's shack was chewing on that old witch he's got laying up in there. That Mammy Water. Like as not this is her blood all over this gal."

Woman touch my face, my hair. "Sami, maybe you'd better go see to your wife. Take water and rags. Take whatever you need. Child, call me Mother Magdalen. Can you speak? Has she said anything, Mr. Peter? Wait, Sami. Does she have a name?"

"Miss Magdalen, I call her Girl."

Woman smile. "I used to be called Daughter, Girl. May I call you Angel, for my daughter?"

"Now, Miss Magdalen, don't go getting attached. Like as not she's a runaway. Or born of runaways and abandoned in the woods."

"Sami says she's his, not a runaway."

"I wouldn't count on nothing African Sami says. I found her in his shack, watching that wolf dog chewing on that zombie wife of Sami's. Shot the wolf. Almost shot the girl, too, wild as she is."

"This golden girl is not wild. Just frightened."

"Ain't nothing gold about this girl, Miss Magdalen, but the reward money I'm going to get for her, as soon as I turn her in. Runaway or not, one thing's for sure. Old African Sami's been keeping secrets out in them woods."

A new voice. "What's this, Peter, Maggie? Something about my gold out in those woods? Has someone found it? A runaway?"

I turn.

"Good lord, Maggie. What in the world is this?"

"Mr. Dennis, this is Sami's Girl. Or so he says."

"Mr. Dennis, this here is a runaway caught in Sami's shack."

"A runaway, Peter? And all your talk of gold and the woods? I suspect there's something you're not telling me. You're my overseer. No secrets, now."

"Mr. Dennis, sir, I only meant-"

Mr. Dennis come close to me. I growl.

Mother Magdalen step between. "Mr. Dennis, she is frightened out of her mind. Let me wash her and dress her, give her something to eat."

"Look how lovely she is, Maggie, tangled hair and all. It feels like ropes of silk. Wash her all you want, but don't you dare cut that glorious mane."

Water. I shiver. Water run like my Wolf blood. I whine.

"Easy, little one. Maggie, I'll hold her still for you. It's all right, Girl. You're safe. I love the feel of a woman's beating heart."

I bite his hands.

"Why, you little cur. Maggie, she bit me."

"Mr. Dennis, let go. I'll dress her now."

Clouds over my head. Tight around me. Woman push me to the floor. Hot warm meat like fire and water. I eat.

"Maggie, maybe you mean to keep hiding my brother's secrets until you've ruined me. But I'm warning you. You've lost your daughter, but you still have a home here. Everything you need. I take care of you. Don't make me sell you and all these people away to recoup my losses. What does this Girl have to do with my brother and the hoard he hid before he died?"

"Mr. Dennis, nothing in the world. It is all in your head. You are starting to sound like your brother did before he died, sir."

He shove her out the way. He grab my arms. "Now listen, Girl. My gold. Do you hear? What do you know about my gold? Is it out there in those woods? Did you hide it for these two? I heard them. What is it you know?"

"The girl doesn't speak, Mr. Dennis. She just grunts like an animal, sir."

Mr. Dennis shove me away. "I'm going to the sheriff for news of a runaway. I'll be back by morning to tell you no one's lost a girl around here. By then, you'd better be ready to tell me the truth about this Girl, and what she has to do with my gold. Or I'll cut out somebody's heart and eat it for breakfast."

He gone. Mother Magdalen say, "I guess we shall see who will be eating hearts around here. Won't we, Angel Girl? Come lie down and rest. I have a room for you."

Long walk. Dark stones. More soft than leaves, I lie down.

I wake to see Mother Magdalen on her knees. "Mr. Jared, you have to help me. You have to push on your side. Or let me get Mr. Peter to help."

Stones move. A man-thing crawl from out the dark.

Bent over stick leg. Sit and rub. Head rise. Dirt, and spiderwebs, and shine things hang off arms and neck and face. "Magdalen, who is that girl? What have you done? Who have you brought in here?"

"Mr. Jared, calm down. This girl will be our deliverance. She is a runaway found in Sami's shack, probably searching for food. She must have been hiding in the woods for years. She cannot speak. But for some reason, your brother has taken it into his head that she knows something about his lost gold. I told you, he is losing his mind over it."

"His gold. *His*, Magdalen? I always *knew* you would take his side someday."

"No, no. Oh, please, Mr. Jared, not now. I never meant-"

"Oh, but you did. I heard you, Magdalen. Dennis's Maggie. That's what *he* calls you, isn't it? And you let him. *Maggie*. Maggot. Vermin woman. Parasite."

"Mr. Jared, hear me out."

Stick man crawl quick grab her. "No, Magdalen! You hear me. It's time to get me out of this hole. I'm losing my mind in there."

He let her go. Crawl back. Sit. "I know what you're up to. You want to help my brother steal back my inheritance. He's the reason you won't come with me and leave this place."

"Mr. Jared, how long did you really think your brother could run this place on the profits from last year's harvest? Master, it has been a year since you and all your parents' savings disappeared, and he is ready to start selling people away. Think, Mr. Jared. What will happen to you when I am gone and cannot bring you food and water?"

"Yes, almost a year. You could have gotten me out of this hole. We should have been gone by now. North. Married, if you like. There are still states that marry African and wight. What woman of any race doesn't want to be married to a wealthy man?"

He pull her close. "But you've gone over to *his* side, Magdalen." Hit her face. I whine.

"No, no." She back away. "Hear me out, Jared!"

"*You've turned against me, Magdalen.*"

80

"Hear me! You and I are caught, Jared. Trapped in our own plan. Nowhere to go. This Girl is our chance to buy time. To make peace with your brother. Return him some of the gold, just *some*. No questions can be asked. I will tell him he must have been right. The Girl has found the stash in the woods somewhere. She cannot talk, Jared. It will take me years to teach her. She will buy us time."

She crawl inside the stones where dark.

He crawl in after her. "Magdalen! Get your hands off my property. I'll kill you."

She come out. Hands shine. "Angel. Girl. Run!"

"*Traitor*!"

They fight. I run from light to woods.

Morning baba find me. Drag me back to Mother Magdalen. "They know about you now, Girl. You don't want to live like a hunted thing. Come, Girl. Mother Magdalen will take care of you."

Mr. Dennis wait for me. "So it's true." His hand in shine things. "Where did you find the pretty things, Girl? Can you lead me to the stash of pretty things?"

"Mr. Dennis, I told you. Let me take care of her, sir. Teach her to speak. Win her trust. Give her to me, sir, to take my Angel's place."

***

Mr. Dennis gave me into Mother Magdalen's care. She has been my teacher and my mother. She tries to keep me safe. But I cannot be safe in this place. There is nowhere here that I can hide from the stick leg man.

Jared. He comes to my stone room at night. I smell his rot before I sleep. I wake to find his hand across my mouth.

"My treasure, Angel. What have you done with it? You're helping Magdalen steal it from me. Where has she put it? She doesn't want to be sold away. Well, would she rather be killed? Would you rather be killed? Would you rather I kill your pickaninny?" He touches my belly, big with child. "Dennis's child. Dennis's property. A theft for a theft."

Mother Magdalen tells me these are dreams, but they are not. I only dream of my wolf and my tree.

***

Dennis had dreams of his own.

While that first baby grew inside me, hurting me, I would wake at night to find Dennis in my room. He stood above me with a candle, lifting my bedclothes to see my belly.

"I dreamed the baby was gone," he would say.

"And now you see it isn't."

He would get in bed beside me. When he slept at last, I would move away so he no longer touched me.

I hated him. But I feared to sleep alone.

When the baby came, a storm broke. Thunder screamed like someone dying. I paced my stone floor and thought of Wolf, how he hated thunder, hated the leak of rain pounding our tree.

I loved to watch the lightning rip the sky. "Open the shutters," I begged Mother Magdalen. "Let me see the storm."

She opened them as lightning flew. I thought I heard my Wolf howl in the thunder.

When I came to, I was in bed. Dennis held my hand. "I'll go get Magdalen."

Mother Magdalen said in my ear, "Let your baby be born, Angel. This fight is killing both of you. Let him come into the world. He is safe. I promise you that Jared is no more."

Candles split the blackness like my baby split my body. Red and tiny. Wet and shiny, like those jewels dripping off of Jared. Was he really dead? Or had I only dreamed Mother Magdalen's words?

Mr. Dennis fed me buttermilk and red wine with a spoon.

I named my baby Sami Wolf Water.

We slept in Mr. Dennis's room, all done in blue, like the sky, and lit by candles all the night.

But best of all, a rifle rests beneath Mr. Dennis's bed. For my dreams of Jared. For one special dream.

The night I woke in the stone room and found my baby gone from beside me. A shadow scraped the stones as it fled.

I ran after it and fell upon it. Touched my baby in its arms. He cried, and his little fingers clutched at mine. I struggled with the shadow, bit at it and snarled.

The shadow howled with pain but would not let my baby go.

We fought in the darkness. And then there was a shot.

The shadow melted into stones. My baby fell into my hands.

Mr. Dennis called for Mother Magdalen and a lamp. They watched me lick my baby clean of Jared's smell of rot and burning.

"He was not a dream," I told Mother Magdalen.

"And you are not an animal. Stop that and give me the baby," Mr. Dennis said.

I growled at him.

"I want you both to come and sleep in my room. Whatever it was that broke in here was marauding for food, Angel Girl. It's wounded now. Look at this blood. This is no place for you and little Sami."

Mother Magdalen did not wash the blood away. Sometimes at night, when I go prowling like my Wolf, I find her in that room beside the stain.

She touches it. Watches it, as if it would move. "Angel, I thought I'd killed him for you. Sealed him in the wall with lit kindling, so you could have your baby. So I could have revenge and peace of mind."

I held her. Tightly, just as I hold my growing belly, ripening with another baby, when I lie at night beside Mr. Dennis and my Sami.

Mr. Dennis is a fool. For how can he protect us from his brother if he believes his brother is dead?

CHAPTER SIX
BLOOD RED AND BONE WHITE:
ROSE WHITE, BORN 1787

I look out through Mammy Water rag door. Night falling fast. Sky gone all pink. Wind picking up quick. It going snow.

Mammy Water got a hold of my hand like she ain't never going let go. What little I can see in her shack is all sad. Her mind full of something she can't quite tell nobody, now Sami dead. She still talk to him. But he don't pass on nothing she say. Nobody around here but Mammy Water can talk right to the dead like they same as living. She got a nerve on her. I look up to her, but I don't pretend to understand her ways.

Understand a little of her illegal talk, though. That be why she hanging on to me for dear life tonight. Trying to make me understand what new vision she done seen.

Us all growed up knowing about Mammy Water and her visions. Change the course of folks' life every time she come out of them dream spells. Dream spells take her back home to Africa. Put her in the land of the dead.

She can look down from heaven and read folks' minds. She can look up from hell and see what road folks is walking and don't even know it. Got powers God give the angels.

Use to come back to us here trapped on the plantation and set us a little bit free. Help us make choices ain't so painful. When it ain't no choice ahead, Mammy Water help folks up and run. Tell them when and how to go. Ain't nobody who listened to her ever got caught. They all made it. Even Miss Angel Girl.

Angel Girl walked out on Mr. Dennis bright and early in broad daylight. She toting her carpetbag all sewed up with flowers and vines. Stepping through the forest still wearing all them jewels he give her to try and make her stay. Walking like she right at home amongst the trees and the wild beasts. She ain't look back. Some womens is just that way. Don't care for they man.

Take me and my sister. Us both named for our ma'ammy wedding present. Shacking up present.

My ma'ammy had got to where she was ready to lay up and die before she have one more baby that Mr. Peter was going sell out from under her. He done sold the ones she had from that field hand she loved. Next Mr. Peter done sold off the babies he had off of her his own self.

My ma'am lay down say "This going be my dying bed. I ain't getting up out this bed one more time in my godforsook life. Man come near me one more time, I chop off his head with my cotton hoe. Watch me."

Ma'am laying up there dying day and night. Mr. Peter come in and whip her something terrible. She bleeding. Look up and say, "Thank you, you fool. You hurry me on up to the judgment seat. I remember you to the righteous God when I get there."

Mr. Peter all scared he going lose Mr. Dennis a good breeder. Run off to Mr. Dennis. Mr. Dennis say "Don't go near her no more. Try see if you can send in Mammy Water."

Mammy Water come out one of her sleeping spells. Look around find Mr. Peter crawling in her shack like a man done lost his woman at the auction block. Peter say, "Mammy I is begging you. Go see to that woman laying up dying because I done sold all her children. Tell her that just the way us do things around here. Tell her get used to it. I can't do nothing with her."

Sami tell Mammy Water what Mr. Peter say. Mammy Water answer Mr. Peter promise to stay away from that woman from now on, she do it. She go make that woman want to live. But he go near her, spirits around her going act right up. Can't nobody answer for spirits.

Mr. Peter must have done believe her. He ain't go near my ma'am since that night.

Mammy Water come in with Sami next day. My ma'am shock. Ask why they done come disturb a woman dying bed. Say she don't want water food nothing keep her from meeting her maker, sit down have a little talk with him.

Sami talk for Mammy Water. Say, we each got us a path. Something only my ma'am can do. She got to live give birth to two gal babies going set all us folks free. My ma'am don't do it, it ain't going get did.

My ma'am listening but don't believe none of it. "How can that be," she say. "Womens born to a field hand can't set nobody free. Ain't free they own self."

Sami say, "Mammy Water say you ain't got to live. But you live, you going have these here baby gals I done told you about. And they going up and set all the hands on this here plantation free. That all

87

Mammy Water know to tell me. You don't have them, they ain't coming to nobody else. Ain't coming to us here. Could save folks from misery. But you got to choose."

Ma'am say, "I don't even believe Mammy Water done put them words in your mouth, Sami. Wise woman just can't talk that foolish."

Sami hush up quiet. Mammy Water done had enough. Mammy Water cross that little dark shack and lay her hand right on my ma'am belly. Lay it there and Ma'am start in to feeling heat. Heat like to burn her up. She start in to screaming. Mammy Water like she don't hear nothing. Ma'am too weak to fight her off. Had to lay there and take it. Ma'am think she done bust in to flame. Burn up and die to ashes. She ain't nothing but a cinder when Mammy Water finally let go a hold of her belly. Get up grunt kind of satisfied and gone. Walk out don't say nothing.

Sami stay behind. "Can I get you something to eat or drink, Sister?"

Ma'am ask him to fetch some clean water. Drink it up, bathe in it. Few days later, she back in the field. Hating Mammy Water for burning up her road to death. She got a thirst to live like a newborn baby.

Mr. Peter keep his word stay away from her. But he look and see my ma'am talk all right to Sami. No time, Mr. Peter done order Sami give it a try see can he stud Sister.

Well, Sami ain't the worse hand to have to stud with, my ma'am say. Everybody know he gentle with the womens. Sami get sent in, womens ain't going have to fight and cry. He going talk to them.

He going wait on them. He going lie to Mr. Peter even Mr. Dennis. Say, "We trying but ain't nothing happen yet."

So Sami show up say "Mr. Peter sent me." My ma'am ain't go for her chopping hoe. She get him some supper lay down go to sleep don't even look at him. Middle the night he must is gone back to Mammy Water shack. He ain't there when day break.

Same thing happen next night and the next. Finally one night my ma'am feed him say all scared, "Look Sami. My belly bigging."

Sami say, "I know it, Sister." Say, "Name me a wedding present I give it to you. Put out word I'm father to your babies. Think it likely Mr. Peter think twice before he sell them."

My ma'am say, "You done something to me in my sleep, Sami?"

And Sami say, "Man in Africa have as many wives as he can love and take care of. I is asking you to be my wife let me bring you something by way a wedding gift. You feel better about these baby gals you going give birth to."

My ma'am ain't go for it. She feel tricked.

Sami bring one thing after another. Ma'am turn them all down. Things he make with his hands, grow in Miss Magdalen garden, probably steal out her kitchen. My ma'am say, "It a shame meet a hand ain't got nothing better to do than pester after a big belly woman. You give me all the wedding presents you want ain't going get you on my sleeping pallet. I suspect you done come after me in my sleep, Mr. Shiftless. You better bring me a axe in case you go

89

crazy try to come near me when I is wide awake. Chopping hoe kill you too slow to suit me."

Soon Ma'am laying up can't give birth right quick as usual. In pain. Sami rip off her rag door build her a wood one. Got a log she slide through to bolt it shut. Ma'am say, "That my wedding present, Shiftless Sami? A door I can lock you out with?"

Womens come help Ma'am get them babies out. Door shut on the biggest storm they done had in them parts. Solid wood door a good thing. Ma'am wish to thank Sami but ain't seen hide nor hair of him since the door built.

Us born, me and my sister, at the end of the storm. My ma'am come out, see two big rose bushes planted growing up the face of her shack. One got roses bloody red, other got roses bony white. They big and bold and clambering up, like to reach around peek in the chinks between the logs. Face to the sun.

Ma'am sling us on her hip and up and hunt down Sami. He digging and planting in Miss Magdalen vegetable garden. Ma'am say, "Sami, how you know I love Miss Magdalen rose bushes?"

Sami point to two graves over at the side Miss Magdalen garden. Say, "Miss Magdalen folks bury there. It ain't many Africans around here you can find where they bury. African child around here ain't got no ancestors to call. Don't know who you calling, don't know who you get when you call. Us all can't see in the dark like Mammy Water see. I see them bushes growing on Miss Magdalen folks' graves. I say, 'Child call on them spirits, always know who she getting.'"

My ma'am took us went away. Never had named us yet. But now she start in to calling us both Rose.

Folks say, "That ain't right. Two gals with one name, folks can't tell them apart." So Ma'am start in to calling sister Rose Red and me Rose White. Start in to bringing us over to Mammy Water shack in the night, when the hands coming in from the fields. Us two the only children Sami got to share with Mammy Water. Us special to her. Learn to talk her talk a little bit, around her so much.

Was there the night after Angel Girl run away to find her stole babies. Seen and heard Mr. Dennis go crazy come find Sami haul him out the shack. Shaking him and screaming he best go find him that runaway brat and haul her back.

Sami ain't say a word. Miss Magdalen come down from the house screaming and crying.

Sami put back out in the field the next day and die. Blood run from his mouth to the dust. Soak in. Folks come running. Mr. Peter flicking his whip ain't do no good. Hoist up Sami carry him off. Miss Magdalen trail behind the hands dragging the dust with her long skirts.

That night, biggest fire ever and folks stomp and cry out. Mr. Peter Mr. Dennis nowhere around. Us all call it The Frenzy. Mammy Water never come out her shack to sing good-bye to Sami. My ma'am sent us in to hold her hand. Say, "Good thing she got you all. Else she be all alone, now Sami gone to God." One us been come to her bringing food water comfort every night ever since.

That how I come to be setting holding Mammy Water hand when the storm come. Pink night sky mean a storm and give you enough light to see through Mammy Water rag door.

She gripping me hard. I look at my hand. Say, "I got the wrong name. I should a been called Bone White."

All year you work that cotton crop you wish you was dead. Chopping, clearing, planting, and picking. You get your hands sliced raw if they ain't tough as a dog claw. Me and my sister got hands ain't tough. I call her "Blood Red" say "I want to be called Bone White." I say, "Look at our hands." She say, "Hush you make me shiver."

Mr. Peter kept his word ain't sent my ma'am back out in the fields. But every lick a work he ain't get out a her, he done made sure to get out a me and my sister ever since Miss Angel Girl run and Sami die.

These days, Ma'am don't do nothing but cook and pretty up the shack. Keep our few little rags clean. Us always got plenty to eat. Miss Magdalen send it, say "Cook for Mammy Water and share."

So every night me or my sister get to carry some supper over to Mammy Water shack sit and talk. Most likely just sit. Mammy Water don't eat. Look like a skeleton with eyeballs staring at you. I always hope she be sleep these days so I can clean up around her place.

She ain't clean now Sami gone. I don't want nobody to see what I got to scrape and shovel out her shack. Take it to the pits and dump it where it belong. Shovel in some clean dirt sprinkle it around. Lonely woman lost her mind and fouling her own place. I wish she could go to peace.

Tonight she won't close her eyes nor let loose my hand. Start in to seeing hearing things. Could swear I hear something breathing like rocks caught under a chopper's hoe right outside that rag door.

I can't stand me no rag door. I must be spoilt, but give me a wood door like my ma'am got, or I can't feel safe. Ma'am say, "Don't put folks down. Who got leisure and logs to build a wood door? Sami tending the vegetable patch was a special case. Don't you look down your nose at folks ain't fortunate, Rose White."

But I can't set up in Mammy Water shack after dark done fell and hear sounds from the woods and be all right. And this night, between the stink in the shack and the breathing outside it, I'm like to die. Can't stay put and can't run nowhere. Ain't a clean spot to fall on, and don't want to get grabbed by whatever outside that rag door making such a ruckus.

I look up see a shadow done fell on Mammy Water wall.

Pink snow light coming through the rag door done got block by whatever breathing out there. Perfect shape of something big bent over spiky hair done got throwed on the wall I sit facing.

Scream. Can't help it. I look at the wall again. Shadow done gone. I on my feet and gone, too.

Hit the outside staring wild all around me. Hunting for that big bent over shape. Don't see it nowhere. Take off running to my ma'am shack. Maybe I can get there before that shape get back from wherever it gone to.

Shack door open. I throw myself through it and slam it shut. Crying and swallowing air, I want to

93

breathe so bad. Ma'am tending our supper at the fire send my sister to me. Say, "See about that gal, Rose Red."

Rose Red say, "What got into you tonight?" Try to pull me from the door in her arms.

Now I got the shivers. Say, "Something out there, Ma'am. Rose Red. I seen it shadow on Mammy Water wall."

Ma'am stop her stirring and spooning up. "What you saying, child? Was something in Mammy Water shack scare you?"

"No, Ma'am. I think it outside."

Ma'am ain't going for this. Say, "Rose White, you don't want to go take Mammy Water her food, you ain't got to make up tales. Just say you ain't up to it. I send Rose Red."

I curl up on my pallet start in to crying for real. Howling like a dog. Tired, hands hurt. Left Mammy Water shack a stinking mess I have to go clean up tomorrow. I just let it all out.

Ma'am set her big spoon back in her kettle come to me. Rose Red got me on one side, and Ma'am got me on the other. They hold me up. Us start in to hugging on each other.

Next thing Ma'am got her hand on my mouth. She staring at her wood door eyes bugging out. Say, "You all hear that, Rose Red, Rose White? You all hear what I hear out there?"

I can't talk with her hand cross my face. Rose Red say, "I hear it, Ma'am."

You could hear a scrape drag. Scrape drag. Getting louder. Till you hear that rocky breathing right on the other side a our wood door. I check quick with my eyes see I forgot to slide that log bolt.

I could have cursed myself. I was so happy to get inside, I done collapsed before I thought to lock the door. That door can get pushed open easy as you please.

And something right outside it now. Thumping on it.

I is up and running to the door with tears still wet on my face. Slam my body against it. Scream, "Rose Red come help me slide this bolt!"

Rose Red up behind me in a shot scrabbling at the bolt with her bloody cotton-picking hands. Can't get her hands to work. Panic and pain. Can't get mines to work neither. My mind gone.

Us shoving on the door and clawing at the bolt. Something on the other side shoving right back. Thumping so our bodies bump the door and us edging across the floor because the door opening up.

Ma'am up behind Rose Red, pushing, too. Yelling at me to get out the way so as she can try to slide the bolt. I scared to leave go the door. Pushing back against whatever pushing to get in. Us all three screaming no. Screaming go way. Jamming our heads our shoulders up against that opening door.

Door slide and something dark and spiky stick in at the open part. Something hard curve look like claws on the tip. Slide in reach around take a little swipe feel for somebody inside.

Us stare in the firelight at this claw thing and scream. Duck out the way still leaning on the door. Hand slide out from under the claw. Reach in feel

95

for somebody to grab hold to. Us leap back so as not to get touched.

My ma'am come throw herself in front of me and beat at the hand under the claw. Tell it, "Get back! Get back, now!" She look around the shack wild-eyed. I know she wish she had her a chopping hoe or a axe tonight. That hand be on the floor.

Ma'am say, "Rose Red, go get me a burning log out that fire."

That loud rocky breath outside the door start in to moan. Voice slide out from inside that moan just like the hand done crawl out from under the claw. Voice say, "Don't burn me, Ma'am. Don't burn me. Help me."

Ma'am shake her wits back inside her head. Grab the burning stick from Rose Red. Still leaning on the door say, "Let me shut the door talk to you through it. You don't mean us no harm, let me shut this here door."

Voice say, "Ma'am, don't shut this door on me."

Ma'am say, "You don't let me shut this door I burn you with my cooking stick. Shove your way inside this house I burn you."

Voice say, "Ma'am, don't burn me. Let me in and talk to me."

Rose Red say, "Start to sound like folks. What is it?"

I surprise myself. Say, "Ma'am, let it in. Find out what it wants. I don't think it mean to hurt us."

Ma'am look down where it done caught hold of my hand. Claw sliding a little off to one side. Hand holding mines firm but gentle. Fingers wrapped around together. Ma'am say, "Let go my girl before I let you in."

Fingers let loose us ease up off the door. Ma'am still got her torch burning. Ease up straight open the door bit wider with the other hand. Get the door off the creature arm.

Good thing I ain't got the door no more. Because I would have made my ma'am a lie. I see her open the door uncover this giant big spiky hair thing with another claw waiting. I ready to scream and burn its eyes out. Ma'am grab me with her free hand bury my head against her shoulder so I can't see no more. Say, "You done give your word not to hurt nobody. Come in talk as long as you can keep the peace."

Rose Red scream and shove something in her mouth. I pull away from my ma'am run and hold Rose Red. Us back away and watch the creature come in.

Take it a long while. It bent over hunchback dragging something. Big lumpy spiky hair body kind of roll and sway when the thing try to move. It heave and roll itself forwards over our dirt floor. Dragging and heaving and rolling its shoulders. Stop, breathe deep. When it all the way inside, it say, "Ma'am, please shut and bolt that door."

Rose Red say, "Don't lock us in with this thing, Ma'am."

She ready to run for the door. I scared Rose Red might go for Mr. Peter. I grab her say, "Ma'am, please shut the door."

Ma'am shut it. Stare at the thing, her eyes wide, her stick burning.

The thing eye her back. Start to rise up. Slow like it growing on the spot. Us see a snout like a dog, empty eye sockets, fangs between pulled back lips. Rise up some more. Dark fur start to ripple. Shake. Slide. The fur slide off.

Fur, snout, fangs, and all slide to the dirt floor. Crumble in a heap. Us look up again. It some kind of man standing there where the creature used to be.

Tall, brown, thick built, got a head full of curl long hair. Head bent down. Breathing hard. But no more rocky sound.

Shaking out his muscle arms.

He kick that big bear fur. Bear fur slide flat to the ground. He got a big wood box at his feet. That must been the dragging sound. Scraping sound. Maybe the rocky breathing sound, too.

Ma'am say, "What that?"

Man say, "My freedom, Ma'am. Can I entrust it here to you?"

She say, "Why me?"

He say, "Because don't Mr. Peter nor Mr. Dennis come inside your shack. You got a wood door and a bolt so can't nobody come prying. And you right on the edge of the woods."

Ma'am say, "Who told you come to me seeking help?"

Man say, "My mother."

Ma'am say, "Who that?"

He say, "Miss Angel Girl, Ma'am."

Us all catch hold our breath. Ma'am say, "Who you?"

Man say, "Let me sit down I tell you."

Ma'am say, "No. You answer right you sit down I feed you. You answer wrong you and that box get out my shack."

"My name Sami Wolf Water, Ma'am."

Me my sister us eyes got big. Us catch hold each other stare. I start creep forwards look him in the eye better. Ma'am say, "Get back, Rose White. You and Rose Red dish this man up some supper out the pot. Mr. Sami, you want to sit comfortable, spread that bear skin out under you."

He say, "Much obliged." Spread his skin out plop down on it. He one tired big man.

I bring him water to wash and he drink it. Rose Red bring him a wood bowl full of burning stew he swallow it down. Lick his lips look around. Ma'am say, "Bring him some more." Rose Red bring him some more. He put the bowl to his lips and gulp again. Ma'am say, "You want some more, Mr. Sami?" He look shame. Ma'am say, "Rose Red, bring him some more." He gulp it again. Ma'am say, "Rose White, quit staring and bring the man some pone."

I go fetch the hot pone baking on a flat rock in the fire. Put it in his empty bowl. He break it. Pull back when it burn his hand. Rose Red snicker. Ma'am give her a look. Mr. Sami play cat and mouse with that pone till he work up the nerve to eat it hot, too.

"Thank you, Ma'am," he say.

Ma'am say, "Us eat better than the other hands because Miss Magdalen steal for us out your pap kitchen. Your ma'am done sent you to the right place to eat good. But look to me like you got a story to tell. Us listening."

Mr. Sami lay back on the bear skin. Look over at that box. He say, "What's to tell is told quick. My father had a older brother. Bear ripped him. Mr. Peter let it. Didn't shoot the bear till he thought it

99

killed the man. Older brother figured it was better to hide out than hang around get killed. So he hid in the house where nobody find him. Miss Magdalen took care of him. They had a girl together."

My ma'am say, "The first Miss Angel. Murdered. She still haunt people, I hear."

Mr. Sami say, "I wouldn't doubt it. When Mr. Jared disappear, my father took Miss Angel lock her up till her ma'am tell where Jared gone."

My ma'am say, "Everybody know she never told."

Mr. Sami say, "So Mr. Jared torture Miss Angel till she dead. Got a mean streak in him can't be satisfied, I hear."

My ma'am say, "Owning folks do that to you. But you ain't told us nothing us ain't heard around here for years."

Mr. Sami say, "Maybe you all didn't know that when Sami brought Mr. Dennis his daughter, Angel Girl, she found the treasure Mr. Jared done holed up with. My father done stole everything from Mr. Jared. House, land, and folks. But he couldn't find that coffin box of treasure."

Mr. Sami thump the box. Say, "Mr. Jared swore to get his treasure back. But Miss Magdalen buried him alive in the house. Tried to burn him to death in the walls. But he wouldn't die. Got out, missing leg and all, and come back to steal me and my sister. Holding us ransom for this treasure."

"Then what you doing with it?"

"Miss Angel Girl learned from Mammy Water how to find us. This treasure going buy my freedom from Mr. Jared," Sami Wolf Water say.

"How that?" ask my ma'am.

"That's what he told me. When I find him the treasure I done cost him, he let me go."

Ma'am say, "You done cost him? How so?"

Mr. Sami say, "He give it to my ma'am to save her life from Mr. Dennis. He say she promised to give it back. Ain't did it. Say I bring him back his treasure, he let me go."

Ma'am say, "You believe a man reason like that? How long he kept you, anyhow?"

"Let's see. I was stole from here about three four years old."

Ma'am say, "He done snatched you away-"

"Hiding me under this here bear skin."

"-and you believe he up and set you free? From what I seen around here, you find him that treasure, he sell you quicker than you can say help. And what about your sister? He promise to set her free?"

Mr. Sami say, "Please, Miss Sister. This my only chance. What can I do crawling around in Mr. Jared's bear skin, hiding from the world? Help me try to get free."

Ma'am say, "You ain't got to beg. I help you. But anything go wrong, I got my gals to lose."

Mr. Sami say, "You got two sweet beautiful gals."

Ma'am say, "Never you mind my gals. What you want?"

Mr. Sami say, "Let me leave my box here. Tell Mr. Jared it been found. Get your gals to bring it to the woods for me. I meet them pick it up. Take it to Mr. Jared, and he set me free."

Ma'am say, "Why you ain't take that box straight to Mr. Jared tonight?"

Mr. Sami say, "My ma'am say that be a mistake. Say make him wait. Say make him make me promises. Say, give her time find where he hid my sister."

My ma'am say, "Leave your box here. Wait a little longer, till Mr. Dennis lights out in the big house. Us all need some rest. But let me wake up catch you near one my gals, I scream for Mr. Peter and that gun of his so quick you never know where the holes in you done come from."

Mr. Sami say, "I understand, ma'am. I don't mean no harm."

But us all oversleep wake up just before cockcrow.

"God help us," my ma'am say. "Now how us get this man out this shack?"

"I know!" I speak up say. "Mr. Peter know me my sister go out to the woods most every day before us hit the field, gather you some kindling. Let's us walk on out to the woods, and Mr. Sami here creep along the ground hid behind our skirt. In case Mr. Peter looking, he ain't going see nothing but two gals out for kindling like he see most every day. Us go running to the field with a arm load of kindling he can't do nothing but holler like he always do. Mr. Sami be gone."

"Go head," my ma'am say.

"Thank you," say Mr. Sami. "That a smart gal you got."

Ma'am say, "I done heard you talk one too many times on my gals. I be watching you from the door. You make a move I don't like, Mr. Peter trigger-happy."

Mr. Sami say, "I understand, ma'am."

Ma'am go throw the bear skin on the box. "You going wear this?"

"I move faster without it."

"Good," she say. "Keep us warm on a cold night. Get going."

Me my sister at the door peek around. Try to look casual. *How you do that?* Start out walking. I squeeze her hand say, "Kindling. Look like you ain't thinking about nothing but kindling."

She too scared to talk back. I feel Mr. Sami kind of hunching along on his hands and feet the same time, brushing up against my leg. Knock me a couple times. Afraid I look shaky. *Mr. Peter must not is up looking because I know me my sister ain't looking casual.*

Woods look long way off. Years away. I thinking back to my babyhood. *Me my sister used to play in the woods till Miss Angel Girl run off.*

Them last few steps to the woods stretching out. I start in to thinking I don't want Mr. Sami to go. *Wish I could look him in his eyes one more time. Hope he come back for that big box.* Think how different he look. Think how strong and brave he look. *Woods leaping away the closer us get.*

Rose Red say, "Ain't us never going get to them woods?"

Mr. Sami scuttling along look up say, "What?"

He bump me. I stumble. Rose Red reach to steady me. Mr. Sami reach, too. I falling trying to push his hand back down below the tall grass.

"Get up," Rose Red say. "You want Ma'am scream for Mr. Peter?"

103

I lay there just seen Mr. Sami's eyes close up in outdoor light. *Green and gold like trees and sun. Dark flecks lit by the falling moon.*

He holding me. *Big brown arms all around me, gentle. Not skinny like Ma'am. Not soft like Rose Red.*

His eyes look startled. Open his mouth to speak.

I feel hands like claws dig in my shoulders. Rose Red haul me up. "Ain't got sense God gave a goose," she say. "Walk, gal. Us all get shot you all staring bug-eye at each other."

Now I don't want to get to the woods lose Mr. Sami. But now I don't want to, us all sudden get there. Blam in the dark woods. He scuttle up rise to he feet. Stand face me stare in my eyes.

Rose Red say, "Come on. Help us gather up some kindling, you."

He ain't move. I can't neither. I think I can see what he thinking. *Can't understand it, though.*

Rose Red say, "You don't move from in front of my sister I'm going start in to screaming at Mr. Peter to shoot you, boy."

He turn kind of look at her. *I'm sorry to see them eyes turn away.* Pull my heart after them.

He look at me one more time. All my feelings leap to him. He say, "Rose White. Words is awful weak."

Rose Red bang into me. Say, "Take this kindling get out of here, gal. You crazy like a loon. Run to the shack before I call for Ma'am."

I take the skinny little bundle run. Scared of what I just done went through back there in the woods. Scared I don't run now, I can't run later.

Ma'am standing in the doorway say, "What got into you?"

"Ma'am, I scared."

"Then you got good sense. Get on out to the fields keep your mouth shut."

Rose Red join me up in my row. Sun creeping and turning the sky purple. She whisper, "Mr. Sami say listen for wolf howl at night. It be him waiting in the woods for that box."

Us chopping and turning the soil despite the snow that fell last night. Mr. Peter a hard and unreasonable man.

I see my hands start in to popping skin and bleeding but don't feel it much. Got my mind full of what I feel on account of Mr. Sami. Would love to ask my ma'am what it might be. But I got a suspicion she don't approve. *Old people don't want nobody to be happy.*

Still got these feelings on my mind when I go to shovel out Mammy Water shack leave her some hot supper. *These feelings good for blunting misery*, I tell myself.

Us all three bundle up in that bear skin next night. Me my ma'am my sister. Snow falling again. *Good to keep warm.*

Snow stop, snow melt, and still no wolf howl from Mr. Sami Wolf Water. "He done forget?" I ask my ma'am. Hurt me to think he forget me alongside that treasure, but I don't tell that to my ma'am.

"Gal, don't be simple," she say.

Next time I ask, she say, "What treasure? What man?"

I shock. "Why," I say pointing to the box cover with a bearskin, "this treasure right here, Ma'am."

105

"Gal, I don't see nothing but a dead smelly bearskin and a box to sit on," she say. "Kind a big for our little shack, though. Now, what man you talking about?"

Rose Red start in to snicker.

"Never mind," I say. I really don't want her to say nothing like that about Mr. Sami. Make like he ain't never was there. I make up my mind to wait quiet.

Time pass I think I must done made a mistake. *Ain't nothing happened like I thought. No such person as Mr. Sami. Ma'am right. Nothing in that box. I been a dreaming child.*

But my heart a changed thing. I start looking around at mens and boys I knowed all my life. And now they look different.

My face burn the snow off the ground, it feel so hot when I see them mens. See Mr. Peter staring in my eyes I like to die on the spot. I ask my ma'am ,"Find me something cover up where my raggedy old shirt getting too tight. Busting at the seam."

She ask why it bother me now I break down cry. Say, "Mr. Peter staring at me."

She say, "God help us. Don't you go take care Mammy Water no more. Neither one of you. I do it myself. I don't think he come in here at night, long as I'm alive."

She take off her head rag show me how to wrap it around cross my heart with it.

Next day in the field Mr. Peter ask me why I got that rag tied round my chest. I say, "Keep off the cold." Don't look at him. Go to sleep crying that night.

Wake up hear a wolf howl.

106

I'm up out the bearskin like a shot. I'm grabbing for the box. Hear Ma'am say, "Rose Red, help her."

I say, "Let me go alone."

But, truth be told, it way too heavy. Rose Red at the door say, "Rose White, go on out there and tell Mr. Sami come back here tote it his own self. Take all three us carry this thing."

Ma'am say, "Go on."

I take off running. Never run so fast so far in my life. Feel like my feet never touch the earth. Feel like flying.

I see his eyes before I see anything. Then I see his smile. Lips like stole fruit in the summertime.

He come toward me up to the edge of the trees. I can't stop running and slam into him. Them strong arms go around me. Pick me up. Us spin around. Topple. Stand. I can't believe he real. Look at him. Them sharp brown cheeks, that scraggly hair. Them eyes green and gold like I remember.

He pick me up carry me further under the trees. I'm breathing hard from running can't talk. Wouldn't say nothing if I could talk.

"What's this?" he say, put me down got his hand on that rag crisscross my chest.

"Keep Mr. Peter's eyes off me," I say.

"Mr. Peter?" he say. Mr. Sami whip his head around like he looking for Mr. Peter in the trees. Long thick scraggly curls strike me in the face.

He whip that head around stare at me again. I all of a sudden scared. Scared to be alone in the trees with Mr. Sami. Scared a his anger. Scared what might happen if I stay.

I push both his hands off me. I say, "Us can't carry your box, Mr. Sami. You have to come get it."

I pull twist get away from them strong hands. And gone through the trees.

I don't hear him behind me. I don't care. I must a been crazy wishing I could see him again. He scare me. I don't feel sane till I see them two rose bushes waving in the starlight front a my ma'am shack.

I come flying into the shack. Go duck into the bearskin. My ma'am my sister still huddle at the door saying, "Rose White, what you up to, gal? That Mr. Sami out there?"

"Yes," I whisper, peeking out the bearskin.

My ma'am ask, "He coming?"

"I don't know."

They groan look up to heaven. Ma'am say, "Rose Red, you go."

"No!" I say.

"Why not?" Ma'am suspicious. "Gal, what happen to you out there?"

"Nothing," I say and start in to crying.

My ma'am come gather me up hold me. "You growing up, I like it or not," she say. "Give anything to keep you little, but I can't. Now what happen out there?"

"Nothing," I say. "I told him us can't carry that box, and then I ran right back here."

Rose Red say, "He coming. I see the grass moving."

Heartbeats later I hear his voice mumble something in the shack. Ma'am holding me say, "Don't you come near her. Get your box and get out."

I hear him say, "Ma'am, ain't nothing happen."

"Something happen, all right. My baby crying."

"Ain't me you got to fear coming near your baby, Ma'am. I say it Mr. Peter you got to fear because I don't mean your gal no harm."

Ma'am sharp say, "How you know so much about Mr. Peter?"

"Rose White say he looking her over."

Ma'am say, "You don't get that box get out a here I is liable to do something crazy."

"You do something crazy to me, you won't have no protection for your gal."

Ma'am make a rude sound. I awful surprised. Peep through the bearskin at her. Ma'am say, "You hiding in the trees, Mr. Sami. How you protecting anybody?"

"I won't be hiding in the trees forever, Ma'am."

Ma'am answer back, "You hiding nowadays while Mr. Peter looking at my baby. Then you come wolf-calling making my girl cry."

Mr. Sami voice sound tight. I pull back the bearskin. Look at him good. He ain't looking at me. Got both eyes fix on my ma'am. Say, "I get this box out a here tonight be back in two three days. You keep her away from Mr. Peter two three more days I be back set all three you all free."

"You got big dreams for a boy ain't got nothing."

Mr. Sami say, "I got me this box."

"And you fixing to give it up."

Mr. Sami look like he just got slapped. "Got to buy my own freedom before I can buy anybody else."

Ma'am say, "So you tell me."

Mr. Sami look confused. "What you want me to do, Ma'am?"

109

"Something got more sense than you give away everything you just done got your hands on."

Mr. Sami drop to the floor sit next to that long box. Rose Red come stay by the bolted door. I look from Mr. Sami to my ma'am. They both look all sudden done in.

Mr. Sami say, "Ma'am, my own ma'am want me to free my sister, too."

"And what you want, boy?"

"I want to free all you all. My sister, you, and your gals. All you all."

"Big plans for a boy creeping round back of the woods."

He don't say nothing more. Up and go to that box. Rip at a lock on it with his hands. Twist and pull. It don't budge.

Ma'am send Rose Red for her big wood cooking spoon. Mr. Sami take it rip it around in the lock. It break. The lock stay. He grab the metal plate hammer into the box. Dig into it with his fingers. Dig till blood spurt. Grunt and groan. Start in to yelling, and Rose Red clamp her hand quick on his mouth. Eyes shut head throwed back he heave and strain.

Metal snap off the box. He crash into Rose Red, and they tumble to the floor. He hold up the metal lock a flapping in his tore up hand. He start in to laughing. Rose Red under him on her back on the floor clamp her hand on his mouth again. But she laughing, too.

Ma'am put me down get a rag and some water to wash the blood off his hands. He digging in the box. Rip the lid off, his eyes so big, I see colors in the dark. He say, "Look. Enough here to buy anything."

Ma'am say, "Boy, what you know about money?" But she smiling.

"Ain't money," he say. "Better than money. Look." He hold up round shiny things in his hands. He say, "Let's us stuff these in the bear paws. They like pockets."

And us scoop shiny hard stuff in our hands and stuff it in the bearskin paws. They pocket pads where he use to stick in his feet and hands to walk and be a bear. Us stuff them full but the box still got more.

He say, "That's enough, Ma'am. I come back and buy you all three from my father. Two three days. I told you."

Ma'am say, "You going buy us with the same money you stole from your father, boy? He be done whipped you till you dead. You ain't going buy yourself nothing but a licking."

He say, "You see. Now help me find some kind a sack to dump this stuff in. Can't tote it in a busted box."

So Ma'am go for her sack stuffed full a pine needles she sleep on for her aching back. Dump the pine needles on top of the bearskin. Say, "Sleep on the bare needles just as good. Here, boy. Take this sack."

Mr. Sami take it start to shoveling in the round hard shiny things from the box. Rose Red and me help. Our hands bumping into each other. Us laughing in the soft light from them shiny things.

111

All sudden Mr. Sami heft that sack and start for the door. Say, "Got to get started before the moon set."

I run after him, start to throw my arms around him. He turn round look at me in the starlight come through the open door. I back off. Wonder what my ma'am thinking but can't turn around to look at her. Don't want to take my eyes off Mr. Sami. Got the strange scary thought, *What if I don't see him no more?*

Watch him cross the grass creeping low with that sack full of shiny things. Can't see the grass move no more. He must done got to the woods. He gone and I still standing at the door staring. Ma'am and Rose Red stand close to me say, "Rose White, child." I shut the door. Us lie down I hear somebody breathing. I can't sleep.

Pretty soon, I hear Rose Red say quiet-like, "Rose White. How it feel?"

I say, "Like living and dying both at once all the time."

She say, "I don't want to lose you. Not to him not to nobody. After Ma'am, you all I got."

I reach out feel for her. Hold her. She cry herself to sleep on my shoulder. I try to think but I just recall Mr. Sami face in the starlight at the door. Maybe I dream on it because cockcrow and I ain't thought of nothing else.

Us in the row chopping. My teeth chattering I say to Rose Red, "I keep you with me no matter what happen. I be with you and Ma'am till the day I die."

She don't say nothing but I see tears roll down her face. Field hands always breaking promises like that to each other. My hands just about froze wrapped around that hoe. I all sudden think how good it feel take a hoe to Mr. Peter head. I ain't never had a thought like that before. Scare me. But I like it.

So sleepy that night, me and Rose Red fall sleep waiting for Ma'am to get back from Mammy Water shack. She left mad saying "How can a body cook with her spoon all broke?" I want to wait up remind her Mr. Sami some day buy or whittle her another cooking spoon. Ma'am and Rose Red shake me to wake up and eat, but I can't. Can't remember what I wanted to say, neither.

All sudden I hear that wolf howl again.

I sit up. Ma'am and Rose Red curl up near me sleep. Fire banked. Ma'am and Rose Red don't move. I whisper, "Wolf call, Ma'am. You want I should go?"

But she don't say nothing. I don't think twice. Up and out that shack in a heartbeat. Barely take time to shut the door.

Fly over the grass. All sudden thought hit me, *What if it ain't Mr. Sami out there? What if it Mr. Peter trying to fool with me?*

I stop dead in my tracks middle of the grass. Moon throw light cast me a shadow up ahead. Look back. Them two rose bushes just a waving me on from home. I want so bad to go to them woods have a look see. I turn look ahead. *I dreaming? That my name I hear?*

"Rose White," someone whispering. Wind pick up my name carry it soft to me. "Rose White. Rose White. Come here, girl. I won't hurt you."

I tiptoe on. My heart give my feet flight. Next thing I know, I'm running again.

Slam into the darkness of the woods. Look around. Wild-like. "Rose White," I hear. "Over here, girl." I follow the voice.

Something quick grip my ankle like fire. I try jump back. It hang right on. I try kick it off. It won't let loose.

Burn and rub into my skin something awful. Scraping the skin raw round my ankle. "Quit it!" I say. "You hurting me!"

Low voice start in to laughing. Evil. Snatch my ankle jerk me round by the leg. Pain shoot up my leg to my knee. I fall down in the mulch. I start to crying out, "Let go! Let me loose!"

Beating at the hand got hold on me. Don't even look real. All shrivel and tough. Bones jutting out. Shiny things hanging off it and clicking together.

I kick at it with my free foot. Another hand fly out the mulch grab hold my other leg. I still can't see no face. Panic take hold. I twist and kick thinking something terrible got me. *Dragging me where?* Reach over grab at them fingers try to pry them loose.

Face rise up out the mulch. Don't know where it come from. Half of it ripped and tore away. Something at the bottom of it open up say, "Girl, you get away from me, I shoot you running."

I stop fighting back. Panting hard, though. Say, trying not to look too close, "What you want with me?" Voice shake so even I can't rightly make out what I'm trying to say.

But Hole-in-the-Face must could understand because it answer right up say, "You must is Rose White."

"Yes," I say.

"I the man own that box of treasure in your shack," Hole-in-the-Face say.

"You a man?"

"Don't you sass me," Hole-in-the-Face snap. "I kill you right now."

I'm working up a nerve. *Since when spirits and things got to brag on they self?* I snatch one leg free say, "You call me out here to kill me? Why you waste time talking about it, then?"

Trying to sound like I think my ma'am would a talked.

Now it got a free hand again, Hole-in-the-Face reach in behind it somewhere haul out a pistol. I seen one before. Mr. Peter tote them. Kill folks kill a mad dog all the same to him.

Seem all the same to this one, too. "You got my gold," it say. "Now you lead me on in that shack get me out my gold back. You try trick me, gal, I splatter your brains out."

"For real?" I say. I ain't trying to sass no more, but I can't rightly make out why this thing here hate me so. I gone cold inside don't know what best to do. It drag pull one my ankles so us start crawling toward the grass. I look up see Ma'am shack ahead. I don't rightly want to lead this pistol-toting creature back to my ma'am and sister. I try to figure what happen if I kick it in the face make a run for it. It try to shoot me, least my ma'am and sister wake up know something going on.

115

All sudden a thought strike me. *What if this Mr. Jared that Sami done told us all about? Come to get the treasure on his own because--because what?*

What if Mr. Jared done killed Mr. Sami? Come back to get the treasure his own self? Going kill my ma'am my sister and me, too? Might as well warn them. Maybe they save they self.

I crawl out little further where I think moonlight strike me good my ma'am look out the door. Count my crawls so they stay even. Cold shaking in my stomach so I think I must going gag soon. *Here go,* I say to myself. *God help me. Spirits help me.*

I tuck my free knee forward like I about to crawl on it. Slam it back feel my foot strike something sharp something soft. *Lips and tooths?* Whatever, it spin away under my foot. I look back quick slam again. Raise up that free leg stomp on that face while I can't see it nohow. It groaning or something.

Hand let loose my ankle. I shove off from the ground with my hands digging in. Shoot forwards kind of walking scuttle like I seen Mr. Sami do. Stay low in the grass till I pass between the rose bushes fling myself at that door. Hear a shot when I push through it. Slam the door and don't forget to bolt it this time in my panic. Ma'am and Rose Red sitting up trying to rub eyes and figure what going on.

"Mr. Jared out there," I say. "Either that or some crazy evil spirit took out after me. I ain't going back out."

They up in a heartbeat at the door with me. "What it want?" Ma'am say.

"The treasure," I say. "Got a pistol."

"Spirit with a pistol?" Ma'am say. "Bolt the door."

"It bolted."

"Why you go out there?"

"Wolf howl."

Rose Red speak up. "It tricked you, Rose White. Must done heard Mr. Sami last night."

Ma'am thinking hard. Breathing fast. Say, "Let it hang around out there make a racket. Maybe it wake up Mr. Peter. Two pistol-happy fools kill each other do me a favor."

All sudden shot crack splinter in the door. Voice low nearby scratching at our ears say, "You got my gold in there, woman. I ain't playing no games with you. Open up that door."

Ma'am at the side a the door yelling back, "You a fool to shoot off that thing in the night. I ain't let you in here. You want your treasure, you welcome to it. I ain't ask that boy drop it off here for you. But you going fool around wake the hands and Mr. Peter be here in no time, all that ruckus you making. I know you, Mr. Jared. You want Mr. Peter round here rip the other half a your face off?"

And she ain't lying neither. Us hear shouts and scuffling because folks up around hunting out the source of them gun shots. Wasn't nobody set to be whipped. Can't nobody think why folks hearing shots in the night ain't nobody planning to run off. They up shouting and calling on Mr. Peter to bring that rifle a his.

Us hear a rustle in the grass figure Mr. Jared done hightailed it back to the woods. Folks banging

117

at the door say, "You all right, Sister? Them gals in there safe with you?"

Ma'am shout back, "Us all right. Shook up is all. You all look around see somebody out there?"

Pretty soon Mr. Peter say, "Sister! Look like somebody try to put a bullet through your door. Open up let me take a look see inside there!"

Ma'am say, "Why?"

Mr. Peter say, "He still round I need to bust him out."

Ma'am say, "He in here you think I be in here with my gals? You get on out to them woods hunt out whatever is hunting us, Mr. Peter. You got a gun what you scared for?"

"Tell him, Ma'am," I say.

"Hush," Rose Red say.

Mr. Peter yell through the door, "Who was it anyway, Sister? I can't hunt what I don't know I'm hunting."

Ma'am shout, "Say he Mr. Jared. I ain't open the door see for myself. You hunt something in the woods got a gun on it you must is found what you hunting for!"

Folks talking fast outside. You can tell Mr. Peter feel challenged. Don't want to believe it. Mr. Peter say, "What Mr. Jared want in there pestering after you for, woman?"

Ma'am snap say, "Look to me he want the same thing you want, pestering after me."

Folks take that up. Feel out Mr. Peter mood kind of scared, and they start saying "Let's us go beat that pistol-toting wretch out the woods, Mr. Peter. What you think Sister hole him up in her house after he done tried to shoot her and her gals? Pass out the guns us help you find him shoot him."

Mr. Peter must a thought he best look into this or Mr. Dennis not going take it too kindly. Say last thing, "Sister, Mr. Jared tell you why he hunting round here after you?"

Ma'am ready for this one. Say loud, so everybody hear, "Whatever shot my door say Mr. Dennis son done broke loose from it and it trying to hunt him back down before he find his pap."

That done it. Folks all fired up. Mr. Peter don't go chase this spirit now, he regret it on the morrow. One way or another, Mr. Dennis going hear, "Sir, your son free and trying to find you, but something hunting to take back your son, and Mr. Peter say it ain't none of his affair."

Mr. Peter gots to go. Is in a sweat. Us could hear him swearing, saying, "One thing I can't stand me no smart-mouth darky. Let me catch you out that door tomorrow, woman, I whip you some manners into that nappy head."

Ma'am shout, "Catch me tomorrow good as you can. Because I ain't opening this door for nothing and nobody tonight."

I reach out hug my ma'am.

Folks outside the door say, "Come on, Mr. Peter. That thing in the woods be done got away, us standing around jawing at a scaredy-cat woman. Let's us go get something teach Mr. Jared a thing or two."

"It be folks can't wait to shoot at a wight man," Rose Red mutter.

Us hear folks walking away. Mr. Peter shouting "Niggers can have hoes, knives, anything got a long

119

handle but no whips and no guns. First nigger I see got a whip or a gun," Mr. Peter say "I shoot on sight no questions asked." And say "Every nigger better be in the field at day break." Then Mr. Peter spit and sputter and can't do a thing but follow.

Ma'am lean on the door, sigh, say, "And I always thought Mr. Jared wasn't nothing but a scary story for childrens. Can't stop counting the miracles in the world. Wish it was some of them good, though. Let's us lay down get some shut-eye. No telling what the morrow bring."

Hard to lay down try go to sleep. I'm staring at the ceiling beams over my head thinking about Mr. Jared hole in the face. *You have to feel for him,* I'm thinking. *Poor man. Face all tore up. Can't walk right got to crawl. Creeping round the earth face in the muck all the time bound to make a body kind of mean. What all this treasure going do for him, anyway? Ain't like my ma'am don't want nothing but her a new cooking spoon. New cooking spoon new sack so them pine needles under her back stay bunched up.*

I roll over look at my ma'am sleep. *I wonder what do she want. She ain't never talked about nothing but me my sister Rose Red. She got her two babies ain't sold off she make it sound like she happy enough. Just fighting to keep folks' hands off her babies is all.*

I sigh roll back over. *I gots to be a better girl. Keep my own hands and eyes off that Mr. Sami.* Soon as I think of him, it all over. *Now what I go do that for?* Now I lay staring at the ceiling wondering what done happen to Sami Wolf Water he ain't showed up tonight. *Mr. Jared done killed him I have to go to Mammy Water learn me a curse. But good.*

Pity a fleet-foot thing. "I'm cursing that Mr. Jared for a creeping wretch if he done kill my Sami," I mumble, trying out my cursability.

Then I startle. *I done called Mr. Sami my Sami? I must be one bold-mouth gal.* I shake my head. *And here I lay just telling myself this very minute how much better I was going to be. No hope for me.* Feel kind of soft and happy though, so now I can drift off to sleep.

Somebody at the door blam blam blam. I wake up sit up. Ma'am trying to roll over get up. "Who it is?" she shouting.

Mr. Peter voice say, "Mr. Dennis send me for your gal."

Ma'am look around eyes big. "Where my Rose Red?" she scream.

"Out in the field where she belong," Mr. Peter shout back. "Crazy old woman, I come for the other one. One seen whatever she seen last night. Send her out here but quick. I ain't got no more time to mess with you. You feel my whip hand you give me some more your black sass."

Ma'am scared. Hop up haul me up. "I'm going with you," she say. She shout through the door, "Give the gal time to wash up. She ain't slept all night spirits and fools banging on the door."

Ma'am sassing good but her voice ain't got no pepper. She scared, all right. Got a rag dripping drinking water and sloshing my face while she talk.

Mr. Peter done took something to the door. Banging away. Sound like thunder and hail falling from the sky.

121

"Quit it!" my ma'am scream. Rush to the door start drawing the bolt. She try to slip out I slip out past her. She hot on my tail. Stand in the shut door glaring at Mr. Peter. You can tell she can't make up her mind to stay guard that treasure or go guard me.

"Ma'am, get you some rest please," I'm begging. "I'm going be all right. Come back tell you what Mr. Dennis got to say."

For a heartbeat look like Mr. Peter raising that rifle barrel going knock my ma'am down with it. "I'm coming with you, Mr. Peter," I say, trying to catch his eyes. His eyes done went all crazy. *Why he hate my ma'am so, I just don't know.*

He haul off reach for me bump into the white rose bush. Look up like he just noticed it first time in his life. "How this get here?" he all a sudden want to know. "What a field hand doing with a rose bush? Where you stole it from and why?"

Ma'am thinking. "Them rose bushes sprung up when my baby gals was birthing," she say. "Come out my house I was told spirits must a planted them watch over my baby gals see don't nothing happen wrong." She hold his eyes steady. He calm right down.

"Come on," he say to me. I pick myself up take off after him. Can breathe all right now because Ma'am done stay put.

Reciting myself a lesson all the way to Mr. Dennis house. *Sassing a dangerous thing,* I tell myself. *Keep folks at a distance and keep them wanting to get at your throat.* I don't know how my ma'am survive.

Ain't never set foot Mr. Dennis house before. It loom tall and big over all the trees. Little square patch of green things trying to grow in the shadow of that big dead bone white house. *Many ways I don't like white,* I think to myself. *I don't like snow, don't like maggots, cotton bolls, Mr. Peter, nor dead animal bones. And this house just like a dead hollow-out bone. And Mr. Peter the maggot crawling in.*

So what I suppose to be, following him? Little black ant, that's me. Can't stop working.

I recall seeing a pack of ants scuttling in and out a dead dog bones once. So now I can't stop thinking Mr. Dennis house nothing but a tombstone. I got the shudders. Don't rightly want to set foot in that house. No wonder Miss Angel Girl took off headed for the woods. *Ain't Mr. Dennis ever look up see that house of his look just like his parents' two tombstones he got round the side of it?*

Tombstones sitting up tall just as dull white as that house they done left to Mr. Dennis. Seem to me resemblance ought to strike him.

"What you gawking at, gal?" Mr. Peter want to know, face all snarl at me.

"I hear tell them two white curve stones mark where Mr. Dennis folks is buried," I say.

"And what's it to a shiftless darky no-good gal like you?" he want to know.

"Ain't nothing to me, Mr. Peter, sir," I say. "Except maybe I was just thinking he get the shivers his house looking so like them tombstones."

Mr. Peter stop dead in his tracks. Look round good like he ain't rightly ever notice before. "Well, I'll be," Mr. Peter say. Them eyeballs a his rolling from the curve gravestones to the curve windows and doors and back again. "Well, I'll just be," he keep on saying, and I all sudden think I know what my ma'am got on him. He scared of death. *Somebody done dished out so much death to others. And yet, he scared a death his own self.*

I say real child-like sweet, "Mr. Peter, sir?"

"What now?" he say all soft because his mind elsewhere.

"What happen to folks when they die?"

He go all pale white like them tombstones. *He scared a death, all right.* "How I suppose to know?" he snap at me. "Wight folks don't talk about them things. Go on back talk that crazy black mumbo jumbo with that gnarl-head witch live over in Dead Sami shack."

"Thank you, Mr. Peter, sir," I say more sweet than ever. "I just do that. Mammy Water talk to Dead Sami all the time. I just sit listen in learn something."

He don't want to hear none of this. He gone ahead of me before I get half my words out good. *Now how he figure I can listen in on them she talk a tongue I ain't allowed to listen to?*

Catch up to Mr. Peter at Miss Magdalen back door. I know I got a power like Ma'am but I best watch it don't go to my head.

Miss Magdalen at the back door eyes fixed on me. She ain't smile. But when I gets to her she open her arms take me inside.

Mr. Peter don't follow us in. Look like he want to get going awful bad. "I done brought her," he say. "Got to get back to them fields. Mr. Dennis want me, I be there."

Take off at a stiff trot.

124

Miss Magdalen watch him shake her head. Turn back to me. "Come on, girl," she say. "Bet you ain't ate nothing today."

Set before me a bowl of steaming mush. She come round behind me while I eat start in to feeling my hair. She say, "These plaits need tending."

Mouth full of hot mush, I say, "I ain't rightly got time for no hair-plaiting, Miss Magdalen."

"But I do," she say, and I feel her start in unwinding my hair. "Rest my mind get my hands in a girl's hair," she say, and I feel that tug and pull tell me I might as well wait a while. *Can't go no place no time soon.*

Miss Magdalen start in to talking. I'm shocked because I can't recall her to be one to say much. She talking about hair and how pretty she done made gals once she get her hands on they head. Who they done hitch up with all a cause of Miss Magdalen done plait they hair.

I ask myself she ever look out Mr. Dennis skeleton house see how many her couples is done split up due to studding and selling off. I don't say nothing, though. No point hurt a woman think she done did some good in the world.

I start in to thinking, *I could use me another bowl of food,* but can't tell how long it take Miss Magdalen to go find her the kitchen out back and fetch it. *She send me, I never make it back. So maybe I just sit here bear up under how she tugging on my head.*

All sudden door slam open. I think this must is Mr. Dennis. Sure enough. "Well, well, Maggie, my dear! Isn't this just cozy? While I'm chewing my nails over this little wench and her nighttime adventures, you're just shooting the breeze, aren't you, my dear?"

I ain't seen Miss Magdalen shoot nothing yet.

She say, "Mr. Dennis, this gal ain't had no time to take care herself. I'm just helping out."

He lay into her. "You want to fix her head just snatch off that head rag she got round her chest put it where it belong. I ain't studying about no nigger naps today. I'm onto the trail a my son."

Miss Magdalen say, "Well just let me-"

He ain't want to hear it. "Gal," he say so I jump. "What this I hear haunts is after you talking about where my son?"

I put my hand up where Miss Magdalen done lit into my head something terrible. "Mr. Dennis, sir," I say my face all scrunch, "it true."

"Who these haunts say they is?"

"Say they Mr. Jared, sir."

Mr. Dennis slam his fist on the table so me my bowl both jump. "Why they studying after some no-count nigger wench like you?"

"Sir, they ain't tell me why they do what all they do."

Blam go that fist one more time. I start in to thinking, *Ain't safe open my mouth round here.*

"Gal, you want me take a strap to you?"

"No, sir."

"Then you best start talking sense."

"Yes, sir."

"Now, what this here spirit got to say to you, gal?"

"It say it hunting Mr. Dennis son back, sir."

"Why saying all that to you?"

126

"A cause I the only one out in the woods middle of the night, sir."

Mr. Dennis look right startle. *I got him that time.* His voice gentler now. "Why you out in the woods at night, gal?"

"Voice calling my name say come here, sir."

"Gal you got any idea why some spirit call you out to the woods? Your ma'am let you out in the woods at night, knowing the patrol come catch you I be done lost me a good field hand?"

"She was sleep and I didn't know what she would a wanted me to do. So I gone."

"You scared?"

"Yes, sir."

"Then what happen?"

"Something grab my leg say it going shoot me. Say it hunting your boy, sir. I kicked it and run home."

"See here, gal. You ain't no way misleading me?"

"No, sir."

"What that haunt do after you kick it and run?"

"Shoot at me. Splinter in my ma'am door."

"You look at it good? What it look like?"

"Got a hole in it face it use for a mouth. All deck out with shiny things. Face all ripped. Rings on its fingers when it grabbed me."

"Sound like Jared, all right. Why you call it a spirit anyway, gal?"

"I don't know. I just thought it was. It so ugly, creeping on the ground."

"You ever heard tell spirits creeping on the ground?"

"No, sir."

127

Mr. Dennis sigh take a deep breath pull up a chair and sit. He look all a tremble more pale than before. *I hope he shook up getting my story out me.* He change his tone: "Might there be anything else you can tell me, girl? It would help me to know anything you might be able to tell me about my son."

"I think on it, sir."

"Let me give you something," he say. "Maggie, what you think this gal might want? Teach her talking to me is a good thing."

I speak up. "Sir?"

"What is it?"

"Can I ask for something, sir?"

"What you want?"

"Cooking spoon for my ma'am."

"How she cook all these years ain't got no spoon?"

"It done broke on her."

"Maggie, get this gal ma'am a spoon. Nothing else, gal?"

"New sack for my ma'am pine needles, sir."

"What your ma'am need pine needles for, gal?"

"Pillow her aching back a night, sir."

Mr. Dennis laugh at that. "Why her back ache a night?" he want to know. "She don't work none."

"She say she done birthed more than a dozen babies in the field, sir. Done broke out her back on her."

He look right down at the table. "Maggie," he mumble at the table top, "get that gal ma'am a sack. Nothing else, gal? You see I be learning you to talk to me."

"Well, sir. I could use me one last thing."

"Tell me about it."

"Need me a shirt more big, sir."

Mr. Dennis look up, surprise. Start in to studying on me. I can feel my face burn all the way to my belly. I die he ask me why I need a shirt more big.

But heaven be praise he say, "Maggie, find this gal some clothes. And don't let me see that ridiculous head rag round her chest next time I call her in to talk to me. Man take good care a his field hands shouldn't have to look at such a sight."

"Yes, Mr. Dennis," and he heave up and gone. Slender man but he walk away heavy. Look kind of sad.

Miss Magdalen wait till he gone and say, "Sit tight, girl, while I finish up these plaits. Folks in the field probably never know how much that man loved Miss Angel Girl and her babies. I know he thinking he get them babies back, she soon come following behind. You see he ain't took no other woman in and give her Miss Angel Girl's things."

I steady saying to my own self, *Now why folks in the field gots to take note on Mr. Dennis troubles?*

She go head answer like she heard my question. "Get Miss Angel Girl and them babies back here, things change for the better," she say.

"How that, Miss Magdalen?"

"When Miss Angel Girl was around, didn't nothing happen to the hands they couldn't tell African Sami to take to her. She light out after Mr. Dennis and he set things right in no time. He couldn't stand to have her cross with him. Crazy over her. Jealous a her dead wolf. Jealous a her pap.

Jealous a her babies. But suit me just fine, man made a flint got a soft spot stick out a mile like that."

"African Sami gone now," I pluck up nerve to mention.

Miss Magdalen quiet. Say, "Your ma'am you gals taking good care Mammy Water out there. You all keep it up, you hear me?"

"Yes, Miss Magdalen."

"Let me go on now find that spoon that sack for your ma'am. I go hunt you up a gown, too. Don't you move now."

I sit feel on my head while she gone. She done plait them rows so tight I think they never come loose. *Probably pretty, though.* I start in to daydreaming on that dress she going find me. *It got to look better than what I squeeze into now.*

She back in no time. Spoon, sack, she put them on the table in front of me. Then she say, "Turn round look at this."

I turn round catch my hand to my throat. I know I stare but I can't help it. "Miss Magdalen, I can't work the field dress like that. That dress look like something Miss Angel Girl use to wear. Mr. Peter take a whip kill me."

Miss Magdalen turn up her nose like she ain't got no good use for Mr. Peter. She say, "I got me a hunch you ain't going be back in that field no time soon, gal. I'm thinking Mr. Dennis going set you in the woods act as bait for Mr. Jared. Don't surprise me none you be baiting Mr. Sami Wolf Water, too. But mens don't necessary think ahead like that."

My mouth drop.

Miss Magdalen go on. "Learn to keep your feelings to yourself, gal. Never do to drop your jaw like that front a Mr. Dennis. He don't need to know no more than you already done told him."

She stand me, peel off my rags, wash me, dress me.

I leave feeling I done learned to be proud humble all at once. My dress soft pink like dawn light. White spider webs hanging off my throat my arms.

Walking behind Mr. Dennis. Miss Magdalen right. He don't want me back out in no fields for nothing today. Want me in the woods. I'm toting my sack my spoon for Ma'am. And another thing. I done begged me another dress to give to Rose Red.

Folks watching me parade behind Mr. Dennis. I raise my free hand wave. Smile all around. I love living today.

Mr. Dennis stop me by my ma'am shack. "Go on in there give that stuff to your ma'am. I go find your sister in the field bring her here to you."

Mr. Dennis going send my sister with me.

Ma'am frown all up want to know what I done did up at the big house to get two new dresses out Mr. Dennis. I tell her, "Ain't did nothing but tell him Mr. Jared hunting his son."

She all a tremble and ain't satisfy. I give her the spoon the sack she throw them on the bearskin. Say she won't touch nothing I got through my shame. I get on my knees start stuffing her old pine needles in the sack my own self.

They awful stiff and dry. I say, "Ma'am, should I go gather you some new needles? I be in the woods all day today."

Ma'am come sit down near me. Reach out hold me say she sorry she lost her head.

Rose Red come in all agitate. Want to know why Mr. Dennis come fetch her from the field. "Why he won't say nothing but 'Get to your ma'am shack right now, girl?'"

I show her the dress she whoop and want to put it on. Ma'am pull out that trusty rag and go for her wash water. Scrub up on Rose Red while I talk about Miss Magdalen and Mr. Dennis and his stupid questions.

Rose Red say, "Let's us go fishing at that little stream in the woods. Bet us catch something tasty for supper. Have us a good old time."

Mr. Dennis hollering, "Get on out here, you two. Ain't got all day wait on you."

Kiss Ma'am take off running. Pull up my skirts so the rose bushes won't snag them. Rose Red do the same. Us having a grand time all dressed up. Her dress not quite like mines, though. Sky color. No spider webs.

I done begged Miss Magdalen for something for Rose Red look like mines but she all strange talking about "Won't do to show up the bride." I ain't seen no bride nowhere in the woods myself, ever since Miss Angel Girl gone.

Mr. Dennis grab at my hand say, "Come on show me where you seen that spirit last night." So I skip on to the woods and he got to let go or skip with me. Rose Red laughing and skipping behind. Us hear Ma'am shut the door.

Get to the woods show Mr. Dennis where everything took place. "Here where Mr. Jared spirit grab me," show him my ankle rub raw, "here where us crawl, somewhere round here where I start in to kicking the spirit face." I all pleased with myself. Hope it don't show too much. *Never do to show certain folks you proud.*

Rose Red say, "Us need some sticks some twine go fishing."

Mr. Dennis speak up. "Go back to your ma'am get you what you need."

Soon she gone he grab my arm. Seem to me these days folks always grabbing on me. He come up close in my face say, "Listen here, wench. Don't sport with me. You see that spirit Jared you grab a hold a him set up a holler. You hear me?"

"Yes, sir."

"You see my son, you do the same. Hear?"

"Yes, sir."

"You know what Miss Angel Girl look like?"

"Not rightly, sir."

"You see a light-skinned negress got a dress on like you, you lay hands on her fetch her home. Hear me?"

"She might think I acting strange, sir."

"Sassing me, gal?"

"No, sir."

"Why you twisting and pulling?"

"You hurting me, sir."

He let go. Stand there staring at me like he want bad to say something but ain't going to.

Soon Rose Red run up, she can tell something ain't right. She look from one us to the other but don't ask no questions. Mr. Dennis stomp off. She set in to checking I'm all right.

"Let it alone," I grumble. "Let's us not let him ruin our day."

She take my hand gentle like tell me I get the first worm.

By high noon us done forgot all about Mr. Dennis, Mr. Jared and all they problems. Kicking our feet in the water like the old days. Roast and eat our fish. Thinking about peeling off our gowns so us can go swimming.

All sudden splash and scream so close by us drop our poles in the stream. "Let them go," I say. "Let's us go find out what was that."

Head up the stream and part the rushes. Come face up on the ugliest something you ever did see. Couldn't rightly believe my own eyes. I had seen him before, but not in broad daylight. *He a worm-eaten earth-crawling carcass, all right.*

Mr. Jared caught in the bushes getting one leg tugged down the stream. Screaming to high heaven. I try to get him to hush. Tell him "Never do if Mr. Peter and the mens come running find you here."

He just won't quit. I reach down slap him and tell Rose Red "Help me haul him free of the stream."

She got her face turn like she going lose her fish she look at him one more time. But she reach down, grab hold and tug. String a white beads break off his neck and he set to screaming.

Us yank and pull and get him out. He lay in the mulch at the forest floor gaping up to the sky like a dying fish. *He one ugly something.* "Ugh," I can't help saying, and take my hands back to the stream wash them good.

Come back to him Rose Red still got her face turn away. I cover my mouth like he smell rot and say, "Folks want to talk to you, Mr. Jared."

Them gape eyes swim round fix on me and my belly heave. He open that hole mouth say, "What for?" His hands steady feeling round see if he lost something.

"Folks think you got Mr. Sami Miss Angel Girl and them." I all the time asking myself, *How you talk to something you can't stand to look upon. I seen field hands whipped to pieces scarred for life ain't turn my stomach not a bit. What it be about this man spirit here distress me so?*

Mr. Jared say "What if I tell folks you and your ma'am got gold stole from Mr. Dennis house?"

"I tell them Mr. Dennis boy give it to me. Think that satisfy most people." And then I go wander away fall against a tree trunk cause I don't feel so good. Rose Red follow after me.

I call out, "Mr. Jared, all us want to know what you done with Mr. Sami and them. Where they at? You kill them or what?"

Rose Red whisper, "Why us don't just call for help?"

"I need to know," I whisper back. "Us call for help they rush up shoot this man. Us never find out nothing."

Mr. Jared lay there fish mouth gaping say, "Boy all right. His ma'am and sister, too. I got them all locked up is all, and I ain't letting none of them loose until you get me back the rest a my box of gold."

I snap angry-like, "How I bring you that gold I can't lift and carry it?"

"Two you all together," he say.

"All three us me my ma'am my sister can't carry that box. What people going say see us struggling toting a box of gold out round the woods? Why you stop Mr. Sami from toting it to you? Clear to me you can't tote it yourself."

He doing that thing fishing round in his pockets again.

"Go on," I say. "Haul out your pistols dry them and start in to shooting them off. Bring Mr. Peter and them running. You ain't got sense to see us wasn't put out here but for to bait you in? You greedy sucker got enough gold on you to buy everybody."

Rose Red draw in her breath like something punch her in the belly. She don't know it be no danger to talk to this wight man like this. *He ducking and hiding his own self. Who he going tell on us to? Us ain't got nothing to fear sassing him.*

"You got good sense, Mr. Jared, you listen to me. Send that Mr. Sami Wolf Water back out here tote that treasure because none of us can't. You holding out trying to keep it to yourself and can't even get your hands on it. Child butt naked figure out this ain't going work."

Rose Red bust out laughing. I'm feeling good warming up. I say, "Try to do you a good turn, Mr. Jared, you ain't got sense enough to take me up on it. Might as well turn my back call the hands to come fall on you. Mr. Dennis want you so bad every hand get a piece a you just might get a Christmas ham out your brother."

Rose Red guffaw.

Mr. Jared got his eye on me stuffing wet powder in his gun.

I can think of one more thing to say. "You going try to shoot me, Mr. Jared, I might just as well scream for help now as later."

Flip on his belly like a fish out the water and start in to wiggling away. I can see he got a wood stick strap to where he ain't got one leg, but he won't stand and run on it. Crawl and wiggle on his elbows till it distress you to see.

Rose Red hold her belly from laughing and gagging both.

Then her face go all grave. "Why you do that?" she look up want to know. "Why you make him skedaddle, Rose White?"

My voice done fell like a stone in the stream. I say, "So he go set Mr. Sami free."

Rose Red come put her arms round me.

Us come out the woods sun going down go up to the big house tell Mr. Dennis us ain't seen nothing all day. I ask my ma'am let me go take care Mammy Water now Mr. Peter got to leave us alone. She say "All right," smiling a cause her new spoon work so good, I guess.

I take Mammy Water her plate surprise to find she ain't fouled up her shack today. She sit hold my hand stare and smile at me. Then she say something I can't understand and kind of ease down on her pallet. Close her eyes let go my hand and I fear she ain't going eat Ma'am cooking for a while, now.

Wake to a wolf howl that night. I sit right up. Ma'am and sister sit up, too. Ma'am got hold me round the waist and won't let me loose. "No," she say. "If it Mr. Sami, let him come to you."

"But what if he don't think to do that?" I want to know.

137

"What use you got for a man can't think that far?" she say and I start to cry.

Rose Red hold on to me, too, and I ain't got no choice but to sit and listen till that voice calling in the woods die down. Kill me not to know was it Mr. Sami. Crush my insides to think he out there thinking I won't come to him. *He just broke loose from Mr. Jared and all.*

When I can't hear it no more, I throw myself down on the bearskin and sob so my shoulders shake. Bite the bearskin in my teeth. Hear the fur popping out the skin. Feel Ma'am sister patting my head. Don't do no good.

I hate this dead skin all that's left of Mr. Sami. I hate these plaits so tight won't let me sleep. Miss Magdalen a double-talking dope think her plaits do something for somebody. I hate this dress with spider webs, too. I hate everything. They don't let loose my head I like to turn round knock somebody hands off me.

I spit out bear fur and manage to say, "Don't touch me," and they stop. *Good thing, too. I was going hate myself tomorrow if I done slug my sister my ma'am tonight. What they have to go and hold me down like that for? What I ever didn't do for them?*

In the dark I hear my ma'am say, "Mr. Sami got a pap be glad to help him get away from that Mr. Jared."

I work on my voice before I can answer back. "Ma'am, you know Mr. Sami don't just want his own freedom. Want it for his sister, too. His ma'am, for all us know."

Rose Red say, "And for us."

Ma'am sigh in the dark. "Well," she say, "all I know you the littlest weakest nobody round here can't help Mr. Sami better than his own pap. You stay out of it from now on. Mr. Sami work this out, let him come looking for you. You think I live all these years ain't learned nothing?"

I already feeling shame how angry I was at my ma'am my sister. *They only mean me good. I know it. I can't look at one time they done something selfish by me. I not even thought to get more for my ma'am than the spoon and sack she used up on Mr. Sami worthless treasure in the first place.* "Ma'am," I say soft. "Ma'am, you sleep?"

"No, Rose White."

"Ma'am, can I give you this dress? Can't do nothing in it. You don't do nothing but stay round the house cleaning and cooking. How I look fishing and swimming in the stream with something like this on?"

Ma'am say, "Thank you, baby. But you keep it. I think Miss Magdalen had good reasons she chose that dress for you. And I know I had good reasons not to let you run the woods in it tonight. Everything be all right. You getting big, but I can see you ain't outgrowed your old ma'am yet. Now go to sleep."

Seem to me by the time folks telling you to go to sleep it cause they know you can't. I lay up staring at them ceiling beams again. *All I recall of Mr. Sami face was his hair slapping me when he whip around at the sound of Mr. Peter looking at my body. Something in there I wish I understood better. Make my belly tight.*

Didn't know I fell asleep. Didn't know I was dreaming. Woman came to me. Light-skin woman. Thick long hair. Dress the color of bones and hung full a spider webs. Blood running all over her body. But not her face. Beautiful face. *Sad.* Tilt her head to one side look at me. Saying something. Blood red pouty mouth open close. *Saying something I can't make out.* Coming close her hands outstretch toward me.

I want to go to her. *I'm afraid to go to her.*

She walking back and back now. I follow. She got her hands toward me. She kind of turn with a smile got her back to me now. *Blood running on this side, too.* She walk into a dark place and I don't see her no more. Wake up in a sweat.

Ma'am holding me. I hold on tight tell her my dream. She don't say nothing.

Next time I wake up I covered with rags and Rose Red washing herself. "Where Ma'am?" I ask.

"Took your dress gone to talk to Miss Magdalen," Rose Red say.

"Why?" I ask.

"Ma'am think maybe that dream was Miss Angel. Miss Magdalen girl. The one Mr. Jared done stab to death."

"Where was us at when all this was going on?"

"Not born yet, I don't reckon."

"Why Miss Magdalen give me that dead woman dress, then?"

"That what Ma'am gone to find out. She say don't move till she get back."

"What if Mr. Peter want us in the field?"

"He going have to take it up with Mr. Dennis."

I lay back sigh. *Don't this madness never stop?*

When Ma'am come in first thing she say, "I hate that house," and don't me nor Rose Red ask why. *She still toting the dawn pink dress with the spider webs on it.* I got mix feelings to see it. I wait to hear what Ma'am going say.

"You all hungry?" she ask.

"No, Ma'am," us both say.

"You wash yet, Rose White?"

"Not yet, Ma'am."

"Well, wash up get dress."

"In that same dress, Ma'am?"

"You heard me, girl. Don't make my life harder than it already is."

Rose Red give it a try. "You learn something, Ma'am, about why Miss Magdalen want Rose White to wear that dress?"

"Learn more than I want to know."

Us wait. Ma'am seem done talking.

I try. "Ma'am, you going tell me why I must to wear a dead woman dress?"

"Since when you fear the dead, child?"

I had to give that some thought. "I ain't sure I do," I say.

"Then wear it. Maybe Miss Angel look down help you fetch back that other woman brought so much peace to this plantation."

"Who was that, Ma'am?" Rose Red say.

"Miss Angel Girl. Just take my cooking spoon."

Like you ever let anybody take it again, I thought. But all I say be "What about your spoon, Ma'am?"

"Before Miss Angel Girl, most the babies and childrens had to eat slop with they face in a trough all together, just like the pigs. After Miss Angel Girl

141

come out the woods and Mr. Dennis take to her, set her up in the big house, she done away with the pig troughs for the childrens. Make him give most the ma'ammies some kind a pot some kind a cooking stick if not a real spoon. Hand them some hambones salt pork or other leavings out the smokehouse. So they can make they cornmeal rations mush a night instead a dry pone, can't go far enough to feed the whole family."

Everybody cook mush instead a pone. Childrens eat with they hands in they ma'ammy shack instead a the pig trough with all the other childrens.

That all Miss Angel Girl did?

Ma'am so old-timey she wear me out. Just like the old folks to think things must is better every time they ain't got worse. *I don't even know what to say about Ma'am stupid pot and spoon story.* So I don't say nothing.

But my quiet ain't never stopped Ma'am from talking. She say to me like her sass coming back, "You ain't done washing yet? You about to scrub that armpit raw."

I say, "But what if I get dreams again?"

"About Miss Angel? Ask her what she want with you. Talk to her. Clear to me the woman got something to tell you, child."

"What about, though, Ma'am?"

"How I know? She come to me?"

Rose Red interrupt. "But why she come to Rose White?"

Now Ma'am make up her mind she going talk. "Listen here, childrens," she say. "Miss Magdalen done told me she took one look to Rose White say, here the gal Mammy Water prophesy going save the peoples round here. She didn't have the idea about Miss Angel come talk to you, Rose White, till you up and ask Mr. Dennis for a dress."

Rose Red clap her hands like she gots a idea. "Maybe Miss Angel put that thought right in your head, Rose White?"

"More like Mr. Peter put that thought in my head," I grumble.

Ma'am say, "Miss Magdalen don't doubt it was Miss Angel. Say spirits float around see all kind a things us can't see. Look a here, gal. You just wear this dress the daytime. Nighttime, us bolt the door I put it on my own self. Miss Angel got what all to say to you, she can say it day light hours. After dark, she best settle for talking to me."

I come hug my ma'am. She surprise cause she don't know how mean I been thinking, how sorry I be sometimes for my temper.

Then I put that dress on slow. Feel like I dressing for my own death dance. Remember folks Frenzy when Sami the African die.

Death and spirits. Maybe I understand Mr. Peter fear after all, for all I don't like him. That teach me to do something mean just to scare somebody else. Now all sudden death can't wait to come hit me upside the back a my own head.

Say to Ma'am, "Maybe I best go hold Mammy Water hand see she got somewhat to say to me."

"No, baby. You ain't out in them woods come sun up, Mr. Dennis be round here."

Rose Red try to sound all chipper. "Let's us go swim today," she say.

"Seen enough of the water yesterday," I say back. "Let's go look where that Mr. Jared done crawl off to."

"He might done got dry gunpowder today," Rose Red say.

"Then let him shoot Miss Angel off my back," I say, and Ma'am look at me real serious. But she don't say nothing. I know I shouldn't a talk like that. Ain't showing respect for the dead. *But why the dead can't just leave me out of it?*

Once us at the stream, I surprise to find Mr. Jared trail still kind of dug into the mulch. Us can see real clear where he done start dragging his self off to. Start in to following. Wind up round in the woods where us ain't never been before. Rose Red say, "I don't like it here."

I say, "Me neither."

"Us lucky patrol ain't swing by."

"They lucky, too. They be done got lost traipsing round up in here."

"Let's us go back."

"Can't. Not till us find where he gone, Rose Red."

"What us going do once us find Mr. Jared? I ain't looking forward to seeing him again. First time made me sick."

I can't answer Rose Red fussing so I don't try no more. I ask myself, *How crazy is a gal who risk her life and her sister too for a man ain't had sense enough to stay free once he got free?* I don't understand nothing I do these days.

Us up round some rocks calls for climbing. Little trees just out the side of rock like I ain't never seen.

All sudden us raise up onto a flat wide rock and I like to fall over backward where I just crawl up from. Us standing smack in front a some kind cave or something. Dark. Can't see nothing inside. Don't want to. *This where Miss Angel gone into in my dream.* I shudder.

"Death in there," I say to Rose Red.

"What?" she ask.

"Death," I say. And I can't walk back nor forward. Root to the spot like one them bitty trees.

Rose Red looking back forth at me and the rocks. "How you know?" she ask.

"My dream," I say. "Miss Angel gone in there. Miss Angel, forgive me for what I said about Mr. Jared shooting you. I'm scare out my mind."

"Well let's us get out a here," Rose Red say.

"No."

"Rose White," she say, "you ain't making no sense. Death in there, us don't need to hang around."

"But what if Miss Angel done lead me here?" I ask.

"Maybe she don't like you," Rose Red say.

"But Miss Magdalen ain't say that," I say.

"Maybe Miss Magdalen don't know everything she think she know," Rose Red say, and I be the last somebody want to argue with that.

"Let me just sit here catch my breath," I say, and I sit down on the flat rock back to the cave. Rose Red sit next to me.

But she won't turn her back on that cave. She face it. She say, "Don't you let me fall backward off this here rock bust my head open down there, Rose White."

I say, "And don't you let nothing come flying out that cave grab me."

So us sit close watching each other back. I sit thinking hard, *What I should ought to do now?*

And it happen.

Voice calling. "Rose White. Rose White. That you? Come here, girl. Come on over here."

I catch hold Rose Red arm. "You hear that?" I ask.

She turn look at me her eyes big as my face.

Voice start up again. "Rose White. Rose White. Don't you hear me call you, girl?"

I say to Rose Red, "Where it coming from?" It sound like it come from all around us.

She raise her arm point to the cave. I turn round slow try to take a look-see. Can't think a one thing might be in there I might want to see, though.

"Who calling me?" I say loud.

Nothing. No sound, no moving.

"Somebody calling me?" I ask more loud still. Now I sure it Mr. Jared up to some stupid tricks. I show him up but good this time. Toying with my name my feelings. *Let him drag out here in the light. Me my sister kick him over the edge the rocks.*

"Hush," Rose Red say. "Let's us get out a here."

"Not till I know who calling me," I say loudest yet.

Rose Red whisper, "You crazy fool, come on."

I can't answer. I stand slow. Sit back down hard. Feel my sister hand grab me hold on. My mouth dropping open. "Oh my good lord," I try to whisper.

Rose Red turn slow from looking at me back to the cave. Look like she don't really want to look and

I don't blame her. *Don't look,* I try to say, but too late. She got to live with it now.

Rose Red shove one hand in her mouth bite down on her knuckles. I try to cover my sister eyes. My own start running hot tears.

Us done seen some gruesome sights. Can't live on a plantation avoid bloodshed. Blood spill, skin get ripped. Field hands got to live with such things. But past certain point, you ain't got to watch a tore up body move no more. You get peace knowing they got peace.

Woman walking out that cave toward me my sister ain't have no business walking. Body running blood so it pool at her feet. Trail of blood behind her look like the setting sun. Dress clinging dripping blood white as bone. *She shimmer like a pond in sunlight.*

She keep coming. I put up my free hand for her to stop.

"Miss Angel," I say. "Go back. Don't come near me my sister. You scare us."

She keep coming. So close I see flesh flapping where she been stab.

Tears running so fast now I can't rightly see good. Got my hand still over Rose Red eyes. Shaking so I fear I got to fall off this here rock.

"Miss Angel," I start in to plead. "Please don't come so close. Please stop. What you want from me? From us? Us ain't never harm you."

Miss Angel keep walking. She so close now I can see her chest rise and fall to breathe. Cuts rip all cross her chest, her belly, open and move with the work her muscles doing. Open and another glob of blood run. Cuts open everywhere globs run

147

together. Thick flow trickling down all over her body. *She so close I see the spider web stuff dance on her skin.*

She hold out her hand towards me. I look up see her eyes. *Oh, them sad eyes. Dark and suck you in. Got in them every unhappy feeling I ever done had, but all at once.*

She betrayed. She can't believe it. She lonely. She trapped. She can't get free from what been done to her. She living in a circle can't shut her eyes and rest. *I can't bear it.* Shut my own eyes tight.

Can't move. Can't feel my own body. But I feel her coming on closer.

I'm praying. "Go way," I say. "Don't hurt my sister me. Us ain't never meant you no harm."

I feel a wave a cold prickle me. Start at my face and work through my body. *She passing through me,* I think, and my mind go blank. Hurt. Cold and sharp prickles like getting beat with a rose bush full of thorns.

Cold got me shaking so my mind gone white. *Cold and white.* Mind fit to bust. I shake so bad till I drop my hand from in front my sister eyes. Think I hear her calling me but I can't hear good. I let go everything.

And all sudden stop. Everything stop. Shaking gone. My eyes fly open. I stare round. I ain't never seen so clear in my life till this here minute.

I look around see Rose Red looking at me. Her face spread wide stiff with shock. I ain't never knew before her eyes got so much yellow in the brown.

"Rose White," she say, "you look different. What happen to you?"

I got to think to talk. I feel all right. I just a minute don't know who I am. *Rose White me? Must be.* Say, "I all right, Rose Red. Nothing happen to me but Miss Angel walk through me. You know what?"

"What?" Rose Red say, but she still don't look no better.

"Everybody dead wrong."

She stare say, "Wrong about what?"

"Why Mr. Jared killed Miss Angel."

"Cause he crazy." Rose Red look at me like I gone crazy, too. "He killed her like that, cut her up, to make her ma'am Miss Magdalen scared of Mr. Dennis and flee the plantation."

"No, Rose Red. He was scared Mr. Dennis kill him and give the plantation to Miss Angel. Pretend she a wight woman and give it to her illegal-like."

New voice speak up from out the cave. "How you know all that?" it say.

Mr. Jared crawling that weird crawl a his out the cave. One elbow at a time, wiggle forwards, one good knee, wiggle up, start on the elbows again.

"Ugh," I say. *Why don't he get up walk on that stick leg his?*

Scrape, scrape. He making his way cross the rock ledge towards me my sister. Breathing hard, say, "You gals ain't know when to quit, is you?" He say, "Well, you right. Was me killed Angel before my wretched brother up and give her the place and the hands, everything, and why not? She mine, flesh, blood, and property too. But what good it do you stick your nose in all that it beats me."

I say, "She trusted you."

He say, "She was scared a me. Ain't trusted me for nothing."

Rose Red say, "Can't blame her."

He sudden turn dark red. Scream, "We talking about my property, you darky slattern witch! The house my property, the land my property, Angel my property, and so is you, too! And you think she died hard, you watch see how you feel when I blow your hard-head brains out. I'll show you how to die hard!"

"Move to the side," I call to Rose Red. She scuttle. I say to creeping Mr. Jared, "I can't figure what you get out a killing me nor Rose Red. She ain't never did nothing to you. You can let her get out a here like she want."

Mr. Jared stop that wiggle crawl to catch some breath bust out laughing. Say, "You tickle me, you little sassy black gal. You trying to give orders round here?" He reach round back like he going for that pistol again.

Uh oh. I ain't got a lot of time to think. I take my foot leap at that hand. Stomp it to the rock and start in to jumping on it. He start in to squealing like a boil live pig. Then he try to do that fish flip over.

Rose Red run up throw herself on that other hand he flailing round trying to catch me. I'm looking round for something I can grab smash him to a pulp. Rage driving me.

Got Miss Angel before my eyes. Got it in my head Mr. Sami dead somewhere, stuck full a holes like her. *Kill this man, who going complain?*

All sudden hand reach grab me out nowhere. I feel myself get shoved back. Stumble sit down hard.

Rose Red get throwed in my lap. I looking round trying to see.

Big back turned to me. Wild scraggly curls whipping in the wind done picked up. Big arms raise that crippled Mr. Jared in the air. He up high against the sun. Screaming, wiggling. His gold and things catch light twinkling and clinking.

I feels for him. Poor tore up man. His eyes full a terror. One bloody hand reach round trying to grab hold to the man going fling his body down.

Rose Red go to duck her head cover her eyes.

I see the body go over. But I can't look away. Hear some kind a dull thump way down somewhere. I stare hard at the big body done flung Mr. Jared down. I ain't rightly seen it in day light.

It turn round. Anger in the eyes dying down.

It Mr. Sami.

He look at me like he wish I ain't seen what I did. I work my way out from under Rose Red go to him. Edge up to the rock peek over. Mr. Jared weird rip body all tangle on the rocks below.

Mr. Sami look down there like he sad. Say soft, "Now I never find out where my sister hid."

"I so sorry," I say.

"Mr. Sami, help us get back home," Rose Red say. "Us lost." Then she start in to sobbing.

Long bloody trip home. Got blood all in my mind my eyes. Can't see think nothing about how I feel for Mr. Sami except it all a piece with the blood I done seen today.

He got his arms round me my sister leading and dragging us home. Rose Red weep like she never use her eyeballs for nothing else again. I can't shed not one more tear. I keep thinking on Miss Angel trusting me. I wonder where she at and do she know I understand her now.

Us drag in home the field hands stop and look. Folks standing up all over the field clearing way the hoes and sacks, turn stare like to recognize somebody. I say to Mr. Sami, "They can't know who you is. Can they?"

He say, "You never know what quiet folks know or don't."

Us get to my ma'am shack, she already out the front door flying. Crying like she knew was something happen. I look down see my dress tore. *Oh, well. Still not bad as the rag I wore up to two days ago.*

Ma'am lead us in the shack like us don't know the way. Tell us, "Stay put." She take off get Miss Magdalen. My head swimming. *I can't think can't feel.*

Soon Miss Magdalen thump thump running back behind Ma'am. "Rose White? Little Sami? Rose Red? What happen, children?"

Us hear folks gather outside. "Going be long night," Mr. Sami say. I smile at him.

Folks up storytelling two days three nights running. Mr. Dennis come down from his bone house eyes wet ring bloodshot. Grab hold hug on his son.

Folks whisper, "Mr. Dennis act like that boy wight kin."

Folks whisper back, "African kin wight kin. That boy the only kin Mr. Dennis got left."

Folks say, "What happen to Miss Angel Girl and that baby gal got stole?"

152

Folks say, "Mr. Jared done took them to the grave."

Revenge a bitter thing.

Mr. Dennis don't make nobody hit the fields. Send down liquor food folks want it. Got Miss Magdalen some maids running back forth from the smokehouse and the cellar. Big celebration.

Third night coming on, Mr. Dennis down at the bonfire with the hands, say to me, "Mr. Sami done ask me what he want. Now you ask me what you want."

I know what he mean but I'm going lead him on. Think I could learn to like this sassing. I say, "I like a answer to a question, Mr. Dennis, sir."

He look touch surprise. Say, "What is it?"

"Would you really have gave this farm to Miss Angel instead of letting it go to your own brother, that Mr. Jared?"

Mr. Dennis say quiet, "You forget she was his property, too."

"And your niece, sir. I ask myself, had Miss Angel Girl knowed how you cared for Miss Angel, would she have come back here by now? Would she have never left?"

Mr. Dennis face drop like it going hit the fire and burn.

All sudden Mr. Sami stand up. Fire light up his face. He fling back all that scraggly hair out the way. He say, "So there you is, you no-count rapscallion," and go to hoist up his pap rifle.

Now, I knowed Sami got his hands on Mr. Dennis big barrel rifle gun though it be against the law. But I figured it was in case Mr. Jared crawl around again.

153

But Sami up here talking to Mr. Peter.

Mr. Peter walk up all wary stick out a hand like to shake make friends.

Mr. Sami raise the rifle.

Mr. Dennis stand up look back forth don't say nothing.

Mr. Peter look like he think folks drunk and playing games. Start in to laughing.

And Mr. Sami pull the trigger. That rifle like to leap into the sky. Smoke everywhere. Some woman scream.

Smoke clear, Mr. Peter a mess on the ground. Pieces of him every which a where.

Mr. Dennis say quiet, "Ain't legal kill a wight man around these parts."

Mr. Sami say, "Then I guess it time take my wife my inheritance whatever you want to give me and get out a here."

"Ain't no need be hasty, son. Gather up some boys get this mess buried right quick. Got us a wedding to throw. Maybe someday you tell me why you done this. Damn good overseer gone to waste."

Mr. Sami say, "Maybe some day you tell me where and why Rose White got this new dress."

Mr. Dennis chuckle slap his son on the back. "Boy, you going find out soon enough ain't nobody never laid a hand on that gal a yours. Her ma'am done seen to that."

Mr. Sami ain't smiling. "Old black woman can't see to nothing much round here these days," he say.

Mr. Dennis ain't stop smiling. Say, "Evident to me you ain't seen Mammy Water."

Mr. Sami say, "Equal evident to me you ain't seen my ma'am lately."

Mr. Dennis frown up like he done miss something. Say, "Truce."

My ma'am come up hustle me off talking about I seen too much blood for one lifetime. But I'm thinking, *Somehow Mr. Peter blood don't bother me one bit.*

Miss Magdalen Rose Red my ma'am wash and dress me. They want to do it up at Mr. Dennis bone house but I say no. I want to get married at my ma'am shack.

Us stand out front the house between the rose bushes. Mr. Dennis say he got authority to denounce us man wife. Some such speechmaking. Fire leaping everywhere. Folks singing, clapping, stomping and dancing. Food flow till folks like to bust.

Us took off. Kiss my ma'am my sister. I sneak off kiss Mammy Water cheek while she sleep. Glad to see she fouling herself again. Normal.

Sneak back tell Rose Red her turn now look after Mammy Water. Mr. Sami done tell his pap us get back two three days. Maybe more. Hoist that bearskin full jewels and that rifle I can tell he going come to love. And us take off for the woods.

Hike all the way out to the cave first night. Spread our bearskin stretch out. Mr. Sami start in to telling me about his life out there after Mr. Jared done stole him away.

Boy growed up lost just miles from his own home ain't knowed it. I cried for him. Held him.

Sami held me and I found out what it was I use to be scare was going happen between us. Two folks become one, doing something like this. Now I

155

feel I never lose my Sami. He always be a half a me.

Strong man gentle a good thing. Can't be too gentle, though. Blood everywhere all over that bear skin. *Why can't I get away from blood?* Seen my blood spilt all over my legs in that starlight coming through the cave mouth and cried.

Sami thought I was a crying from the pain. I let him think it. *Field hand old as me seen so much blood still crying at the sight a shame.* Hate to let him know I so weak-minded.

He want to stop me crying. Sami help me dry-scrub my blood off the bear skin and us hike down the rock went swimming in the starlight. Love to see the moon on my Sami face. Put me in mind that night in the trees when I first scared myself, falling in love with him.

Us stayed in Sami's cave hunt around for Sami's sister and ma'am every day. Stayed out there a solid week. Miss Angel ain't troubled my sleep again. But I sure wish she would.

I would a loved to ask her where Mr. Jared flung down body done got off to. He ain't nowhere round them rocks.

Me and Sami done searched high and low and everywhere. Look each other in the eye and say, "Now what?"

CHAPTER SEVEN
BEAT BACK THE NIGHT:
HEAVEN, BORN 1786

In the woods a tree is there,
where The Saver finds a bear
curled and sleeping in his lair.
With blood and treasure at his paw,
he opens wide his fanged jaw.
The wolf will leap out from his maw.
Wolf of blood and crystal eye,
emit the death-bird with your cry.
Fatal death-bird,
fly.

The last note of my song lingers. My fingers brush the cutting strings of the mandolin in my lap. The last note ends.

I have sung to sleep the sun. Stars rip the sky to sparkling shreds. Now is my time. I can delay no longer.

I have called to my mother, the wolf. She and the phantom wolf who raised her must find me. Have they scented my sorrow? Can they track it to me?

I have done all I can to draw my mother here. Tomorrow will be too late. All my yesterdays were too soon.

Shards light brittle sky over the maze of woods beyond my barred window. Have I learned my lessons? Would my old ma'ammy have been proud of me?

Tonight I rejoice that my old ma'ammy and my books were taken from me. Their loss drove me to become the Saver. I have learned strength from persecution.

My Enemy will learn that the weakest is the strongest. The girl I was is gone with ma'ammy's stories. Tonight I will call death to my Enemy with the songs he taught me.

Time is passing, playing into my Enemy's hands. Already he recovers from his contest with my brother, the bear. Tonight my enemy comes to sell me for my virginity and my songs.

He has always said he would. Always is now. The final battle with my Enemy must be fought tonight.

I am ready, seated in my ma'ammy's chair, all of her still left to me.

One arm of the carved rosewood is a bear's arching back. The other is a wolf stalking on two legs. They point their muzzles up to the headrest where the birds soar.

Between their beaks tumbles something brilliant one of the birds has disgorged. What is it they battle to seize between them?

I have turned this question over and over in my mind.

Wood is deceptive. It gives only shape. It does not give color or texture. I fear the death-bird's Enemy has disgorged a crystal.

This is the crystal ripping the eye socket of the wolf in my song. The song made itself over the years. I would never have wished the manifestation of my Enemy's soul to be a crystal.

How does one defeat crystal? It is enchanted. It generates its own magic. A crystal soul is why my Enemy was flung from the cliffs by my brother, the bear, and yet he lived.

Did he live because his soul is crystal and could not be smashed within the cushion of his body? I hope his soul is not crystal. My life has been spent in the search for my Enemy's soul.

The mandolin slips to the floor from my hand. It hits the planks with a hollow thump like the sound of my Enemy's flesh-wrapped bones when they hit the rocks where death fled him.

My soul lives in my wolf mother's tree. My old ma'ammy taught me, before she was taken from me, that The Saver was hung from a tree. This must be the same tree where The Enemy perched as a loon and croaked as a toad and slithered as a snake, deceiving the weak.

The Saver's blood dripped and fed the tree. So we are all Saved by his blood. My mother and her phantom wolf circle the tree of knowing, sniffing the Saver's blood. My thoughts feast there. All who seek may know the Saver and be Saved.

Except the Enemy. He is evil and cannot be Saved. If I feast on the Saver, must I not vanquish The Enemy? Or so my ma'ammy used to say. It is the blood.

I shed blood in my solitary time, after my ma'ammy was sold away and before the Death Angel came to me in her silver mirror.

The Death Angel beats back the night and my solitude and fans sleep from my face with enormous bright wings.

I used to fly alone and insubstantial to the tree of knowing and weep for my lost mother and brother and feast on The Saver's blood. Now he has given me my own blood.

Hot blood bursts from my body when the moon rises full. The shock used to drive me from myself. But I have realized that the shedding of blood is the Saver's gift to me. Now I embrace the bleeding.

I feel beneath the rosewood seat a jutting nail. I center the pad of a finger against it and press the finger quickly with my other hand. The pop of resistant skin. Deep pain flows to the warmth of running blood.

I wipe each bar of my prison window with a bloody stripe to consecrate it. I picture my blood dappling all the trees. My wounded hand makes flinging gestures. My fingers strike the bars and send nervous shocks up my arm. My weakness is sprouting into strength.

I wait for the waxing moon to rise. May I never see its full white face through these blood-smeared bars again. May I be free of this place next time the full moon comes.

Time is a lie. I am outside time. I am a point in eternity. My destiny eddies in a burning stream. It waits for me. I will go forward and fear nothing.

First I will distract my guard. I will satisfy his greedy watching with a sight of my helplessness. Then I must go to all who shared my life in this tower and say good-bye. If I win this contest, I will never fly to them from my tower again.

When I am free, I must live in the world and take my place in it. I must learn to live in the flesh.

Not the blood. Not the night flying and visions by day.

I rise and go to the folding silk screen, lurid with vines and flowers. I reach behind it to the fragile chamber pot my guard expects. Already I hear him rustling at the door.

I turn my back on the silver mirror and the shadow lurking within it. My day's wash water slides its milky thickness into my porcelain chamber pot. I carry the filled pot to the door and place it on the floor. "Open the door."

The bolt grates across rough metal. The door edges ajar. "Take this." I shove the fragile pot with the toe of my slipper.

The guard forces his torch just inside the opening door. Its leaping flames splatter me. His eye, just beyond, devours me.

I kick the pot at him. It tumbles and splashes its contents on his leg. I shove the door shut. "Slide the bolt!"

He persists, imploring. How I hate him. "Take the supper tray away. I refuse it. It's been ruined. Don't disturb me again tonight."

His hands stroke the massive door between us, placating with the sibilant brush of dry skin on splintered wood. He has done these senseless things since my Enemy brought him to replace my ma'ammy.

"Go, or I shall tell your Master Jared that you wasted my food again tonight."

He is still. I hear him slowly slide the bolt. He thumps heavily down the wood slat steps that circle up my tower.

161

This is how it is. I breathe without a sound. I listen. Stealth is his step when he comes and my noiseless breathing as I wait to hear his loathed coming.

At last the soles of the guard's booted feet shush their way back up the worn and splintered steps. His body slips into its place at the foot of my bolted door. He will sleep there miserably all night.

No matter. He cannot open the door without my leave. He fears what his master will do to him. Tonight my value in coin remains my protection from my guard. Tomorrow my value in coin will be my degradation. Unless I have faced and defeated Jared.

But first I must face her.

I turn to the silver-framed mirror where my Death Angel waits.

Since my blood first ran, and my old ma'ammy was taken away, and the lustful guard and haunted mirror were brought, I have always found *her* waiting there. Never myself. I have never seen my own reflection. Perhaps I have none.

I face her silver-framed glass cage. There is no need to call. She is always there, waiting for a sight of me.

Her eyes weep their eternal sorrow. She raises her blood-dripping hands. I draw back. Not from her. From my own impulse to hold her ever-freshly-sliced body against my whole one.

"No, Angel. I will not fly with you tonight. Tonight I refuse you and gain strength as myself. I will set both of us free, myself from this tower and you from me."

Her eyes deny my hope. I raise my chin and draw back further. "I am on my way to say good-bye to all the companions of my loneliness. You are the first. Good-bye, friend of my nightmares. You with your wings to false freedom, Angel."

She is a fountain of blood. It pours from her everywhere. I have never drunk her blood as I have drunk The Saver's. I turn my back on the Angel's sorrow-filled eyes and bleeding wounds. The rush of her wings calls me.

Fly free. Join me and soar from this place in your dreams tonight. Come to me. Let me come to you. Free me. I need you. Friend.

The rising crest of one wing and the crown of her head start from the mirror in a shimmer of silver that catches starlight and flings it at me.

"No."

She falters. She retreats. The shining head and feathered wingcrest recede into the falsely flattened plane of the mirror. Her massive wings beat in a futile blur beyond the glass. She returns to waiting. Her eyes rebuke me. I wonder what our relationship would be if she were free.

"Angel?" Can I trust her with one question? I have never trusted her fully. But tonight there is something I very much wish to know.

I will risk her lying resentment. She cannot harm me if I do not trust her. But I may secretly believe her. "I may die in my contest with my Enemy tonight. Will I join you if I die? I hope to. But if in death I do not go to you, where will I go? You are Death and know about such things."

Friend. Her sorrowful eyes widen in panic. *Do you mean Jared? He killed me. He has no mercy.*

163

You need me. Do not go without me. The feathers surge from the mirror again.

"Stay. I deny you. I refuse you. You lie even now. You were never killed, Angel. You *are* Death. You call me friend and betray my faith in you."

She shakes her head in such violent denial of my charges that bloody droplets spray the inside of the glass. Her still-beating wings smudge the spots and spread them in streaks. She presses her hands against the red smears as she leans close to force me to look into the eyes of her bottomless grief.

I rush from her and throw myself into the circle of my bed cushions. The Death Angel cannot see beyond the drawn bed curtains or feel me out of the tangled eiderdown.

I close my eyes and will myself free of my reclining body. I rush from my human warmth in a hot burst like monthly blood.

The Angel's chill fingers reach from her mirror and grasp at me in passing. The prickling numbness of her touch ends when I am through the bloodied bars of my window and soaring beneath the infinite black sky.

Easiest farewells first. I will go to the cave of my brother, the bear.

I become mist. I spread myself through the woody labyrinth. I hover above the rocks where my brother, the bear, sent our Enemy crashing. I weep vaporous tears upon the rocks that returned my Enemy to life. Then I gather the folds of my sorrow and drift into the cave as softly as a sigh.

My brother, the bear, lies curled on his bearskin with his wife. She is the color of tree trunks and very fertile in her love. Her love grows through the

164

bear like strong roots. His jagged bearskin dissolves into his future human flesh. He is now more bear than he was when forced to hide in its skin.

My brother, the bear, slumbers in sensuous affection and passionate rage.

His wife's mind searches for the Death Angel. She seeks my voice and calls to the Angel I rode to her. I pull outside the tree trunk's tangle of love, whispering, "I face our Enemy before the sun rises. I will never come to you from the tower again. I wish you happiness. Good-bye."

My brother, the bear, stirs. His wife reaches for him. "Sami, you hear something?"

The bear sweeps his bride close and murmurs to her. She is comforted and nestles between his body and his arm. A wedding ring of ivory from my grandmother's home and youth glows on the bride's finger. I feel the banked fires of distaste she has for this ivory ring.

Grandmother's ring. Grandmother. Hers is the name of wading through time. I call her and see pooling flames in an eddy made between a young girl's legs. My grandmother is a young girl in a flaming stream, waiting for me to free her.

I tumble along the mulch floor of the forest and the dust of the still cotton fields toward my grandmother's abandoned body. Her body can be seen ahead as I skim the broken furrows in the starlit night. I swarm to her portal and pour myself through it.

Grandmother's rag door flits away from her shack in the bare breeze my spirit stirs. "Grandmother. Will you think of my battle?"

Breathless, I circle and caress the aging body. I exude the lavender scent of regret. I leap and pour myself about her.

Grandmother's clean body puckers in unsullied folds. I lean close to absorb the purity of her dying breath.

She could strike horror into my Enemy's mind if she opened her eyes upon him, her terrible eyes that I love most of all. She keeps her eyes closed in dreaming and shuts in the sights they have seen.

One is as strong as one has been weak. She draws The People to her through her weakness.

The Enemy never embraces his weakness. Therefore he is never as strong. This is my advantage.

My night is the wide deep space where everything uncreated waits. Beyond the night is the lapping water of the world. Grandmother's spirit stirs the water of my creation where it leaps in flames between solid shores. I cross the desolate sands the river girl crossed to chaos.

I reach the spilling mouth of eternity's river and flow against the current to where its first blue torrent burns. Here is the river girl who ceaselessly wades.

She shines with sunlight, fire, and water. I watch her legs in the fiery eddy where my paused destiny circles. How long can Grandmother hold back my destiny?

The wading girl gestures with wonder toward the eddying water-tipped sparks beneath her. She inclines her head and smiles. Firelight dances on her white teeth. The ivory ring encircling her finger glows red.

I look up to pine trees pointing above a patch of sodden earth. I am at my lost ma'ammy's grave. The mound rises like a pregnant belly from death.

I have seen the pregnant bellies of women bent like grain stalks in the cotton fields, quivering taut bundles. So is my old ma'ammy's grave expectant.

"Pray for me."

I press the mist of myself into the moist earth that shelters her. I mingle my mourning with her decay. If only she could caress me with ghostly hands.

Salt is the taste of sorrow. Blood and tears.

I have tried for years to shape the fine black lines again in my mind and read what Ma'ammy read. When I am free, I shall find old and fragile books. "Ma'ammy, look for me if I die."

Just one embrace. Oh, for a moment's touch.

I am a mist of desire. The People gather in the field. Their rough empty sacks scrape the broken ground. I plunge among them and spread myself about their cracked pale heels. Their feet slide into me and are warmed. Their enjoyment excites my anguish.

I sense despair. I turn toward it with appetite.

I should resist. I should leave this field of misery and resignation to find my Enemy.

Even as I reason, I track my keen desire to wretchedness. Here is a man freshly whipped and sent to bend the pulling fresh scabs on his back over the burrs and weeds in the field.

Feel me heal you. Let me touch you.

I spiral up his taut high calves and ragged clothes to his shredded back. I arch along it. I slide like thick salve from his waist to his neck, curve along his chest and belly and up over his back again. I am dizzy and exuberant.

I can soothe you. Want me.

He straightens. I encircle him and draw him into me. *Take me. I need to be felt.*

He cannot resist.

Tension flows from his torn back and shoulders in sudden sweat in the morning's chill. Can he stand, if I do not hold him? He bends into my embrace that I have become. I hide his trembling, a current against his humiliation. We are sealed from the world.

Give me your pain. Feel my care.

I hold him in my vastness, a vibrating quiver.

I drink his tears until he falls to his knees. Someone calls out to him by name.

I disperse in every direction and am gone.

Shamed, I gather myself where the field meets the woods. Life. Touch. Belonging. All denied me. Tonight I cannot give in to loneliness.

Tonight? Already the stars dim. The night flees.

I have lost time crying at Ma'ammy's grave and lingering in the whipped man's pain. The black of night fades to gray. I fly through the woods. My call scrapes the trees.

It is as nothing that I seep under Jared's heavy door.

My Enemy's room sits below and beside my tower. I waft to his draped bed.

Twisted upon his useless leg, spittle oozing from an open corner of his scarred mouth, Jared sleeps. He has not risen to come for me.

Outside I hear the mirthless cackle of a loon. Could that be his spirit? I seep back out under the door and lumber in the shape of the bear toward its prey.

I find the loon perched atop the tree of knowing. I fling myself against the wide old tree, disemboweled by lightning.

The loon lurches into the air.

I shrink and strike the ground with the force of my pull inward. Wings and talons sprout. I shove off the earth, after the escaping loon, my Enemy's spirit.

It wheels away. I rise above it and dive, talons reaching toward its head.

I hit it with an impact that sends us crashing together across the highest branches of the forest's trees. The loon's head splits between my gripping talons and the pine branches.

Then the loon is gone.

It has shrunk to a snake narrower than the destroyed loon and slid from my grasp.

I watch it hurtle to a thick branch, wrap around it, and slither down the tree as I fly past.

I rise, circle, return. Sight is sharp and fury strong. The serpent tunnels into the ground at the root of the tree of knowing.

Before I've reached the earth, I am the wolf and must leap the last feet. I land with legs flexed and paw after my prey. Soft earth flies behind me toward the dawn.

The snake's head rears from the earth and snaps my paw. Pain shoots up my foreleg. My jaws snap the snake's head. I shake the snake's whipping body. Its hard little head and pointed tail slap my flanks.

Bear! Maybe the snake's poison will be lost in the bear's huge mass.

The bear is repulsed by a small struggling thing in its mouth. I scrape the thing off my tongue with a furry paw that tastes sharp and sweet. I see a toad hopping fast from me.

I lumber after it, only a little dizzy. The fleet Enemy bounds toward a nearby brook. The scent of fresh water and fresh fish revives me. I leap and try to land on the toad with my splayed heavy paws. Maybe I can crush it. It dodges. Its nimble top-heavy shape dazzles and repulses me.

The toad lands in the brook and is lost. I splash into the water, slapping around as if fishing.

Bird!

Even as the cramps of shrinking overwhelm me, my eyesight sharpens. I perceive the movement of the toad's bloating throat and blinking eyes. I have swooped my talons into its pale belly before its bulging eye can blink into mine one more time.

Now I will learn what the core of my Enemy's soul really is. My pitiless talons and beak, unable to taste, shred the squirming toad. Suddenly my frenzied talons and beak are filled with flying feathers. It seems I had not entirely destroyed the loon. It is back to cover its master's treasured soul.

My talons cling to the loon's bulbous body. I beat back its frantically flapping wings with my own. How long can this dying bird fight to get away? I grip its writhing throat with my beak. *Wolf!*

Can the wolf grasp this barely-pinned bird?

Rapid shape-changing stuns me. The loon flips from under my two right paws before I gather my senses. The wolf's bared fangs snap until they seize the loon's throat. I jerk the bird's head skyward.

Blood spurts in a dark fountain into the brightening sky. Is it dawn?

The wolf is colorblind. I cannot be sure. I stare at the night's transformation into day when the crystal dislodged from the loon's severed throat hurtles downward into my upturned eye.

Back in the tower, my body sits up in its cushioned bed. I sway as my spirit flies back into me. Screaming, I claw at my eyes.

The guard's garbled shouts bring me to my senses. I am in the prison tower. I was in the midst of a vision, battling for my Enemy's soul and my destiny.

I feel around my eyes with my fingertips. Nothing but pain. I must return to the vision. I lean forward and part my bed curtains. Dawn has not yet stained the sky.

I press myself back against the eiderdown and will myself into the suffering shape of the wolf.

Its head is down. It wriggles and whimpers as it paws its punctured eye. The paw scrapes the protruding crystal but cannot dislodge it.

A firm human hand grips the bristling fur of my mane and hauls me almost upright. Another hand wraps around my snapping jaws. A thumb presses into the vulnerable space beneath my jaw and challenges my panic. Two eyes stare into my sighted one.

I am stilled. I try to understand.

I am staring into the beloved and merciless face of my mother, the wolf. "Don't move."

One hand releases the mane that covers my hunkered shoulders and hovers above my wounded eye. I am about to jerk my head from her, but the hand has already shot forward.

It gouges into the soft tissue that cushions the crystal. My skull has exploded.

The maiming hand shoots skyward like a bird trailing red plumage. The dripping plumage is my blood. The fingers hold the blood-washed crystal to the rays of sunlight.

The wolf-woman laughs.

She releases my snout and bends down to look into my remaining eye. "Open your mouth and take this back to your body."

The wolf's jaws close on the jagged crystal and its own smooth blood. It turns and leaps over the dew-damp forest floor.

Again I sit up in my bed in the tower. My eyes are shut tight. I will not open them until I have recalled who and where and what I am.

I am in the prison tower where I have spent almost all my life. It is dawn, and I have the crystal of Jared's soul in my mouth.

I swallow the mouthful of the wolf's blood and probe the crystal with my tongue.

What more can I do? I remember my hope of the night before that the crystal just might be hollow, like bone. Hollow and holding something softer inside.

My tongue works the crystal over to the side of my mouth and wedges it between top and bottom teeth. I press.

My mouth fills with saliva that drips. I can hear the guard's jumbled mumbling outside my door. Does the man not know that he cannot speak?

Find a fault. Press with my teeth. Move my tongue away.

I hear cracking. Something chips. My teeth or the crystal, I cannot tell. I press harder. A large chip flies from my tooth and runs on saliva out of my mouth. I clamp tighter. The crystal cracks at the top.

I have created a fault line in Jared's soul. Now I can break it.

My heart races toward Jared's life in my hands.

I press one hand to the crown of my head and cup one under my faltering jaw. I force myself to bite down on the crystal again. The crack splits the crystal into splinters.

I open my mouth. The shards and saliva run onto my bedclothes. Whatever was inside the crystal tumbles into my hands.

I hardly dare touch it.

It sits in my hands in a pool of warm fluid. "Wolf, bear, death-bird, give me your fearlessness. My prey is here in my hands."

Blurry vision clears in both eyes.

Between the pieces of shattered crystal, falling away and catching the colors of the morning light, lies a brown egg.

With my left hand, I pick away the sticky pieces of crystal clinging to the egg's shell and drop them into the saliva pooled in my lap.

I cup my hands together around the egg.

If it contains a live animal, I do not wish it to escape. I will have to squeeze it to death in my hands.

This is my Enemy's soul. The egg pulses like a beating heart.

I press my hands closed. Resistance, a pop, and splinters of eggshell jab my palms. Thick cool stuff oozes to my fingers.

I open my hands.

Just an egg. His life was an egg, and I've smashed it.

Jared is gone.

I throw back my head and laugh in a wild new voice I've never before heard from myself.

CHAPTER EIGHT
BABIES DON'T CRY:
ROSE RED, BORN 1787

Shadow man wasn't nothing but the truth coming to me so I could see it clear. Like the truth always do to folks, the shadow man scared me. The truth was I was going be ate alive in the big house. And I was only there for Rose White.

Going on sundown, when the sky wash everything red, Rose White and Mr. Sami came out the woods from they honeymoon. Was a pale woman with them. Us in the fields, we watched her weaving and laughing and stumbling like folks do when they drunk. Or crazy.

Folks dropped they hoes and stood straight to see. We was getting used to the strange and the not possible happening right regular round that plantation.

Folks been waiting on Mr. Sami. They was in a hurry to start telling on Mr. Dennis. Tell about that whipping took place soon as Sami and Rose White left. Tell about food and family cut down and sold off. Mr. Dennis called it payback for what he done paid out for the wedding feast.

Mr. Sami came humping along under the bearskin with his rifle sticking out before and behind. Then two more people came struggling together all joined at the hip and pulling away at the top.

It was Rose White and this other somebody. But the other somebody kept kind of falling away. And you should a heard how she laughed. High, deep, and on and on. Her laugh wasn't nothing but screaming. Made my hair rise on my head.

Her head was rolling. She would toss her head back, close her eyes with the red sun on her face, and calm down. Next thing, no reason we could see, she bust out with that wild laugh again.

Folks looked at each other like, *Now what?*

I dropped my hoe ran home to Ma'am. She was outside the shack by the rose briars.

"Ma'am, Rose White and Mr. Sami is back from the woods. They got a crazy somebody with them."

Ma'am wiped her hands, chewed her bottom lip.

They came to us through the field. People parted a way for them, calling out a welcome and breaking out a smile. Then they fell in behind and followed them.

Rose White got up close to me and smiled like the old days. Then she cut a look see at the woman she was holding. I did, too.

The crazy woman rolled her head back, eyes shut.

Mr. Sami said, "Ma'am, Rose Red, meet my lost sister, Heaven. She came to us in the woods."

Soon as he said my name, the madwoman leveled her face at me. Parted her eyelids, her eyeballs kind of swimming round behind the lashes, and let her eyes find me.

Gray color. Drained. Skin too pale. Like fresh milk when it done lost all the cream off the top.

"Red?" Sami sister whispered.

"Yes, Miss Heaven," Rose White said. "This my sister, Rose Red."

Miss Heaven pulled away from Rose White. Came up close to me.

"Rose *Red*?" She reached out and touched my cheeks with cool fingers. "Blood is red. Blood is sacred. Your name is special. The color of blood."

My mouth fell open. I couldn't shut it.

"Will you be my friend, Rose Red? I don't have a friend, now that I've left the tower and the Death Angel." She leaned in like to tell me a secret. "Sami and Rose White don't understand me. But I could talk to you. You could tell me about living in the real world. How people do it. I've been shut away, you know." Her fingers combed my face.

By this time, Miss Magdalen had come running. She fell to weeping and begging Sami and Rose White to come up to the big house, wash, rest up. She asked about Mr. Sami mother, Miss Angel Girl. Was Miss Angel Girl coming home to stay, too?

Rose White shocked everybody. She started crying. She said she missed her ma'am shack. Didn't want no parts of that big white bone of a house.

Mr. Sami fell to fussing with her. You could see they already done had this particular spat many a time. "The big house is your home now," he said, which of course ain't helped nothing. Rose White cried harder.

Folks slid they eyes at each other and started to whisper it was a shame her carrying on like that, seeing as how she was the new mistress of the place and married to the man who was going to change things for the better.

Miss Heaven got hold a that word "bone."

177

Now she was all up in Mr. Sami face talking about did he know bones was hollow, and if the house was a white bone, who was the blood in the marrow?

Ma'am didn't do nor say nothing just yet. Studying the situation. I should a kept my mouth shut. But you know me.

I said to Rose White, "Hush crying, girl. Folks liable to say you ain't got good sense. I can come help you get settled in the big house. You ain't got to cry."

Ma'am laughed. "Now that seem to me a good idea. Mr. Sami, you give us leave to come with you and help Rose White get settled in?" Then Ma'am hugged up on everybody so folks wouldn't think nothing too strange was going on.

I brushed Miss Heaven fingers down off my face and didn't look at her again. I wasn't going there for her. At least, I ain't thought so.

Ain't took till we was sent up to bed I real-eyes my mistake. Ma'am was sent off one way, to a room near to Rose White.

Poor girl, I mean Rose White, was going to be lost with that rifle-crazy husband a hers in a bed so big she could have got shot and died in it, and me and Ma'am together couldn't a never found her body and dragged her back out. Would a had to bury her under all them white things stuffed with feathers. What people need to sleep among feathers for? Ain't birds.

And look. All that space, and I was sent off to yet another room where I got locked up with Miss Heaven. People talking fast about how newlyweds needs to be alone. Bury people in a bed like that, you can't even find them, they must is alone, seem to me.

People telling me I'll be a companion to Miss Heaven. Give me a big word so I can't real-eyes what they was pulling on me.

That Miss Heaven. Rolling her eyes all round the room, still on about the Death Angel and the blood and The Saver, and how he got her here safe. And my special name. Rose *Red*, how she said it.

I held her like a baby and sang her to sleep. I kept my eyes open. I had a plan.

The minute I heard her breathing calm, I peeled myself out from her arms and headed straight to Miss Magdalen back door.

I was fuming. Thinking to myself, *People lying in my face telling me I'm free. Wrapping my body round some crazy woman like to drink my blood in the middle of the night ain't my idea of being free. Get me back in the cotton fields.*

But a big house like that when it get quiet will set you to looking in dark corners. With all the people either sleep or gone, and that crazy woman dreaming upstairs about how red my blood run, the house itself got to feeling like it had eyeballs watching me crawl through its belly. I was rushing down the hallways to get out.

The hallways was like pig intestines when the belly get split. Dark and red and bulging, twisting and turning so you can't see where you going.

Wasn't no light on the walls, neither. Candles was blown out. The mirrors that might a shot me some light from the window full of colored glass was all took down. So there was starlight shining through the colored glass just at the far ends of the

179

hallway. But the middle, where I had to go, just sat breathing dark like a beast slit belly.

It was that crazy Miss Heaven, cutting up and screaming about the mirrors and ripping off the old covers and smashing at the glass with her fists, that made Mother Magdalen decide to take them down.

My hands hit the smooth wood of the stair rails. I rushed headlong down. I was breathing like I been running through the woods, scared.

The steps turned and confused me. They went on till I thought I must a got on the wrong ones. They ain't seemed this long when I went up with my candle, holding Miss Heaven on my other arm.

At the bottom step, I seen a bare light glint and disappear on the carpet at my feet. Come from over that way.

I ain't asked myself what might give that light. I just took off, hoping and following.

I could see a door open, and past it, the shape of Miss Magdalen outdoor kitchen and the edge of the hands' quarters beyond. I rushed ahead.

I was near about smack up on Miss Magdalen back door when I real-eyes was a man's back framed in it. Huddled in on itself.

I must a made a sound. He turned and looked at me. "Rose Red? Girl, what's with you?"

It was Mr. Dennis. I was so glad it was him and he sounded almost kind, for a change, that I grinned and fell right into one of them chairs at Miss Magdalen big table, where we all had our supper, as soon as he said, "Sit. Join me."

That must a been hours before when we was sitting at that table earlier tonight, blowing on hot stew and laughing about the changes Mr. Sami was going make round here.

And that whole time, Mr. Dennis had stood at the door. Staring out back at the rain. He was there to greet the field hands that wandered up, they eyes all downcast, calling out good wishes to the newlyweds and stooping to put a word in Mr. Sami ear, tell on his pap.

Sight to shock sore eyes, field hands greeted at the back door by Mr. Dennis.

What was he looking for? Miss Angel Girl. Now, it kind a strange to see a woman who got everything walk out and give it all up. Slave woman, too. But even more strange is when the man been left long enough for the children to come home grown, and he still waiting at the back door, watching for her.

"He could a been to town plenty a times and bought him another woman, by now."

"I hear he done just that."

"You know what I mean. Someone to be his woman and stay here with him."

"Wight Englishwoman staying round here cost too much."

"But give a African woman a taste a freedom, I don't care how light-skinned she is, she get ideas and ain't take no more orders from nobody."

"Poor man can't win for playing cheap."

Guffaws.

Mr. Sami hushed up the whispers round the table. "Man can't help loving and hoping," Mr. Sami mumbled into his stew so drops of the hot meat sprayed folks sitting close by.

And I said to myself, *Just listen at Mr. Sami Wolf Water. Him crawling in the woods with the wild beasts, how all of a sudden he think he know so much about "man"? He going tell people that men who own other men is just like the men they own, whip, and kill?* Got on my last nerve.

But didn't I sound just like Mr. Sami now, feeling sorry and asking myself was Mr. Dennis standing there ever since folks had kissed and wept and said good night? For hours?

"Mr. Dennis, I didn't expect to find nobody down here, sir." My voice had questions in it. I could hear them myself.

He ain't seemed to take offense. He said real soft, "Neither did I expect company. But I'm pleased to have it."

He studied me a little close in the dark. His arms was still crossed. The rain had started to fall, like it do sometimes toward evening at the end of summer. Looked like he been there so long, rain done splattered on him. But he ain't seemed to pay it no mind.

I stopped smiling and looked at him back. What was he thinking so hard?

"May I ask what you're doing up and about, Rose? It seems a little dark for touring the house and a little late for traipsing outdoors. A little wet, too."

Should I make up a story about how I figured the chamber pot was for Miss Heaven, so I was on my way to the ditch?

But Mr. Dennis had turned from me to reflect on the rain and night some more, like he had just answered some question of his own. "Wet for walking, if she didn't know for certain how to get back here. It's been so long."

I knew who he meant. Miss Angel Girl. I didn't say nothing. Didn't believe he was talking to me, anyway.

Long silence, him looking at the rain and me watching his back curved toward the doorframe. Then he said over his shoulder, "Miss Heaven fall asleep okay, Rose Red?"

"Yes, sir."

"You couldn't sleep yourself, I guess."

"No, sir."

"Neither could I. Sleep, that is."

Me so use to talking familiar with my ma'am and sister, I up and said, "I'm sorry, sir. Sometimes folks just let you down. Not that they mean to, though, sir."

"Rose Red. That's your name, isn't it? She doesn't care if she lets me down. But I did think she'd want to be here for the children. I just *knew* she would come back as soon as both her children walked through this door." He looked hard at me like I should explain Miss Angel Girl to him.

Had a been Rose White talking, I would a said, *Clear to me you ain't knowed everything good as you think you did. So why you going on about it now? Let it go.*

But this *was* Mr. Dennis, even if he wasn't quite himself. So I kept still.

All that rain on his face made him look like he was crying. I ain't seen many men cry in my lifetime. I seen men whipped raw and ain't cried.

But losing a woman, you know, from giving birth, or selling off, or just laying herself down in

183

the field to die, I seen men cry like newborn babies. I guess it just something about men and they women that do that to them.

I did what I seen folks do with a crying man. Went up and put my hand on Mr. Dennis. I didn't worry it might be too familiar because I was new to the big house and ain't supposed to know no better. *Don't matter to nobody what I do,* I told myself. *Tomorrow I be back in the fields, anyway.*

I put my hand on Mr. Dennis shoulder and stood close. I looked out and watched the rain fall with him. So he wouldn't be so alone.

After while, he looked at me some more.

I could see him move out the corner of my eye. I looked at him back and quick dropped my hand. I had been thinking about the woods and my ma'am shack and the roses blooming I was going miss in the morning if I didn't wake up back home. His staring startled me.

"Don't go," he said.

I put my hand to my mouth. "How did you know, sir?" I must a looked scared of how he could read my mind.

So now he looked puzzled. "You took your hand away. I assume you're on your way back upstairs to bed." He moved even closer, studying me good. "What did you think I meant, Rosie?"

I was embarrassed bad and looked back out toward where the woods made a dark bunchy line past the fields.

"Oh," he said. "Come on. You don't like the big house? I don't believe it. Where were you thinking of going, Rose Red? Back to your mother's cabin?"

I said low, "To the woods." I was scared I said it. I crossed my arms over the cold in my stomach and looked at the ground where the rain was striking up dirt and making it mud. I wouldn't a never said it if him and me hadn't a been talking like I might talk to Ma'am. About how people feel and what they want.

Mr. Dennis put his fist on his hip and leaned back against the open doorway. Then he made one of them sounds folks make when they kind a sick and tired of you. "What is it that could draw a woman away from a house that has everything for her, and out to the wild woods?"

I struggled. All I knew at that time was my feelings. But how you put words to those? You can say the woods, but you can't say what they mean to you. So I said, "Mr. Sami been promising folks they going to have they freedom," because that almost gave me the right to want to go somewhere Mr. Dennis didn't understand.

"Ha!" It wasn't a real laugh. "Sami doesn't know as much as he thinks he knows about running a plantation of this size."

The rain stood on Mr. Dennis face and made it shine in the dark. It must a been something wet shining on my cheeks, too. Because Mr. Dennis stared at me a long minute and then reached his fingers out to my face, like his daughter Miss Heaven had done.

He touched the wet. "Have I made you cry?"

Something in his voice so soft got right to me. I put both hands on my face and cried for real.

His one hand still there touched mine. I could hear him saying something, but I couldn't tell what.

I felt a dreadful fool. I hiked up my apron to dry my face.

"Excuse me, sir." *I should say something more*, I thought. But I just took off running toward my ma'am shack.

Mud flew up between my bare toes. Felt good to run.

I hadn't got past Miss Magdalen vegetable and flower patch when a hand jerked on my arm and spun me around. It was Mr. Dennis, face frowned up scary in the rain. "Where the hell do you think you're going, girl?" He started in to shaking me. "And what do you think I'm supposed to tell Sami and Heaven when they wake up, and you're not there? 'Well, Rose Red decided to take a stroll in the woods in the dark and the downpour and maybe meet up with some patrollers-who knows?-and I thought it was a good idea'?" He didn't let loose a my arm.

I have a temper. I started in trying to snatch my arm back. I been struck for that kind a thing by Mr. Peter and the bullies in the field, but I don't care. If he couldn't understand my feelings, Mr. Dennis still ain't had no call to make me sound such a fool.

"Whoa!" Mr. Dennis grabbed the other arm. "What's with you, girl? Have you gone crazy?"

Crying make you lose your manners. "Ain't nobody crazy round here but your daughter, Mr. Dennis. And I'm getting back to my ma'am shack before Miss Heaven drink my blood and make me crazy, too." Then I ducked my head, waiting for his hand to land on my face.

186

One of his hands let me loose and pulled back, like to strike. But nothing fell. I looked up around at him.

He was standing staring at me dead serious. Rain ran his hair down into his eyes. He had to blink a lot. But he didn't look angry no more.

He jerked his head toward the house. Rain tossed off the ends of his hair. "Come on. Just come back with me, and we'll talk. You can't run off, girl. Not to your mother's place and not to the woods, either. Nobody's given you your freedom, yet. You go where I say go, or you'll be caught and whipped till you scream for mercy. Now, come on. Let's get out of this rain."

He must a knew I wasn't going run no more. Too scared. But he kept hold a my arm, anyway, till we was back in the house with the door shut.

"Sit down." He fell on his knees to build up a fire in the fireplace.

I had never seen such a thing. "I get that for you, sir." Had my misbehaving turned the order a things so upside down that here was the man who owned everybody, on his knees doing grub work?

"Stay there," he said.

I sat still till he came back wiping his hands on his pants. I hate how men do that. I guess it's because they don't wear no apron. I raised my own raggedy old apron up. "Clean your hands for you, sir?"

He threw back his head and kind a laughed for real. He sat in the chair next to me and held out his hands.

I wiped them till he took the apron out my hands and closed his fingers around mines. He

187

could stare till it wrack your nerves. Till I felt like telling him leave me alone.

"Tell me. Why do you really want to get out of this house? You've spent your life in a shack that was hardly better than living in the open woods. Seems to me you'd be tickled to death to be in a house like this, Rosie."

I had to look away. I hadn't never spent much time talking to Mr. Peter and none to Mr. Dennis. How could people talk so down to you and still wait for a polite answer?

When I looked back at him, I could see he meant no harm. He really wanted to know. "Folks got they druthers, sir."

The firelight hit his eyes from the side. He had the same eyes as his daughter. I wondered how eyes so misty on Miss Heaven could be so icy on Mr. Dennis. Gave me chills.

"Tell the truth," he said. "Is there somebody out there in the quarters you want to be with tonight?"

"Everybody I care about is upstairs sleep."

"Don't lie to me. A girl as pretty as you? Come on. I've had my eye on you a little while now. I'd say you've got about four or five boys out there hoping you'll come to them tonight." He chuckled again. It had a ugly note to it.

He was hitting a real sore spot with me. I figured a blow or two upside my head wasn't going to be nearly as bad as listening to what he was working up to say. I stood up.

"Wouldn't want Miss Heaven to wake up alone, sir. Good night, sir."

He got hold a my wrist. "The fire hasn't dried you yet. Stay."

I looked at him. His voice wasn't hard. But I would just as soon he didn't spare me blows and make me owe him favors. So I ain't moved a muscle.

Only my mouth dropped open because he said, "Please."

He let his eyes go up and down my dress and put his other hand at my waist. "Look," he said. "Your dress isn't nearly dry. You'll catch a chill if you leave the fire." He looked back up at my face. "So, tell me, Rosie. Don't you care about one or two of those young hands out there?"

"Not in particular, sir."

"Why not?"

I shrugged. "Seem to me it ain't no use, hands picking out somebody to care about, sir."

"I see. Can you tell me why you feel that way?"

"Not without giving you offense, sir."

"I won't take offense, Rosie. Tell me."

Now, why was he asking me a question that he had to a knew the answer to before I was even born? *Well, let him hear it, if he wanted to so bad.*

"You take a notion, you sell folks apart, sir. I love my ma'am and my sister, so I figure I love two folks too many already."

He studied me real hard real long. The fire danced and snapped. I could see he was good as his word and wasn't going get angry. But I couldn't figure what he must be thinking. Nor why he would ask such a question.

"So tell me, Rosie. Can you make your feelings do what you want them to?" He made a sound like he was getting ready to laugh at me if I said yes.

189

Thing about the way he laughed most a the time was, it wasn't like nothing was funny.

"I don't have to make my feelings do nothing, sir. They ain't never gave me no trouble."

He went on ahead and laughed. Then he rubbed one hand up and around my waist. I got a cold squeeze in my insides. "Sounds to me as if your feelings haven't been pushed very far. Maybe your mother managed to scare those boys out there away from you." He was back to studying my dress.

But I didn't feel like it was my dress he was studying. He pulled at my sides. "Sit here with me." I landed on his lap.

He put one hand to my head and pulled me close to his face. I felt something soft go up against my bare neck. "Warm," he said, and I felt his lips move on my skin.

I shivered. "What was that?" he asked. No doubt about it. He was making his lips move over my skin on purpose.

I tried to stand. He held on. "I want to go now, sir." I struggled a little with his hands.

He slapped at my fingers. "Let go."

I turned on him my hate-fullest stare. But I sat still.

He studied me till a slow smile took over his face. Then he laughed like he had found something funny at last. "I never thought I'd see the day I'd have to envy one of my own field hands."

"Who, sir? Me?"

"Don't be a simpleton. Nobody in the world is as innocent as you pretend to be. I envy whichever boy you're protecting right now."

"Protecting, sir?"

"Yes. Protecting. And don't try to make me think you don't know what I'm talking about. You're the one who brought up selling people away from each other."

He leaned back in his chair and studied the fire. I made a move to get up at last.

"Stay. I told you that already. Your dress isn't dry, and I don't want to be alone."

I looked toward the stairway out a here and back up to Miss Heaven room. I didn't know when I had it good. I had tears spilling out my eyes. Sometimes I cry easy.

"Now I've really made you cry." He pulled my head down till it was on his shoulder. "Listen. You're young, and you've never seen anything but my farm. On the other hand, I've been halfway around the world and back. So, let me teach you something. The way the world works is, some people have power, and some people have none. I have a great deal of it. And you have none. On the other hand, that doesn't mean you have nothing. I've watched you a little while now, and I can say for a fact that you're one of the sweetest little things alive in the world today."

He pushed my chin up to look at my face. He ran his hand down my chin to my throat and cupped and dipped it around the curves of my breast.

"You're frightened. I can feel your heartbeat. Don't be afraid. Tonight, I'm just going to talk to you. I have my reasons. Do you want to know what they are?"

"No, sir." I shook my head in case he didn't hear me.

"What if I taught you to care about me, Rose Red? What if that's been my mistake? What if you didn't want anything in the world more than to be with me? I bet we could make each other happy."

I sat up as far as he would let me. "Can I move sit on the bench, sir? I can't listen sitting on you like this."

"No." He eased my head back down. "Now, it's like I said. You have no power, to speak of. That may be unfair. On the other hand, I have plenty of power. And everything that comes with it."

His hand left my breast and started stroking down my skirt from my waist to my knees. I could feel little round patches where the dress was dry and hot and where it was still damp and cool as his hand moved over them, topside my leg, underside my leg, inside my leg.

It was that blue dress he gave me when he took me and Rose White to the woods to bait Mr. Jared and Mr. Sami. I wore it ever since I got it.

I liked how it fell against me and moved like water in a stream. Until now. Now I felt like Mr. Dennis hand was running along my bare skin, and I wasn't wearing no dress at all. I wished real quick I had my old scratchy too-tight burlap rag back on.

"You're beautiful," he said.

He looked up from stroking my leg and looked at me close in the face. "Angel Girl was beautiful, too. But she was wild inside. I knew it the first day I saw her. I should have just sent the dogs out after her, when she ran away. But I wanted her to want me and come back on her own. Does that make sense? All these years."

He shook his head. "Tell me something," he said. "Why do people want what they know they can't have?"

His fingers started up at my face again. Down to my neck and that same breast he liked so bad. But this time his eyes stayed on mines. "You're not the least bit wild, are you, Rose Red? But I think I like you." Another real laugh. "I sound like some kind of schoolboy. I know I like you." Smile left. "Could you learn to care for me, Rose Red? If I were very nice to you for a very long time, could you learn to love me from your heart? This heart."

He folded his hand soft around that breast and tried to scoop it out of the dress, but the dress wouldn't let him. He gave up and put his mouth to the cloth. I told you it was thin.

I hadn't never in all my born days heard of a man taking suck like a baby. I didn't move nor make a sound. There was a pull from that breast ran all through my body.

"Mm," he said after a while.

I said so low I couldn't hardly hear myself, "Mr. Dennis. You said you wasn't going to do nothing but talk to me, sir."

He bit into the breast through the cloth. I cried out.

He stood up quick. I couldn't fall because he was holding on to me so tight. "Come on." His voice was real deep and kind a scratchy. He bent to scoop his arms beneath my legs and around my back.

My breast hurt where he had bit me, and it felt like ants was running everywhere he touched me. "Let me alone, sir." I ripped at his fingers and twisted out of his arms. When his hands slipped a little, I ran.

It was hard taking them steps so fast in the dark. I fell a couple of times. But I got to Miss Heaven room and had the lock turned on the door before Mr. Dennis caught up to me.

I could hear him breathing on the other side of the wood. "Let me in."

I didn't say nothing. I wanted him to think I was away from the door, maybe hiding in the bed with my head covered.

"Rose Red?" he whispered hard. "I know you're listening. I said let me in."

I decided I best not move from the door, or he might hear me and know I was up and around. I was thinking the next day would see me in a powerful lot of trouble for this night's doings. I was forever going to feel naked in this dress, after tonight.

"Honey," Mr. Dennis said, "open this door for me. This is my own house, Rose Red. You know I could have you punished for running from me. Twice tonight. You've lost your head. But I swear I won't hurt you if you open this door. Now."

Maybe I best obey at that, I thought. I quiet undid the latch and slid the door a little open. I ain't looked at him, though.

He reached in and caught my hand. "I won't scare you again. Look at me."

I looked up at him. Couldn't see him good in the little light full a colors coming from the window at the end a the hall. Just the shape of his face on the side. Places where his hair kind a curved away and fell behind him. Surprised me how the shape of it was pretty.

"I promise I won't scare you again tonight." He pulled me through the doorway toward him and over to one side so he could push the door shut behind me. I backed against the wall. I leaned on it and felt how I was trembling.

Something I knew very little about was going on here.

"Don't fear me." He leaned into me against the wall and put his mouth on mines.

I smelled something like trees burning and tasted something like the air when you get too close to a bonfire. His mouth sucked at my tongue and teeth and lips. I had never heard of people doing so much to each other with they mouths. I stopped breathing. My heart beat too fast for breathing, anyway.

There was a hot heavy bundle all of a sudden between us, pressing into me. It started to burn me, right there at the top of my thighs. He pressed it harder. Was it him?

"Soft lips," he said in my mouth. He pulled away and brushed his lips across mines one way and another. "I'll teach you what to do with them." He put his mouth full on mines again. Something wet and thick slid into my mouth. His tongue? He licked my lips and took his tongue away. "Someday soon. Quite soon."

He took a deep breath and moved back from me. The heat was gone. He reached around me, behind me, and shoved the door open. He pushed me backward, inside the bedroom. He watched me while he shut the door.

I felt sick. Dizzy. Cold.

I crawled in Miss Heaven bed with my damp and dry dress still on and shivered till I fell asleep.

Miss Magdalen came in and woke us in the morning. I couldn't believe I had slept till the sun was high.

"You're on Miss Heaven's bed?" Mother Magdalen looked kind a concerned at me.

"Nobody told me nowhere else to sleep."

Miss Magdalen smiled. "Well, if Miss Heaven wants you there, I guess it isn't up to me to make you sleep on the floor."

What? I asked myself. On the floor? I can do that in Ma'am shack, and don't have nobody chasing me up and down the stairs and got they hands and mouth and hot things all over me, neither.

"Get moving, you two lazybones." Miss Magdalen was all cheery. "We've got to make some nice clothes for all these new gentlepeople."

Was a old man brought in from the stables who knew how to work with leather, set to measuring all our feet for some "simple" shoes, how Miss Magdalen put it.

Miss Magdalen hunted up some bolts of cloth, old and stored up from when Miss Angel Girl used to live here. Mr. Sami would get some of Mr. Dennis things that fit all right. But Miss Magdalen sent me and Rose White and Miss Heaven and Ma'am into a little room with stone walls and floors where women measured us and stuck pins in cloth up against us.

Ma'am said she wouldn't never get used to being called "Miss Sister." Rose White just called all the maids "miss" right back.

196

Only crazy thing Miss Heaven did was, when she saw the bolts of cloth being unwrapped, she ran and knelt down next to a dark red one. "Make my and Rose Red's new dresses out of this one."

A seamstress said, "Miss Heaven, I think that light wool will be way too hot up until the snow falls. Why don't we look at some of this peach-colored silk, here?"

Miss Heaven just ran her hands over the dark red. "Rose Red and I will have all our dresses made of this, and nothing else. Do you understand me?"

Seamstress looked at me. I said, "Don't make me no difference," and she set to flopping the cloth off the bolt.

Miss Heaven wrapped her arms around herself. She started singing about animals and eyeballs and wandered out the room. I was so glad.

I was trying to get alone with Ma'am and Rose White and tell them I was going to have to move back to the shack that very night. I was thinking to only complain about Miss Heaven. I was way too shamed to say a word about Mr. Dennis.

But Ma'am kept trying to get off alone and talk a little with Rose White. I had a tight feeling inside. Why couldn't Ma'am nor Rose White turn around and ask was everything all right with me?

End of the fitting, when we was outside the sewing room, I said, "Rose White, you think that new red dress going look fitting when I get back out to the field?"

Her mouth dropped open. I could see it in the dark of the hallway. Got you back, I said to myself.

Ma'am spoke up. "Rose Red, don't you give your sister no hard time. Us done promised to stay and help her get used to this place. Ain't time to start going back on our word. You mind me like you got some sense." Ma'am had her hands slapped upside both hips so it felt like home round here.

"Excuse me, Ma'am. But folks done lied to me, telling me I'm here for my sister, and all the time fixing to lock me in a room with that crazy Miss Heaven."

"Why you call her crazy?" Rose White had nerve to say.

"Because I got two eyes to see and a mouth to talk," I said right back.

"What she do crazy to you?" Rose White didn't know when to quit.

"Always on at me about blood and about how she see things ain't there."

"Don't sound crazy you listen to her good." I told you sometimes Rose White don't know when to quit. "You and me seen Miss Angel ghost our own selves, up there at Sami cave. You done disremembered that, Rose Red? Seem to me seeing things ain't there just the other side of living." Hands on her hips, too. Since when she talk to me like that?

"Well, she ain't crazy to you, Rose White, why you ain't sharing her room and watching her see things all night? Let me tell you what. She crazy or not really don't make me no never mind. But I'm here to tell you ain't nobody going lock me up one more night with some cackling gal can't get her mind off the bleeding and the dead."

Now Ma'am started in on me. "Rose White your own flesh and blood, Rose Red. Maybe you don't want to hear nobody talk about blood because you done turned your back on your own blood kin. You thought about that, gal?"

Ma'am always did speechify.

"That Miss Heaven you so had enough of, too. Gal raised up by the one man hate her in the whole world, locked in a tower with a runaway for a ma'ammy, and that woman killed under her nose when she was just a bitty thing. Some woman-eater off the chain gang with his tongue cut out his head, set to ma'ammying poor Miss Heaven after that. Miss Heaven got the right to be confused and can't think straight."

It was clear to me I wasn't going to get they help to get out that house and back to my shack and my fields unless I told them some of what went on between me and Mr. Dennis. And I just couldn't do that. I left all hangdog.

I was glad to get back to Miss Heaven. She wanted to take a walk together in the garden after our fitting. Sitting under the grapes and roses at the willow path with her head on my lap kept her quiet and gave me time to fume.

Why didn't that gape-mouth Mr. Jared prop up on his stick leg and shoot that creeping Mr. Sami before he could come bust up my family this a way?

I decided I just best learn to stay locked in Miss Heaven room at night. If I wanted to run away, I'd have to try it in the daytime.

That night, Mr. Dennis came knocking at Miss Heaven door. Must a read my mind again.

It was after Miss Magdalen had dressed Miss Heaven for bed and plaited her hair, and I had sung her to sleep. Her head was still resting on my chest like I was old enough to be her ma'ammy.

Knock knock knock. Knock knock.

I right away wanted to think it was Ma'am or Rose White, come to see about me after all.

"Rose Red?" Mr. Dennis whispered.

Oh no, I thought.

"Come and open this door," he said louder.

I took my time getting loose from Miss Heaven and sashaying to the door. I was trying to think what could Mr. Dennis do to me if I didn't do what he wanted.

Yelling? Slapping? Whipping? None of it seemed like something I was ready to go through just at the moment.

I opened the door.

Mr. Dennis reached in and took my hand. "Come down and let's sit together. I won't frighten you tonight. You have my word."

We sat in the dark, candles blown out and the back door wide open, come breeze, bugs, or stink from the outhouses and ditches. There wasn't no fire in the fireplace. I guess because there hadn't been no rain to cool things off.

It was a long time before Mr. Dennis said anything. I had started in to thinking maybe I had misjudged him all wrong.

But after while he took my hands. He studied my fingers till I was shamed of the places where you could see picking cotton had cut them up. "Rose Red, tomorrow we're going to try to find wherever it was my brother-or whoever-hid Miss Heaven. I have two reasons for searching that place out. First, I'm thinking Miss Heaven may have things there she'd like to have back. Second, Sami thinks there's a chance that their mother, Miss

Angel Girl, might be waiting for them there. He wants to come along."

He looked up from my hands to my eyes. "Would you like to come? I know how much you like the woods."

"You want me to come take care of Miss Heaven, sir?"

"No. What is it? Scared to come, Rose Red?"

"Not rightly scared. At least, not for myself."

He had moved his hands further up my arms. He was holding me just above my elbows. I wondered what would happen if I leaned a little away from him. I sat still and ain't moved.

"Are you saying you're scared for Miss Heaven? Is that the only thing that bothers you?"

"Yes, sir."

"She isn't going. Only Sami and I, and a couple of hands to help carry things back here. So you don't have to worry about her."

I fixed my eyes to stare outside, so I could look past Mr. Dennis. How nice it might be to be out in them woods.

And maybe Mr. Dennis wouldn't act like this in front of Mr. Sami. We might even find Miss Angel Girl. And she could be the one to care about Mr. Dennis and make him happy.

"Thank you, sir. I be very pleased to go with you all."

Mr. Dennis smiled. "Good girl."

Then he settled back and took my fingers light in his hands. He told me how he loved the woods much as I did, and how when he was younger, he spent all the time he could out there until Mr. Jared got clawed by a bear, and then he had to take over the plantation.

I woke up shamed to find myself on Mr. Dennis lap again with my face on one of his arms. He was stroking my body with the other hand. Just like the night before.

I jumped up. "Excuse me, sir."

He didn't try to stop me. Just smiled. I took off up the stairs in the dark again saying, *See. Everything going be all right. He let me get away.*

And he didn't even come knocking on Miss Heaven door, neither.

But didn't folks look strange gathered out behind the big house in the morning when they real-eyes I was going with Mr. Dennis and them. Eyes sliding everywhere. I could see something was bad wrong, but Ma'am wouldn't tell me what.

Ma'am just said, "You make sure you stick by Mr. Sami and tell the mens keep they hands to they self. All of them." She came close up and whispered, "That go for Mr. Sami, too."

Ma'am went up to Mr. Sami. He was strapping a pack on a horse. Kind a. He looked mean like always when he didn't know what he was doing.

He wouldn't look at Rose White for nothing. I thought maybe something went wrong between them. Maybe she asked to go, and he said no.

Serve her right if she want to go and can't, I said to myself. I was mad at her for bringing me here and turning her back on me. But sad if I was missing a chance to have a good time with her in the woods again.

"Mr. Sami," Ma'am said loud enough for everyone standing around to hear, "now I be counting on you as the gentleman you done become to make sure my baby don't suffer no humiliation, out there alone in the wild woods with all these mens. She suppose to be in training to be a lady. Ain't that what you all done told me, sir?"

Mr. Sami stopped his fiddling with the saddle pack. "Ma'am, I thought I asked you to please stop calling me sir. It's really not fitting, your being my wife's mother. And you know you don't have to ask me to guard your daughter's virtue. Her virtue is mine, now."

He looked around and all the sliding eyes looked away.

Mr. Dennis glared on all sides so I could reckon-eyes him from the old days. He said, like if to his son, "If people get it in their heads to tarnish a girl's name, I'll just have to un-hang my whip and put it to some good use." But then he looked like a new thought all a sudden sneaked up and hit him upside his head.

Mr. Dennis looked quick over at the two hands from the field, picked to join us in the woods. His face spread wide with shock. He set in to studying them till I myself had to blush. His eyes ran up and down they bodies like he had a just noticed how lean and strong them two was.

I don't know who picked them to come with us. They was, in fact, two special young men to me. But no way was I going let on about that.

I backed over to my mother. "Ma'am, maybe I should stay. I don't think something's right."

Mr. Dennis must a heard me. He clopped his horse up close to my side. "Rose Red, get up on this horse ahead of me. You don't have to know how to

203

ride. I'll hold you on here. Sister, you don't have to worry about your girl. I'll take care of her my own self."

"Yes, sir," Ma'am said, but her eyes said, *Oh no.*

Mr. Dennis hooked his arm around my waist and hauled me up on the saddle.

Then he went right on talking into everybody silence and staring. "You two boys get on up there and drive that horse pulling the cart. Stay behind my son and in front of me. Keep your eyes to yourselves. You know I mean it, don't you?"

My heart was flying. I couldn't catch nobody eyes no more but Ma'am and Rose White, and they looked in a tizzy.

We could hear Miss Heaven off crying in the house.

"But I ain't seen Miss Heaven to say good-bye," I said, twisting in the saddle to face Mr. Dennis.

"Haven't, Rose Red. You *haven't* seen Miss Heaven to say good-bye. Maggie, make sure Miss Heaven knows that Rose Red's gone riding, and you'll be looking after all her needs for a while."

Then he clicked his tongue to his horse. Mr. Sami did the same. The cart jerked and bumped on the stones up ahead of us.

I made up my mind to breathe shallow so my belly wouldn't poke out and touch Mr. Dennis arm. *And if I don't turn and look at him, I'll be all right,* I told myself.

But being up on a horse is like flying. It wasn't no time before I wasn't thinking of nothing but how the horse muscles rippled under my legs and how pretty them bloodthirsty fields could look to you when you wasn't working in them.

We had to skirt around in the woods, finding good trails. The hands was having a gay old time off the farm. And I got to where I was just twisting and turning to see around me, and didn't care nothing how Mr. Dennis arm might rub and bind.

It was probably plenty a times my face brushed his when I turned, but I didn't even pay that no never mind, since he acted like it didn't mean nothing.

And then we got to the cliffs at Mr. Sami cave. We all looked up while Mr. Sami talked about flinging Mr. Jared down, and how the body disappeared from where it hit.

I didn't look at the spot. I kept my eyes on the cave.

"Rose Red, what are you thinking about?" Mr. Dennis hot breath hit the back a my ear.

I made up my mind to talk with my back to him. "Sir, that's where me and Rose White seen Miss Angel ghost. Miss Magdalen daughter. Not your woman, that we out here hoping to find."

He took my chin in one hand and tugged so I had to turn around. I kept my eyes down. Didn't help.

On the horse, our two bodies was wedged so tight, I like to died seeing how folks at the plantation must a seen us. Our bodies was one from our bellies to our toes. You couldn't a slid a finger between us.

"Rose Red, what if we're not out here to find Angel Girl?"

205

I made like I ain't heard nothing and asked to go take care a my needs. I slid down and ran to climb rocks and slip between trees and get away.

We camped there under Mr. Sami cave. I stayed away from Mr. Dennis the rest of the evening. But when we was sitting around eating the supper I tried to heat in them little pots with stream water, Mr. Dennis got it in his head to tease me into telling about Miss Angel ghost. He just had a mind to make me talk. Had he forgot there was still folks who believed he was the one killed Miss Magdalen girl? Why would he want to bring her up?

Mr. Sami listened to how the ghost walked through Rose White and told her things. "The ghost must have led me out to save you two," Mr. Sami said. "I saw a light move out of the cave and followed it. There was Jared, threatening you."

"So that's how Rose White knew who killed Angel and why." Mr. Dennis tapped his spoon on the side of his eating pan.

Mr. Sami said, "Makes you wonder." One of the hands I used to fight with when I was little and first started working in the fields said, "Sure enough."

His voice sounded soft, and I wondered if he knew I was feeling down. He hadn't never had neither a kind word nor a kind look for me. But I looked up at him anyway.

Sure enough, he smiled at me for the first time in his life.

I was moved. I wasn't never one to turn down a kindly act. I smiled back.

And then I seen Mr. Sami eyes move. I looked to see what he was looking at.

Mr. Sami was watching Mr. Dennis watching me smile at that hand I had always called Bully.

I left to wash up the cooking things in the stream and take my own bath. But I couldn't enjoy my swim for thinking what it looked like to see Mr. Dennis thighs running alongside mines on that horse.

I had to get dressed before my body got dry good. I just kept feeling uneasy, sitting on the grassy bank with nothing on. And when I came trailing back to the campsite, my dress already getting muddy from the swampy wetness, trying to carry all the pots and spoons in one trip, Mr. Sami offered me to sleep in the cart.

I was surprised. It had been parked a little behind the trees where the fire was protected from a breeze, so it was off alone. I ran to unroll my blanket in there and claim it.

I tried to soothe myself to sleep thinking how pretty the leaves waved and covered up the stars, and then the stars would come out and blink between the leaves again. I couldn't wait to see the moon rise overhead.

I woke up to the sharp sweet earth and green things smells of the woods. The sun was high. I had missed seeing the moon.

Well, maybe the trip would take long enough so I might have at least one more night under the sky. Wasn't nobody needed me back home so bad they'd up and die if I took a few more days.

Or was there?

Come to think of it, who was tending Mammy Water these two days and nights since Ma'am and I moved out a our shack? Starting on the third day. Mammy Water could a died of thirst by now.

I sat up straight in the cart and watched pink and yellow wash over all the gray till the pine needles and leaves started shining green.

I would just have to ask to go back. Mammy Water, Miss Heaven, my mother, and my sister, they all needed me. Even if they didn't always act like it.

It wasn't that long a walk to get back that I couldn't make it in a solid day.

A face came up near me, over the edge of the cart. It was the other hand. The one used to stick up for me when I was little and first got sent to the fields. I always called this one Boyfriend.

Struck me I ain't looked at him much since he got all grown up. I smiled at him, now, and then I felt real sad to think how much a stranger I felt to him.

"How you doing these days, Boyfriend?" I knew Mr. Dennis had got everybody afraid to talk to me, so Boyfriend wasn't going speak first.

He smiled big. Leaned on the cart like we was back at home, leaning on our hoes in the field to chat. "Oh, can't complain, Rose Red. And you?"

"Could complain if the trees ain't had ears," I said, and Boyfriend laughed.

His laugh put me in mind of when we was bitty children, scamps really. Whenever Mr. Peter sent Boyfriend to find me in the woods, he'd gather kindling for me along the way. He knew I was always off shirking my duties, and he just never wanted me to get whipped for it.

Boyfriend would laugh when he'd finally catch up with me, off skinning up trees or skinny-dipping in the streams. Then he'd hand me the bundle of kindling so he could take a turn. He saved my hide many a time and ain't never called me on that debt.

Fear of loving hands took me away from Boyfriend.

I was fixing to ask him his mind about that when I heard Mr. Dennis voice real sharp, "Boy! What'd I tell you about hanging around that cart when you're not driving it?"

Boyfriend was off like a shot, a pot banging on his leg that he was going to fill with water for morning coffee.

Mr. Dennis came to me frowning. "Did that boy bother you, Rose Red?"

Look in my eyes and see how much I hate you, I thought. But all I said was, "Boyfriend ain't never been no bother to me. We been friends long as I can remember." I remembered myself, lowered my eyes, and said, "Sir."

"Hasn't ever," Mr. Dennis said, his voice still all hard and not too pleasant. "He *hasn't ever* been a bother to you." He kind of turned his back on me and crossed his arms.

"That's just what I said, sir." *Unlike some other people I could name if I didn't mind getting my back whipped raw.* "Boyfriend always been a kind and good friend to me. Sir."

"So you call him Boyfriend," he said over one shoulder. His head turned toward me but his eyes ain't quite reached me. "Why don't you tell me why you're the only person I've ever heard call that man by such a name."

209

Well, I didn't really see no need to answer that question. Boyfriend was special to me. Kept me out of trouble many a time when I couldn't understand what a field hand's life was supposed to be like, how they was supposed to act. And so I gave him a special name. That was all.

But how do you make somebody reckon-eyes that when he don't want to? No way was I going to beg Mr. Dennis to be a part of what I used to have with Boyfriend, not right when I was missing it the most.

Well, not unless Mr. Dennis got set to whip me for not talking.

And besides. Speaking of talking. I was getting right tired of Mr. Dennis telling me how to talk, too. *Folks tell you how to talk, it's like they telling you how to think and what to feel.*

"No answer," Mr. Dennis said. "I thought not. I guess you're not willing to tell me, either, how 'kind' that hand's been to you. Nor just what 'kind' means, in the first place, when we're talking about naked little boys and girls out rolling in the dust of the fields together. Like wild animals." He was getting worked up.

And so was I.

Who put us naked in the fields like wild animals? This man here. And now who shaming me for it? This man here. And why? Because maybe I had a happy couple a minutes he can't lay claim to and take from me now.

Something boiled up in me hot and ugly.

"Oh, I answer you, all right, sir," I said. "You ask me, I think 'kind' mean somebody treat another body in such a way as to make them glad they alive,

210

even if it got to be out rolling in somebody's field, the way you put it. *Sir*."

No way was I going to cry today. Not in front of this man here. No matter what he made me talk about. No matter what he made me say. *No crying*.

"You silly little ignorant wench. Don't give me any religious prattle about the Golden Rule. Where'd you get a chance to learn that hypocritical doubletalk, anyway? You never tended my mother." He looked back around at me and came and leaned against the cart with his arms still crossed.

"Now, Rose Red, I asked you a straight question and never got an answer. What the hell do boys and girls tussling out in the field have in mind when they start talking about kindness? There's something here you're not telling me. I'm waiting."

I looked from one of his eyes to the other. There was a hardness there that just didn't go with the quiet in his voice. That cold, which was getting right familiar when I looked in Mr. Dennis eyes, ran from my throat through my belly, turned back on itself, and settled in. My stomach cramped on me.

There was a lot I didn't know about coming in from the fields to work in the big house. But one thing I could figure out for myself. This man didn't have to ask nobody permission to do anything to me.

Anything.

You never know how lucky you been till you face to face with the man that own you and want something from you that you ain't want to give him.

Maybe it was time for me to get out the cart and act everyday. Go find Mr. Sami and get him talking to me while I fixed breakfast.

211

I started climbing out the cart. "If you excuse me, sir, I don't have no notion what you on about gold and all that. Maybe you mean Mr. Sami and Mr. Jared and that treasure hunt they done spent they life on."

Mr. Dennis arms flew uncrossed. He grabbed my shoulders. "I think you know good and damn well I'm talking about you cutting your eyes at those two boys last night."

He had stopped me short with one leg flung over the cart's edge. "Doing what?" I said.

"You *heard* me, girl."

"Well, sir, I *heard* you, but you ain't make no *sense*. Cutting my eyes? I ain't never!"

"Rose Red." He shook my shoulders. My head jerked. My neck snapped and burned. He wouldn't stop.

Felt like splinters from the cart slid right in the softest part a my leg. I held on. Couldn't fall forward and didn't think to duck back into the cart. Couldn't think. Couldn't even see.

"Father!"

The snapping and jerking stopped. My neck twinged at me. I squinted to clear my tearing eyes.

Mr. Sami came between the trees. He held his rifle pointed at the ground and stared like little kids do the first time they see they ma'am and pap get knocked down.

"Father? Sir? Is something wrong?" Mr. Sami looked quick from Mr. Dennis to me. "Rose Red, what are you doing, hanging on the cart like that?"

Mr. Dennis let me go. He backed away, lifted off his hat, and ran one hand through his hair. "I seem to have bred up a batch of sassy little smart-mouth girls around my plantation, Sami. That's all."

"Sir, would you like me to talk to Rose Red about something? Because I think-"

"Boy, I'll remind you that I've been running things for a long while around here before you showed back up." Mr. Dennis slapped his hat back on his head.

"Sir, I just thought-"

"I didn't ask you for your thoughts, Sami."

Mr. Sami got quiet. He gave me one last look full of doubts before he pulled back. And then I was alone with this man I didn't understand.

Mr. Dennis leaned upside the cart and looked like he was studying his boots.

Just follow Mr. Sami, I told myself. *Not even ten steps, and you be out a here and this be over.*

I picked my leg off the splinters and slow climbed on over the edge. Just before I dropped to the ground, Mr. Dennis came quick out a his staring spell and caught me.

I was so surprised, I stumbled and almost fell on my face in the dirt. Mr. Dennis didn't let me go. We stood staring at each other.

Empty-headed. That was me. Mind got blew with that chill wind rising out my belly.

Hadn't nobody never treated me like this. Quick mad and quicker sweet. Blaming and pointing fingers and then grabbing and holding on.

"Rose Red, why would you want to badger me? Telling me how kind some naked little pickaninny out in the fields used to be to you. What good do you think that'll do?"

213

"Badger you, sir? I ain't said nothing it wasn't no call to say to you. Ain't I got to answer your questions when you ask them, sir?"

He didn't say nothing to that. It's hard to get used to being stared at by somebody up so close got they hands on your body.

"Sir?" I said, real soft so couldn't nobody in they right mind take offense, "I need to go back home. I'm real worried about the people I'm supposed to be seeing to."

"You mean Miss Heaven?"

"Yes, sir. And my sister and Ma'am and Mammy Water, too." *And me coming on this trip was a big mistake,* I thought. *Biggest I ever done made yet.*

"Mama. Your *mama.* Stop talking like a field hand. And why do you have to see to all these people, Rose Red? Nobody else can take care of the sick and downhearted, but you?" His voice was soft now. Maybe he wasn't quite so mad no more. I couldn't be sure, though.

"I just ain't at ease staying away from all them right at this time. Sir."

Thought came to me to just do things everyday. *Something around here bound to turn out as it should if I don't let on I be in a panic.* Real careful, I said, "Can I go boil up that water for your coffee, sir? That field hand must be back from the stream by now." *No way you going hear me say Boyfriend name again.*

"No. Leave it." Mr. Dennis set in to watching my mouth move. His tongue came out and licked over his lips. I remembered that mouth business in

214

the hallway the other night. The cold dived back down to my belly.

"Yes, sir. Maybe I should get breakfast for everybody, sir? So we can leave camp real timely? I heard Mr. Sami say yesterday that we need to ride most-"

"Rose Red, just be quiet." He closed his mouth.

I closed mines. *Act everyday,* I told myself.

But where was everybody at? Was the cart parked that far from the cooking fire that we couldn't hear nothing and nobody but ourselves breathing?

I could hear birds singing. Birds always sing in the morning, no matter what be happening to you. And something was sure happening to me. I just couldn't tell what.

That heat bundle was growing again between his legs and mines. When had he pulled my body up against his so tight? And why didn't I notice till it was too late? Was I getting used to this? Was this what he wanted to happen to my feelings?

Get out of his arms. I just had to get out of his arms, and then I could for real act very everyday. "Sir, I better go." I tried to sink down, slink back.

He tightened his arms and hauled me tight up against him. "Rosie-"

I kept twisting. I bent my elbows to force space between us. "Sir, please let me go." Panic burst in me. Excuses bubbled out a my mouth. "I got to wash up. I think I hear your son calling. What if he found Miss Angel Girl?" Mr. Dennis snatched at my arms, trying to pin them at my sides. I yelled, "I need to go take care a my needs something terrible, sir."

215

"Father."

We both heard the shout. We both turned toward Mr. Sami. But I snapped out of it first and got one arm free.

Mr. Dennis turned back to me quick but missed grabbing that arm back.

I twisted back the other way and my other arm flew loose from his grip.

I took off running. I could hear Mr. Dennis calling after me.

And splashing my face at the stream, there was Mr. Dennis reflection in the water.

I jumped to my feet to face him. Had he been watching me take care a my needs behind that tree over there? I was burning embarrassed.

"You following me, sir?" Getting respect back into my voice was a real trial.

"Yes, I am. And if your mother had raised you to mind your betters, I wouldn't have to chase you down like this. I'm trying to talk to you about your own good, little girl."

He bent down toward me. I rose and backed off.

"Don't be scared of me, Rose Red. That's the last thing I want, for you to be scared of me." But he wasn't letting me put no distance between us.

"Sir, it's how you act that be scaring me."

He stopped moving in on me just a minute to hold up his hands, like folks do with horses. "Just stay still and let me talk to you, girl. Can't I just talk to you?"

"Mr. Dennis, you free to speak to anybody you choose." I finished the thought in my mind. *Sir, you*

*own me. How can I say no? And why you got to
make me say yes?*

He reached out and took hold of my wet hands.
Here we go, I thought. "Please don't back away any
more," Mr. Dennis said.

I started in to tremble.

"Rose Red, how am I supposed to get through
to a girl like you who doesn't know enough to
understand what I'm offering? Like kindness. What
do you know about it? A field hand who brings you
an extra scoop of water? Is that it? Is that the only
kindness you can understand? You see I'm giving
you the benefit of the doubt."

Giving me?

He touched my face. I could feel it was wet
with stream water. "No. Don't cry." He laid a hand
on my chest. "You're frightened again." He raised
up one of my hands and slid it inside his white shirt.
"Feel my heart. I'm frightened, too."

What did he have to be scared about? He could
quit this. I couldn't make him quit.

I could hear my blood pumping in my ears. I
hadn't never felt no body shaped like his under my
hand in my life.

Flat. Broad. Hard. And *hair*?

I had never one day in my life wanted to know
what some man's body felt like. Now here was my
own hand telling me things I ain't even wanted to
know. I wasn't never going to be the same girl I
used to be. I gave in and sobbed.

He took my hand off his chest and raised it to
his mouth. He kissed my fingers one at a time.

217

The cold turned over in my belly. Bottom of my belly went into a knot. Then the knot melted and ran.

The sky got bright. I hadn't never felt nothing as soft as lips on my fingers. My skin everywhere felt like it got lit with struck flints. A sound came out my mouth.

Mr. Dennis took his time and finished with my fingers. Now he took both my hands and laid them behind his neck. He grabbed my waist and tugged me up snug against him. He smiled in my face like I was a child and this was a game.

I tried to smile back. My lips trembled, though.

"Rosie, do you know why I really planned this trip?"

"So you could find Miss Heaven's tower and her ma'am. I mean, mama. I mean, your woman. Sir."

"No. Because I remembered how much you loved the woods. The day you got this dress, I saw it in your eyes, Rosie. You have to understand. I thought you were a dream of a sweet little girl, when I saw you all spruced up and in this silky dress. I didn't realize you'd grown from a sassy ragamuffin to a shy young lady. You did things to my feelings that made me question my whole life. All my pride over whether or not Angel Girl would come back. And there you were, not a two-minute walk from my back door. No, look at me. I could have sent for you, Rosie. I could have had old Peter bring you up to the big house, whether you liked it or not. You do know I have that right, don't you?"

"Yes, sir."

"But I didn't do that, darling. Why didn't I? I said look at me. You can't answer that question, can you?"

"It don't seem right I should speak for you, sir."

"I want you to care for me, to *want* to come to me, Rosie. It's that simple. Every minute since you moved into the big house, I'm trying to get you to understand this one point, little one. But you just don't know enough about life to appreciate what I'm offering you. Do you, now?"

I was miserable. "I don't know what you on about, sir."

"I don't want to make you be mine, Rosie. That won't give me what I want. I want you to choose me. *Choose* to love me. Why are you pulling away?"

"I'm not. Sir, stop. Stop, please, sir."

Mr. Dennis had put his lips to my face and started kissing up the wet from my cheeks. "Your tears mean you care. I've touched you. I love these tears."

He snatched me up against him. Felt like I was crushed against a rock. I closed my eyes. I heard him say, "I love you."

Then his mouth was on mines again and that tongue slipped between my lips. But this time it was smooth and tasted like stream water.

Mr. Dennis bent me backward with how hard he pulled me into him. That hot bundle was a burning rock between my legs. It had nothing to do with me, and I didn't want it. It was all Mr. Dennis, working it into me so hard it hurt.

I felt his hand right up against the bare skin on my leg. I opened my eyes and seen that Mr. Dennis was bunching my dress up in his hand.

Panic flew, white and blinding. Whatever this was, I hadn't chose nothing. A beating was better.

I made two fists and started hitting at Mr. Dennis head where he sucked at my breast. I was going to get whipped bloody. No doubt about it.

He grabbed on harder and bit, grunting and gouging into my skin. His muscles went hard like iron rods and powered me down.

The forest floor rose under me, swamp and mulch. I screamed when my back sunk into it.

I looked up at bright sky through the dark crowd of trees and hanging vines. The wind was knocked out a me.

That rock body ground into mines and pressed me into pine needles and slime. There was no sweet feeling now. The burning bundle hammered and tore at me. The face over me, looking down at me, raged, red and awful. Teeth gritted. Mad. His fist between us jerked at his breeches and punched me in the belly.

Air wheezed at last in my throat. I breathed in, screamed, and closed my eyes again.

A hand cupped my mouth and drove my head backward into the rank tickling moss.

A knee jabbed mine apart. I jerked my body, trying to turn away, against Mr. Dennis weight and driving fury.

"Father! Father!"

Mr. Dennis raised his face and yelled, "Ah!"

He came away.

He sat up. Glared over beyond me at somebody I couldn't see. Climbed off my body and sat in the mud and muck.

My breath came back so fast it hurt. I rolled onto my face. Pushed off the ground. Got to my knees, shaking.

I crawled away toward the river. I couldn't hear nothing. No birds. Mr. Sami and Mr. Dennis wasn't talking.

I splashed my face and lay on the bank, wiping my face here and there a bit with my apron.

I ain't tried to wash all the muck off. No matter what I washed, I knew I wouldn't get the feel a Mr. Dennis off me.

It's some people in the world can stop crying when they want to. Ma'am is one of them. I ain't. My tears was a waterfall from my heart to the earth where I wished I was buried.

Breakfast was cooked and cold while me, Boyfriend, and Bully waited for Mr. Sami and Mr. Dennis to get back to camp. I sat on a log by my cooking fire, keeping the coffee water hot and staring round me at the woods wasn't never going look the same. Boyfriend whistled a tune I used to love.

I looked down at myself and started wiping the mud and green things off my dress and skin. Then I took off my headrag and started in to unplaiting my hair and fixing it back good and smooth.

Mr. Dennis kept telling me I didn't understand. He was right. I didn't.

Freedom. Funny thing how bad you think you want it when you ain't never had the chance to find out what it is.

But Mr. Dennis had got me out the fields and into these woods I loved so. Twice now.

I could look round one time, and the leaves and pine needles waving over my head was just Mr. Dennis hair falling over my breast, and the sun flicking light on the carpeted ground was how his eyes shined when he talked about his feelings for me.

Then I could look again, and the woods was where Mr. Dennis shoved me into the ground to hurt and humiliate me.

I had my hair all unplaited and was just starting in to plait it back when Bully piped up and side, "Look at her. Hair all wild and butt all skinny. Wouldn't nobody want her but a wight man, anyway."

I looked up.

Boyfriend said, "And ain't nobody wanting you, nigger, but the worms waiting for you in the burying ditch."

Bully stuck out his chest. "Maybe I got something waiting for you, nigger."

Boyfriend stood. "Then you best hope it keep on waiting. Cause if I get my hands on it, I'm like to rip it right off your ass and shove down your throat."

"Hey!" Mr. Sami jogged up, his rifle at the ready. Bully eased back down on the ground and frowned at my feet.

Boyfriend sat and picked up whistling where he left off.

Mr. Dennis strolled up slow. "You all keep at it. Way I feel, I could use some coon hunting. Act up again, and see if I don't mean it."

I waited for somebody to say I wasn't nothing but trouble. Everybody looked at the ground when I brought them food. I was grateful nobody said it.

I looked in the pot and real-eyes I had dished the food up to everybody but me. I was glad I ain't had to try to eat nothing.

Mr. Sami asked me to climb up behind him on his horse. The day wore on and the woods worked magic. By sunset, my soul felt peace again.

That night after supper, Mr. Sami gave me the cart again to sleep in. This time, it wasn't so far from the men and the fire.

Fresh from my bath in a pond, when I was fixing to scramble up the side of the cart and tumble in, Mr. Dennis came up behind me and asked could he give me a boost.

"I rather you not, sir." I looked around and couldn't see Mr. Sami nowhere.

But Bully was off to one side, letting on he wasn't listening. So I knew he was.

"The harder I try, the more you refuse me," Mr. Dennis said.

"You told me I could choose, sir. But you ain't never let me choose nothing." Was I whining? I hoped not.

"Didn't you choose to come out here to the woods?" Mr. Dennis crossed his arms and waited for an answer.

"Yes, sir. But I didn't understand what was going to happen."

"There you go, pretending to be innocent." He leaned upside the cart. I looked at the ground and waited for this to be over.

"Rose Red, all I want is for you to choose wisely."

"How you know I ain't already done that?" I bit on my lip because it was shaking. I real-eyes I ain't said "sir" and looked up to see how Mr. Dennis was taking it. *Should I sneak in a little "sir" while he thinking and not listening?*

The worry, little as it was, brought heat to my eyes. Was I ever sick of crying day in and day out. *I swear babies don't cry like I cry since I moved to the big house.*

"I can give you anything," Mr. Dennis said. "Don't you understand that? I can be anything to you. I am already everything to you, whether you accept me or not. How can you turn me down? Fight me off? What do you think this is about, little girl?"

His slid his hands up my arms, tried to draw me near. Stopped at the resistance. "Just tell me what you want, and watch. You'll have it. I can be gentle. Give me a chance."

I sobbed.

Mr. Dennis slammed his fist into the side a the cart. "Look at me begging a damn field hand!" he shouted. I reached for the back a my leg, where I had just finished digging and pinching all them splinters out from this morning.

"Who do you think you are, Rose?" Mr. Dennis finger pointed right at my eyes. "Don't you know what I am to you? Do I need to show you what I can do to you? Don't you realize I don't need to beg you for *anything*?"

"Then don't, sir." Too much crying make you crazy. Make you forget yourself. I was reckless. "I don't like you begging me nohow, sir."

Mr. Dennis looked all round at the stars splitting the sky. Then he looked at me and took my hands. "Enough. Just tell me what you want from me. I'll get it for you. I'll do it for you. Then you'll understand me, right, Rosie? Just tell me."

Really? My mind flicked open and shut like a butterfly wings. "How about that freedom Mr. Sami done promised everybody?"

Mr. Dennis threw down my hands. "Freedom," he said. "What is all this senseless darky jabber about freedom to you, you ignorant child? You'd never even been off my property until I brought you into these woods. Do you understand that freedom would take you away from my plantation? You'd lose your mother and sister because your sister belongs to my son now. And he's too brown and illiterate to be out in the world without me for protection. You'd be the little renegade running off with some freedom that won't do anything for you but land you into trouble like you've never seen. You need me, and you don't even know it."

Mr. Dennis took my hands back. "And I need you. You don't know what that means. Everything I am, everything I own, including you, I could give to you. Our problem isn't freedom. Our problem is that you don't know what love is. I know you're falling in love with me. I can feel it when I hold you. You're just an ignorant child fighting your own happiness."

He had me there. Maybe I didn't know enough to know if I was in love. I remembered asking Rose

White how love felt when you had it for a man. What had she told me? "Like living and dying all at once all the time."

That was me all right. *So this love? This running and melting from Mr. Dennis?*

I remembered Rose White running in the shack to hide from Mr. Sami, all up under Ma'am. It made me sad. *So love ain't nothing but confusion.*

And tiredness. I was so tired.

"Sir, would you go head give me that boost up into the cart, please?"

He looked surprised. He looked like he wanted to say something more. But he seemed to a thought better of it.

He bent and laced his hands down where I could fit my foot into them and get hoisted up easy.

I looked over Mr. Dennis head and seen Bully snickering behind his back.

I lay in the cart shivering, despite I was wrapped tight in my blanket. I wanted to go ahead on and cry, but I couldn't quite think what was so bad, or why.

Then I thought to look again for that pretty moon. It would be good to remember the moon out here under the trees, once I was locked back in that big white house with Miss Heaven and Mr. Dennis, both.

I turned onto my back and kept my eyes to the black sky. I stared till I drifted to sleep. I woke to a face staring down in mines.

It was sharp eyebrows pointed up at the top and lines wrinkling and dipping all along the brow. Hair shot out like spikes in the ground all over this man's head.

And who was he? Craziest eyes I ever seen, just eating me whole and live.

I screamed out. His hand was already slamming down hard on my mouth.

I started in to kicking on the cart for noise and yanking at his spike hair to pull his head away from me. I got just enough room to put my elbow between us and drive it in his face. Again and again.

Then something real hard seemed like it went right through the side a my head. I let go. Of the man, of my kicking, of everything. I couldn't make myself keep doing nothing.

Next time I woke, it was with my body sliding and slamming against the splintered walls of the cart. My blanket was tangled around my legs so I couldn't get free. I grabbed around with my hands to get a good hold on something.

I could hear men shout. I saw Boyfriend and Bully backs up ahead of me, at the front of the cart. Bully whipped the horse reins. Boyfriend pointed and shouted, "Over there! I think he ran over that a way."

Far up ahead, I heard a rifle shot. Mr. Dennis yelled, "This way! I heard Sami fire a shot over this way."

The cart creaked and banged over roots and sank into mulch. *Why they let Bully drive this poor horse?* I thought.

I flew through the air and slammed my shoulder against the front a the cart.

"Damn," Bully shouted. "Us stuck."

I looked over the edge. Boyfriend leaped down to pull on the horse by the bit.

"What's going on?" I asked Bully.

He turned on his bench and glared at me. His nostrils was flared, he was so mad. "You tell me why that fool can't pass round them guns! You tell me that." He slapped the reins on the horse back. "Get out a there!" he hollered at it.

I heard Boyfriend saying gentle, "Come on, you. You can come on, now. I got you!"

Bully turned back to me. "My chance to shoot a wight man and get thanked for doing it, and I get stuck behind with the master's whore." He swung a backhand slap at my head. I tried to duck. But he grabbed hold of the cloth at my back and used it to haul me over the edge of the cart. My legs pulled free of the tangled blanket as I tumbled over the side. The cool forest floor caught me.

Bully yelled, "Get up and push the cart out the mire, wench!"

Then I heard a shout. More shouts. The cart rocked away from me. I heard quick punching sounds.

I pulled myself up and came around the cart in time to see Boyfriend and Bully going at it.

They moved fast. It scared me to see so much power let loose in a frenzy. They crashed between the trees, down into the mud, and tumbled up against the cart, slugging and slamming. Shouting. Voices deep and harsh, bellowing like bulls.

They knocked into the horse, all out a control, and it got even more skittish and skipped sideways trying to get away. I ran to hold the cart up from tumbling over. If the cart pulled the horse on its side, seem to me something in the horse might get broke.

I was on the side away from the fight, pushing the cart steady, and couldn't see what was happening. But somebody was gagging and coughing. I prayed it wasn't Boyfriend.

Then past that sound, I heard horse hooves clop up fast. *Oh, let it be Mr. Sami, calm them two men down,* I prayed.

I heard a riding crop slice the air. I heard that mean little scream it make when it hits flesh.

I let go the cart and ran round the front of it. It was Mr. Dennis done rode up and laid into Boyfriend.

Bully was on the ground holding his stomach and heaving. Boyfriend had his arms up over his head, to shield himself from the blows. His shirt was ripped to rags and red welts rose up under every strike.

"Stop! Stop, Mr. Dennis. No, please. I can't take it no more." I ran straight between that crop and Boyfriend.

Mr. Dennis swooped his whip arm down around my waist and slammed me up on his horse.

His horse was unsettled by all the racket and wheeled away from where Boyfriend was still bent under his raised arms. When the horse settled, it was Bully standing sheepish by and trying to offer up to Mr. Dennis the crop he dropped to grab me.

Mr. Dennis took it and yelled, "Get on away from here! I'm not gone two blinks of an eye before you two randy bucks are up to your tricks. You two forget we're supposed to be on the trail of Jared's hired thug, out here. This is not the place and she is not the woman for you two to be squaring off!"

I said, clinging to his shirt, "Mr. Dennis, *please* don't yell no more. I just can't *take* it, sir."

Boyfriend turned and looked up at me. His eyes was red and full a hurt, but they said something else. I couldn't tell what it was. But it calmed me down.

I let go Mr. Dennis shirt and sat up to steady myself on the horse. Bully reached up to help me. *Ain't that the cotton field pecking order for you? Nerve!*

I pushed at him with my foot. Mr. Dennis said, "I told you get, boy."

The horse turned. I heard the cart start behind us and scrape forward on the path.

"Where we going?" I asked.

"That was Jared's hired man who attacked you in the cart," Mr. Dennis said. "Sami tried to follow him back to wherever Jared's hidden out." He looked ahead, not at me. "What did he do to you?" he asked.

"I think he hit me. My head feel broke open."

"What else did he do to you?"

"Scared me."

"Nothing else?"

I thought, *Hitting and scaring was enough.* But I held onto my head with one hand and Mr. Dennis shirt with the other and ain't said nothing.

After while he stopped the horse and wheeled it to look back at the men on the cart. We was only still a minute. But he took it to say, "You see what comes of refusing my protection?"

When I do that? I asked myself. I wasn't going to be able to stay on that horse and listen to more of Mr. Dennis crazy goings-on. I swung my leg over

230

so I could straddle the horse and face forward and let go Mr. Dennis shirt. I wrapped my fingers in the horse mane.

As we trotted, I thought to myself that I was fast getting uncommon sassy. It felt like I was going crazy, my own self. Maybe it was catching.

We clopped slow into a clearing and saw a low house under the high moon. Looked like it was made from muddy stones, reeds, logs, and swamp muck. It had a tower rising crooked off to one side.

Mr. Dennis hopped down off the horse and led it up to the house. A powerful stench hit us, and he bent double and cupped his hand over his face.

I pulled off my headrag and wrapped it round my mouth and nose. Mr. Dennis stood straight and turned to wave his hand back toward the cart behind me. Bully ran forward and took the reins from Mr. Dennis. "Hold the horses out here," Mr. Dennis mumbled to Bully through his hand.

I was still tugging my plaits straight when Mr. Dennis reached up and pulled me off the horse by the middle. He took my hand behind him and went straight up to the heavy front door.

The stench round here was even coming through the rag round my face. I turned back and seen Bully was looking right glad to tend horses stead of breaking down the door. I guess shooting wight men ain't looked so fun when you got to go in a place stink like this one to find them.

Mr. Dennis pulled out a pistol from round his hip. He waved it back at Boyfriend. "Come with me," he called through his hand.

Boyfriend made a good guess what Mr. Dennis was talking about and came on.

231

The door was so low, we all three had to stoop to walk through it. Seemed odd Mr. Dennis didn't neither knock nor call out.

Front room was dead dark. I ain't seen no shutters from outside we could a pushed to let some more a that stink out.

"Stay here," Mr. Dennis said and pushed me back against a wall with his free hand.

I squinted my eyes to watch Boyfriend and Mr. Dennis creep forward in the dark. Somebody knocked into something hard and swore.

"I give up," I heard Mr. Dennis say. "Boy, get over to that cart and see can you find a couple of candles. Bring them here lit."

Boyfriend came back in behind me quiet carrying the lit candles. I seen there was something about being here disturbed him bad. He caught sight a my eyes and made his face tough.

Boyfriend passed me without saying nothing, just handed me a candle in passing. It flickered when it changed hands. I looked around. I could see a plank on four wood legs in this room, with a bench knocked over in front of it, a stacked-stone fireplace, and a small bed had its curtains closed.

Mr. Dennis waited for Boyfriend and the candles in front a the little closed bed.

That smell. I had seen and smelled enough dead hands dumped in the burying pit, next to the latrine trench.

Rot so you can taste it. Rot got to slime. Pure stench.

I weaved on my feet a little. I had closed my eyes and ain't knew it. *Don't fall*, I told myself.

I opened my eyes. Mr. Dennis slipped his pistol between the bed curtains and slid them apart. Boyfriend slipped one wrist in-between the parted curtains and pushed them a little wider open. Him and Mr. Dennis studied something inside on that bed but hard.

Then Mr. Dennis kind a went down on one knee. He took off his hat and covered his face on the side so I couldn't see it. I watched his back heave.

Sounded like wood planks was getting ripped off the floor. But it was a dirt floor ain't had no wood planks. It was Mr. Dennis. Being sick.

Boyfriend turned from the bed and looked down toward Mr. Dennis. Seemed to be studying him, real thoughtful. The bed curtains fell soft back in place.

Boyfriend stopped studying Mr. Dennis and looked up at me. He started coming towards me.

But halfway, he melted to the floor like he ain't had no bones. His candles hit the dust and got snuffed out.

I went to him and held my candle high and tugged on him with my free hand. It was slow going. After while, Mr. Dennis staggered up and picked up Boyfriend feet to help.

We all got outside and fell in the clearing. I pulled that headrag off my face and laid on my back staring up at the round fat moon. *Funny how the outside smell so fresh after you been cooped up inside.*

We laid there breathing. After while I turned my head to Mr. Dennis. "What you seen in there, upset you all so?"

233

"I think it's my brother Jared. Dead."

"Why you all so distress? I thought he wasn't nothing no more but a heartache to you." And he wasn't never nothing but a pain to the mens in the field like Boyfriend.

"Rosie, I'd be upset to see anybody or anything that looked like that. He'd been left dead in there so long." Mr. Dennis coughed in his throat. He sat up and spat. Then he lay back down.

I thought of the bones in the burying pit. "Then you don't know it be him. Could be anybody in there."

Mr. Dennis shook his head. "No. I couldn't tell anything by the face. It was-well-gone. Decayed beyond recognition. But the body was short and had a peg leg. It was Jared, all right."

Mr. Sami clopped up on his horse. Handed his reins to Bully and came sat near his pap. "Lost him," he said.

Mr. Dennis sat up again. He looked over his shoulder at me. "You're sleeping next to me for the rest of the trip."

I looked at Mr. Sami. He ain't said nothing but, "Did you all look in the house yet?"

Boyfriend rolled over all a sudden and gagged. He opened his eyes, looked at me, and frowned.

"You all right," I said.

"Oh, lord," he said.

"We have to do something with the body," Mr. Dennis said to Mr. Sami.

And they started talking the strangest dishonor of the dead that I done ever heard. Cream-making that man. I looked up at the sitting moon and couldn't think what kind a men was these would do

234

such a thing to somebody couldn't never harm them no more.

Burn him, and he already dead.

"Set fire to the house and clear off the grounds, and we won't have to worry about prowlers desecrating the place," Mr. Dennis said.

"All right," Mr. Sami said. "Shouldn't we go up and have a look at that tower room?"

The tower door had to be kicked in. All the men took turns stomping at it but Bully. He still had hold the horses, because they ain't liked it here and was skittish.

The door at last flew in on Mr. Dennis. He fell forwards on some splintered stairs circling up and away.

Mr. Dennis picked himself up. "I'd best go up first."

Seemed like we waited forever, watching his candlelight grow small and faint. After a long time, Mr. Dennis called down, "Rose Red. Come here and see this."

I went up slow, testing each slat with my foot before putting my weight on it. The circle a light spread from my candle fell on the mud and stone walls around me. *Who would a thought to trap a child here? And why?*

The heavy door was standing open. I went in.

The walls was all the same stone you could see from the outside. Thick piled up on top of each other. There was a round bed with drapes hanging from a hook in the ceiling beams, pulled almost shut around it. Shiny folds of drapes curved in and out.

There was a tiny table with a lady's things jumbled on it, silver shining and glass like clouds.

235

Under the table was a small trunk, band dull like hide.

And on the wall above was a mirror shaped like a egg, framed in silver worked all round with tangled leaves and vines. It looked like the grape and rose arbor trained up near Mr. Dennis folks grave.

It curved and glowed like the haloes around my candlelight. "Oh," I said. "Is that me?" I reached out with my free hand to touch my face in the glass.

My face was oval like the mirror but with cheekbones like a cliff ridge where the candlelight got caught. I was colored like night and the woods and red rose petals. My eyes sloped uphill, big, round, and pointy at the tips like a cherry pit, shining like the night sky and the stars in it. My lips curved and dipped, cutting sharp lines at the soft edges, puckered at the outside ends like dimples. The hair that curled at my brow caught and twined together in plaits that bent thick and stiff over my shoulders. Everything about me was shining, deep-colored, and soft. I held my candle and stared.

A pale hand reached from behind me and touched the side of my face. It fell and dipped and rose, following the lines a my body.

Mr. Dennis came out the dark behind me and held his candle out to the side opposite mines. Now I could see myself even better. "Have you never seen yourself in a mirror before?"

"No, sir."

He took hold my body round my waist with his free hand. He bent his head down and buried his face between my neck and shoulder.

236

This time I ain't felt no panic. Strange feelings ran to overflowing my heart, but I ain't wanted to run.

"Father." Mr. Sami voice from down the stairs. "We're coming up."

Mr. Dennis pulled up his face and turned toward the sound of Mr. Sami voice. "You can stay here and look at the pretty things," he said. "I'll go to the door."

I looked around in the candlelight.

A chair, carved full a living things, and a cloth painted with flowers and birds so lively you could smell them and hear they wings beat. There was a fiddle, big-bowled, laying next to the chair. Above that, a dark square in the wall must a been a window. Between the metal bars, soft light spilled to the floor.

I bent to pull out the chest from under the table. I set my candle into a pool a wax on the little table so I could pull the gowns out. *Is it women in the world ever get to wear such things?*

I pulled three gowns out, one after another. They colors was so rich as not to be real, not from the earth or sky but flower colors, lined with lacy and glittering things that draped and swung and made noise when they struck each other.

I stood and held one a the gowns against myself in front a the mirror.

"Those were my mother's," Mr. Dennis said behind me. "She was an elegant lady. She should never have had to live in this wilderness."

Boyfriend behind me said, "I'll be."

I turned, still holding the dress. Boyfriend and Mr. Sami was at the door, looking big and stooped in the little room. They stared around and at me.

Mr. Sami went slow to the bed, like he ain't really wanted to find whatever he was looking for there. When he pulled apart the drapes, moon and candlelight caught and shined.

Mr. Dennis went to join him. I folded the gowns back into the chest, got my candle, and followed. Boyfriend came up to the bed beside me.

Kind of pooled in the middle of the bed was something crumbly, shiny, and sharp. Wrapped all round this and dried to seal it was something the colors of blood and a runny nose been left too long.

I looked round at the men. Till they spoke up, I wasn't going know what to make of it.

Mr. Dennis looked over at me and said, "Has Heaven hinted to you, Rose, that her jailor might have broken in and violated her?"

"No, sir."

Mr. Dennis looked over at Boyfriend. "You boys start hauling all this stuff out. Except the bed. Leave it to burn. The rest was my mother's. I'd give a lot to know how Jared got it out of my house and up here."

He put his hand on Mr. Sami back. "Come on, son. There's nothing left but to burn this place to the ground."

The hut went up first. Flames danced high and licked at the trees. We had cleared brush back in a big circle far from the house and tower as we could. But that fire was hungry. Smoke ran to the sky so thick you couldn't see the moon.

"Rest in peace, Jared," Mr. Dennis said near me. "It's over." Flames threw red flickers on his face. His lips spread, smiling.

I was uneasy. What if it was Mr. Jared they found in there, but he wasn't dead? What if he was just sick? Powerful sick, to set up such a stink. But I been in Mammy Water shack. If me and Rose White ain't cleaned it every day, her shack could easy a stunk almost bad as Mr. Jared hut.

I watched how Mr. Dennis was all a sudden so at ease and thought, *What if Mr. Jared wasn't dead till his brother burned him in front a us all?*

Then I thought, *Why would I think such a thing? What's got in my head?*

I would have to find a chance to ask Boyfriend what he had found in that bed.

The tower leaned in like it was praying over what had happened inside it. The stones fell inside, in a pile.

The men walked away. I was still standing and staring and worrying myself over whether or not a man kill so many hands might a also killed his brother while I was watching, when Mr. Dennis rode his horse over to me.

"Ride with me, darling," Mr. Dennis called down to me.

The sun was rising and wasn't nothing left but little fires licking at things wouldn't burn no more. Sleep was closing my eyes standing. "You can sleep, and I'll hold you," he said.

I felt Mr. Dennis haul me as usual by my middle onto his horse. I dozed sitting up. I dreamed about the fire and the stones from Miss Heaven tower falling in.

Looked like early evening when we stopped to camp. I was beat.

The men went to a pond to wash off the smells a Mr. Jared death. Boyfriend sneaked back to camp with rabbit for me to add to the beans in the stew. I said, "How you get this? You ain't got neither snares nor a gun out here."

"Don't need them. I'm quick."

I smiled, but it took a while. I had to think was it okay or not, if I had to talk later with Mr. Dennis about smiling at Boyfriend. Maybe me and Boyfriend could keep it secret.

"Boyfriend, you seen Mr. Jared dead in that house? I mean, before the fire burned it all down?"

Boyfriend looked at me serious. He chewed one lip at the side. Old habit. Showed he was thinking through how he ought to say what he ought to say. "I can't tell you what I seen, Rose Red. Stink and fear got to me. I seen somebody on a bed with a stick for a leg. That's all I can tell you." He elbowed me gentle. "Ain't going help you eat this supper you cooking, though, to think about what I seen. Besides, I know what you thinking. Who was that in there and why we had to burn the place down. Right? Well, get your mind out other people business, girl. You never did know how to stay out a trouble."

Funny how that teeny rebuke, nothing really, should hurt more than all Mr. Dennis yelling and shaking and slinging me to the ground.

Boyfriend reached out touched my cheek. I was afraid and leaned away. He said, "You can't go on like this, not eating. Was a time you use to love

240

rabbit. Here. Let me at that knife you got, and I skin this for you."

"Boyfriend, don't think I ain't grateful." And then I real-eyes was something about the way he said "love." I didn't cry again, though, till Boyfriend went to join the other men swimming.

I washed myself with the pots after we ate. The whole time, I felt wrong. Like I wasn't on my own.

I kept looking around. *Nothing.*

That night, Boyfriend and Bully slept on either side the cart, in case a thieves. I slept between Mr. Dennis and Mr. Sami.

We was all antsy. No joking nor storytelling. Fell asleep heavy and quiet.

I woke up in gray morning to Mr. Dennis arm flung over me. He was leaning on the other elbow, watching me and smiling. "Little girl, how would you like a room of your own?"

"Pardon, sir?"

He made like to tickle my belly, get a smile. "You heard me correctly, darling. You know, all those pretty things we're carting back to the farm were my mother's. They were left in her rooms, after she passed away. Now, if you like, you can have what used to be my mother's bedroom and all these pretty things in it. What do you say, Rosie? A room of your own."

The thoughts troubling my mind the day before flew right out my heart. Was this what Mr. Dennis had always meant when he talked about what he could do for me?

I sat up so his arm slid off me.

He sat up, too. He stopped smiling and watched me. "My mother's things are special to me. Like you are. I'd like you to have them."

None the other men moved. I thought maybe Mr. Sami was really sleep, but I doubted Boyfriend and Bully was. But what did I have to hide?

I leaned over and hugged Mr. Dennis close. "Thank you, sir." I felt his lips going up and down my neck, as always. *Maybe I might someday get used to it. Learn to like him. Maybe.*

When I jumped up to go get water for coffee, Mr. Dennis was still looking after me, smiling.

On the ride that day, I let myself rest back against Mr. Dennis. He seemed pleased. I wanted to be all right. A room of my own with beautiful things in it. I was going be happy. *I want bad to be happy and be shut of worry.*

The going was slow. When we stopped that evening, we hadn't got far. I felt good but for a little worry nagging way at the back a my mind.

After washing the supper things in a rushing stream, I slipped off my dress and waded into the water.

A room of my own. Love was being took care of. Was that what Mr. Dennis said? Why did I feel like I had missed something? Something kept slipping away from me.

The water was chill like I liked it. I splashed it on and watched it roll down my skin like stars flashing and falling in the sky. I bent my knees and pushed off swimming.

Swimming clears your mind. *What was that about love and two people giving what the other one wanted?*

I stroked my arms lazy, careful to stay to the side where the water wasn't rushing too bad. Maybe it would come to me.

What was that? Moving over there.

I stopped swimming and started to tread water.

In the dark piling up under the trees along the bank, a shadow. Moving sharp and quick.

I caught my breath and stumbled over some rocks, trying to get my footing in the current. *A man there*.

Where was he now?

"Mr. Dennis?" I called out.

"Who out there?" I shouted. "Don't play. Answer me." I didn't mean to shriek so. But the chill in the stream went right through me. Somebody was still there behind the trees and bushes on the bank, but he just wasn't going to answer.

"Mr. Dennis." My voice cut my throat. "Is that you?" After I hugged him today of my own free will, would he have call to be doing this kind of sneaking and peeking?

He knew I was coming round to where he wanted me. He ain't needed to carry on no more.

So who might feel he had cause to hide and creep so to make your skin crawl?

Boyfriend wouldn't.

Bully, then? *Trying to get my goat*.

I pushed off from the bank and back-paddled toward the middle of the stream. The current tried to sweep me. I kicked against it. "Hey, Bully. Don't you fun me, now. You want me to have to tell on you to somebody?" Now it was time for Bully to start swearing and telling me how no-count I was.

243

But he didn't say nothing.

No sound. Just the breeze blowing. Maybe some crickets starting up. A frog or two.

I stopped kicking quite so hard. The current caught me. It tugged. Hard. I couldn't fight it.

"Help!" I called out. "Somebody!"

I struck out paddling against the stream. It swept me on. I couldn't get my feet to stick on the rocky bottom nor pull with my arms to get me back to calm water.

I started into a rush downstream.

My toes and heels bruised. Rocks jut out and cut me, but when it came to standing on one of them, they wasn't nothing but mud, reeds, and moss.

I spun around, front and back, kicking and flailing. I just turned face forward into a fast pool when I got slammed belly first.

Water rushed on. I curved belly down over a smooth hard something that rose out the water and scratched my face. I was smack against a jut of bank at the drop of a little waterfall.

I crawled up onto the bank, getting my numb legs out the stream. I curled up and shivered.

The sun had long went down. The earth was cooling fast. I tried not to backslide into the stream.

Every now and again I would snap to and ask myself how come nobody came looking for me but the man on the bank, in the shadows.

I stared there. Was the shadow man still waiting and watching me, trapped here naked? I felt he was.

I kept looking for him. I curled tighter and shivered some more. Seemed like the night should a long been over. I must a dozed, scared and cold and all.

I woke with a jump.

What was that? Did I see shapes move?

I could hear twigs and pine cones snap. I pressed myself flatter down against the rock. I tried not to breathe hard. I didn't want the shapes to hear me.

I heard voices. Not loud. They drifted across the rush of water noises.

"Rosie?"

"Rose Red!"

I sat up.

"Look!"

"There she is!"

I flung my arms over my naked breasts.

"What on earth is she doing out there?"

"She ain't got a stitch on!"

"Nigger, don't look! Rose Red, hang on!"

Splash. Splash.

Two of the shapes went into the water. They fought the current and came on towards me, arms curving up and into the fast flowing water.

I searched the water to see the men coming at me. All a sudden I got real frantic.

Felt like I best not trust nobody.

Four hands reached up and slapped water onto the bank where I sat. Drops sprayed me. Two faces rose up over the water and hands. Boyfriend. And Mr. Dennis.

They hands reached up toward me.

"Come on, girl," somebody said.

No, I thought. *They don't understand. Not back to the stream bank. Don't take me there.*

The shadow man was waiting there. Somewhere. I had seen him.

245

I pulled back. No way was I leaving this bank. I was safe here. Not scared no more.

Four hands scrambled and grabbed me. I screamed.

"Easy, little one!"

"Hey, girl! We ain't doing nothing but getting you safe back to camp."

I kicked out at them. I felt crazy. Scared, wet, and shaking so my teeth chattered. No way I could explain myself.

Get away, I thought. *Don't take me where that man is waiting. You won't be there to keep him from me. You don't understand nothing.*

Mr. Dennis caught one a my feet and yanked till I got close to the edge a the bank. Boyfriend reached up and caught my other leg. The two of them eased me into the water. I scraped my back on the reeds and dirt.

The water cooled the places where skin was broke. Boyfriend and Mr. Dennis slid they hands up to grab at my arms. I started yelling. I don't think I was saying words, though.

Dipping and diving under, they dragged me between them back to the far bank.

Bully and Mr. Sami came to the edge to help haul me out. I sagged between them. Something dry got wrapped round me.

Voices kept talking. "You're safe now, Rose Red."

"Everything going be all right, child."

"Look at her eyes! She scared out her mind."

I was angry and kept pulling away. Felt like strong arms kept catching me back up to my feet.

I heard a fire crackle. Something rough and shiny was dragged onto my body. Though I heard the fire and felt the weight of the heavy clothes, I couldn't get warm inside.

Chill had got through me. Felt like it was running through my body in my own blood. And I couldn't stop crying again. Somebody was holding me and kept tugging some kind a wrap around us both.

I woke in blue morning still shivering. I could hear my throat still making crying sounds, but no tears would run.

I looked to see who got a hold on me. It was Mr. Dennis. We was sitting near a fire.

He woke when I did. He gave me the oddest smile I ever seen out of him. "Ready for some hot coffee, little one?" He went to slip out the blanket, like he was going to get the coffee.

I grabbed his arm, my eyes staring wild. I couldn't help it. "That man. That man in the shadows. Where he at, Mr. Dennis? Please don't let him at me, sir."

Mr. Dennis knelt and held me by my arms. Tried to look in my eyes. I could see his face there, but I had to keep looking round. *What if the shadow man sneak up on us?* I searched scared all round the trees.

"What man?"

"In the shadows, sir."

Mr. Dennis called the men and woke them up. They pushed off they blankets and came close to hear what he was saying.

247

"What man is she talking about?" Mr. Dennis said. "Did any of you catch sight of a man, when we split up to search?"

Everybody said no. But Boyfriend said, "But that don't mean it wasn't no man out there. Somebody made off with her dress, sir."

Sami said, "Maybe we'd better just get out of here and get back to the plantation as soon as we can."

The coffee was so hot it scalded my throat going down. It didn't warm me worth nothing.

We clopped slow onto the plantation grounds. The cart had a slowed us, but so had I. I was wrapped in blankets and one a those heavy dresses that used to belong to Mr. Dennis ma'am. I ain't had no chance to feel pretty. I was heartsick and dozing so Mr. Dennis had to keep propping me back up between his arms.

Folks followed us from the fields to the back of the big house. Mr. Dennis new overseer, new name a Whip Man because he was whipped to make him carry the whip, led the way.

Folks' greetings died on they lips. I opened my eyes good as I could and seen worry on they faces. *These the folks use to kid and fuss with me every day,* I thought. *How I miss them!*

A few children in rag shirts ran fast ahead to Miss Magdalen, calling out, "They back! Mr. Dennis, Mr. Sami and them back!"

I heard Rose White calling me before I seen her. When we clopped up to the house, Ma'am was holding my sister back. Miss Heaven come running, too, look like from the direction of the quarters.

Seemed everybody had they eyes straight on me. I tried to smile or say something. I worried that, weaving and drowsing and dressed different like I was, I must a been a sight.

"Easy now," Mr. Dennis said, and let me down off his horse into Whip Man hands. Whip Man looped his whip over his shoulder. He reached and held me and for just while he carried me, I felt real safe.

I looked round for Ma'am and Rose White. My eyes cleared up on a sight like I ain't never seen. A woman with thick wild hair branching out every way from her head and falling almost to her knees like leaves on a weeping willow, was standing in front a me. And round her long skirt was some kind a silver beast, circling and watching me.

I shook my head, afraid I was dreaming. And they was gone.

Whip Man hauled me on in the house and up to Miss Heaven room. I passed out on the stairs. It felt so good to be held by arms solid and strong.

Next time I opened my eyes, it was Ma'am and Miss Magdalen faces over my body, stripping that heavy gown off me.

"Don't take it off," I said, grabbing on Ma'am hands. "You take it off me, I'm a catch my death."

"Hush, child. Look at this gown, Miss Magdalen. Where my baby get such a thing?"

"It was Mr. Dennis's mother's favorite ball gown. No doubt, we'll learn what this is all about after the men have eaten and rested."

Pain and shivering led me to sleep. I kept finding myself back at that stream, running and splashing in the water, climbing on the bank to get away from that man in the shadows.

Swimming to the other side, trying to get to the campfire.

The stream and the fire. The stream that chilled me, and the fire that didn't warm me. Pain and chills. My life had turned into dreaming and tossing in pain and cold.

I opened my eyes.

Light came through lace at a window. A hand held mines. It was soft, but with calluses riding over the palm. Rose White.

She sat in a chair near my side the bed and leaned near me. I looked round. Fire in the hearth. I shivered, getting used to the sound and feel of my teeth batting each other.

Miss Heaven was stretched out sleeping on the other side a me, breath soft and quiet.

Somebody worked the latch at the bedroom door. Trouble getting it loose. I watched the handle move. A little up, a little down. A click.

The latch gave way. Door swung in, creaking.

Ma'am came in toting a tray of steaming things. "Girl, you ain't gave us all a fright." She set her tray on a table next to my side the bed. "Rose White," she said. "Rose White. Wake up, now."

Rose White shot up straight like she ain't been sleep at all. "I'm fine, Ma'am." You know how people do.

"Girl, quit," said Ma'am. "Go on get out a here and let this child drink down her broth."

Rose White gave a little jump and hugged on me. We laughed like when we was little.

Ma'am looked real pleased till I said, "You all, why it so cold around here? It ain't summer no more?" scooting back under the covers.

"It still summer. You just sick," Ma'am said.

Rose White arms still around me. "Rose Red, what happened out there? Won't nobody tell us nothing."

Panic crept in on me. *The shadow man. Don't talk about it,* I told myself. *He might hear.* "You all, believe me, I don't remember nothing."

Ma'am put her hand on my forehead. "You here and safe now. Get some hot food in you. Us talk another time."

Ma'am had brought me green water steaming in a cup and bowl. "Broth. Miss Magdalen boiled up some vegetables from her garden and sent you the juice. Plucked some herbs from out a there, too, and boiled up tea."

I wasn't happy. I took a few sips out the bowl. Bitter on my tongue and sharp down my throat. "I been sleep, Ma'am?"

"I'll say."

"How long?"

"Oh, don't worry, baby. Two three weeks now, I reckon."

"How come I ain't in my room Mr. Dennis promised me?"

Now Ma'am ain't looked none too happy. "He promise you a room, Rose Red? What room?"

"The one used to be his ma'am. And Miss Angel's. Plus with all them pretty things he took out Miss Heaven's tower. He promised me they be mines, too." My lips set to quivering.

"He ain't told nobody nothing about all that. Fact is, Miss Heaven mother done come out the woods, and Miss Magdalen done put her in that room. Moved in all them pretty things, too, you talked about bringing from Miss Heaven tower. Powerful pretty things."

"Miss Angel Girl done come back? Mr. Dennis wife?"

"That's right. While you all was out traipsing the woods, she done come back here on her own. Still don't nobody know where she done hid out, all these years. She ain't staying but till she get Miss Heaven to light out a here with her. She done told Mr. Dennis, Mr. Sami. Ain't here for nobody but her little girl."

I was thinking. It was hard, with my brain all fevered. "So, if she go back to wherever she came from, maybe I get that room, after all."

"Maybe, child. Don't look likely she go, though, if she waiting on that Miss Heaven."

"Why not?"

"Ma'am, don't," Rose White warned. I looked at her, stunned. *Since when us girls tell Ma'am what to do?*

Ma'am lowered her voice. "Miss Heaven done took a terrible liking to the Whip Man. Can't nobody talk sense to her. She say she going out to see to Mammy Water for me or Miss Magdalen, spare us the trouble. And the next thing us know, she done hightailed it to find Whip Man and they off alone somewhere. His woman near on to lost her baby, trailing them two everywhere. Fell in the burying ditch and twisted her leg." Ma'am shook her head in her old disapproval of folks with crazy ways.

"Folks be right glad, though, if Miss Angel Girl would just fetch Miss Heaven and get. Not just cause a the Whip Man and them goings on." Ma'am cut her eyes at Rose White, to stop her before she could ask Ma'am to hush again. She whispered. "It something right strange round here. You don't know Sami and Rose White done try to share out the farm animals with the people. Paying them for working, they say. But animals been disappearing. Folks fear it Miss Angel Girl wolf taking them."

"Miss Angel Girl got a wolf? Don't they kill people?"

"Bite the hand that feed them," Rose White intoned.

"Angel Girl herself got one hand all curl up where folks say that wolf done tried to pull it off. Folks scared any day now that wild thing going start in to stealing babies."

Ma'am put her hand on me. Pushed me gentle. "Listen at me scaring my sick baby with stories about these crazy folks and they nonsense ways. You ain't need to study about them and what they done got up to. Just lay on back down. Rest and get better, now."

She sat on my edge the bed and held me till I couldn't open my eyes no more. I ain't heard when she left.

"Rose Red?" It was Miss Heaven whispering next to me. "Why would you want a room of your own? Don't you want to be with me?"

I looked over at her. She was too close. Her face was like a child. All open. "You been listening in on me and my ma'am?"

She put one her cool hands on me. "Welcome back home. Don't you want to be with me anymore? I need you."

I sighed and shut my eyes.

I felt her arms go round me. She put her face on my shoulder. "Stay with me. They've brought that evil mirror here. Promise me you'll never look into it. I never go into my mother's room, even though she's covered the mirror over for me. I trust her, but not it. Promise me you'll stay safely in this room."

I opened my eyes. "What you got so against mirrors?" Against my will, I recalled my first day moving in here, listening to folks running down all the long halls, snatching mirrors from the walls while Miss Heaven screamed.

"Death waits in them," she said.

She wasn't going to make no sense now. I closed my eyes and made believe I was back asleep. Soon I really was.

Dreamed I was running through the halls a this big white house looking in the mirrors on the walls. Was Mr. Jared face in all of them looking back at me, melting.

I would scream and his face would bust out burning. I took off running to the next mirror, trying to find myself again. Down the next twisty bulging hall, hearing his burning head in the mirror I left behind, laughing loud like screaming. Like Miss Heaven screaming and laughing the day I met her and moved into this twisting, bulging house.

Mr. Jared burning hands reached out grabbed on the walls and pulled him out a the mirrors I ran past. His burning skull turned to seek me out.

I ran down the stairs. I headed toward starlight. Miss Magdalen back door stood open to the night.

The shadow man would be standing there. He would turn to watch me running towards him.

I woke too scared to scream. I sat with my covers bunched to my mouth, shooting my eyes round the room, looking for the danger. I knew it was waiting. But where?

Seemed sleep was set to overtake my life. I couldn't count on staying wake long enough but to see Ma'am or Rose White come to feed me or wash me. I couldn't tell nobody my bad dreams. Too weak from not eating and not getting well.

The dream changed. I was in the woods. I could hear a fire crackling, but the closer I got to it, it still didn't warm me. Sound of a stream rushing.

Sound of a man cracking through the shadows, hunting me.

Sometimes I would wake and peel back the bedclothes, shaking, and try to stand. I had to get out. Get away.

The room would dip and dive. My stomach would get light. My knees would give out from under me.

Next thing I knew, I'd be waking up again, trying to stand.

After while, I could make it to the window. I would slip my hand between the dark red drapes and the creamy lace. And see him.

The shadow man. Real. Staring up at me. Face a shadow. Body a shadow.

He would slip away.

I would wait, but he wouldn't show himself again before I slipped back into bed next to Miss Heaven.

He was there. I knew I ain't made him up. I had a reason to be so afraid. Plagued by dreams. Reaching out in my mind.

I got to where Mr. Dennis came into my dreams. Mr. Dennis was at the campfire with his hand in the air, waving and calling, "Rosie!"

I was trapped in the stream, fighting my way from the rock into the deep water.

I got to the opposite side and gripped the bank. The current snatched at my hands and hauled my body downstream. A hand reached down and clamped onto mines, pale like Mr. Dennis hand. Held tight.

I looked up. "Oh, thank you. Thank you for helping me."

A shadow would fall as I raised my face. And by the time I got my head up out the water, I wouldn't see Mr. Dennis face above me. It was a face all covered in shadow. Its hands tried to tug me out the water.

I would wake trying to scream. My throat was too dry. I would cough and snatch at air.

Then one day I woke up on the floor in front a Miss Heaven fireplace. My face was so close to the flames, I had to scoot back for fear sparks would light in my hair.

I was shivering like as if I had just hauled myself out the stream. My teeth clacked. "What could be wrong with me?"

I could a crawled right in that fire in my sleep and been-what was that word I heard from Mr. Dennis and Mr. Sami?-cream-made.

`That's what was happening to me. I was being slow cream-made. Just like they done to Mr. Jared.

Sure enough, he wasn't dead and melted when we found him. Just sick and sleep. Like me. And Mr. Dennis and Mr. Sami and them came along and made him cream.

I stared in Miss Heaven fireplace and my mind just flew. I could see again the tower licking flames to the black sky and smoke rolling up in fast black clouds, clearing the air a that terrible stink. And the hut underneath it where a man lay burning and ain't none of us moved a finger to save him.

He was a danger to everybody. But who wanted to be burned to death? Cream-making.

The tower finished burning red and the ring of stones fell in. Like the bone ring on Rose White finger she hated so. Like this bone house she hated, too. I should a listened to her, coming out them woods, hauling Miss Heaven home.

A idea was coming clear to me. Bones. Circles. Red and white.

Red and cream at the window where I looked out to see the shadow man skulking, hanging round the red and white roses, the red grapes, the white gravestones. Circles of red and white, and me trapped.

But past him, the willows and oaks that led to the woods. To safety. Freedom.

I had to get out a here. Wasn't no place safe for me but the woods.

I curled up and lay shivering in sweat till the door opened. Miss Heaven ran to me, knelt, and lifted my head up onto her lap. "What's wrong, Rose Red?"

"I'm being cream-made, Miss Heaven."

"What is that?"

"I'm going to be burned to death."

"Who's trying to burn you? I'll tell my father. He'll protect you."

What could I say? I ain't wanted to tell on her father to her, waving me on toward the fire that wouldn't warm me till I got in it and burned. Maybe even crazy Miss Heaven would try to tell me it was just a dream. How do you tell people some dreams be more real than real life?

I just said, "I got to get to the woods, where I be safe, Miss Heaven."

"The woods?" She stroked my head and seemed like she was thinking. "I don't want to lose you. And I know how to get you to the woods, Rose Red. Don't let anybody in this room until I get back. I'll lock the door and let myself back in with my key."

Not long till I heard the latch working again. A big thing prowled in all hunkered down on four paws, gleaming silver.

I seen its eyes yellow like the sun, shining. I reached out my hand.

"Wolf Water," a low voice said. The big thing circled round me once, twice, keeping its eyes on mines, and settled in a lie-down around me. Its bushy tail flicked once.

"He likes you," that same soft voice said.

A woman came and settled down next to me on the floor. Her gown spread out round her feet. It was the woman with weeping willow hair dressed in a color like new spring leaves.

She reached out a hand to pet the beast. I looked at her other hand.

I pulled back from it. It was all curled and dangling from her arm, like oak leaves dry and curl in winter before they drop off the trees. Long shiny scars ran up that hand, wrapped round her wrist, and headed toward her elbow.

"Who you?" I asked.

"Mother Magdalen called me Angel, but my father called me Girl."

"Miss Angel Girl."

"Miss Angel Girl is my and Sami's mother, Rose Red." Miss Heaven slid my head up onto her lap again. She started telling Miss Angel Girl how I couldn't be safe till I got to the woods.

Miss Angel Girl said, "Will you come now, Heaven? I'll take Rose Red and care for her, and she'll get better, if you'll come."

Miss Heaven bowed her head down. "You won't take her without me? But if I go, who will take care of Mammy Water?"

"There are other people here to care for Mammy Water, Heaven. You and I have missed our lives together."

Miss Heaven studied her carpet.

It was clear to me that I wasn't getting to the woods if Miss Heaven didn't agree to go along. "The woods ain't so far you can't come back of a night and see-" I wasn't going for this stuff about Mammy Water one bit "-whoever you want to see." Whip Man. *Gal, you ain't fooling nobody.*

This got Miss Heaven looking up. "I'll come with you, Mother, if you'll let me come back here whenever I want to. Just to visit. Not to stay."

Miss Angel Girl stood up. Her silver beast stood up, too. It circled round me and Miss Heaven. Its tail brushed my face and tickled. It smelled like dark earth, like you find under trees where the grass don't grow. "We'll go tonight. We'll support Rose Red between us. Get her dressed for the cold, Heaven, and I'll be back when everyone is sleeping."

"For the cold?" I asked. "But it be summer."

Miss Angel Girl laughed. "No. The snow is about ready to fall. You've slept for months, like Mammy Water." Her animal slipped out the door behind her. Miss Heaven got up to lock it.

She went to the big wood wardrobe and started pulling out clothes. All deep red like old blood. I remembered the fitting before I went in the woods with Mr. Dennis and them. Did Miss Heaven have clothes made for me while I was ill?

I was going to get better. I was feeling stronger already.

I made my way to the window and parted the curtains and drapes. Sure enough. The shadow man slipped into the dark.

I didn't have a thought for Ma'am or Rose White or Mr. Dennis. I didn't think what it would feel like if I never knew what became of Mammy Water or Boyfriend. I didn't care about nothing but getting away.

Miss Heaven wasn't much help dressing me in one a them red dresses. But after while, sitting on the bed, I strapped on a pair a simple leather shoes that old man made everybody.

Miss Heaven brought me out a big thing like a blanket, all red. She wrapped it round me and pulled its hood up over my head. "Wear my cloak, Rose Red. I haven't had one made for you, yet."

"But what will you wear, Miss Heaven?" She ain't answered. She went out the room, locking the door and telling me she was going to bring me food.

I got near the fire and fell asleep. I woke hearing the lock turn. Miss Heaven came in quick and knelt down near me. "Here. Drink this." Coffee. Strong. And some kind a sweet bread. I got most of it down.

"Heaven? Are you ready?" Miss Angel Girl whispered from the hall.

We came out, me leaning on Miss Heaven shoulder. Miss Angel Girl came over, her beast circling round her skirt. He gave her room to slip her good arm round me.

"Are you ready?" she said. "Once we start, we have to keep going until we get to my tree."

The wolf went ahead of us down the hall. Its silver fur caught star and moonlight through the colored glass window. It headed down the stairs without looking back.

I kept looking round at the walls to make sure all the mirrors was still down. I'm getting just like Miss Heaven, I thought to myself. Maybe she ain't crazy after all.

When we got to the bottom of the steps, Miss Heaven was breathing hard. How far could she help her ma'am carry me?

Her ma'am with but one good arm. I had to try hard to keep my eyes and my mind off that ripped one.

How could we be safe with a animal eat the hand that feed it?

I thought about what my ma'am said. First folks chickens and pigs disappeared. Next, they children.

All on account of this animal here. And I'm running away into the woods with it.

For a minute, I hoped Mr. Dennis would be at his place at Miss Magdalen back door. Maybe he could say something to make me feel safe here. Then I thought, *No. What if it be the shadow man waiting there?*

I reached to pet the wolf. It looked at me with them yellow eyes over one shoulder. It slipped its head down low and trotted toward the back door.

"Come on," Miss Angel Girl said.

The silver wolf paced round in a circle. Miss Angel Girl let me loose again so she could unlatch and open it. "Wolf Water," she said to her beast, "stay close."

It trotted out under the starlight. Went a little ways and then doubled back around to circle our legs.

I looked around and like about couldn't reckon-eyes the place. It was the back a the big house, all right, but it was all changed.

All the shacks in the quarters had little gardens outside the front door. Cold was ending the growing season. I could see where vegetables had been. Cornstalks and squash vines. Even a few orange and red flowers. Some rose vines.

And most the front doors wasn't no more rags. Somebody had allowed the people wood and time to make doors. Almost everybody had a new wood door, shut against the chill.

We didn't pass close enough by Mammy Water shack for me to see what she had for a door. So I asked.

"Sshh," Miss Heaven said. "People have doors to protect their chickens and pigs, now." She looked at Wolf Water circling our skirts. "And their children. Since Mammy Water's alone, I don't think Sami and Whip Man have had anyone make her a door, yet."

That didn't make no sense to me. Sami and Whip Man ain't real-eyes that if Mammy Water was alone, she needed a door more than anybody? Or was they hoping she'd get ate and stop pestering people with her visions?

I looked toward where my ma'am shack bordered on the woods. Had anybody planted a garden there?

I stopped dead still.

"What is it?" Miss Angel Girl said.

"I seen something move. By my ma'am shack."

We all looked. Nothing.

"What did it look like?" Miss Angel Girl wanted to know.

"Like a shadow."

Miss Heaven said, "A shadow of what?"

"Shadow of a man." I was spooked. "I think we best go back."

"Wolf Water can kill a man," Miss Angel Girl said. "Come on."

But once we dragged up to Ma'am shack, Wolf Water wouldn't go past it. He kept sniffing in front a the shut door.

"Wolf Water," Miss Angel Girl kept calling, "stay close."

He ain't budged.

"I can't keep going, Mother," Miss Heaven said. "Let's let him check around inside, and then we can rest there."

They helped me to the door. I tried to open it, but I couldn't. "Somebody done drew the bolt." My voice shook. "On the inside."

Miss Angel Girl let loose a me to slap her leg. "Wolf Water, come!" She grabbed the ruff of fur loose at his neck. "Let's get to the woods!" She took off leading her beast, ducking low through the grass.

I dropped to all fours. "I can crawl on my own, Miss Heaven. You try it, too."

I had to keep hiking that wool dress away from between my knees, and the cloak every now and then snagged in the grass. I dropped lower and lower against the ground till I was dragging myself on my elbows.

We made it barely up under the trees when I fell over on my back and ain't moved.

Miss Heaven crawled over to me, breathing hard. "Where's my mother? Do you see her?"

"Here." We looked around, hearing the voice but seeing nothing.

The silver wolf came from between some trees, flicked that bushy tail, turned, and went on.

"Let's follow, Miss Heaven. I can make it walking now."

I pulled myself up between two close trees. I grabbed a hold a one to steady myself on my feet. Then I pushed off. I could make it if I threw myself from one tree to the next.

The cold that had hold a me shook loose. I was burning. Sweat poured. I stopped, propped on a tree, and fumbled to flip off Miss Heaven cloak.

"You take it, Miss Heaven. I don't need this no more."

She was shivering so her teeth chattered. She swung the cloak round her shoulders and went past me trying my trick, stumbling from one tree to the next. "Mother!"

And that silver wolf slipped into the starlight between the trees, flicked its tail, and slipped ahead again.

Miss Heaven followed her mother's wolf, and I followed Miss Heaven. Every now and again I turned to see if the shadow man followed us.

We went on so long, seemed to me wasn't nothing but my mind still working. Beating like a heart. Saying, Go on, girl. Next tree. Breathe. Next tree. Go on.

I had scratches ripped in my dress where I flung myself against them trees. We had took a way I wasn't used to. I was lost. I was desperate to keep my eyes on Miss Heaven blood red cloak flicking through the shades a black that was trees and shadow. I lost her once and stopped in a cold panic. Where was I, surrounded by black on black, looming close?

Sky, forest, wet muddy ground, all looked the same to me. Bulging blackness. "Heaven? Miss Angel Girl?" My calls started in a whisper.

265

Then I heard the wolf howl, a long sound, started low, but rose and grabbed at the hair on my scalp and pulled it up.

I listened and waited till that long rising wail fell and died away. Soon I saw Miss Heaven cloak swiping past the tree trunks, red on brown. Like blood on my hands in the fields, I thought. But all that was over. I hadn't worked in the fields in months. And might not never again.

Miss Heaven took my hand and led me on without a word.

Then we got to a clearing. So much light came through from the distant sky that grass growed there.

In front of us was a blasted tree. Looked like lightning took a fiery ax and hacked out its insides. Miss Heaven and me fell to the grassy muck before the big empty tree.

The wolf came round from back a the tree. It carried something in its jaws, big and pink-fleshed. It was already tore up. Bones was swinging and glowing underneath the bright yellow eyes.

It dropped the thing near us. Me and Miss Heaven tried to scoot back. It was a pig head, almost whole, singed like it had been roasted.

Somebody must a roasted the whole pig and then cut most the meat off the bones.

Wolf Water looked round behind his back, once over each shoulder, and then lowered his head and snapped the pig skull.

"Somebody's been here." Miss Angel Girl followed the wolf. "Someone's brought chickens and at least one pig here to my tree and roasted them. There are bones and beaks scattered all

266

around. And the pine needles I've stacked for a soft place to sleep have been covered with feathers and squirrel skins."

She sat down near us and rested her good hand on Miss Heaven, her bad hand on me. "Heaven, Rose Red, I've tied some corn pone and a drinking gourd inside my skirt. Do you want any?"

I drank some a the water and got away from the splatters of bone and pig flesh Wolf Water shook off his muzzle. "Where we sleep at?"

"In the tree," Miss Angel Girl said.

It was hard to crawl up and through the slit in the tree belly. But once inside, it was dark and cozy like my ma'am shack before my life changed.

I snuggled down on the feathers and little brown skins. The pine needles crunched. Another mother and daughter to share my night, like Ma'am and Rose White. Miss Heaven spread her cloak over us all.

The wolf leaped in and circled, stepped on us with his sharp dry paw pads and scratched us with his gray claws.

I dreamed about fishing in a shallow pond in mild sunlight, in a old rag dress, kicking my feet to make the water spray.

I woke alone in the tree trunk. Ants was everywhere. I needed to stretch my legs and get off my one side. I pushed off Miss Heaven red cloak and started in to pulling myself up and out that slit was the front door.

Sunlight all around. The air was chilly, but it smelled pine and fresh.

Miss Angel Girl came round the tree, scraping together bones with a bundle a twigs she had in her good hand for a broom. "Good morning, Rose Red. I'm collecting these to keep predators away. They'll feed Wolf Water a good long time." She stood up and reached under her skirt. "Here's the last of the pone." She tossed it to me.

I unwrapped it from the rag and bit in. Dry, crumbly, and some a the best food I ever ate.

"Where Wolf Water and Miss Heaven at?"

"I think Heaven ran away, back to the farm. I've sent Wolf Water to find her." He must not a found her. He came back towards evening, all alone.

I had spent the day dozing and gathering my strength in the clearing. I was glad of that wool dress. It kept me warm. Miss Angel Girl came to me with roots, berries, nuts, and water in her gourd.

"I'm going love it here. I'm going to get strong again. I love the woods."

She smiled. "My father raised me in the woods, trying to get me free of the plantation." She kind a cocked her head over to one side like a wolf do. "You know, when I was little, I always wanted my mother with me. When I got to be big, I always wished I could have my son and daughter with me. But it might be nice to have a sister, finally."

"Oh, I know about being like a sister. I been a good sister to Rose White."

"That's not what I mean. You don't have to be *like* a sister. You already *are* my sister."

"How so?"

She settled back on the grass and looked at the sky. Wolf Water came out a no-place and settled near her so his head could rest on her leg.

"Mother Magdalen told me, when I was expecting Heaven, how I came to be born. I always knew I was Mammy Water's daughter. But I wondered why I and my son had no resemblance to her or Sami. So Mother Magdalen told me about how, when Sami was bought, and Mammy Water was sent with him, she arrived at the farm already in that strange walking sleep. Sami would leave her in his shack to go out and work the fields. Mother Magdalen could see that Mammy Water was with child. She knew how much her own little daughter had saved her own life, so to speak, so she thought that if this woman in her terrible sleep could survive and have that child, maybe it would make her want to live in the world, too. Mother Magdalen came whenever Sami was out, fed the woman, and tended her body. Then, one morning, Mother Magdalen came and could see that the birth had happened. But the baby was nowhere to be found.

"She couldn't start asking questions. If Sami had killed the baby, that would be stealing from Mr. Jared. Sami would have been punished for it, mutilated or killed. So Mother Magdalen just hoped the baby had been born dead and asked no questions.

"Then her own daughter grew up and was killed. Mother Magdalen thought she'd lose her mind. She spent nine months in agony. It was a pain like childbirth, she said. It got stronger and stronger.

"And then one day, nine months to the day after her daughter was killed, I came to her. She said it was like she had come to life again. She said it was just like her own daughter had been given back to her. Like life was giving her a second chance."

"To do what?"

Miss Angel Girl said, "To protect me. To protect her daughter and keep her safe. But I only wanted to show you that you and I are sisters because we have a mother in common. I was born from Mammy Water's body, and you were born from her spirit." She looked at me across the blades of green grass and smiled. "Your mother had you because Mammy Water came and laid her hands on your mother's belly. Sami claimed all three of us. He was a good father." She looked back up at the stars. "I can't imagine a better one."

"But Angel Girl, if you know Miss Magdalen love you so, enough to kill a man for you, why you stay gone from her so many years?"

"I've never stayed away from Mother Magdalen. How would I have survived out here, without her? It's Mr. Dennis I left."

I thought, *Maybe I can keep going back to my ma'am, too.* "You tell Miss Heaven about that? Why she run away, then, back to the farm?"

"She's in love. A man is not a mother. And a place to visit is not a home. I can't tell Heaven to come here and give Whip Man back to his wife. I wish I could." Her voice died away. I could hear her thinking, *But I'm not that much of a mother to her.*

Angel Girl stood up and Wolf Water leaped to his feet, wide awake. "Let's get into the tree for the night. There's not a man back at the plantation who you want, is there?"

"No." But I looked back through the trees. What if there was a man back there who wanted me? That man in the shadows.

270

But Wolf Water could kill any man, Angel Girl had said. We was safe out here, running between the trees and the plantation with Wolf Water.

The snow fell. I got stronger and happier than I had ever been in my life.

I still slept a lot. I might wake to find myself alone in the tree, wrapped in Miss Heaven red cloak against the cold, with Angel Girl sliding hot food from Mother Magdalen through the slit. Or I might wake in the clearing, with a low fire roasting something Wolf Water or Angel Girl caught scuttling through the woods.

Every day I got out the tree to walk some. Sunshine, snow, or pinpricks of sleet, I wrapped myself in my cloak and set out.

I couldn't believe I was at last free in the woods. I wouldn't miss a day of it. There was streams and nests, bayous and caves to see and climb and wash in. And once I seen anything in the speckles of sunshine between the thick-hanging vines and trees on a sunny day, I had to go back and see it iced with snow or washed and sparkling with rain.

Me and Angel Girl would walk, laughing over nothing while Wolf Water circled our legs and ran ahead. We talked about our lives. Sitting perched on a marshy ledge, or skating stones across a icy pond, or wrapped up tight together under her brown wool shawl and my red cloak in the tree, Wolf Water tail flicking our faces. She was the first person I ever told all about Boyfriend and how he kept me out a trouble when I was a little wild girl being made into a farmhand, and how Bully picked on me. About

271

Rose White and how we shared almost everything together.

Angel Girl helped me see that some a my fears back at the plantation was just fever madness. She doubted folks cream-made live people. "That would be a waste of money." She hadn't heard of it. She guessed that only dead bodies got burned. She hated Mr. Dennis and made no excuses for him. But Angel Girl was sure wasn't nobody in that house meaning for me to get burned.

So I was shamed to tell her about the shadow man. I could figure out for myself he wasn't nothing but a fever fear. Probably just some leaves blowing in the wind under the pines.

My fever fears was suffering that brought me to a good end. Living out here in the woods I loved, with a sister I never knew I had, was a good end to my sad story.

My mind cleared and my body healed. I wanted to go back and make sure Ma'am and Rose White knew I was safe. And see them a little again, like Angel Girl was free to do with her two mothers, Mammy Water and Mother Magdalen.

Angel Girl never even so much as brought me news about them. "How is my ma'am doing? Can you find a way to let Rose White and them at least hear I'm safe?"

Angel Girl would pass me some food and drink and say nothing to me but how was Wolf Water while she was gone.

I thought it was odd that she always left him behind with me. She must not a felt she needed protection in the woods.

After a while, I started to fume. Angel Girl knew all about the people she loved. She could even sneak up the stairs and peek in on Miss Heaven sleeping.

But I couldn't even send word to nobody. Wasn't like I was asking about Mr. Dennis and that room he promised me, and that mirror where I was so beautiful.

"I don't want to lie to you, Rose Red," Angel Girl said. "It just isn't safe. Not even Sami knows where my tree is. All those years he was stolen, I would go visit him in his cave. I found him, but I never brought him back here."

"I ain't wanted to visit Mr. Sami."

"You want to visit his wife."

"I want to visit my sister. And I don't need to talk to her. Just let me set eyes on her, Miss Angel Girl."

"Not yet."

"When?"

"I don't know. Heaven's knowing where this place is already endangers our secrecy here. Don't press me to make promises that will turn out to be lies."

I stopped asking.

I had got strong, hadn't I? I could someday soon make my way back to the plantation alone, find Ma'am and Rose White, and let them know I was safe nearby. It would be done and I'd be back in the tree before Angel Girl even knew I was gone.

I waited for a nighttime rain or even snowfall, in the hopes that Wolf Water wouldn't smell my tracks.

Rain or, better yet, snow like I wanted was a long time coming. But one night, when we was sitting in the clearing to eat our pone and ham, I the sky glowed pink.

I put down my ham, so I could sleep light on a emptier stomach. Wolf Water came and licked it from my fingers. I petted his ruff a fur. Angel Girl watched me and smiled.

I woke that night and pulled myself out from Angel Girl arms, to look through the slit in the tree. And there it was.

Snow piled and fluffy, hushing and fluffing the woods.

I looked round at Angel Girl. She lay still. The snow threw a glow into the tree hollow, on Angel Girl and Wolf Water sealed eyelids.

I thought to myself, *She won't never know. Till I get my freedom to go back and forth and visit.* Then me and Angel Girl would get along better than ever.

The woods glowed from the pulpy swollen ground up, sweeter in its bright darkness than day. The snow whispered, making its way through the thick woods, hushing like a ma'am singing a lullaby. I listened and heard nothing but the song of the snow.

But what had I seen?

A shape. A shadow. Fast in and out a the glowing dark trees.

I stopped. Wrapped my cloak tighter, pulled down my hood so as not to be seen.

I waited till the cold crept in on me. With the cold, that old fear came creeping.

No, I thought. *No. No more fear.*

I moved forward again.

The path down to the plantation was this way. Funny how Angel Girl tree was not so far, really, but up and off in a direction that led away from the road to town and the other farms.

Again. A flicker between trees where it wasn't no reason for a shadow.

The snow-light don't cast none.

And the moon and stars couldn't be seen for the trees and the snow clouds. So what was it that threw that flicking shadow?

I turned and looked back where I came from. Could I find my way back if I needed to? Fast?

Funny how I hadn't doubted it till now. "Stop that," I told myself like I figured Ma'am would do. "Stop scaring yourself and go ahead on."

I put my mind back on Ma'am and Rose White and how they would cry and hug me when I got there.

Again. *No doubt about it, this time.*

Up close. A shadow shot from one tree trunk to the next, right in front of me. Shadow shape of a man.

I couldn't move.

Think, I told myself. *Think what to do, and do it quick.*

I couldn't think.

Fear was on me. I couldn't do more than breathe out little white puffs of air and look straight ahead and wait.

Run, I told myself. *Run back to Angel Girl tree, calling out for Wolf Water.*

No. This is what she feared. Me taking off and showing the world where was her tree.

Tears stung my cheeks. I had forgot about all this crying.

I didn't think. I just lifted one a my feet out the snow-crusted muck and put it soft down. Behind me.

Now the other foot. Soft behind me. *Keep going. One foot. And the other foot. It must be somewhere I can turn and run,* I thought.

I turned and ran.

The cloak whipped around me. I tried to snatch it and hold it close. My feet sank deep in the soft new snow. Snow fell into my simple heavy leather shoes. Fell in, melted, and sloshed under my feet while I ran.

My breath was sharp in the cold. I hadn't run in so long a time. Could I run for long?

Sharp breath in and out. Raking my chest like claws.

Maybe I didn't need to run. Maybe it wasn't no shadow still following me. Breathe.

I stopped, weaving and dizzy and trying to catch my breath.

No sound.

I turned around in a full circle. Looked.

Nothing. Nowhere. Just the shush a the snowflakes settling.

"Ah!" That scream came from me.

I was down in the snowy mulch, my face shoved in deep. Tiny flakes a snow and spatters a mud shot in my mouth and nose. Something hard landed on my back. Pressed down like to break me in two. I couldn't breathe to scream again.

I struggled, reaching my hands behind me. I hit something hard. And moving.

Arms. Hard hands grabbed and squeezed both my wrists in a grip I couldn't break. One hand slammed through the snow and mud till it got to my face. Pressed in. Slush squeezed against my cheeks and nose. The hand shut my mouth.

The hands worked to flip me over.

I looked up, hating to see what I must see.

My tears burned and cleared. He brought his face down close to mines.

I screamed into his hand.

The shadow man squatted on me. The glowing snow between the trees still threw his face in shadow, but his body was hard and heavy.

I knew at last who he was. This was the face I had woke up to in the cart. It wasn't a dream. It wasn't a fever fear. It wasn't me being cold and scared in the stream.

It was real. He was real.

Miss Heaven's jailor, freed from Jared, who had come to steal food at Mr. Dennis camp and found me in the cart instead. He had led the men to Mr. Jared, dying on his bed. And then he had followed us back to the plantation.

Now I understood the shape always hiding outside Miss Heaven's window. Following us when me and Miss Heaven and Angel Girl escaped to the woods.

So this was who locked himself in Ma'am shack and left them bones roasted and scattered round Angel Girl tree. Ma'am had said something was stealing folks new chickens and pigs. I even understood why Angel Girl left her wolf behind with me when she went through the woods. She knew the shadow man was real.

277

I fought to get out from under him. He rose to his knees, shoved me, squatted again. His eyebrows shot up. Wrinkles danced across his forehead. He took one hand off my face. He reached at my throat and started pulling the cloak ties.

I at last got my mouth open.

My scream flew out my throat and went up over the trees. It hung in the air.

I drew shaky breath to do it again.

He stopped fumbling at my cloak. It was spread away from me like a circle a blood. He got up on his knees to snatch up my dress. I bent my knees to kick him.

I seen his fist near my face. I heard a crack. Light broke my vision. I couldn't see. Another crack. More light. Then I couldn't feel. Not the cold. Not the fight that I hoped was still going on. Somewhere was my body, and I couldn't do nothing for it.

I could hear, far away, someone snarling like a beast. Was a beast eating me? My eyes was closed. I had to open them.

It seemed to take a long time. I kept passing out and waking to remember what I had to do. *Open my eyes!*

Trees swam over my head, dipping inward over me. I sat up, propped on my elbows. Nothing pushed me back down.

Shapes in the snow wrestled. The silver curved back of a wolf leaped and twisted, keeping its jaws clamped tight.

Under that twisted face, them jagged brows. Clamped at the shadow man's throat, squirting

278

blood in a bright stream over the black mud splattered with white snow.

I sat in the snow and cleared my eyes on the sight of Wolf Water ripping that body in parts and pieces.

Angel Girl hadn't told the whole truth. Wolf Water ain't just killed that man. He ate some of him, too.

CHAPTER NINE
MY SOUL'S GLASS COFFIN:
ANGEL, BORN 1767

I lived in an oval of light. I lived in a glass prison and saw a world through it that sliced my heart with longing as if with a knife.

I do know the feeling of a knife slicing my heart. I've felt it. Not just the first time, the time that killed me. Many times.

I have also known no time, rocking on the flow of things that must be as they are.

It was that first act, the murder that ended my life, that taught me what I had always been in life. Property. Less than human. I had not known.

I was almost an adult. I was ready for marriage, my mother Magdalen said just days before Uncle Dennis tied me to my bed and locked me in my room. Ready for marriage with some brave free man who would take me from the plantation and the constant threat of enslavement. And still I knew nothing about myself in that threatened slavery, neither who I was nor what hopes were allowed me.

It was that act, my murder, that taught me. Then it caught me and held me in my reflection, to gaze in longing at the lost world where I had held nothing but a threatened place.

I pressed my face to the glass and gazed at what had been my room, where I lay on my bed and watched as my murderer crept to me.

The stones moved slowly from the wall, one by one.

I lay watching from my bed. I sweated so much fear that I could smell it.

Even the first time, as I waited to be killed, I knew what would happen. Whenever I found myself free of the glass and stretched on the bed, I knew what would happen again.

When he had moved enough of the stones from the wall, the man who said he gave me life crawled through. My maker. My murderer. My father.

On hands and knees, he came. Slowly. Staring first at the floor where he crawled and then up at me. "Say nothing, Angel. Do not betray me." Mr. Jared dragged his body first on one ridged solid knee and then one strapped knee socket, his peg shooting stiffly out behind and to one side as he crawled.

He slipped a crabbed hand on the bedrail and pulled himself up to sit near me. He leaned close and put a rag to my face. "We never thought your Uncle Dennis could be so ruthless, your mother and I. We never thought he might do something like this to you, to frighten you into betraying me. You are frightened, aren't you, Angel?"

"No, Mr. Jared."

He sighed as if weary of a tiresome world and a wayward child. His voice grew insistent. "Of course you're frightened. There's no need to lie to me. I know you. I made you. I own you, and I know you better than you know yourself.

"You are frightened of your Uncle Dennis. You wonder what he will do to you. He will frighten you into betraying my whereabouts. And then he will kill you. Your mother has been foolish to believe

281

his lying hints that he would ever free you and will you his property."

"No, Mr. Jared." I shook my head so it shook my body. Uncle Dennis's ropes pulled at my wrists and ankles.

Mr. Jared's face flushed. The scars purpled and puffed. "Yes, you will tell him, and he will come to kill me. Then your mother, my own disloyal *property*, will survive me and live on to serve my murderer. How can such a thought be borne." Flecks of his spittle sprinkled my face.

"Please, Mr. Jared. I won't tell Mr. Dennis. My mother won't tell. I know she won't."

Mr. Jared grew serene. "Won't you help me do what is right, Angel?" The twisted scar that shaped his mouth smiled. "Yes, you will help me. Just as you should." He spread and folded his rag on my bed, mumbling, "Let me help you to silence. People like you don't know courage. You have no concept of loyalty. Your mother courts Dennis's lies. All lies, Angel. He has tricked your mother, but you will help me set everything right."

When he was pleased with the stringy rag rectangle, he leaned in closer. I smelled the rot at the site of his lost leg. I smelled the bear claw wounds inside his mouth, where moisture and darkness kept them fermenting. I pitied him as much as I hated and feared him.

My mother could have healed those claw wounds with herbal poultices. She had begged him to let her apply the poultices inside his mouth. But he feared poisoning and would let none of her plants pass his lips.

I saw myself and my kneeling murderer in my silver-framed mirror. Mr. Jared jerked his rag between my teeth. He shoved my face away from him so he could knot the gag at the back of my head. "Angel, remember. Silence when my brother comes to ask you about me."

I heard my mother's running footsteps on the stones in the hall. My shout was muffled in the rag. My tongue tasted its salty grime.

Mother banged on the locked door. She shouted for Mr. Peter to come shoot the lock away. The pounding of her fists became the running footsteps of my death.

"You are afraid of being hurt." Mr. Jared's contempt lifted his lips against its scar. "What do you know about being hurt, Angel? You were born to serve and suffer. You neglect your duty to me. You dare fear for your own safety. Betrayal!" He grabbed at his chest and groped inside his stained linen shirt.

He yanked something out, leathery and wrinkled. He raised it in one hand. It was the lost leg.

He held it by the ankle, above the foot, which twisted up like a cane handle. "This is suffering. To lose everything to a greedy upstart younger brother, even my body. Even Magdalen. This is wrongdoing. You have no idea." He brought the cut end of the leg down on my skull.

The bone struck between my eyes and stunned me. The smell of old decay swarmed around my head. I retched into my gag.

Mr. Jared flung the leg from him. It bumped the stones scattered where he had come through the wall.

Outside my door, my mother pleaded. "Please don't do this. Whoever's in there with my baby, I'm begging you. *Anything*. I'll do anything, let you do anything, help you do anything. Please don't hurt my child."

If I had fainted, would I have been spared imprisonment in the glass?

Where do the dead go? Where should I have gone?

Mr. Jared pulled a gleaming silver blade from his belt. The point gleamed in lamplight. Light ran to the knife's tip and trembled there, pooling and stinging my eyes.

I watched the bright knifepoint puncture my flesh. The first stab sent pain racing to my brain. After that, every little opening sliced into my body filled my mind with more terror than agony.

My body burned and blood rushed to soothe and heal. I glowed red with my flowing death. My healing blood sheathed Jared's silver knife, dripped, and fell uselessly back to me.

I turned from the trail of bleeding punctures toward my silent bedroom door. My eyes opened on my oval mirror. I saw through a mist of tears and weakness my blood-washed body reflected there.

My whole soul flew to my reflection, as if on wings. And I was embraced in the glass.

Held. And rarely released.

My death was a drop like rain that drew all my life's light and continued falling, with me caught inside.

I have sometimes flown free. I have sometimes drawn someone to me in my loneliness.

Such exquisite aloneness.

I used to press myself to the glass until I drew away in horror from its cold. I lingered behind the mirror and watched my breast's blood shrivel in dark streaks along its surface.

I plotted to draw others to my isolation. When people turned to me in passing, I would fix their gazes on reflections they most wanted and feared. For women, grace and loveliness. For men, tenderness reserved for babies and the dying. For children, a friend who offers no rebuke.

I waited.

But the only friend I drew was Heaven. I drew her as a child and lost her as a woman. She had no need of beauty or friendship. She only wanted freedom.

Her imprisonment was my freedom. Was I wrong to yearn to be seen and sought?

I mourned my loss of the living Heaven as others later mourned her death. I did not mourn her passing, for I knew she had not died.

I waited hungrily for the birth of her child.

When the child was born, and Heaven lay searching for a sanctuary from death, I flew and held the new little life in my ever-bleeding, ever-empty arms.

The others had abandoned the baby to weep over Heaven's death throes. I raised the newborn from her cradle, carved by Whip Man with hearts and flowering vines.

I held Heaven's forgotten child and made it a gift of my heart full of love.

For the long hours of that lovely night, I held the baby and named her Solace. I beat my wings against the world that shut us out.

It was someone else who later named her Snow White.

Those who were not clustered to mourn Heaven's death inside the big house gathered instead against the slow drag of their own dread out back in the quarters. They circled a hasty fire whose flames shot toward the full moon, to watch Mammy Water's corpse dance.

It danced in spirals. It started with its arms dragging the soft dark dust, as if weighted by its grave. Then it turned and raised its arms higher as it turned. Its skeletal fingers grasped at the sky's placid moon.

As Mammy Water's body danced, everyone finally knew what I had long known. That Mammy Water had been dead since Heaven returned to the plantation. Nearly nine months. Dead and decaying, untended, in her shack.

Everyone had gotten used to the stink that defined Mammy Water's life. Everyone knew Mammy Water never ate. Everyone knew, and lived well with the knowledge, that she lay with her mind and breath flown from her body.

After Rose Red's escape to the woods, no one did more than peep through the rag door of Mammy Water's shack, look around for fresh waste to dump, find none, and sneak away to breathe sweet clean air. Heaven's excuse to run through the quarters searching for Whip Man-that she wanted to tend Mammy Water-was a welcome lie for everyone.

Mammy Water's soul had left without a glance back at me. I was not a good sight for a soul newly set free, lingering in mourning about the plantation, searching for Heaven and my mother. Every soul swept toward its distant light without a look, a prayer, or a last word for me. "Come away, lost one."

As if the sight of me might curse eternities.

Mammy Water's soul was gone. But Heaven's soul was newly freed. It rushed to lift Mammy Water's drying body in the remembered gestures of dance around a fire.

After her death dance, Heaven still didn't go away. She stayed to dance the corpse again and again. The dead have no time. Time circles itself in one moment of truth. That truthful moment is eternity. One might spend it dancing, I suppose, though there must be brighter ecstasies.

No one could interrupt the mourning women who ringed Heaven's deathbed that first night, to tell them that Mammy Water's corpse had risen from its shack and danced. Mother Magdalen, Rose White, Sister, and Girl, who had stolen my name and my mother.

All of them circled Heaven's pale body and wept and whispered throughout the night. They held her cold fingers and prayed for her peace. They prayed selfishly for their own loved ones.

Girl prayed for her wolf, who watched the flames and the death dance from the edge of the woods. Sister and Rose White prayed for Rose Red, who hid in Girl's hollow tree. Did Mother Magdalen pray for me to find rest? I could not bear to listen to her prayers at Heaven's deathbed.

It was Sami who came down from his dead sister's room to Mother Magdalen's back door and heard that death was dancing. Sami left the house for the quarters, to watch this horrible miracle.

It was hard to tell what Sami learned. The cloud of his thoughts cleared on images of rage and power, a bear. He frightened Rose White out of her tenderness. I watched their solitary prayers shape the mists of their future together.

To leave the plantation and start anew would be their salvation and almost all the farmhands'. I held baby Solace and watched a beleaguered community's prayers become what would be.

Rose Red would have her happiness, wandering her wild woods in the surprised passion of her love for Boyfriend.

Sister would leave the plantation with Sami and Rose White and their caravan of sharefarmers, unaware of the unearthly battles to be won and lost, freedom at such great price.

Not I. Not Whip Man and his family. We would be left behind here.

I passed that blissful birth night fanning Solace with my cooling wings. At dawn, I lay her gently in her cradle.

Sami came to his sister's deathbed and murmured in Mother Magdalen's ear what terrors he had seen in the night. Mother Magdalen gathered that numb courage that was her life's legacy and went quietly down to the quarters.

It was full morning. Rose White, Girl, and Sister put down Heaven's stiffening hands to crowd around the waking baby. I whispered her new name to them. "Solace."

Rose White squinted into space. "I feel something, like a spirit, trying to speak to me. Maybe this baby already got her a name. What you all think? You ain't heard it? 'Salt' something. Salt lip. No. Salt lick. No, that don't make no sense."

Girl said, "Could it be Heaven? Is she saying Saul? There was a hand who used to bring me berries, when I was pregnant with Heaven, and he was named Saul. Or Sally? Remember Sally Jane, Sister? She used to make me laugh so. But I don't think Heaven knew her."

"Yes," Sister agreed. Yes what? This was nonsense!

"Solace!" I insisted. I willed myself to appear. But without Heaven's powerful faith, appearing was too much for me.

Should I go in search of a mirror? But who would look into a mirror, over Heaven's dead body? Besides, there were no mirrors in Heaven's room. Did no one know why she feared them?

"Sauce?" Sister suggested timidly. "Wouldn't no spirits be trying to name the baby Socks, would they?"

Rose White clicked her tongue. "Sound like something you call a cat with white foots. 'Sop?' Did Heaven like to sop her corn pone in pot liquor, Angel Girl? I know I love to sop me some pot liquor. Ma'am, I'm is hungry all the time these days. You think I could be in the family way?"

I flew in disgust in search of Mother Magdalen. It hurt to be near her, but at least she always heard me.

I found my mother just forcing herself through Mammy Water's rag door. The reek of Mammy

Water's shack held new meaning for Mother Magdalen, and this was difficult for her. She entered with guilt, her head bowed. Hadn't she been through this before? I, too, had died while left in her care.

I folded my wings and drifted in behind her. Resentment brushed away sympathy. Resentment anchors the one who dies to those who will survive.

"Murderess," I whispered to her. She had taken another daughter in my place while I lingered, less than dead and far from living.

Mother jerked her head toward me. Then she looked away and shook her head as if to empty it. She always heard me. She always shook it from her.

"I let her die," Mother said aloud. "I let you die." Pity moved me. I drew close and swept my wings about her.

"She died the night Heaven came back home. She died for Heaven. She died for Solace. Look how she waited, how she has decayed, Mother. She was waiting to die."

Chill and snow had preserved the cadaver. Occasional fires hastily lit to warm and light the dreary shack had not thawed the body. But the warmth of spring and summer now revived the rot and vermin that would eat away at the corpse.

Mother gave herself to my comfort. Comfort raises hope. She reached beneath the ragged burlap that covered Mammy Water's corpse to feel if there might still be a pulse.

Mammy Water's withered fingers closed on Mother's wrist. The dead body used the strength in Mother Magdalen's pulling away to lift itself up.

Mammy Water's corpse sat up and lifted eyelids above flattened sockets to look at Mother Magdalen.

Darkness and the recesses of an emptying skull are tempting to the weary. I felt the curving maze of Mammy Water's skull pull Mother Magdalen inside.

Heaven might pull anyone who dared to challenge her dancing death into the skull's twisted turns. But I, cursed to wander life's glassy reflection, still needed my mother alive.

Solace would need her, too, when the sharefarmers followed Sami away. Heaven must not take my mother, yet.

"Mother, death is a long journey in a dark tunnel, if you're lucky. If not, its brightness scorches your eyes until you wish you could not see, and burns your heart until you no longer remember what it was to feel anything but remorse. Resist it, Mother."

Mother Magdalen shook her head and broke her gaze from the skull's sockets. She suddenly seemed to notice the glowing little pieces of bone that made a bracelet around her wrist.

Mother screamed and jerked her arm away. It did not come free of the skeleton's grip.

"Let her go, Heaven," I said.

Heaven swung the skull's face toward me. A layer of loose dry flesh fell from the neck.

The sockets sucked at me, inviting me to lose my loneliness in them. Heaven worked at the body's shriveling lungs and rigid throat. She pushed airy, gasping noises out through the mouth cavity. Up and down went the jaws still full of white teeth, their clicks echoing in the throat.

Mother Magdalen screamed and jerked her arm again.

"Angel," the corpse wheezed, "lonely. Look. Come."

"I am looking, Heaven."

Mother Magdalen's eyes searched wildly around the dark shack.

"Heaven, I have seen a bleak time for this plantation. Your daughter will need my mother's care. Solace. Leave my mother for Solace. If you must have someone, take me. I want to get lost in that endless fleeing. Look at me. I come willingly."

I spread my wings in hopeless triumph. How could Heaven take me? Death had denied me.

Heaven turned Mammy Water's skull to the wall and let the air wheeze from its slack jaws. The body slumped back onto its pallet, thinly wrapped bones clattering as they fell.

Mother watched the corpse and struggled to her feet. She swayed in the stale air, still looking around and rubbing her reddened wrist.

Then she hurried from the shack, her skirt sweeping dust into little spirals in the sunlight.

I was left staring at the only friend who had abandoned me in my exile. "Fool to refuse the refuge of death. Heaven, you could have been gone from here by now."

I drew my wings closer about my bleeding image and floated from the shack, careful to touch nothing. I would have nothing to do with Heaven's defiling of the death for which I longed.

Each day, Heaven lay and gathered strength to force Mammy Water's corpse through its nightly dance.

Each night, I held the slumbering Solace in my sliced and bleeding arms and sang to her. She learned to coo for me. The sweet sound healed me. I thought I saw wounds close.

We sang to each other as the corpse danced. Sometimes I carried Solace to a window, where I might see her maddened mother.

Mammy Water's corpse shuffled to its nightly dances wearing a faded rag wrapped around its hips and falling to its ankles. The cloth was wrapped tightly enough and knotted at the top, so that it did not shake loose from the dwindling skeleton.

Each night, the dance became more horrible. Flesh fell under Heaven's careless use. First the feet were scraped bare in rolling clumps. Then the flapping arms waved shredded flesh like rags. The body turned and dipped in Heaven's abandon, and the dancing thighs rubbed their wisps of flesh away against Mammy Water's wrapped waistcloth. Bones jerked, and skin ripped from dried ligaments fluttered to earth. At last the damp insides, clinging in webs to the pelvis and ribs, fell away in shreds.

The face and firm breasts were the last to fall. The people and I watched the gleaming ribs topped by dried firm breasts turn and turn. Only the decay of her hair was hidden from us. Mammy Water's head remained covered by a thin wound rag. We watched the lost beauty of Mammy Water's face turn and turn beneath the changing moon.

Baby Solace was indeed as white as snow. But she had Mammy Water's African face.

Solace grew lips as full and defined as dark rose petals beneath her rounded nose. Solace's

293

cheeks rose and her eyes opened long and wide, as had the living Mammy Water's.

Solace was Mammy Water's beauty born in its enemy's image. Someone had raped the newly captured Mammy Water. I had watched and mourned as Heaven's prison guard raped Heaven.

And yet, all that misery produced Solace. Horror runs from beauty, and to it again.

Uncle Dennis believed that Whip Man was Solace's father.

When Heaven could no longer hide her pregnancy, Uncle Dennis scourged Whip Man for disgracing her. Heaven beat against the windows that kept her from her hanging, bleeding lover. She had to be carried from the bloodied glass to the bed where birth and death awaited her.

It might have been best if Whip Man had not survived this second scourging. He was hideous to see. His wife nursed him, as he couldn't open his whip-scarred mouth to eat. Sister came to their shack to hold the baby as the father nursed. His survival was another ugly miracle.

When Uncle Dennis returned to the plantation, he did not wish to see Mammy Water's breasted bones dancing around her small fire. Sami insisted. Uncle Dennis walked behind him, his eyes squinted under the brim of his hat. I left the sleeping baby Solace to follow them to the scene.

Women had learned that the dancing skeleton stopped to circle the first fire it found. No one wanted the dancing death to circle the quarters. So they had gotten into the habit of lighting a low fire outside Mammy Water's rag door as the sun set.

Children and babies were hustled out of the dancer's eyeless sight.

When her gleaming finger bones poked through the rags and caught moonlight, the fire was already leaping.

I drifted close behind Uncle Dennis. "Your plantation is death. To stay here is death." I let the breeze of my slowly beating wings chill him.

He shuddered in the fire-lit night. "What can this mean?"

"I don't know," Sami said, searching the crowd for sight of Rose White. He did not want her here to see this sight. He had a vague dread of what it might do to their unborn child.

Rose White, instead, had the enslaved woman's thirst to understand. She came and contemplated the mysteries of the death dance every night.

All the women watched, wondered, and waited. While they did, I left to gather Solace again to my beating lifeless heart.

Bodies and souls shape each other. Good or evil.

As nights passed, women noticed the corpse no longer reached toward her watchers in Mammy Water's gestures of sharing visions and power.

The corpse became more frenzied. Its mindless dance, in turn, drained Heaven of her own fragile innocence.

The death dance became the dance of our lives, at the plantation. Who was the slave, and who the enslaver? What would become of the freedom now promised by Sami?

Uncle Dennis fled and bought a house in town. He married a wealthy widow, as he had always threatened my mother he might. He returned to the plantation to leave Sami carefully-worded freedom papers he spent a full night drafting in Mother's back room.

In the morning, he confronted Rose White. "I could have sent patrollers with hounds out after your sister."

"I know."

"I didn't free her."

Rose White tried to look defiant, as Rose Red would have wanted to. "I ain't thought you would."

"She can't leave with you and Sami. I haven't willed her to him. She's still mine."

I flew down behind Rose White and whispered, "She was never his." Rose White turned so that her face settled into my shoulder. I raised my arms around her. "Rose Red is safe," I said.

Most of the freed people left with Sami and Rose White for their new faraway property, where death would not be dancing. They were to be called hired hands now. Boyfriend, however, followed a wolf call into the woods.

Sami abandoned Whip Man and his family to starve or survive as they might on the fallow plantation, watching Heaven dance.

Mother Magdalen stayed to tend my grandparents' graves, to care for Girl, and to wait for Solace's footsteps to sound in the house one day. She stayed to feel me near.

As Sami and Rose White's carts pulled away, my soul flew to its bright grave in the mirror.

Mother Magdalen covered my mirror with a black silk cloth. "Enough. Rest, Angel. It is time to rest."

I woke to find myself shut inside the mirror.

Did my mother mean to deprive me of escape? Or did she mean to free herself of my suffering?

I beat my thick useless wings against the black silk shroud my mother used to seal my soul's glass coffin. I shrank back with my sliced arm over my eyes to shield them from the world inside the glass. I was pulled into my murder again and again.

I lived on the outer edge of my death, dying, falling, and waiting, floating face up to the blinding light that terrorized my glass prison.

I thought, Will I never be freed again? Why did my mother do this to me?

I drew to the soft black veil and called out before the light sucked me again into the mirror.

I fell into a bright pit of despair.

Then, one day, voices drew me from my misery.

Women's voices. Mother. And someone I didn't know.

I came straight up to the mirror's face and pressed my fingers to its blackened surface. I breathed as living people breathe. It fogged the glass a little.

"See me," I called to the stranger. "Save me. Unveil me. I will give you gifts no one else can give you."

"What is under that cover, there on the wall?" the stranger asked my mother.

"Just a mirror," my mother said. "Please, Miss, don't unveil it. It has seen sad things."

The woman had drawn close. I felt her warmth. I saw her breath stir my mirror's black veil.

"Lift the cover," I urged her. "See yourself as you have always wanted to be seen."

"It has seen murder," Mother said.

The woman laughed. A bright sound. I drew back against its light. "Oh. That old superstition. Why, that hardly-" She was going to say that hardly made sense. I didn't care how she dismissed my torment if she freed me.

"Lift the veil," I said again.

I cupped my hands with the full light of my prison and raised them, brimming, to the glass.

When she lifted the black veil, light flowed through her eyes, her skin, her teeth, her hair. She seemed a magical creature to herself.

She stared at her reflection in my eyes.

"You are beauty," I told her.

"Beauty," she repeated after me. "I might have married better, you know, Magdalen. Not that I would have you repeat this to Master Dennis. I know he wed me for my money. I wanted his family's old name. But I might have married for love."

She stopped and turned in confusion toward my mother. "Oh." She put her fingers to her lips as if to silence them.

She needed beauty. We would trade her beauty for my freedom.

I tried to fly through the glass. My wings hit against it. I was too weak. How long had I been imprisoned?

I flew to the glass and sought the lady's gaze. "Why, most of the furnishings in this room are quite valuable. I'll have them moved immediately to my townhouse. Oh." She touched gloved fingers to her lips as if to silence them. "I do mean, of course, to Solace's house."

She faltered. "You know, I understand poor Master Dennis's ambitions for her. She is so pale that I myself have taken to calling her Snow White. But with Dennis gone, I can't protect her from what she is by birth and blood. It will be best for her to return here, until such time as we learn what has become of Master Dennis."

Solace? My mind searched and found a young woman lonely and softened with that wash of sadness that made vulnerable girls so appealing.

Solace. Coming here? And would my mirror be unveiled and waiting when she arrived?

At sundown, my mirror was loaded into the widow's waiting carriage. She held it on her lap and gazed into its depths throughout the jolting ride back to town.

"How lovely," she murmured to me.

"Yes, how lovely you are in me."

I didn't see Solace until she was sent to the plantation. She came into the widow's room in dripping rags like Mammy Water's.

I shed my love about her. I poured rays of light upon her from my glass.

The widow tossed the black silk over Solace's reflection. I cried out as the veil settled again over my mirror, swallowed again into the mirror's belly of light.

My mind was burned free of all thought as I fell into the glare of the mirror's pit. I floated again in its bright agony, waiting.

As always, time was lost to me.

Until I was pulled again to the mirror's calm surface.

The lady stood before me, drawing away the veil and searching for a glimpse of her lost beauty. I cupped the light she sought and poured loveliness upon her. She smiled and gave herself over to the enchanted vision.

Her hunger fed me. I would grow stronger, I told myself. Might I not become stronger, eating her need, than I had ever been?

And then what steps might I not take to free myself of both my mirror and the reliving of my murder?

I stretched my wings behind the glass and searched with my eyes for glimpses of the world beyond. I ate the lady's adoration day and night, as she preened before me. I drank her trembling joy.

"What shall I do with my hair today?" I poured golden light to glint among the strands. "What shall I wear?" I gilded her bare body with my prison's glow.

I devoured her need without pity. She grew weak and anxious. I grew stronger. My murder faded from me.

I drew to the mirror's pane and peered outside. No blood marked my fingers' passing along the glass. Was I somehow freed of the murder that had trapped me here?

Murder. Betrayal.

The widow came to me in excitement about her new lover. "What shall I say if my lover asks tonight?" She wanted me to scatter shards of wicked light to sparkle in her eyes. I painted, instead, the images of bloody murder in bright spinning pools upon the glass.

This new man would destroy us both.

The widow wished to see nothing in my mirror but her beauty. When I withheld it and showed only the other, deadly vision, she grew frantic.

She leaned close and withdrew, cursing me. Her eyes darted over the mirror's surface, studying the scene of her lover's betrayal even as she denied it. Enraged, the lady covered my glass again with the veil.

I swirled in the blinding lights but flapped my strengthened wings to rise above despair. I closed my eyes against visions of Mr. Jared's knife, returning. I would not be trapped forever in my own murder because this lady denied hers.

I would fly to the mirror's edge and wait for the veil to be removed for the last time.

"Mirror? Mirror? Am I no longer fair?" A trembling voice pulled me from floating in my pain. The veil slid in ripples to the carpet. I heard its hushed rustle as it landed. I made my voice rustle like the whisper of silk on wool.

I flew forward. My wings lifted and fell, waiting. I smiled through the light.

"Come," I whispered to the widow. She leaned in close. Her nose grazed the glass. Tears smudged as she moved.

"Come," I insisted. I beat my wings and surged silently forward. "Come into the lovely light." I pressed my fingers through the glass.

The tips emerged on her side, sparkling and silver. Her eyes flew wide.

"Come live in my light," I said, pushing my arms through the mirror. "Come to this shining world. Reach in."

I beat behind the glass with my strong wings. The current drove me further forward and lifted the lady's wisps of hair about her face.

She closed her eyes. I caught her in my shimmering hands. "Come into my light. Come into your loveliness. Here is your joy."

I gripped her body. We surged back into the mirror on the pull of my beating wings. The widow broke through the glass with a rush like blood and water at childbirth.

She spilled through the silvery pane against me.

I let her fall from my hands. I rushed past her through the rippling glass. My wings scraped the silver frame. My hands flew to cover my face. Heat and light and shivering cold swept past me and through me.

I fell forward and lay still, my eyes squeezed shut.

Had I broken free?

Everything around me was still and silent. The mirror's blinding lightness was gone. Heaviness enfolded me.

I opened my eyes. I saw my body, whole and clothed in the white nightdress in which I had been murdered, stretched on the flowered carpet.

I rose to my knees. The weight of my wings pressed my back so that I swayed on my hands and knees. I turned to look back into the glass.

I breathed deeply and watched my wings stir. The air they moved fanned my face and lifted me to my feet.

I faced the mirror, and the face I saw reflected there was my own. A calm smooth oval, my face, but more serene than in life.

I gazed at the flowing lines of my unbroken body in the glass. Where were the bleeding slices, opening and shutting like mouths to tell on Mr. Jared, my maker and my murderer? Sealed? Healed. No trace of them left. Not even scars.

Could I at last be done with dying?

I spread my glistening many-feathered wings. They filled the room. Sky colors in my wings fanned out around me.

I floated above the floor. I looked down at my body. Was it truly solid?

I beat my heavy wings. They shot me forward toward the silver-framed glass.

I lifted a fist and slammed it down on the mirror's face. Pain raced from my fist up my arm.

I withdrew. Jagged cracks broke the glass's surface. I floated backward through the room until I saw my whole reflection in the splintered mirror. I was radiant with a light that shone from inside me.

I glided to a window and shoved it open on the night sky. Stars. A crescent moon, hooked like the arm that holds a sleeping child.

I looked down in the softly lit darkness to my body. It still glowed. I had an inner light, as if I had swallowed the mirror's glare and escaped.

"So this is how angels are made," I said.

I gazed at my glowing skin in starlight and wondered if it is the blood of angels that heals.

CHAPTER TEN
WANDER THE WIDE HEAVENS:
SOLACE, BORN 1804

I was happy when I left step-grandmother's house in town.

I only knew the town house. Grandfather told me of the plantation when I was small and he used to visit. His eyes would fill with water and sad longing. He looked away from me, in our fashionable parlor, into a place where his heart was still soft.

That was when I was allowed to sit in the parlor as my step-grandmother taught me to be a lady. Only when grandfather was home.

He was rarely home. His visits were great occasions for both of us, step-grandmother and me.

She would dress in her rustling satins and laces and perspire in the shaft of afternoon sunlight streaking rays upon her favorite velvet chair in the parlor. Sweat would bead on her upper lip and drip into the aromatic tea in a lavishly flowered cup.

She would smile and show grandfather her self-control.

I was allowed into the parlor in flounced dresses of pink satin and white lace. I was served creamy teacakes on a wrought silver platter. I held them on a tiny painted china plate that matched step-grandmother's teacup and wiped my lips with a lace-trimmed napkin. I saw the splendors of grandfather's travels as he spoke.

My favorite place to visit in grandfather's memories was his plantation. He had not been there since I was a baby. But the place claimed his love. He always wished he might go back. He said so whenever he came home to us.

I had never set foot outside the townhouse except to hang laundry in the cobbled patio behind the cook's kitchen. I might have wished to go anywhere. But loyal to grandfather, I, too, wished to go nowhere except to his plantation.

When grandfather was gone again I was returned to the attic where all the maids slept, in dresses sewn from cloth too stained or tattered to make good cleaning rags. I would dream of grandfather's visits and his promise that his plantation would one day be mine.

In my dreams, grandfather would come again and lift me in his strong arms and hold me to his neck that smelled of sharp sweet cologne. He would laugh deep in his chest and tell me the wonderful things he loved about me. He would carry me away to his beautiful plantation, where I would sing in the parlor the lullabies I'd learned from the African maids.

I kept one lullaby in mind. Grandfather had sung it with me in one of our parlor visits.

Step-grandmother had left the room to see why our tea tray was late in coming. I was so happy to have grandfather with me, and step-grandmother gone, and a lovely lace dress on, and teacakes coming, that I began to kick my shiny leather shoes so that the big black bows on top flounced, and I sang my special lullaby.

Grandfather smiled. When step-grandmother returned, frowning but silent, I stopped singing.

Grandfather said, "Where did you learn that song, Solace?"

Step-grandmother looked at me quickly. She did not like Africans to sing in the parlor. Africans were not to eat teacakes, nor wear satin and lace, nor sing so that gentlemen might clap for them when they were done.

Step-grandmother always spoke as if it were a bad thing to be an African. But I was pleased. If I were African, I would not have to grow up to be like step-grandmother.

"I don't know where I learned that song, Grandfather."

"You must have remembered it from the plantation," he said. "Though I don't see how you could've. You weren't even old enough to talk when I brought you away." He looked suddenly quite sad. "There was a woman at the plantation who sang that song," he said.

Step-grandmother said, "Are you telling the child about a nigger woman, Dennis? For I am not at all sure that it is good for her to hear about the habits of nigger women. Despite her fair skin, her natural inclinations are already resisting my best efforts to help her become a lady."

"Of course, my dear. You must excuse me." He was silent a while. But as I selected the very creamiest teacake from the tray, I heard him whistle my lullaby.

"Dennis, I fear your travels have affected your memory of polite behaviors. One does not whistle in the presence of a lady."

"Of course not, my dear." By the time I bit into my cake, he had begun to whistle again.

Step-grandmother left the parlor without asking to be excused. She did not return. So grandfather and I sang the lullaby in harmony together. He described to me the lovely African women at the plantation for the rest of that afternoon.

I was always pleased when step-grandmother left me alone to entertain grandfather. They rarely got along. I feared she would one day drive him away.

He began to visit us less and less often. And then he never came back.

Step-grandmother began to wear heavy black satin dresses. She spoke to men in black suits whose tall hats had been handed to me at the front door.

I waited at the entrance to the parlor. I listened to their talk about courts and judges and laws. I held their long high black hats and searched their faces for a sign that they knew grandfather was a good man and his loss to us was a terrible thing. They grinned and bowed to step-grandmother and showed no sign.

Sometimes I stood in the front foyer and stared at the closed massive front door. I willed grandfather to come through it and catch his wife and these men plotting his legal death. I stared at the door while tears bathed my face from not blinking. I called grandfather with my mind and my memories of our long lovely talks in the parlor. I called him from the paddleboats, steamboats, and pony trails to come home to me.

This never brought grandfather back.

I was very pleased when I learned I would be going to the plantation. I would have liked to have owned it, as the gentlemen in black hats said grandfather willed. But step-grandmother assured me, throwing a veil over a silver-framed mirror she'd stolen from my plantation, that Africans shouldn't own colonial property. Laws were changing because Africans were only fit to work the land for Englishmen, and even that had to be forced out of them. Africans were naturally lazy and inept, step-grandmother explained. All the newest sciences said so.

None of this explained why she hid the mirror she'd stolen from my plantation. "I wish I might own the farm, since that is what grandfather willed. But even if I may not, I will work day and night to make it productive for him again, as he remembers it."

"You may make it productive for me. It is I who have had the care of you all these years. It has not been easy. Your grandfather abandoned us both and is no more."

I spread my rag skirts and curtseyed. We-or rather, step-grandmother-had everything grandfather owned. How could we-she-complain?

And I was sure grandfather wasn't dead. If he were, all the hope would have gone out of my world. But it hadn't. Yet.

I was bursting with happy hope when I was handed into step-grandmother's carriage to be driven to the plantation. The day was gray and dark inside the house. Candles and fires had to be lit for work to be done and for visiting gentlemen to be greeted.

I was no longer allowed to claim the gentlemen's hats at the front door. A very special friend of step-grandmother's had said to me that I was an extraordinary beauty and had asked her my price, kissing her hand.

Step-grandmother's eyes had flown to me, waiting in the door with the gentleman's hat, and raked my body up and down. I felt my rags, already a disgrace in comparison to the other maids' neat simple dresses, to be no clothing at all.

Another woman was called to hold the gentleman's hat until he was ready to leave. And I was made to stay well out of sight from then on, cleaning in the kitchen when gentlemen called.

So my leaving for the plantation was delayed from morning until teatime, due to my having to hide in the kitchen from step-grandmother's flow of gentlemen callers.

My face burned with eagerness by the time step-grandmother's coachman handed me into her carriage.

"Happy, Miss?" He gave me a tender smile.

I was too excited to be ladylike. "Oh, yes, Mr. Tim. Very happy."

Step-grandmother said she was through allowing me to pretend that I could ever be more than a common nigger wench. So grinning at the carriage driver was probably all right now.

No one was at the door to wave good-bye to me, as step-grandmother always did with her most special visitors. Never mind that, I told myself. I waved to the empty doorway, pretending the maids had come out.

When I arrived at the plantation, I would pretend that grandfather himself stood on the verandah stairway to wave me home. And if there were no verandah stairway? Well, he would just have to wave me in from the road.

I settled into the coach to enjoy my very first view of the town where I had been raised.

The buildings were enormous and all different. They were made of bricks, and more rarely, stone, like grandfather's townhouse, or of neatly planked wood, like the attic room. They were grand and tall, with flowers and trees neatly trimmed before them. Or they were small and seemed broken in odd places.

Women and men and children walked and ran the streets in a hurried freedom I would never have imagined. They seemed very determined to get somewhere. It was impossible to believe that they each had someplace to go. I had never had anywhere to go.

I leaned from the carriage window and stared shamelessly.

Africans and those who were not African mingled strangely. They walked head on toward one another until they nearly met on the wooden boards of the sidewalk. Then, with a shallow bow of courtesy, the Africans would step quickly into the street until the others had passed. Their faces never lost their busy, pleasant expressions.

Some of the Africans were dressed much more elegantly than the people for whom they stepped into the street's churning mud. All this sidestepping had left their clothes mud-splattered. Step-grandmother would never have stood for having to splatter her gowns for grubby strangers.

But then, few people on the streets were dressed as grandly as step-grandmother dressed every day. Even fewer of them were dressed as poorly as I.

I looked down at my rags and blushed to see how my thighs shone through the threadbare cloth. Why had I never noticed? "I suppose one gets used to things," I said to comfort myself. But I withdrew from the carriage window. I hated wondering if the people outside might be watching me, as I watched them. I didn't like to think how I must look.

To cheer myself, I began to sing the forbidden lullaby. I must have sung myself to sleep.

I woke in thick darkness. I spread my hands out around me. I could feel that I was still in step-grandmother's carriage. It wasn't moving. We had stopped.

"Mr. Tim?" He didn't answer.

If we had arrived at our destination, it was odd that I had been left sleeping in the carriage. I thought with disappointment of having missed my vision of grandfather waving me home to his plantation.

I worked at the latch on the carriage door until it gave. The door swung sharply away from my hand and opened.

Thick trees all around. Birds chirping and fire crackling. Rustling and snapping along the ground. I was surrounded by barking, chattering, twittering animals, new sounds lively and confusing to me.

I took a long step from the carriage to the ground and looked around.

Green billowed up from the dark earth all around me. It rose toward the sky where it blocked out the light. Or was night falling?

There was the small fire. The coachman looked up from it as I drew near. He frowned. Smiled. "You won't starve, Miss Solace. I seen to that. This boar here should feed you good for tonight. The master old plantation should be that a way." He pointed.

Mr. Tim stood and hoisted my satchel from the ground. It looked odd. I came closer to see it in the crowding green darkness. It was caked with what looked like blood and mud in a red brown mix.

"What have you done to my satchel, Mr. Tim?"

He shook his head and pursed his soft lips. "Child, you don't know half the trouble you in. Listen to me good, now. You eat what you can off this here wild pig, and then you hightail it off in that there direction." He pointed where he had before. "You going find the plantation, if you keep running and don't look back nor stop to fret."

He bent toward me, as people do with children. "Now, I done always heard you was a brave little gal that don't cry for the meanness some folks do to you. Tonight ain't the night for crying, Missy. Tonight the time for running till you get where you be safe. You hear me? I done already took so long out here, shooting and cooking that there wild pig, the widow going be wondering whether or not I done like she told me with you. And I ain't. So I best hurry back to town and make my lies look good."

Confusion. Understanding scraped at its edges. "Please don't leave me here."

"I got to leave you to protect you, girl."

"Why, Mr. Tim?"

He sighed. Lifted his cap. Rubbed his scalp as if to relieve a headache. "Listen here, and be a big girl. The widow don't want you to make it to that plantation, child. I was suppose to take you just to the edge of the trees and-" He looked away from me. He frowned again. Then he said, "Look a here. Don't never try to go back to the widow. Don't never try to write her nor ask her for one blamed thing. Be glad you alive, and let her believe you dead."

I backed away from him. That was a word I had never thought of for myself. "Dead?"

"Yes, Miss Solace."

Eager to claim my grandfather's plantation and make it productive fore him again, what had become of me?

Even as I asked myself, I knew. Step-grandmother had planned to be free of me. Grandfather was gone for good. If I disappeared in the woods, who would question it?

"I'll need my satchel, Mr. Tim. It has my free papers grandfather wrote and, well, you know, sir, personal things." My face burned, but I held out a steady hand.

"Sorry, Miss. The widow wants something of yours to come back to her beat and bloody. Proof you died. I thought you could stand to lose this here sack better than-" He nodded toward my ragged dress.

I pulled away from him as if he had reached for it.

"Better to lose your free papers than your life, Miss Solace. The widow can't live forever. Someday, who knows?" He walked to the carriage

313

and slung my muddied, bloodied satchel inside. He hoisted himself up to his high seat and snatched up his reins. "Get up!" he said to the horses and flicked his whip above their heads.

The carriage had trouble turning on the wild country road. The horses reared and whinnied and bucked, frightened by the strange scents and threatening predatory sounds. Mr. Tim lost his scowl as he calmed them.

I ran along beside the rearing horses and pleaded to be taken along. I had never begged for anything as I begged not to be left in the darkening, crowding woods, alone.

Mr. Tim never looked at me again until he had the carriage turned and ready to head back toward town. He pointed his whip at the roasting boar on the fire. "Fill your belly good on that pig, now." He pointed his whip away toward the thickening trees. "Then head that a way. Don't you fritter away no more time jabbering in the dark at me, gal. You ain't free no more. Patrol find you, you going wish I had a did what I was told to do to you. Don't you be too backward to get my meaning. Now, get."

He flicked the whip so it snapped. The horses leaped forward, and the carriage lurched behind them and rolled on. They clattered down the road.

I stood watching and let sobs shake me. What had I done to deserve this? How would I ever find my way? I looked where Mr. Tim had pointed.

Could one actually walk between these trees on the treacherous mud, blanketed by nothing more sturdy than soft moss? I had always walked on carpets and floorboards.

I backed away from the roasting boar. Its gelled eyes stared at the woods' green ceiling. Its bristles burned, and the smoke stank. Its tusks curled the blackening lips into a snarl. Grease leapt from between the sizzling teeth.

I turned toward the plantation and ran.

It was easy to kick up sticks and flecks of mud in the dash across the narrow beaten road. After that, nothing was easy.

Trees loomed above me and tilted in upon me as though they would fall. They waved and crowded closer together when I tried to pass between them. Often I covered my eyes and ran blindly, or I could not have kept running.

I fell. Vines along the ground rose and twisted about my ankles. The heavy wooden clogs I wore rubbed my toes and raised blisters. They popped and ran inside the clogs.

I don't know when I kicked the clogs to the coiling vines and left them behind. I felt the wild woods close upon my torn feet.

As I ran, I thought, *Step-grandmother hates me. I'm not safe in her home. I'm not safe in the woods. Maybe I won't be safe at the plantation.*

Maybe I won't find the plantation.

I went on stumbling and falling and untangling myself from dangling vines and humped roots to run again while night dropped its sudden black blanket.

I ran until I couldn't see. Then I fell onto something sharp and bumpy and sat. I stared into a darkness that had no limit.

Had the ground before me fallen away? I suddenly no longer trusted that the ground would be there, if I stood and put out a foot. If I moved from this spot, I would surely fall into nothingness, like sky. I put my face on my arms and cried.

"Miss Solace?"

What was that?

"That you weeping, Miss Solace? Answer me, child."

The voice drew closer. I looked up.

In the black that softened the harsh shapes of the forest, I could just make out a figure bent over itself like a bush, carrying a barely lit taper. It rolled as it moved toward me.

Bushes don't have feet, I thought rather wildly. *That's why it has to tumble and roll so.*

I stood. I kept my eyes on the hunching, rolling, speaking bush.

"Miss Solace? That you, girl? Answer me, now."

I opened my mouth. Wind sucked noisily down my throat but did not come out again. I had no voice.

I felt myself sink. I fell to the muddy cushioning ground. Tired, I thought. Hungry. Frightened. Tea. Something to eat.

The forest went away.

Warmth lifted me. Bunched muscles worked under my belly. Someone was carrying me.

I opened my eyes and found myself flopped over a bent back. My body curved around the sudden rises on the back of the creature that carried me.

I raised myself, my hands on its back. I could see the back and side of a cloaked head, no face, but the light of the taper that glowed beyond the hood.

It held me with a broad arm to its rolling muscles as it stalked through the woods.

I looked all around in panic. There were no trees beside and behind us. But ahead, I saw tiny houses like chicken shacks and one big house.

The creature stopped and turned its head toward me. The hood covered its head and most of its face. It held the taper on the other side of its head away from me, so that the light fell into my face.

A scraping, whispering voice came from inside the hood. "You come to, Miss? You want I put you down now?"

I stared into the empty hood so hard my eyes hurt around the edges. I was alone in the woods with a talking monstrous thing. "Help!"

I hammered the monster's shoulders and back with my fists. I struck its humps. The edge of one hand caught its hood. The light behind the creature's head streamed forward across the side of its face.

Thick coils of skin roped over each other and curved around the creature's staring eye. The skin glowed and darkened in the light as though it were made of rusted iron.

We stared at each other. "Miss Solace."

I screamed.

He must have let me go. I slid from his shoulder and took off running across a field of prickly thistles that snagged at my rag dress. Sharp things stabbed into my oozing feet.

"Miss!" The muffled voice was always close behind.

Firelight off to one side, among the shacks. I could make out flickering flames and one moving shape. I ran toward it. "Help me."

The creature shouted from behind, "No, Miss Solace." I had nearly reached the big house when I stopped to stare at the figure moving before the stone-rimmed fire.

This could not be.

The creature that turned to me now was nothing but yellowed bones stacked loosely above each other. It clattered rhythmically as it moved in a slow stomp dance. When the dancer circled between me and the fire, I could see the fire leap in the spaces between the bones.

The dancer had once been a woman. As she danced, she kept touching the fine bones of her fingers to the knots that held her ragged turban and wrapped skirt in place.

I felt the warmth behind me of the humped creature I had tried to escape. "Miss Solace," it said at my ear, "come away from here."

I grabbed handfuls of my hair and shook my head, trying to clear it. Something was wrong with me. I had fallen into a nightmare and must waken.

I screamed into the high black sky.

I woke with a throbbing in my head so heavy I could hear it in my ears. I squinted into the darkness.

I was in a darkened room, surrounded by the shadows of bulky furniture. I could make out two heavy posts at the foot of the bed where I lay, holding up a sagging canopy. The canopy leaned in toward me as though it must soon drop.

Thick drapes outlined a window. Only the barest silver light struggled through the filthy pane. A table and chairs with sides and legs carved like flower petals stood out in the window's meager glow. On the other side of the bed, I could make out more looming shapes, but not what they were.

The air was too close and heavy to breathe. It smelled of damp dust, rotted fabric. Something else decayed.

I coughed. I had never slept alone, or in the dark. I had to get out of that room. I had to get out of this house and find my grandfather's plantation.

I pulled back the heavy bedclothes. Damp and dust brushed my cheeks. I sneezed.

My bare feet swept the thick wool carpet on the floor. It hushed my steps. Ragged holes where moths had eaten snagged my toes. I stumbled.

Each time I fell forward on my hands, dust rose into my face. I coughed and wiped my face on the rags that used to be my skirt.

When I made it to the door, I found the huge latch rusted. I lifted and shoved it down with all my might until it gave way.

The crack as it opened echoed up and down the long silent hallway.

I pushed the door open wider and crept through the doorway to stand in the threshold. I turned this way and that to see where I should go.

At one end of the long corridor, I saw a pattern of stained glass cut in jagged, senseless patterns in the wall. I turned from it and moved toward the darker end of the hall. I felt my way along the walls. My fingers brushed framed portraits and mirrors hung with dusty cloth. Between them on the darkly glowing walls, sconces jutted into the hallway. I felt in the saucer of each sconce for flints and found thick candles draped with cobwebs and littered with brittle winged bodies.

My fingers gathered sticky cobweb threads that crackled as they pulled away from walls and sconces. I finally stopped to peel them, rustling and resisting, from my fingers. They clung to the wiping hand. I reached to wipe it on a wall.

I grazed another heavy frame and swung it forward. It settled back with a thump. As it settled, dust and chattering noises burst past me. Something scratched my cheek and snagged the tangles of my hair in passing. I heard the jerky flap of thin wings beating against my ear.

I grabbed into my hair and seized something soft. It drove pricks into my curled fingers. It squeaked and kicked and flapped in my hand.

It wriggled and clawed. I heard the roots of my hair pop from my scalp as I pulled.

When the thing and my hair were pulled free of my head, I threw it to the floor, the furred body and flapping skin squirming beneath my bare foot.

Tiny teeth daggered my foot until I jerked it free and ran on, still forced to feel with my fingers along the walls.

I rounded a bend in the hallway and nearly tumbled into empty space. I threw my hands out.

I landed on carpeted steps and slid. My fingers clutched a banister. The grab wrenched my shoulder but stopped my fall. I sat hard on curving steps that swept away below me.

I pulled myself back to my feet and stood, panting. My toes found the next step. Again. And again.

My hands slid along the wooden banister, gathering clumps of dust. Pocked carpet muffled the steps' creaking each time I eased my weight down.

Crackly cobwebs swept into my nose and eyelashes and clung as I descended. Wispy threads fluttered in and out of my nostrils as I breathed. I brushed at the cobwebs with my free hand as I went on.

Suddenly, I reached the bottom. There were no more steps. The banister curved away from my hand and ended.

Now where should I go? To one side was darkness. I had had enough of that.

To the other side was a circle of golden light. I went toward it.

I came into a room lit by a bellowing fire. From the rafters dangled tied bunches of drying plants and vegetables. Iron pots and skillets hung on the walls and from hooks in the ceiling. Clay bowls and wooden spoons seemed piled and stacked on the walls' many shelves. Sewing things and odd snatches of dusty ribbons, wooden combs, long knives, and tangled twine jammed the cooking utensils.

A fireplace lined with blackened stones nursed the blaze that drew me. A kettle nestled in the fire puffed steam from its spout.

There was a large wooden table in the room's center. Chairs with armrests opened wide and heavy benches ran along each side of the table and along the room's stone walls.

On the side of the table nearest a massive outer door, I saw a huddled figure.

It was cloaked in burlap, its head hooded so that I couldn't see the face inside the thick folds, the burlap bunched around the figure's shoulders and clutched at its neck. I saw no skin anywhere.

Could my dream of a dancing skeleton have been real? Was this the skeleton, hunkered down before me now? Or was it the monster who had carried me through the woods?

The figure turned the darkness of its empty hood toward me. "She here, Miss Magdalen. At the door."

I fell back, thinking to run from the room. But the firelight had blinded me. I couldn't see into the darkness I had just run from.

A hand caught my wrist.

"Let go!"

Another hand clamped my mouth. "Sshh," a woman's voice said.

The hands drew me close against a warm, soft body, and the woman spoke. "Miss Solace? Don't be afraid. What are you afraid of, child?"

I lifted a finger and pointed at the hooded figure. It still hadn't moved. But the way the blank space inside the hood remained aimed at me, I felt that it watched.

The woman swept her long eyes toward the hidden watcher. Purple shadows curved along her eyelids. "That man there? What makes you afraid of him?" She lifted her long hand a little from my mouth.

"It's a monster or a skeleton. I saw monsters. Strange things."

She threw back her head so her golden throat showed and laughed. She encircled me with both arms and hugged me. "He's neither. He's Whip Man. He was the dearest friend your mother ever had. You can't be afraid of him, baby."

322

She took my hand and led me into the room. The blank hood followed my movements. "Does she look like Heaven?"

The hood nodded. Once up. Once down.

She sat on one of the benches by the table and pulled me onto the seat next to her. We faced the empty hood. "You must be kind to Whip Man, Solace. Here, we all watch out for one another."

"There was a skeleton. I saw it. Dancing."

Sobbing sounds erupted from the hood. Its shoulders rocked with the force of its sorrow.

The woman said, "Oh, where are my manners? Solace, call me Mother Magdalen. Are you hungry, baby?" She started to rise but sat down again. She seemed hesitant to let go of my hand.

If she did, I was ready to run for that massive door beyond the shuddering hood.

She watched me. "How did you hurt your head?"

"Something in the hallway got tangled in my hair. I had to pull out hair to get away from it."

She clicked her tongue and shook her head. With her purple-lidded eyes still on me, she said, "Whip Man, maybe now that Miss Solace is here, we'll clean this place and fix it up."

The hood moved.

Mother Magdalen put her hands into my hair. "It's not bad. The scalp bleeds a lot for a little hurt. But did the bat bite you? That might be a sure sign of rabies. They are normally shy creatures. Now, you promise to sit tight, Solace, and I will get what I need to take care of this."

"Ma'am, how do you know my name?"

She laughed again as she got up. "Why, I helped name you, little one."

I brightened. "Really, Mother Magdalen? That means you must know the people at my grandfather's farm. You must know where it is. Can you get someone to lead me there? I'm sure they're expecting me."

Bent over a bucket in a corner, she looked back over her shoulder at me. Then she looked at the hooded figure. It had stopped its sobbing and shuddering and sat huddled in on itself. She said, "Solace, this is your grandfather's farm."

"No."

"Yes, child."

"Not Mr. Dennis's place."

"Yes. Mr. Dennis's place. Or rather, your place now."

"That's not possible."

"Why ever not?"

"I've always heard from grandfather about his plantation, and this isn't it at all."

Mother Magdalen came back to me with a clay bowl half filled with water, floating plants, and clean rags. She set them upon the table. "Your grandfather hasn't been here since you were a baby, Solace. Things change."

"Not like this." I pressed my hands to my face to fight back the pain of her cleaning and the sight of the hooded man.

This was it? The end of my lifetime of dreams?

She was saying, "Don't despair, dear. We can fix things up at least a little bit," when the heavy door behind the cloaked figure creaked open.

A woman's head, tightly wrapped in a clean faded turban, poked around the door's edge. She was a ruddy, pretty woman with a smile that shone. Sunlight spilled in through the open door upon her and around her. "So there you are, Whip Man. You still hiding out and eating Mother Magdalen good corn bread? Now you know I can't get that yoke on that boy by myself." Her voice held the familiar mix of chiding and doting that the maids at the townhouse reserved for men and little children.

Everything about this woman bathed in sunlight struck me as normal and comfortable in this weird and deathly place. Maybe she could make sense of what was happening to me. Maybe she would tell me where my grandfather's farm could really be found.

I rose to speak to her. She looked at me and caught her breath. I smiled. "Ma'am, if you would please tell me how to get to Mr. Dennis's plantation, I'd be so grateful. You see-"

I had pulled from Mother Magdalen's hands and reached the woman. She fixed her eyes on me in something that looked like shock until I was quite near.

Then she swung a sharp slap against my cheek. I staggered back and fell against Mother Magdalen.

The cloak said, "Rhea! Don't you never dare."

I stared, horrified, as the cloaked figure rose from its bench, enormous and bent at odd angles, to seize the pretty woman's arms. She struggled in its grasp and glared into the hidden depths of the hood. "You would raise your hand to me for her? After she ruin your life and mines, too?"

I cringed to the think she was staring straight into the monster's wrecked face.

It pulled her by the wrists through the massive doorway. It turned and blocked the sunshine to stare back at me one last time. Holding both her wrists in one wealed hand, it reached with the other to shut me and Mother Magdalen into the house.

I sank to a bench. "Why did she hit me?"

"Let me get you cleaned and dressed in something fit to be seen. You're the mistress of a large plantation now. We can't have you in rags." Mother Magdalen touched my head. I flinched away.

"Solace, there was a time when I loved to do a young girl's hair. Yours needs tending badly as any I have ever seen." She turned toward the stairway that led upstairs, saying as if to herself, "But I do not seem to have it in me anymore."

I sat alone and looked at the door that led outside. I couldn't think why this woman, this Mother Magdalen, would lie to me. But this couldn't possibly be the sweet place of grandfather's memories. I was just going to have to escape and find his place as well as I could. Surely the people at his plantation should be out looking for me by now.

I stood and went to the door. I grabbed it and heaved it open. It creaked.

I stared at the dust and cobblestones that glared in the sunlight. As far as I could see were splintered shacks like chicken coops and a weed-choked field beyond.

I couldn't even guess which way to go.

"What are you doing, Solace?" Mother Magdalen had returned to the room with a dark red dress crumpled in her arms.

I looked at her and tried to smooth the desperation from my face.

"I just thought I'd have a look at my property." I was in the habit of lying to step-grandmother. I was good at it.

"Well, you really should not be seen in those pieces of rags, Miss. So come in and let us get you washed and properly dressed."

She peeled the rag gown from my shoulders, and I held my hair as she washed my back with the rags and water she'd used on my bleeding scalp and the bat bites. Then she handed me the rag so that I might finish washing myself.

When I'd slipped my rag gown to the floor, she lifted it from around my feet and tossed it into her fire. She dressed my washed body in the dark red gown. "This was your mother's, Miss Solace." She buttoned it, and I watched it clutch and curve around my body.

The gown was musty and more than a little moth-eaten. But it was more beautiful than anything I'd been allowed to wear for years, ever since grandfather stopped visiting.

Mother Magdalen put a plateful of crumbling corn bread and a wooden mug of coffee on the table. "You haven't eaten, Miss Solace. The widow tried to have you killed, didn't she?"

"I think so, ma'am."

"I thought she would. That is why Whip Man went to search for you, when the day passed and you did not come. You are safe here." She hefted the bowl of dirtied water onto her hip. She pulled open the door and was gone.

Now was my chance.

I yanked the door open and stepped out. Dust rose around my bare feet. I blinked back the sharp sunlight.

When my eyes got used to the glare, Mother Magdalen was nowhere to be seen.

I began to walk. I might as well cross the field and get to the woods. Maybe I would stumble upon someone willing to tell me where grandfather's farm really was.

The path outside Mother Magdalen's back door carried me past a little cookhouse and garden with two small mounds on one side. Firm vegetables gleamed among the plump green leaves. Rose vines climbed from the garden over large pretty stones on the mounds and up the side of the outdoor kitchen.

Then I reached the shacks.

They were proof that this could not have been grandfather's plantation. He was a kind and good man. These houses could never have been livable.

They were tiny and built of thin splintered planks that had never seen paint. The shacks' doors stood open to reveal dirt floors. None had windows. Animal droppings littered the doorways. Square furrowed plots between the shacks, like fallow gardens, sprouted flowering weeds and wild greens.

Far to one side leaned a shack more weatherworn than the rest. Shreds of something filmy that might once have been rags flittered in the doorway without a breeze. The stone circle before the shack's doorway held the ashes and charcoal of a recent fire. The earth around the stones was well trodden.

Had I seen a dancing skeleton?

A spasm of fear shook me. I waited for it to pass. I must keep going. I could get away from here. I had daylight ahead of me.

I found myself before a broad field.

I could make out the shapes of three people. They all seemed to have turned to look at me. One was the hunched figure of Whip Man. Another, hands on the hips of her faded dress, was the woman he had called Rhea. The third was not Mother Magdalen, as I had feared.

It was a slender young man with a Y-shaped wooden plow tied by crisscrossed ropes to his back. The plow's rusted metal nose dove into the earth behind the young man's bare feet.

His body was tightly muscled and glowed bronze with a light coating of fresh sweat. He held the ropes away from his skin and watched me watching him. "Miss Solace?" he called out. "You hunting something out here, ma'am?"

I thought I should turn and run. But I came closer.

The young man' s face was like Miss Rhea's but took smoother turns at the cheeks and brow. His mouth looked soft, the lips puckered with smile pockets at the corners.

"Do you know me?" I called back.

Miss Rhea gathered the dim folds of her once-colorful skirt and ran from the field.

Hunching and limping, Whip Man followed her. He turned often to glance back at us and pull his hood low with a twisted hand. Dust rose and clung to the trousers that dangled beneath his burlap cloak. They disappeared as if swallowed by one of the shacks.

"Why does she hate me?" I asked.

"Cause a her babies," the young man said. I jumped a little at the deep softness of his voice up close. He looked at me and smiled. "You done cost her all her childrens but me."

I stared at him. The steady dark eyes never wavered. "I? How?"

"You don't even know what Mr. Dennis done left behind him here, does you? Well, it ain't hard to figure. Ain't nobody never told you how folks keeps a bull from calfing a heifer?"

"No. What does that have to do with your mother?"

"What? You mean it too, don't you?" He chuckled, and anger left his face. "Why don't you help me out this thing, and us leave my pap to figure my ma'am," he said.

His pap? He couldn't mean that Whip Man the monster was his father. Because he was beautiful.

I began to sweat. The drops trickling from my armpits tickled down my waist.

I moved close. I reached to touch the ropes burying themselves in his shoulder. My fingers touched his skin instead.

It was cool and smooth.

He said, "Slide them down over my shoulders."

I slid my fingers over the sloping muscles of the shoulder nearest me and on down his arm. When my fingers reached his, he took my hand.

I looked up at his face. His eyes were wide but steady. I had surprised him.

I had shocked myself.

What, what had I just done? Stroked the flesh of a stranger with pleasure and abandon.

I stumbled back. I covered my mouth with one hand. "I'm so sorry." What else could I say? "I'm really sorry." I backed away further.

"No, it ain't no problem, Miss Solace. Just-"

"No. I can't help you. I can't. I'll get Mother Magdalen." Weeds and stones cut into last night's burst blisters in my feet as I fled back toward the house I had just escaped.

A safe place to hide. From these people. From myself. From the world outside my grandfather's townhouse.

If only I could have died when he did. There was no place for me without him. There was no place for me anywhere.

What would become of me?

What had come over me? What was I becoming?

I reached the back door of the big house and heard Mother Magdalen call to me from the direction of the shacks. I yanked the door open and got it closed behind me before she reached me.

I kept running. Blindly, through the fire-lit back room, up the curving staircase and down the bent hallway, tripping with my toes jammed into carpet holes and clawing at shredded cobwebs that touched my face. When I stood again before the jagged lights of the stained glass at the end of the hall, I turned toward the door that stood open.

I hoped it was the room in which I'd wakened. I never should have left it. I stumbled inside and shut the door behind me.

A quiet dark space to be alone. Not clean and familiar like the attic. But I had lost the attic, and this room would have to do.

I leaned on the wall just inside the door and slid down to sit in the tightest ball my body could make. I wrapped my arms around my legs. My face pressed into the itchy wool at my knees.

Maybe I could sit here like this until somebody very kind found me and explained to me what had happened to my whole life and all my hopes and everything I wanted or knew about myself, in just two days.

How could I have touched that young man?

I tried to think of any young men I had ever met. If any of step-grandmother's callers had been young men, I hadn't been able to tell. Their bodies were covered in layers of cloth in all kinds of weather. They moved as if they fought for space against the air around them.

But this young man's body shone. His eyes and voice were tender. He laughed, even with that terrible yoke on his back.

The yoke!

I raised my face from my knees.

I had meant to get Mother Magdalen to help him out of the wooden plow. But I had run right by her without a word.

Now what would he think of me?

What must he think of me already? What could I have been thinking?

Of how he glowed. There had been no one, since grandfather disappeared, that I had wanted to touch so badly. Or wanted so to touch me.

Why should I wish a stranger would touch me?

Because I was lonely and frightened, and the dream of my life, coming to grandfather's plantation, was ruined. And I had no other dreams.

I should go back down and get Mother Magdalen to help him. I couldn't bear to go back down.

I stared into the room's darkness, as impossible to see through as my future. I bit a knuckle and shook my head.

What choices had I? I couldn't sit up here forever.

A light tapping sounded on the door next to me. I held my breath and waited for the tapper to go away.

"Miss Solace?" Mother Magdalen said. After she'd said it a few more times, the door worked its way slowly open.

I sat absolutely still.

The slender bulk of Mother Magdalen's shape came into the trickles of light that spattered the threshold from the stained glass in the hallway. Her silhouette moved its head, searching for me.

"Miss Solace?" she called again. She called several times. Then she backed from the room and closed the door.

I had just done another strange thing.

I had run screaming from Whip Man, whom everyone else treated as normal. I had tried to rush to Miss Rhea for comfort, when everyone else knew she hated me. Then I put my hands on a young man, naked to the waist, whose name I didn't even know.

And now I was hiding from Mother Magdalen, who had washed me, dressed me, and tried to feed me.

I wished I had eaten. I wished I were a part of these people's lives. I wished I had always known them and didn't find them strange.

How would I ever come to be a part of this place? How could they ever forget how oddly I had behaved my first day here?

Could I stop behaving strangely? Control myself? I couldn't even recognize myself. Get up and go tell Mother Magdalen to take that young man out of the yoke, I told myself. I didn't move.

The urge to get rid of yesterday's food and drink gave me brief sharp twinges. They went away. I dozed.

I woke with a need to stretch. The room was dark, as always. I wondered where a chamber pot might be. I put my hand on the floor to push myself up and clutched dust-balls.

Why did no one clean this house?

I groped my way to where I believed the room's solitary window to be and felt for the drapes. Lumps of dust and empty insect bodies floated onto my head as I tugged at the pull strings. I shook my head and brushed at the debris.

The drapes opened to lacy curtains. They were eaten through in places. They had once been very fine.

Night had fallen again. I peered at it through the window.

In starlight, willow trees and wildly flowered walkways curved below. The trees moved so that I could see two more mounds like the ones outside the cookhouse. But these had carved granite stones at one end instead of the river rocks all around I'd seen at Mother Magdalen's garden.

I turned from the window to search for a chamber pot.

I worked up my nerve to reach under the sagging bed. Lots of wispy things brushed my fingers. But here was something cool and curved. I pulled it out.

Success. A lidded chamber pot. I tried not to look inside it before squatting over it.

When I'd lidded the pot and returned it to its hiding place, I thought that the next day I might begin by cleaning this room and claiming it as my own. Perhaps people would be kind enough to pretend I hadn't acted such a nitwit, my first day here.

I could deny it no more. This dreadful place was indeed my grandfather's farm and my destiny.

It was the young man who'd convinced me. He'd named grandfather, out there in the field. "You don't even know what Mr. Dennis done left you here, does you?"

He had said it all. Could my grandfather possibly have known the state of decay I'd find when I'd finally inherited his plantation? The young man had understood my loss and confusion. It felt good to be understood.

I returned to the window and pulled aside the shredded lace to see outside. Full starlight softened the dipping willow leaves into shades of silvered green.

And in the silvered light, something moved.

What was that down there?

I pressed my nose to the musty lace and grimy glass. It passed under the willow trees and emerged near the carved granite stones.

A very large dog with hulking shoulder blades. It hunkered up onto one of the mounds, spread its large paws, and lifted its muzzle.

Its fur shone black and gold-tipped and bristled from its body. Its black-rimmed lips trembled open. It began to howl.

All the world's sorrow, and mine too, trailed in the wake of the dog's song. I put my fingers to the glass and leaned my forehead on the pane. The howl ended in rippling waves like sobs.

Its black-rimmed eyes turned fully upon me.

Could it see me? It seemed to stare. I stared back.

The beast lowered its head to the tall grass. The golden black bristles on its back rose and seemed to move as if in a breeze. The fur tightened, curled, seemed to lift away from the animal's skin.

The curls fell away to bare a long neck. The neck's brown skin flowed down, wrapping shoulder and back muscles that were rounded by hard work and whittled by lean eating.

The changed creature raised its head to me again.

I cried out and hid away from the window.

I had looked into the eyes of the young man in the field.

That could not be. I must have been mistaken. I moved to stand before the window again.

The young man sat in the deep grass. He held my gaze and raised an arm to rest it on his knee. He lifted his fingers and gestured, Come here.

I fled the window. I bumped into the bed, trying to get to the bedroom door.

No. Better not go out that door. Maybe I was safest in here. Could I hide? Where?

What had I just seen?

"Don't be scared," a voice said behind me.

I turned and bumped into a bedpost, backing away. Silhouetted in my doorway was the outline of the young man.

"Don't be scared, Miss Solace," he said again. "I got my trousers on, and I ain't coming in till you says I can."

His outline was cut sharply into the room's darkness. The stained glass seemed to be on fire behind him in the hallway.

I couldn't see his face. But I saw the smooth shape of his close-cropped head, the long muscles I had touched, and his chipped waist and hips.

Below the ragged fringe of his trouser legs, his ankles disappeared into the carpet. He had appeared so quietly. Were his feet still paws?

He came forward and stretched out a hand. "May I come in? Or will you come downstairs, Miss Solace? I know you ain't ate since you got here. I got you some squirrels roasting."

"Was that you outside my window?"

"Yes, ma'am."

"What-I mean-what are you?"

He laughed and shrugged a little. "A man."

"No. Was that a dog with you?"

"A wolf, Miss Solace. Why don't you come down eat? Everybody been looking for you all day. Everybody worried us done lost you already." He started toward me again.

"No."

337

He stopped. "Come on, Miss Solace. I ain't hurt you. I done waited all my life to see you come back here to the farm."

"All your life? For me? How could you have ever heard of me?"

He tilted his head to one side. "Shucks. I was raised on tales a you and what you going do for us all when you come back. Save the plantation and everything. You sit and eat with me, I tell you the work cut out for you round here." He laughed, his eyes still on me.

"Raised on tales of me?" I said. "That makes me feel old."

His hand reached mine. "Truth be told, I was surprised my own self to see a pretty young thing walking up here owning the place. But I ain't complaining." Did he never lose that light chuckle?

"But the wolf-"

"Don't be scared. I had to do the wolf. Couldn't nobody else find you. But I wouldn't never hurt you. I just ain't want you lost and scared out in them woods again." His fingers tugged mine. "Come on," he said. "Eat and you feel better."

"So the wolf was you. I'm supposed to believe that."

"Don't hold it against me. I can be real sweet."

I shivered a little, and the impossibility of his being a wolf was lost in the greater hint that sweetness might ever be an issue between this young man and me.

He nodded in the direction of the cold fireplace screened by dusty spider webs. "Us could be alone downstairs. You ain't have to see folks and explain nothing cause everybody sleep. But you rather have a fire here? I could fetch up them squirrels I done caught for our supper."

I had never eaten squirrel. But I was starving. And he was kind and mild.

"I'll eat with you," I said.

"That's better." I saw a flash in the dark that must have been the light of his smile. Then he was gone.

I was standing on the threshold, waiting for him, when he bounded back down the hallway.

He jumped when he saw me and pretended to be startled. He clutched the large bowl he was carrying to his chest. "Miss Solace. Now you scaring me."

I had to laugh.

We sat at the table by the window to eat his squirrels. Dimly, I could make out the sizzling shapes of five curled and crisp animals, stripped of their skins, skinny, and headless. He picked up the sticky carcasses one at a time and peeled off strings of flesh for us to share. "Ain't hunt so good today," he said. "I use you for a excuse and say I couldn't keep my mind on the hunt." More chuckles.

"Why not?"

"Told you. Afraid you done run off."

"Why should that bother anybody around here? Everyone seems so strange." I chewed and thought. "Everything seems so strange."

"How you figure that?"

"Nothing here is like my grandfather's stories. They were marvelous." I tried to look as if I were wiping grease from my mouth as I swiped at my sudden tears.

His voice was tender. "Tell me some them stories, little girl."

I poured out my heart's treasure chest of grandfather's memories. Sweet women, the seasons, the songs drifting in from the field, and the lure of the wide woods beyond. I ended by singing the lullaby.

"You do tell it like you done lived it," he said.

"I've lived nothing else."

I had forgotten the tears. He reached over without a word of excuse or apology and wiped them for me. "It all still here," he said. "Just changed a little, maybe."

"You talk like you know my heart. And here I am going on about myself to a hungry stranger in the middle of the night. I don't even know your name."

"Boy."

"Boy? But that's not your name, is it?"

"Ain't never been call nothing else."

We licked our fingers, and I asked him to tell me his stories about me and the plantation.

He said he couldn't think of what to say. And everything I asked brought me the answer, "Miss Solace, I can't tell you about that."

I finally accused him of not wanting to tell me anything.

He rubbed his fingers up and down his dark trousers and stared out through the window. "Then don't ask me no more. Sides, day be breaking soon. I best go so you me both can get some shuteye."

I reached for his hand. "No, don't go."

He returned the squeeze. "Now what you on about, ma'am?"

340

"Don't call me ma'am. Or I'll have to start calling you Mr. Boy."

"I might could get to like the sound a that. Why don't you try it out?"

I laughed.

The laugh died. "Mr. Boy, please don't leave me alone in this dreadful room."

"I don't want to go, Miss Solace. But I be one dead hand in the fields tomorrow if I don't get some sleep tonight."

"But you can sleep here. Don't look like that. I never slept alone in my life before last night. I was either in the attic with the other maids or in a pretty little room near grandfather's, with a ma'ammy holding me. You've made everything so much better. Please don't go."

"Miss Solace, don't beg."

"Don't call me Miss. Be my friend, Boy. I don't have anybody anymore."

"Look Miss-I mean Solace-sound to me like you just scared. It ain't nothing to be scared about. No, hold on. Course I stay." His hand on mine was gentle. "Maybe in the morning, though, you should ask Mother Magdalen to let you sleep in her room."

He held onto my fingers before I could pull them away. "Anyhow, ain't nobody looking for me till daybreak. I done had a shack to myself for few years now. Only, I gots to be out a here by sunup, Miss Solace. You wake up alone, you know I had to get to them fields before folks come a looking and asking questions."

"I'll help you wake up, Boy." Still holding hands, we found our way to the vast dark bed.

I lay in my itchy red dress and felt the strongest embrace of my life. How could he sleep and still hold me so tightly?

The sweat that had dried on his cool skin had a clean scent. There was the smell of fur.

"Were you *really* a wolf, Boy?" I asked as I fell asleep. He breathed softly and didn't answer. It must have been a trick of some kind. Something I misunderstood. *I'll ask him in the morning*, I thought.

But I didn't.

In the morning, I woke to women's screaming.

The sound shot me straight up in the broad dusty bed. Sunlight streaked between the parted drapes. It was full day.

Boy leaped to the window and flung himself at its sash. He shoved at it until it scraped up the frame. As his arms rose above his head, his body seemed to darken and drop to the floor.

I ran to him. But he was no longer there. The black and gold wolf paced along the wall and snatched up Boy's abandoned trousers in its jaws.

It circled behind me and crouched to leap through the open window. I cried out and ducked as it hurtled above my head.

It landed on the open ledge and scrabbled with its hind paws, shredding dry rosy wallpaper. Then it hurled itself from the window toward the grass below.

I leaned over the ledge to watch it fall. It seemed to swim through the air, twisting its spine and paddling with its rear legs.

It landed with a muffled thud and a high-pitched yelp. It dashed over the green mounds and through the dipping willows, tripping over the trousers that trailed from its mouth.

I turned toward the bedroom door. No time to think about what I had just seen. The screams seemed to be coming from inside the house. They rose and fell. Shouts interrupted them and died away. How many people were in this house?

I might hide in this room and wait to learn what was going on. But fear would grow as I waited, and I would suspect that secrets were kept from me.

I had to go down.

Finding my way was much easier than it had been the day before. Harsh sounds rushed around me and pulled me running down the unlit hallway and stairs.

I came through the doorway into Mother Magdalen's back room and froze before a strange scene.

A woman with sweeping ropes of dark golden hair raised an arm to cover her face as she ducked and dodged falling blows. Her other arm dangled, curled in upon itself, at her side. A silver wolf larger than Boy skulked and snarled before her feet. It snapped at the people who came near her.

Her attacker was another woman, dark in color and the most beautiful that I had ever seen, even in her frenzy. This second woman screamed, "You lied to me, Angel Girl! They don't burn live people? They don't cream-make nobody who ain't already dead? Then tell me why they put Boyfriend out a his pain with the fire instead of a gun. You tell me that! Pieces of him all over the ground, and the patrol can't but soak him in lamp oil and light a fire to him!"

She threw up her arms and bared her teeth in a shriek that raised the hair on my scalp. "No! NO! *NO!*" she cried out. Spittle and tears spattered her face. Something long and silver-colored caught firelight and glinted in her hand. One of the chopping knives. "I couldn't do nothing. They had me tied," she wailed.

The woman dropped to her knees and covered her face. Mother Magdalen made a grab for the knife. The woman looked up and held on. They struggled.

The woman grabbed at Mother Magdalen's head, to push her away. Mother Magdalen's turban got caught in her fingers and unwound. It slipped down over her face, uncovering two thick white plaits wrapped several times around her head.

The beautiful dark woman pulled away and got quickly to her feet. She faced the woman with the silver wolf and what must have been Whip Man.

He cowered between the three women. His hunched back brought his face to a level with the women's waists. His cloak had fallen away. He was hideous to see.

His face and head gleamed with raised scars. Tight rings of hair grew in clumps on his head between the wheals. One of his ears seemed nothing but a jagged gap.

He seemed to want to avoid head blows. His mouth twisted and collapsed upon itself as he shouted, "Stop, now," his arms upraised to fend off blows, jabs with the chopping knife, and attacks from the wolf.

Miss Rhea had snatched up Whip Man's fallen cloak and tried to toss it over the frantic wolf. She batted it at the animal's snapping snout hissing like a cat, "Down, Wolf Water! Where your manners at, you nasty thing? Back, you!"

Suddenly the heavy door nudged open and Boy threw himself into the fray.

He grabbed the wild-haired woman and shoved her out through the open door. He shooed her wolf out behind her with a shove of his foot on its flank. It snapped back at him as it sidestepped, trying to regain its balance and crouch.

Boy slammed the door on them and leaned against it to face the woman with the knife.

I came out of my shock and shouted, "No, Boy!" I threw myself between him and the chopping knife.

I felt his strong hands grab me from behind and fling me down to the planked floor. I slid a little and felt splinters glide into my soft palms. Stunned, I turned and looked back up over my shoulder.

The woman with the knife had come out of another screaming fit to lunge at Boy. I watched as her blade flew in an arc toward his head.

His hands seemed to come from nowhere and arrest the woman's wrists in midair. His dark knuckles bulged. His arms trembled. They stared into each other's eyes. "Back," he spat at Mother Magdalen, easing up behind the woman with the knife.

Whip Man had snatched his cloak from Miss Rhea and now threw it over the knife-wielder's head. Miss Rhea jumped forward with twine to tie the cloak at the woman's throat while Whip Man made a grab at her waist.

Whip Man and Boy brought her down to the planks and held her with one knee each. Boy leaned forward and bit into the hand that still clung to the knife.

The burlap rose and fell at the woman's face as she cursed and sobbed. Boy finally wrenched the knife from her bleeding hand. I heard his open-handed slaps strike the cloak and the face beneath it. He shouted, "Let go, Heaven! Leave her. What she done to you? Let her alone!"

Heaven? Wasn't that my mother's name?

Dazed, I put a hand to my head and crawled to a bench to sit beside Mother Magdalen. She was panting and trying to retie her turban. I lifted my splintered hands to help her, but they shook so that I couldn't.

"Enough!" Whip Man's muffled voice shouted. "She done passed out, Boy."

I heard sounds of movement but couldn't look back down at the unsettling scene on the floor. This violent new Boy frightened me, and I couldn't bear to look at Whip Man uncovered any more.

"What done brought this on?" Boy demanded. I could hear that he had stood and come closer to me.

Mother Magdalen had gotten her turban wound. Now she knotted the ragged ends. "You heard," she said. "Boyfriend got lynched and burned last night. Patrollers must have heard about Mr. Dennis being declared legally dead and thought they'd go have some fun. You know how they feel about freemen. Angel Girl must have come on the scene and cut Rose Red down from the tree, to bring her here to the-"

Mother Magdalen quickly looked at me, as though she had said something she should not have.

Boy barked my name. "Miss Solace."

I looked at him.

He said, "Seem some patrol owe you the cost a field hands who was your property now."

From somewhere in the room's firelit depths I heard Whip Man say, "Boy, don't get the gal in over her head soon's she show up round here. She ain't got no man going go to the law for her and fight. For all we know, she best lay low so that patrol don't come banging on the door talking about pay for the dogs them two wolves done killed."

"Two wolves?" I said.

Boy gave me a sharp look. Not a frown. But. Did his family not know that he could change his shape?

But Boy couldn't have been there. He had been with me.

Or had he? Where had he been before he came to my window?

In the woods, fighting patrollers and killing dogs.

Could a man think while he was a wolf? I felt a second wave of fear mix and flow through my strong warmth toward Boy.

Beyond Boy, I could see that Whip Man had come closer and was watching me.

Miss Rhea said, "Us all going stand around counting dogs and wolves, and Rose Red knocked out and bleeding on the floor? Boy, you ain't had no call to chew on her so. Now you two mens don't know what to do with yourself heft this poor woman and carry her up to Rose White old room. What you

347

think, Miss Magdalen? That room ain't so bad? Bed ain't going fall in, they puts her on it?"

Mother Magdalen rose on unsteady legs and asked the men to follow her. They lifted Rose Red's body and carried it between them.

Her face was still covered. Her arms dangled behind the men's hips and struck the doorway as they went through.

I was left alone with Miss Rhea. I turned to her, still dazed. "Did Boy call that woman by my mother's name? I thought my mother passed away when I was born."

Miss Rhea reached for me and buried her fingers in the mass of my hair. She started pulling tangles apart. I flinched and pulled away. "Gal, your head a wild mess. You want I fix it up for you?" Her voice was tender in the room's red darkness and startled me.

I said more gently than I intended, "No, ma'am. Thank you. Shouldn't we be out looking for that other woman? The one with the wolf? Maybe she's hurt."

Miss Rhea snorted. "You mean Angel Girl? Don't even talk to me." She came around behind me and tucked my head backward into her belly. Her middle cushioned my efforts to pull away from her finger-combing and plaiting. "That wild woman been taking care a herself long as I can recollect. I done had me enough a wolves and bloodshed for one day. Let her go on get out a here. Child, sit still. You knew how you look, you be begging me to get these naps out your head."

The men came back. Boy grinned suddenly at us and slapped his mother on her rear. He was evidently pleased at the sight of our getting along.

"You knucklehead, where my switch at?" Miss Rhea asked him gently, moving her hips out of his reach. "Get out a here and go ask Miss Magdalen she got anything go with that corn bread steady burning on the fire."

By the time everyone had dipped corn bread into buttermilk and sipped scalding coffee, chitchat was making its way around the table. I was surprised and pleased when I realized that people were going to dismiss my strange behaviors of the day before. No one even asked me where I had hidden myself, or why I had come back. I was grateful to them.

When the men went to the field, Miss Rhea amazed me by offering to help me clean as much of the house as we could in one day. "After today, I gots to get back to my own chores," she explained.

I spent the day doing the filthiest work I'd ever done in my life.

When I was alone, admiring my cleaned room that evening, Rose Red's cries tore down the hallway. I went to find her and comfort her as best I could.

But the patterns thrown onto the hall floor from the sunset's light through the stained glass caught my attention. Hadn't the stained glass had no pattern?

But on the floor at my feet now, I could clearly see the figure of a man.

I turned around to look at the stained glass window. It still looked like random shards of glass bursting through the wall. I looked back down at the floor. The window's light formed a man.

Or was he a beast?

His brown hands raised to claw the sky. He reached for the daggers of light that a blazing sun hurled earthward. He seemed to scream. He rose in his agony from a dark earth so mingled with his body that only his hands and face were clear.

The patterns on the floor shifted and blurred. Was that blood on the creature's claws? And what was the white stuff that floated just past his grasp? Cotton bolls?

I knelt to touch the lights on the floor. They looked so oddly real.

Rose Red's cries ripped through my reverie. I rose, tried to remember where I was and why. Of course. The hallway and Rose Red.

I went quickly through the darkness in search of her. I tapped at each door and called out, "Rose Red? It's Solace. May I come in?"

No one answered at any door. On my way back toward my room, I stopped before one of the many covered frames on the wall. Even through its black silk veil, I could tell that the frame was elaborate and well wrought. The veil stirred as I breathed.

Cobwebs draped it on all sides and grayed its sunken face. I reached to lift the veil and see whatever it covered.

"No, don't," Mother Magdalen said from behind me.

I jumped and turned to her. "Why not?" I could see her face only in shifting shadows and colors from the stained glass.

"Heaven, your mother, had all the mirrors in the house taken down. All but one. That one, I only covered when she died, as it had been hers. In time, of course, I put these others back. But they need to remain covered."

"Maybe it's time to uncover them, Mother Magdalen."

She frowned and shook her head. Rose Red's cry sounded again. Mother Magdalen said, "Oh, my!" and bumped past me down the hallway. She stopped at a nearby room, pulled a chain of keys from her apron pocket, and let herself into it.

I heard desperate weeping while the door was briefly open. Then it was shut and locked and all was silent.

That evening, there was a light stew served in clay bowls in Mother Magdalen's back room. Everyone but the woman with the wolf sat down to enjoy it.

Rose Red was changed. She was mild and sweet in her every word and gesture. I stared. I couldn't believe the difference in her. For her sake and mine, everyone talked of old times at the plantation.

No one remembered it as grandfather had. They spoke fondly of lost friends and family, but I heard too of daily weariness and resentment. It seemed a given that the bleak poverty of their present near-freedom was better.

Their loves sounded secret and deep. Their hopes seemed to have been fleeting, and their joys were seized with abandon and rage.

I asked myself, *How does one give back stolen lives? Hadn't grandfather and I spent hours*

351

relishing the memory of these people's enslavement?

I felt ashamed.

Maybe I could begin to give them their ownership of this house and these lands. For surely it was more fair that they own it than I. Maybe I could learn to protect them. What had Mother Magdalen said about patrollers' feelings toward freemen?

I said, "Is there a formal dining room in this mansion? Wouldn't it be pleasant to take supper all together in a real dining room? I was rarely allowed that at the townhouse."

Rose Red looked at Mother Magdalen. Whip Man's hood turned to face Miss Rhea. Boy stared at me.

I said, "And there are so many rooms in here. If you'll help me clean them, you can all move in." I smiled hopefully. "It must be better in here than in the shacks."

Mother Magdalen said, "Miss Solace, you sound like a child."

"I've never been as alone as I've been here," I insisted. "I'd rather have the house full of people than full of dust and spider webs."

Miss Rhea laughed. "Well, I'll help the child clean. I ain't never seen so pale a woman work so hard in my life as I seen her do today."

I returned to my room that night cheered and pleased with myself. My bedclothes had been stripped and scrubbed and were hanging outside. So were all of Heaven's red wool dresses and yellowed lace underclothes, pulled from the moths and bats in her wardrobe and chests of drawers. So I could not change clothes again that night but would have to sleep in the same prickly dress.

I stretched on my bare stuffed mattress, folded my arms around my face, and gave myself up to an exhausted sleep. I woke to the sound of tapping at my window.

I sat up and wiped my face. Wet. Puffy. Had I been crying in my sleep? I pushed myself off the sagging mattress and went to the window. Dirt sprayed the glass.

My heart beat fast.

Boy was down below in the grass. He gestured, *Come here.*

I went down the hallway toward the stairs. I paused at Rose Red's door and heard weeping inside.

I went on to Mother Magdalen's back room. The heavy back door was bolted shut. I had trouble lifting the bolt. But as soon as I did, Boy pushed it open from his side. He slipped inside and shoved it shut with his back to it.

Boy said, "Miss Magdalen surprised me and locked the door. I ain't knew if you needed me tonight or not."

I threw my arms around his neck. He drew me closer yet and held me.

We sat up that night on the big bare bed stripped of its canopy. The pointed posts made shadow-throwing spires. Boy told me people's secrets.

That grandfather had wed and lost Angel Girl, and that she was Heaven's mother, and my own grandmother. That Rose Red was my aunt whom grandfather had wooed and lost, as well.

The secrets I had longed and dreaded to be told threatened my world. These emotions broke every rule I'd been taught about civilized behavior. Could these stories be true? Boy told them as simply as he'd told me how to roast squirrels.

I had not known the world I was living in. How does one own one's beloved? How does one hurt one's owned beloved so that she runs away?

My ignorance of grandfather's real past at the plantation gave way to pity and contempt.

I watched Boy sleep. He was all in the world that I could say I now loved. Loved? I would have been proud to say so. I, raised a misfit, had found someone to hold dear.

Yet, didn't I own Boy? Did people who owned other people actually love them?

Our peculiar institution, as grandfather called it, was truly strange. It gave people to others in a closeness that brought out the most vulnerable feelings, ruled less by conscience than by secrets and deceit. If anything Boy had told me was true.

I came up close against Boy and wondered if grandfather wandered the wide heavens and saw that I had become just like him. I, too, had trapped my slave into loving me.

Dared I learn, too, what grandfather had really done to Whip Man? What more must I look at in myself, if I learned that? I put my arms around Boy's lean muscles and smooth skin and slept.

Life at the plantation fell into a pattern that filled the emotional emptiness of my childhood.

My days were spent scrubbing, cleaning, sweeping down cobwebs and running from bats dislodged from the rafters by my broom. My screams were nothing but happy laughter. Miss Rhea helped me clean and helped Mother Magdalen garden, cook, and care for the bedridden Aunt Rose Red.

The cooking was just simple garden stews, wild meats, and healing herbs, to be served with baked corn bread or pan-sizzled corn pone. The smokehouse's store of hams and sausages was depleted years before.

My nights were spent rocked in the warm arms of a storyteller who built my existence for me from scratch, in tales of daring and despair. Like grandfather, Boy told me at length of lives past that I had never known. But his people were of flesh, blood, and dreams of their own, as unlike grandfather's lovely portraits as it was possible to be.

I reveled in Boy's tales and never realized until morning that he had still answered none of my questions.

"But Boy, did I see a skeleton out back in the quarters that first night? If it wasn't a skeleton, what was it?"

"You know, your own great-grandma'ammy, Mammy Water, used to dance and prophesy for the people. I ain't never seen her my own self cause she was old and gone when I was still crawling my ma'am shack butt naked. But I heard how she would get up from her deep sleep and come outside the shack. Folks be gathered round a fire, they eyes all bugged out, they questions on they tongue, cause you know they thought she could fix they lives better."

"And did she, Boy?"

"Sure enough, babygirl. Why, I remember my ma'am told me about this woman." And I would settle into the glorious world of my unknown great-grand and wake to the hurried kisses of parting.

One night, I was determined. "Boy, the skeleton. Nothing but the skeleton. Now. Tell me." I folded my arms across my chest. That should show him.

We had grown so familiar that I now slept in the yellowed cotton and lace underthings that had been Heaven's. My arms and ankles were bare. I knew Boy loved to touch and stroke them.

But now he looked concerned. He reached for me. He gently pulled my arms apart.

And he tickled me without mercy.

I screamed. I fought him off with slaps and squeals.

He pursued. I rolled off the bed and landed on the thin carpet with a loud hollow thump.

Boy's face above me, peering over the edge, said, "Sshh!"

I slapped a hand over my mouth to stifle the giggles. He reached over the edge with one hand to help pull me back up onto the bed.

When we had collapsed together, holding each other and declaring a truce, all questions but one had flown from my mind. "Why can't we just tell your parents and Mother Magdalen that we want to be married?" I asked.

He lifted my face from his stomach so he could look at me.

"Is it Whip Man?" I asked. "I've figured out what happened to Whip Man. My grandfather thought he was with Heaven like grandfather was with Miss Angel Girl, right? Like I want to be with you."

"Yes," Boy said.

"You and your parents think that maybe you and I are related."

"Brother and sister. That's what my ma'am think. My pap say no."

"And you, Boy? What do you think?"

"I tend to believe my pap, Solace. You think I be here if I thought for sure-" He let his voice trail away. He lay down and didn't look at me any more. I thought I saw his eyes moisten. This wasn't what I had intended.

"Well, weren't Aunt Rose White and Uncle Sami Wolf Water some kind of cousins or aunt and nephew through Sami the African?" I argued. "You and I can be like them."

It was a long while before Boy said, "You born free, Solace. You ain't got to carry on like you got some master studding you with your own kin."

"What are you saying, Boy?" I sat up. I slipped one hand under his cheek and tried to turn his face toward me.

Ever tender, Boy looked at me and gave me all his pain.

"I'm not stuck with you, Boy. Nobody chose you for me." I tried a little laugh. "You and I have the opposite problem. Everyone wants to keep us apart."

Everyone, for me, meant grandfather. I could only imagine his horror if he had imagined that Heaven's daughter would someday love and beg to marry Whip Man's son.

"You love me, Solace?"

357

I nodded yes.

Boy didn't say anything. He sat up and leaned in toward me with his soft brown lips slightly open. Below his moist mouth, I could see his long fingers reach for the ribbon that tied my cotton underdress.

"I love you," he said with his mouth to mine.

My heart flew up toward the light touch of his fingertips. Was this how we would stop being brother and sister? Had we ever been brother and sister?

A loud banging on the bedroom door.

Boy and I threw our arms around each other and stared at the moving latch. Someone worked it up and down. Someone banged again. A woman called softly, "Solace? I heard noises."

I pushed away Boy's hands and scrambled from the bed to the door. "No," I heard Boy whisper behind me.

But suddenly I was afraid to be alone with him and glad of the intrusion. I yanked at the latch. The door swung open.

Aunt Rose Red stood in the hallway. Light from the stained glass danced all over her sleep-softened face.

"We missed you tonight at dinner, Aunt Rose Red. How are you feeling?"

"Child, sometimes my spirit get the worst of me." She gave me a sideways glance and a smile and invited herself into my room. "Solace, I ever tell you that you the spit and image of Heaven? Heaven died when you was born."

Aunt Rose Red's eyes on my face got really dreamy. "Everything changed for all us. I thought me and Boyfriend was going to be more happier

358

than everybody, running wild through the woods forever." Her fingers trembled at her shivering lips. "But he dead now. Hung from a tree. Pieces-" A sob shook her. "Solace, pieces was cut off him. Worst places you could think of. And burning."

I put my arms around her.

"Burning," she said again, clutching my shoulders so that her fingers hurt me. After a while she pulled back a little to look at me. "Solace, he screamed till he died. Looked like he wasn't nothing but charcoal, and it was still screaming. At me. Telling me run. Till you couldn't tell the words no more. But I knew what he meant."

She put her hands to her eyes. Her shudders grew larger and wilder. I pulled down her hands and forced her slanted black eyes to see mine. She said, "We ain't had no kids that lived, for me to remember him by."

I had wanted to offer myself to Miss Rhea for the children she couldn't have with Whip Man. Now I wanted to offer myself to Aunt Rose Red. "You can come tell me about Uncle Boyfriend any time. I love old stories, Aunt Rose Red. Like how you didn't know how to be a field hand. What was that you told me? Uncle Boyfriend used to go to the woods and catch you fish? Or did he gather your kindling?"

Aunt Rose Red laughed and shoved at me like women used to in the townhouse kitchen. "Go on, girl," she said. "Kindling. No, both. Everything, really. Anything."

This relief wouldn't last long if we didn't settle into it. I pulled Aunt Rose Red gently to the table under the window, and we sat. A black and gold wolf crawled from under my bed to settle at my bare feet. I reached down and patted its head.

"Come here, boy," Aunt Rose Red said and patted him, too. I caught my breath. Did she know this was Boy? Did everyone at the plantation know that Boy was a wolf?

Rose Red said, "Solace, you *look* like Heaven, but you *do* like Angel Girl. That must be why I like you so much."

I thought, *Aunt Rose Red thinks I love wolves, like my grandmother, Angel Girl. But actually I love a man who doesn't have the freedom to refuse me, just like my mother. Heaven.*

The thought was bitter.

The night wore away as Aunt Rose Red told me about her life. My feelings about these women at the plantation were my vengeance against step-grandmother. With them, I colored my dingy past and spilled it forward into a passionate future. I would be like them someday.

The moon had set by the time Aunt Rose Red's stories ended for the night. She had just finished asking if I'd like to go with her to visit the little graves of her stillborn babies that dotted the forest where she and Boyfriend used to wander. Then the mild flicker of colorless light at the bottom of my lace curtains was splashed with the dramatic wash of dawn.

Boy leaped to his paws. He cast me a frantic look and dashed to the bedroom door.

"Got to let him out," I called over my shoulder to Aunt Rose Red and followed Boy down the dark stairway.

The paintings and mirrors in the hall had been uncovered and the walls cleaned. Enough light filtered in to see by. I never stumbled anymore.

I flew happily down the long curving stair, leaving the stained glass like scattered flower petals and the oil paintings of pale ancestors behind me. Boy's black fur bristled in the gray light.

I had to struggle with the heavy bolt at Mother Magdalen's back door. "You could get up and help me, Boy," I scolded.

He whined. The bolt slid. I scraped the temple of my forehead across the door, skidding behind the moving bolt.

Good-byes were hard enough for me every dawn without having to wrestle with the back door. I'd really have to make Boy sit down and listen to me on this point.

I shoved the door open. It spread wide a view of the gardens and shacks and the lightening field with its clumps of hardy weeds.

Oh no. What was that?

Over by one of the shacks, the rundown one. What had I just seen, flickering and moving? A low fire?

I stepped from the back door's threshold to look more closely.

Boy circled my legs and brushed them with his hard body, as if trying to push me back into the house. "Stop it," I said and shoved at his side.

When I looked up, the silver wolf was leaping toward me.

The wild-haired woman, Grandmother Angel Girl, was running behind it. Her slender body sprinted up the path from the weather-beaten shack

361

with the rag door and blocked my view of the fire over there.

"Wolf Water! No, now! Get back here," Grandmother Angel Girl called.

The wolf stopped and crouched just ahead of me and Boy. It growled and rippled its lips. Its nose crinkled in upon itself.

Boy backed up, growling, too.

The silver wolf made a fake lunge at Boy. Grandmother Angel Girl grabbed its hackles in her good hand.

She looked up at me. "Sonya-no-Sophie? No. Solace? You are Solace, aren't you? Heaven's baby? I'm your grandmother, child."

Her lean face was smooth and tightly covered by honeyed skin. The wild hair held only hints of weeping willow gray. She didn't seem old enough to be my grandmother. She smiled.

"Yes, I'm Solace." I saw Boy rush away from behind me. I wondered for a moment what he would do for trousers, having left his only pair under my bed. "Where have you been, Miss Angel Girl? I hoped you would come back after the fight."

"I didn't go far."

"Please come in." Would Aunt Rose Red go crazy again at the sight of Angel Girl?

But Rose Red had not waited up for me. Day was breaking, and as always, she had gone to lock herself in her own room. I dressed and gazed at my emptied room and wondered what it was I didn't understand about her. Then I smiled to think how narrowly Boy had protected our secret when I panicked the night before. I went back downstairs quietly, listening for Aunt Rose Red but hearing nothing from her room.

In the back room, Mother Magdalen was hugging Angel Girl while a kettle steamed on the fire. Wolf Water huddled under a bench and dozed.

Mother Magdalen jumped and cried out, "Solace, look! It's your grandmother, Angel Girl, come to see you!"

"We met already," Grandmother Angel Girl said.

"Met already? You mean, during that awful fight?"

Angel Girl laughed. "No. This morning."

Was she going to tell that I'd been letting a wolf out by the back door at dawn? But Boy and I weren't ready to face everyone with our love. I looked at Angel Girl with pleading in my eyes.

Her smile never faltered. She said, "Solace must have heard Wolf Water yapping outside. She came down to open the door."

Mother Magdalen said, "I've been bolting the door at night. I guess I should have thought that maybe you'd come back and not be able to get in, honey."

Grandmother Angel Girl hugged her. "I'm in now, Mother Magdalen. Let's have that good coffee and corn pone. And I don't want any of your dry corn bread today. Give me greasy pan-fried pone."

Mother Magdalen relaxed with a happy laugh.

Angel Girl never lost her secretive smile. She sipped her coffee and said, "Good. I miss this when I'm gone." She reached down to pat the sleeping wolf. "But I wouldn't miss my times with you for all the other pleasures in the world," she said to the top of its head. Then she looked straight at me. "Loving a wolf is special. But it might be hard for other people to understand how a lonely young woman and a lonely young wolf come to feel about each other."

Mother Magdalen said, "What crazy backwoods talk is this for a city-bred child to listen to, Angel? Besides, you have not been young for a very long time. Neither has your wolf."

Grandmother Angel Girl laughed.

There was pounding on the door. Whip Man and Miss Rhea came in and shared greetings and hugs with Angel Girl. I went for more mugs and coffee. I couldn't bear to see anyone pull Whip Man, even in his burlap cloak, into a hug. It looked like hugging death. Besides, I hated him for possibly being my father and keeping me from marrying his son.

At that time, Boy's being a wolf had not struck me as a reason we might not fully enjoy our love. *Can Grandmother Angel Girl and I talk about this some time?* I wondered. Was she hinting to me that she knew Boy the wolf and Boy the man were one and the same being? I sat at the table and moped.

I woke with my head in a platter of corn pone. "Go on upstairs and get some sleep, Solace," Mother Magdalen said as she tugged me to my feet.

"Must a been up all night chit-chatting with Rose Red," I heard Miss Rhea whisper as I left. I dragged to my room and flopped on my bed. Sleep. Sweet, sweet sleep.

Tap tap. Tap tap tap.

I raised my head and turned to look at the window.

Dirt and rocks.

I went and looked down. There stood Boy, a pair of Mother Magdalen's bloomers stolen from the laundry line and wrapped around his hips.

I shoved open the window. I covered my loud laughter with a fluttering hand.

"My trousers," he whispered fiercely. He frowned to show that this was not funny.

I pulled the trousers out from their hiding place and threw them down to Boy with many waved kisses. But nothing could make up for the laughter. He snatched them from a crumpled heap on the ground, turned his back to me as he slipped into them, and dashed off to hang Mother Magdalen's linens without another glance at me.

I crawled back across my bed thinking that we'd have to clean and ransack my grandfather's room soon, so Boy could have trousers to stash all around the plantation.

Grandmother Angel Girl stayed. She and her wolf took a room downstairs that had been hers long ago.

Aunt Rose Red took me down there to visit with her that first night and said, "I wish that widow hadn't a took away that magic mirror before Solace could look into it."

Grandmother Angel Girl and Aunt Rose Red were at peace again. They told me they were sisters of a kind and explained it was through Mammy Water.

Boy and I talked it over throughout half of one solid night. But we couldn't figure a way that their being sisters could make any difference to us.

We got sleepy and grouchy and had our worst argument ever. I told Boy that if he really thought he was my brother, he'd better get off of my bed. He left and sat at the table by the window. I demanded to know why Boy had lied and said he believed Whip Man when he said he wasn't my father.

Boy said it didn't matter what he and Whip Man believed. What mattered was what we could get everyone else to agree to believe because we all needed to trust each other and work together at the plantation.

"Solace, what would happen if we were married and your grandfather came back all of a sudden? You still ain't even figured out what your grandfather did to my pap after Miss Heaven had you. What would he come back here and do to my folks, if he thought they let you marry me?"

I hadn't thought of it like that. Boy and his parents, Mother Magdalen and Aunt Rose Red, even I all still belonged to Grandfather, like cattle, if he was alive.

That was the first time I ever felt horror at the idea that my grandfather might be alive somewhere and might come back.

I shouted, "Grandfather is dead and can't come back!" Then I felt sickened, as if my words were a wish that killed him once and for all.

I'd betrayed the only love of my childhood. For Boy. Look what loving Boy had made me do.

I thought about telling Boy that I hated him and didn't want to marry him anymore, anyway. But I couldn't do it.

So I fell asleep sobbing alone in the middle of the bed.

The next night I stayed even later in Grandmother Angel Girl's room. I listened to her and Aunt Rose Red talk about where Rose Red's babies all might be buried.

Did everybody around here have to look like and talk about death all the time? Whip Man and buried babies. It was enough to make you give up on living.

When I felt worn out, I said good night to my aunt and my grandmother and dragged myself upstairs to go to bed.

I didn't want to go. Now that Boy and his parents had moved in, he could have sneaked to my room anytime. And somehow, it was more miserable to think he was in the house and *wouldn't* come to me than that he was out of the house and *couldn't* come to me.

It wasn't until the door was closed and locked that I felt I wasn't alone.

I slipped from my dress, fumbling with the buttons and trying not to think, for soon I would know, and having hoped might make the hurt worse.

I got under the covers and slid across the bed, which seemed to have widened while I was out of the room. Finally, I felt gathered warmth in the mattress under me and touched soft skin ahead of me.

Boy turned, woke, and reached for me.

We didn't say anything. By morning, we would never wonder again whether we had ever been brother and sister.

367

Long after dawn colored my lace curtains, I lay in bed shivering from the emotions our passionate discovery of each other had given birth to in me.

I couldn't bear to let Boy out of the room. I couldn't bear to think of sitting through one more breakfast while Boy strolled out and grabbed a hoe for his day's work in the cotton field. I couldn't bear not to hold him close.

I wept and clung to him. Boy said he'd stay.

Mother Magdalen was the first to come see why I hadn't come down to breakfast. She tapped on the door.

Boy slipped under the bed as I rushed to the window and opened it to air out the room. I worried how my underdress might look from behind, but there was neither time to take it off nor a mirror in which to check it.

So I quietly unlatched the door and leaped back into bed before I called, "It's unlocked, Mother Magdalen."

She came in and flipped back my bedclothes. I gasped and clutched at them.

"Just as I thought," she said. "Blood everywhere. Your monthly. Well, as a rule, I do not hold with young girls carrying on about this kind of thing. But you have been working hard. You are probably just worn out. I will bring you a good cup of raspberry tea. Not as soothing as spearmint, but for some women, it is good for monthlies and pregnancies, too. It is even good for some nursing mothers. We will see if it works for you."

As soon as Mother Magdalen left, I leaned over the edge of the bed and called under it to Boy. "Did you hear what she said, Boy? Pregnancies. She

368

knows about us. What do you think will happen now? Do you think we can get married? Maybe we're married already, if everybody knows about us and accepts it."

The wolf's eyes shone in the dark under the bed. He snuffled. Dust shot from before his nostrils in little clumps. Of course, he said nothing. He couldn't say anything.

I hated it when Boy did the wolf just when I needed him to talk to me.

That day, I found out that everyone I knew at the plantation loved me.

Everyone but Rose Red came by, at least for a few minutes, to see how I was doing and to bring me something. Even Whip Man came and brought me wild eggs to choose from, so he could cook me a couple and help me get stronger.

I had to look away from the dark space in his hood while he talked. "Miss Rhea would do anything for eggs, at a time like this. But you gots to be careful they cook just right, really hard. Or a woman get more sick just trying to eat them."

He said he knew how to cook eggs right for an ailing woman, and his strange muffled voice sounded proud.

I searched into the darkness of Whip Man's hood to see what he meant by "a time like this." I couldn't see anything. Not even the light of his eyes.

Miss Rhea came by while I ate the first egg. It tasted great, as Whip Man had promised. Woodsy and tangy. Sweet and mellow. You'd never have guessed it was cooked by a man who looked like a walking corpse.

"He do take a pleasure in his eggs," Miss Rhea said as I ate. Miss Rhea hadn't brought me anything. She asked what I needed.

"May I have a loaf of corn bread to nibble on throughout the day?" I could throw pieces of it under the bed for Boy, along with the second egg.

And then I asked Miss Rhea for a mirror for my room.

I told her where to find the one Mother Magdalen had once stopped me from uncovering. Miss Rhea came struggling in with it and propped it on a chest of drawers. It was indeed elaborately wrought and beautiful to see, taken from the darkness of the hallway. Miss Rhea said, "If I could find Boy, I'd ask him to fix a strong nail in the wall to hold it up. You know where he done got off to today?"

I was flattered that she would ask me. "I think he wanted to go to the woods and fish last night. Maybe he overslept out there, it's so dark under those trees."

"You scared a the woods, gal. What would you know?" But I could tell by her tone that she believed me and thought her son was shirking his work. "Lollygagging," she muttered as she left. "Wait till I tell him Miss Solace was sick and had need of him. Then he going feel like the big knucklehead he be sometimes." That made me pleased with myself, for having covered for Boy so well.

Until Boy crawled out from under the bed and rose beside me, his fur smoothing and slipping into shiny skin. "Why you say that to my ma'am?" he demanded.

370

I handed him the corn bread wrapped in a tattered clean rag and the little wooden plate with one egg left on it. "So now you're a man, after I've been dog-sitting all morning. You know this wasn't how I meant for you to stay with me. Now, why did I say what?"

"I ain't no dog, and you know it," he snapped at me. "Why you say I been fishing, a all the fool tales you could a told? Now I gots to hightail it to the woods and catch me some stinking fish for my ma'am. And if you ain't satisfied I been here a wolf, how you going feel when I ain't here at all?"

My pride sank to embarrassment. "Well, I didn't think of it that way." My embarrassment turned to anger. I turned my back to him. "I'm not afraid to be alone any more. If you have to go, go ahead."

My anger ran to regret. I waited, forgetting to breathe until I felt Boy touch the back of my shoulder. It was scary waiting for him to make up when I didn't know how to.

"You knows me good, Solace. I always did love to sneak off fishing. I just can't stand to be gone far from you is all, babygirl."

So we had to lock the door again and give ourselves up to the joy of finding that we still loved and were loved, hoping everyone would assume I was asleep and leave us in peace.

When I woke, Boy and most of the corn bread were gone. The egg had been left in its little plate on my table. I knew what Boy would say. It was meant to help me feel better, so only I should eat it.

We had deep-fried fish in the formal dining room that evening. The lace tablecloth ripped as we passed plates over it. Mother Magdalen looked embarrassed. We all told her the pretty place to eat made us feel special.

Grandmother Angel Girl and Aunt Rose Red sat up with me in my room late into the night.

They chatted at the table by the lace-curtained window. The silver wolf lay at Angel Girl's feet and rubbed his nose with one paw or flicked his heavy tail. He kept glancing up at me with something that looked like resentment. "Does your wolf need to be let out?" I asked Grandmother Angel Girl.

"Does yours?" she said to me.

Boy stopped by in the doorway and leaned against the doorframe. "Solace got a wolf?" He put one hand on the hip of his ragged dark trousers.

"You ought to know," said Aunt Rose Red.

Boy looked like he'd decided to ignore her. "So, Miss Solace, how was them fish I caught for you all?"

"Really good. Thank you, Boy."

"I hear you was doing poorly today," he went on.

"And I heard people calling me Rose Red, but I ain't run in here acting like it was news to me." You know who said that.

I scooted further under the covers and pretended I was falling asleep. Maybe the women would leave. I was definitely no longer enjoying their company.

But Boy didn't know when to quit. "So how you ladies doing, Miss Angel Girl, Miss Rose Red?"

Grandmother Angel Girl said, "Well, Boy, some of us work all day, so I guess we're tired. But you wouldn't know about that these days, would you? I mean, some people would call your kind of work pleasure. Though I'm sure it leaves you tired enough."

Aunt Rose Red snorted with laughter.

Boy seemed to be getting irritable. "You ain't going tell me now, ma'am, that Miss Rose Red done took to working during the day? I was right sure that spirit a hers got other plans."

"Boy." That was me. And I didn't even know what he was talking about. Nor did I really want to find out.

Spirit, cloak, dancing skeleton. Too many ugly mysteries, frightening secrets, threatened the love I was trying to enjoy.

Grandmother Angel Girl's silver wolf raised its head and growled at Boy.

I couldn't take it any longer. "Boy," I said, "thank you for stopping by. Good night. Everybody, I'm sleepy. Night, all." The covers flew over my head and shut out the candle and starlight. I peeked out in Boy's direction, to see if he was leaving.

"Oh, well, right, good night," he said. He pushed himself off the doorframe. "Good night, Miss Rose Red, Miss Angel Girl."

Aunt Rose Red said, "You suppose to name the old woman first, if you got any manners left. That's her," pointing at Grandmother Angel Girl.

"Good night, Miss Angel Girl, Miss Rose Red."

Grandmother Angel Girl said, "You forgot to say good night to Wolf Water."

"Good night, Wolf Water."

Aunt Rose Red said, "You forgot to say good night to Miss Heaven."

I flipped down the covers and looked at her. "Miss Big Ears ain't sleep after all," she said.

"Madam Big Ears," Grandmother Angel Girl said.

Boy grinned at me. "They just funning now."

Aunt Rose Red said, "No. We been through funning long time ago. Now we getting dead serious, Boy."

Boy said to me, "You want me to stay, Solace?"

"Excuse me?" Grandmother Angel Girl said. "We don't even bother to say Miss Solace before company anymore, Boy? Have we forgotten ourselves?"

"I gave him permission," I said feebly.

Aunt Rose Red said, "And who gave *you* permission to give *him* permission? You ain't know everybody life depend on you round here, little snot-nose gal? Patrol knock at the door, you going have Boy slip his arm round your waist, say, 'What you all gun-toting, torch-burning, nice wight gentlemens want with my nigger woman ain't no more free than I is, today?'"

"Go easy on her," Grandmother Angel Girl said.

"I just done went easy on her," Aunt Rose Red said. "Now I'm fixing to light into some Boy over there."

"Don't blame him. I made him-I mean-I made him fall in love with me," I blubbered.

Aunt Rose Red said, "Skip it. Heaven done already used up that lie on Whip Man. Rest a us ain't never figured out how a grown man can heft a plow but can't push a skinny little gal off of him."

"Aunt Rose Red-"

"Solace, I wasn't talking to you no more, noway. Less you want some more a my tongue I was saving aside for Boy, I suggest you butt out."

"Boy, I'm sorry," I said.

"What for?" Grandmother Angel Girl said. "Love is a good thing in an ugly world."

"Tell me about it," Aunt Rose Red said.

"But people in our situation have to think about consequences," Angel Girl went on. "Solace, can you really be loyal to Boy for life? He can't help being loyal to you. You own him. He has no choices. Do you really want to take advantage of his helplessness? And what about loyalty in the face of secrecy? What if no one must ever suspect that you're an African woman in love with an enslaved man? Love in those circumstances is painful."

I sat up and shouted, "How would you know? You dare come in here shaking your finger at me about love! You've never loved any man, Miss Angel Girl! The man you had, you hated and left. That was my grandfather, a kind man! Who are you to tell me who to love and how?"

Aunt Rose Red said, "So much for going easy on her. You want I should smack her upside her head now?"

I screamed, "And you, Aunt Rose Red! Talk about doing people some good with your love. After Grandmother Angel Girl left my grandfather, he turned to you, and what consequences were you thinking of when you left him, too? Look at this place!. Abandoned and decayed, because *you* left *him* and so *he* left *it*. What kind of good could you have done if you had stayed? Point your fingers at yourself and answer me that, Aunt Rose Red!"

Grandmother Angel Girl said, "Dennis turned to you, Rose Red? You poor frightened thing. Why didn't you ever tell me?"

Boy said, "Solace, you don't understand-"

"-Nothing," Aunt Rose Red finished for him. "Gal got a head full a Mr. Dennis and high horse."

Boy said, "I been in the wrong, you all. She been asking, but I ain't been telling. Let me talk to Miss Solace tomorrow. She come around. I swear it. She come to understand. *Please*, you all. Please give me another chance to talk to her."

Silence. "Please, Miss Angel Girl. Miss Rose Red."

The women turned to each other and rose as if by silent agreement. They left with the silver wolf, gesturing and arguing in hushed voices all the way.

Boy gave me a look full of sorrow and worry as he left behind them.

I left my door open, in case he decided to come back.

"Solace. Solace, wake up."

Grandmother Angel Girl leaned over me. Aunt Rose Red came over to the other side of the bed and sat down where she could reach and take my hand.

"Yes?" My voice was faint.

The women looked at each other. "You go head tell her," Aunt Rose Red said.

Flecks of gold, honey, and candlelight shone in the pupils framed by Angel Girl's long auburn lashes. "Solace, this place is different from other places. Death lives here. But death leads to a kind of life. A different kind of life. You have to know what you're choosing, when you choose to be a part of the life here."

Aunt Rose Red leaned her face in close to mine, blocking out Grandmother Angel Girl's. "You scaring the child and ain't made no sense, yet," she chided. "If I had to hear it from you, I wouldn't have idea the first what you talking about."

"Hush, Rose Red."

"You hush! Look at her. You got her all pop-eye and open-mouth. What good you going do folks gibbering like a dimwit?"

"Well, you tell it, then! I swear."

"I would a swear too, I talk so empty-head like you just done!"

"Well, we've got a responsibility, Rose Red! I don't know where to start, but we can't leave these children stumbling in the dark."

Stumbling in the dark. That was my whole life in a few words.

I started crying. I couldn't help it. Both women hugged me. All they said after that was that everything would be all right, and I was not to worry.

It occurred to me that these were the people who would probably be willing to tell me all about that skeleton and anything else I might ask. But I couldn't bear to ask. I had to admit that I really didn't want to know. After all that I had said and done, I really only wanted to be happy.

Rose Red and Angel Girl sang me the special lullaby as I fell asleep. Their voices blended and ran into my memories of the girl I had been in the townhouse attic, waiting for my grandfather to come back and hold me as Boy could now hold me.

I woke to full sunshine and washed and dressed slowly. I watched my naked body in the new mirror as I washed it. Did I look different?

I felt different. Grown. Loved and frightened, all at once. Claimed by Boy's love.

I hoped I was saved by it, too, from every shadowy fear that had ever pursued me. I dressed and wondered if Boy liked the dark red dresses I had from my mother, Heaven. I wondered if I liked them.

When I went down to breakfast, Mother Magdalen and Miss Rhea went up to strip my bed and wash my bloody sheets. I worried all day that they would be able to tell the blood was not menstrual but virginal. I worried all day about what Boy had promised my aunt and grandmother that he was going to tell me. I wondered how to stop him.

I didn't have to stop him. That night, men came with torches, and everything changed.

Grandmother Angel Girl and I were working late, cleaning the parlor. The other women were cooking supper, except for Aunt Rose Red, who always stayed in her room way past sundown. The men were just coming in from the field.

Angel Girl and I heard horses' hooves first. Then shouts. Deep angry shouts that wanted violence.

"They came," Grandmother Angel Girl said. Her wolf rose from a corner of the parlor and came to her.

Fists pounded the front door. The flicker of torches threw light through the grimy parlor windows.

Angel Girl said, "The patrollers. Probably coming to demand a reward for catching Boyfriend. Or payment for the dogs that we killed."

We? I glanced at Wolf Water. His ears pressed back. His lips quivered in a soundless snarl. "Get him to come with me to the door, Miss Angel Girl," I said.

I opened the door.

Firelight flared all around. The men moved their torches closer to my face.

Their faces had bloodshot eyes and were pale in the firelight, and twisted. Their bodies stank heavily. "Who you?" one of them demanded. "We seen lights."

"I, sir, am the owner of this property and of the people working it!" I shouted. *Softly,* I told myself. I said more calmly, "Who are you gentlemen, and what are you doing on my private property?"

"Your property, ma'am? Ain't this place abandoned?"

"In a manner of speaking. But now I've inherited it and moved in with my niggers. You must be here to see me. All right. Here I am. But I don't take kindly to being accosted by strange men on my own property in the middle of the night. So why are you here, and what do you want?"

Somebody swore and said, "What them? Some kinda dog?"

I looked down. Two silver wolves brushed by my legs, heading for the patrollers. Their eyes glowed in the patrollers' torchlight.

The man in front shouted, "Them's the critters killed our dogs!"

379

I shouted, "So, you're the men who killed my nigger!"

We shouted together, "You owe me for my losses!" We stopped shouting and sized each other up.

The lead man grinned. I waited.

He said, "Ma'am, you got the wrong patrol. We ain't lynched no lone nigger. We lynched us a pair. Man and a woman. You ain't lost a man and a woman both, then the patrol you looking for ain't us."

The wolves stalked toward the horses, hunkered down.

"I think you'd better get out of here," I said.

The lead man raised his rifle to aim at one of the wolves. "No!" I yelled. I reached for the muzzle of his rifle.

A third wolf knocked me over. I looked up from the verandah floor to see Boy's black and gold fur shining in torchlight as he grappled with the fallen lead man.

"Hey!" The man shrieked. "Somebody shoot this thing," he called out between his shrill cries.

I crawled between the fallen man and his mob, covering Boy with my body. "Let go of him, Boy," I pleaded.

The men bolted. One of them leaped off the verandah, dropping his torch onto the dusty drive, and swung onto a horse's back.

The other two wolves attacked. Blood and foam swirled in the rising dust.

Dogs yelped and flipped into the dust to lie still. Horses nickered and reared. Pistols and rifles fired, and horses shied below their riders, frightened by the sound.

I wanted to call the wolves off. But I feared them.

One clamped its fangs on a horse's throbbing neck vein. The rearing animal rolled its bloodshot eyes and whinnied in terror and pain. The horse's rider tried to take aim with his pistol at the wolf.

The wolf's fangs dug into the horse's broken hide. Its hind legs dangled as the horse pawed the air.

"Oh no," I said.

Boy had abandoned the lead man. He bounded away with the other silver wolf, giving chase to escaping patrollers.

"Help me!" the lead man bellowed next to me.

I turned to him. His legs and face were pulpy gore. I realized he couldn't see to crawl away. I couldn't look at him as I touched him. I whimpered as I dragged him to the edge of the verandah. "Somebody, take this man on your horse!" I cried out.

"My gun," he said.

I found his fallen rifle and pressed it into his hands. "Get out of here, you fool," I said. "You can't see to shoot anything. Someone come get this blind man!"

Several shots rang out. The wolf that had latched onto a horse's neck fell, twitching, in the dust. The horse sank on its knees beside its killer. The rider leaped off as the horse rolled to its side and its eyes slid up toward a sky where the sun had set but the moon had not risen.

"Boy! Wolf!" I shouted. I clapped my hands and slapped my legs. How do you call wolves out of a blood frenzy?

The man who had shot a wolf off his horse came over to the verandah and slung the bloodied lead man across his shoulders.

"Call them off," he spat at me.

"Get off my property," I spat back. But I was sick at heart.

I'd just learned that even Boy as a wolf was nothing but a wolf. I couldn't call him back. I couldn't make him do anything.

Boy and the unwounded silver wolf soon galloped back down the mansion's front drive. They ran past the lone patroller who struggled to carry away his blinded leader.

The man stumbled backwards as the wolves shot past him. Then he righted himself, hefted his screaming friend more securely, and kept trudging.

Boy came to me on the verandah and licked my hands and face. I stared at him in a daze. Flecks of blood dotted his coat and snout. Did I know this creature?

Had I loved it? Made love to it?

How could I have?

He whined and nudged my neck. Then he trotted into the house. The silver wolf circled back to its fallen companion. It nosed the other and whined.

I left the bloodied verandah to kneel in the dirt and run my hands along the wounded wolf's fur.

Was this someone I knew?

What were the people I had come to know and love? Witches? Demons? I didn't know enough about such things.

The wolf opened its eyes and whimpered as I explored it for wounds. I finally found that it had been shot in its foreleg, probably above the heart. I looked up toward the house. Would no one come to help me?

"We'll get her," Boy said, coming down the verandah steps. Whip Man hunched and rolled in his grotesque walk behind Boy.

"You get inside, Solace, and let Mother Magdalen take care a you. You was real brave," Boy said and put his hand on my arm.

I stared hard at Boy in the gloaming. I snatched my arm away from his touch.

"Boy, help me," Whip Man said.

His head was down as he attended to the wounded wolf. It whined and jerked as they searched for safe handholds on it. Boy kept looking up at me.

I backed into the house and into the open arms of Miss Rhea. "Poor girl," she said.

I pushed her away from me. She watched me warily. "Solace, now," she said.

I put my hands out against Miss Rhea. "Stay away from me." My voice shook.

"Solace?" The new voice came from behind me. It was Mother Magdalen. I swept her into my horrified gaze.

She looked at Miss Rhea. "What's wrong with her?"

"Scared, I guess," Miss Rhea said.

Whip Man and Boy wedged themselves through the door with the limp wolf between them.

"No!" Mother Magdalen wailed. "Not my child! Not again!"

Miss Rhea said to me, "Go get rags, gal. Go get water and rags to tend to Miss Angel Girl."

Angel Girl? My newly claimed grandmother? A wolf, not a woman?

My grandfather had loved her. The thought filled me with revulsion.

"I'll do it myself!" Miss Rhea snapped and pushed past me out of the room.

I stared at the little group crowding around the wolf on a low divan. "Go get a blanket to cover her," Mother Magdalen said to Boy. "She's changing back. Hurry."

He ran past me, pausing only a second to touch my cheek and look into my face. I glanced at Boy. Then I looked back to the hanging hind legs that shifted and slimmed and became long reclining calves and thighs with Grandmother Angel Girl's honey-colored skin. I heard her moan.

Whip Man turned his hood toward me.

I backed out of the parlor. I turned and ran up the stairway. I had to get away. I had to think.

What creatures had I been begging to share my life with me? What were these monsters all around?

What pits of loneliness had driven me to love them?

I felt my way down the hall toward my room.

I searched for the stained glass to guide me. I looked up at its scattered colors.

Scattered? Why had I ever thought the patterns in the stained glass were either of a man picking cotton or even just random nonsense? Look.

That was not dark earth at the bottom of the glass's picture. It was a lapping fire swallowing whole bodies.

Those were not cotton bolls that floated in the bright sky. Those were skulls snatched down into the greedy flames.

Nor was that a man picking cotton. It was a burning beast of burden, clawing at the elusive fresh air above his field in flames. Only the bright placid sun remained the same as I had seen it before. I backed away.

"Solace?" The voice was gentle and close behind my ear. I jerked my head around. Aunt Rose Red smiled tenderly at me. "You all right, Solace?" Her smile disappeared. "What done got into you? You done had a bad scare?" Her voice got deeper. "Something happen downstairs? I thought I heard yelling and hollering."

Some strange light seemed to me to flicker just in the dark depths of her tilted eyes. Her beauty suddenly looked quite bestial to me.

Why did she stay locked in her room every day, long after she had recovered from the lynching wounds that had brought her back here? What did the patroller mean when he said his men had killed a man and a woman?

"Aunt Rose Red," I said low so she wouldn't hear my voice tremble, "Did you die with your husband, Boyfriend?"

She looked only a little taken aback. Then she smiled again. "Boy told you, didn't he? I guess he figured me and Angel Girl wasn't the only ones could run around telling other people's secrets. Well, I got it under control. You know, the coming back. I stay up all night, wear myself out, and then the spirit that take me can't do nothing but sleep all day." She chuckled.

Then she lowered her voice. "Almost all day," she said. "I been thinking. Seeing as how it is your own ma'am, after all, maybe you come in with Angel Girl and Mother Magdalen and try to reason with her. Get her to let go, leave me alone. I ain't afraid to die."

I backed away. "I don't know what you mean about my mother. But why were you so angry with Angel Girl? When it happened."

She looked puzzled. "She thought was Mammy Water she was taking me to. Of course, it wasn't. The dancing skeleton was Heaven in Mammy Water's body. All us knew that but Angel Girl. Besides, I ain't wanted to live on without Boyfriend, anyway."

"Why didn't Angel Girl save Boyfriend, too?"

"I done told you, he was burned to ashes. Look at Whip Man. Who want to live his life the walking dead? What you all a sudden asking all these questions for?"

I was almost at my door. "Why are you always talking about finding your dead babies in the woods?"

"I guess I must be like any woman lost the man she love. I want one our babies to keep, Solace," she said.

I threw myself through my doorway and pounded the lock shut before I started screaming into the solid wood of the door. Whenever I paused for more breath, I could hear Rose Red call, "Solace! Solace, now."

What had become of my life? I had been a blind and love-starved orphan, wandering willingly into an open grave just because arms reached out from it to hold me.

Get out! Could I get out? How? Where would I go?

I envied grandfather his being dead. Death. That's what this place was. Death that lived.

What had Angel Girl and Rose Red been telling me that night? Something about death and living.

I crawled fully dressed onto my bed and pressed my face into armfuls of pillows. I thought how peaceful it might be to suffocate in the pillows and have nothing to figure out in the morning.

The morning. Morning after morning, I must wake up and face these creatures.

Tap tap. Tap tap tap.

Dirt and rocks pattered against my window. Habit and slow-dying hope drew me toward the familiar sound.

I didn't open the sash. But I looked down through the worn lace.

Boy stood below, staring up at me.

I saw his mouth move. *Solace,* he was saying. His hand gestured, *Come here.*

I drew from the window and pressed my back against the wall next to it. I stared at the door. Soon, wouldn't Boy be knocking there?

What had he done my first night alone here? Hadn't he come in? He must not come in tonight.

Was the door securely locked? I went to check.

I put my hand on the latch and held it in place. I was going to miss unlatching this door for Boy.

How could I? How could I have put aside what I had seen that he was? How could I have held him to my heart?

I had built my fragile new life on loving Boy. He had made everything else all right. How could I have walked willingly into this despair?

The latch moved against my hand. "Go away, Boy."

"Solace, let me in."

"No."

"Why you doing this?"

I said nothing.

He said, "I thought you and me was in love, Solace."

"Don't remind me. It makes me sick to think I loved whatever you are. What are you, Boy? An animal? A walking dead thing, like your father? And Rose Red? Who else around here is dead and walking and talking, Boy?"

Silence. Then, "I ain't neither a animal nor dead. I ain't but a man who love you, Solace."

"I haven't seen that you're a man."

"I can't help what you ain't seen. Don't mean it ain't more to me, just cause you ain't seen it." His voice wavered. Then, more firmly, "Solace. Don't do this to me. Not after what us been to one another. I love you."

I savored the sound of his words. I had heard them almost every day since my arrival at the plantation. And yet, I had not heard them enough.

I was greedy for them.

Boy said, "I thought you love me, too."

"I don't even know what you are. How could I love you?"

"I told you, I ain't but a man. Try to understand."

"Why should I try to understand what disgusts me?" I put my fists to my mouth. I scared myself. "You scare me," I said.

The latch moved. I grabbed it again. "Go away, Boy."

"You need me, babygirl. I can't go away."

I screamed. I searched for words. They poured out of me. "I don't need you! Monster! Beast! Dead thing! Wild animal!"

"Don't. Don't, Solace. Us in love."

"Love?" White panic shot through me. Had I really loved such an abomination? Something that chewed a man's eyes in its mouth? Held it to me and fed it my soul? I had, hadn't I? Then what did that make me?

The words I'd wished I could have said two nights before finally found their way out of my mouth. "I hate you, Boy!"

"No."

"Yes!"

"You don't mean it, Solace. You don't even know what you saying."

"*Mean* it? I *am* it, Boy! I am nothing but the hatred I have for you and your godforsaken people! Get away from my door! What am I doing? Talking to a thing that doesn't even exist!" *There.*

I could hear him crying now. But he still didn't leave. I would have to block the door, if I could.

I ran to the far side of my dresser and laid both hands on it. I leaned my weight into it and tried to

389

push it toward the door. It wouldn't budge. The mirror perched on it rocked a little and was still. What else could I move?

I ran to my bed and grabbed one of its posters. I leaned back on it, trying to walk it toward the door. My arms ached at the shoulder. Nothing else happened.

I could still hear Boy's sobs. I couldn't bear them.

I knelt in the center of my bed with pillows pulled over my head down around my ears. I mashed my face into the mattress's softness. It rose around my nostrils and mouth and swallowed my cries.

My mind gathered all the pictures of the life I'd lived at this place and everyone's words and threw them at me.

What had I done? What had I been?

What to do? Where to go? How to get out of this place that couldn't be truly real?

Legs and arms changing to furred limbs. A woman raising tiny skeletons from their forest graves. Opening my door to a man who was a wild thing. And all under the hidden gaze of a staring creature in a dark hood.

I woke. I'd been dreaming. I must have cried myself to sleep. Just like a child.

I wished I were a child again. No. I wished I'd never been born.

Now, how could I get out of this deathtrap?

I lay down on my side and lifted one end of the pillow from my head. I could hear nothing.

I looked at my window. Starlight brightened it.

I rose and found the edges of the heavy drapes and pulled them shut. The room returned to the darkness of my first morning there.

I felt my way back to the bed. I had scrubbed and cleaned all day, and my body ached. I was hungry. And so thirsty.

Thirsty.

What could I remember about that?

Vaguely, as if from a world that never was, came to me a picture of Mr. Tim, the carriage driver, at the townhouse. He was at the kitchen door complaining to his wife, the cook. Their boy had forgotten to water the horses. They were weak and slathering. "Don't he know living things die in days without they get no water?" Mr. Tim had said.

Days. Just days, and every problem I ever had would end.

I sighed and placed my head more comfortably on my pillows.

At last. I could resist the urge to open the door to Boy's warm arms just for a few days. I could resist throwing myself at any cost back into the circle of companionship the creatures in this house offered me.

Days, and my loneliness would be over. Once and for all. Forever.

I drifted back to a restless sleep.

I seemed to drift in and out of vivid pictures and sharp emotions for a long time. I seemed to cry, whether sleeping or awake. I seemed to always be reaching out for someone's hand to help me. To pull me up, away, to safety.

There was no safety.

I would wake and pull my hands back in against my curled body. Had any time passed yet?

I woke to find that my mouth had swollen. My tongue melted into the roof of my mouth and pressed against the sides of my teeth. It hurt to move it. Breathing hurt my throat.

I swallowed over and over again, though nothing went down. I rose from the bed thinking of where I could find water.

I stumbled to my chest of drawers and splashed water from my china pitcher into its washbasin. Water.

I couldn't quite see it. But I could hear its gurgle and smell its wetness.

I cupped my hands into the tepid liquid and raised it to my face.

No. I splashed the water on my face and let it run into the china bowl.

How could I have forgotten? Why couldn't I have forgotten for just a little longer?

I was so thirsty. Were these people really monsters?

I scooped more water from the basin and brought it to my face again. It hovered under my chin.

Again I splashed it on my skin and let it run away.

No. I would not torture myself. My only hope was in dying. I could never figure out, by myself, what I had come upon in this place of impossibilities. I could never go back to the only world I'd ever known. I had nowhere to go.

Dying is a sure thing, a safe thing to do, I thought.

I put the basin on the floor and emptied the pitcher into it. There was all the water.

I stripped off my dress and underdress and stood in the basin on the floor. I stooped and washed my whole body with the water.

There. Now it was fouled. I could never drink it now.

I dried myself with the dress and pulled my underclothes back on. Then I thought, *Maybe I should wear the dress.* The wool was itchy and hot. It would make me sweat and lose my body's water.

I pulled on the hated itchy red wool dress.

I lay down again on the bed. I couldn't sleep. I felt refreshed. What if my body had absorbed the water I'd bathed in, through my skin?

I went to the window and opened it. I began to spit down onto the grass below. If I'd taken in water, I'd just get rid of it.

Why hadn't I thought of all this before? Why hadn't I begged step-grandmother's driver to do as he'd been told, and kill me? Why had I wanted to survive?

Because I knew so little about anything, that was why.

How strange to have graves beside one's house. And weren't there more of those odd mounds by the side of Mother Magdalen's vegetable garden?

Whose were they? Did the bodies in those graves rest?

I spit into the grass some more. *I should pour my dirtied water out, to make sure I won't drink it later,* I thought.

"Hey, watch out!" Boy smiled up at me, his face tense and hopeful in the gray light.

Was it dawn? Evening?

I slammed the window.

"Solace," I heard through the glass. I drew the drapes the color of old blood over the creamy lace curtains.

Darkness buried the room again.

I got into bed under all the covers so that I might perspire the life fluid out of myself a little faster.

I was roused by the sound of something slamming my door. Voices called.

"Solace? That's enough, girl." Mother Magdalen.

I heard a body hurtle itself against my solid door. I went back into a hazy sleep I couldn't seem to resist.

It was so good to sleep. It softened the suffocating feeling of my tongue swelling to fill my mouth and block my lungs.

Slam. Slam. Slam.

"No use, Boy," I heard Whip Man say. "That door ain't never going give."

Miss Rhea's voice woke me. "Let her die, she want to. After, us just tote her round back to the death dancer, like Angel Girl done with Rose Red. That bring her right round." Voices rose in agreement and argument.

"No," I said.

How could I have overlooked it? Even in death, I wouldn't be safe from these creatures, these life-taking, life-giving freaks.

I crawled from the bed.

What had saved Boyfriend from being brought back?

My hazy mind struggled with vague dreadful pictures of a body hung at the neck from a tree, burning.

Fire.

If a body wasn't livable, maybe it couldn't be forced to live.

Anything to escape.

I was too dizzy to walk. I crawled across the floor to the fireplace. Once there, I pulled myself to my feet and felt around the mantel. Where was the flint? Did I have any kindling?

It took a lot of fumbling and striking and puffing my scant breath to get a fire going. I almost fell forward and shoved my hand into the new flames. I pulled back in terror.

How foolish of me. Soon I'd throw my whole body into that large inviting fireplace.

I fed the little flames some splintered wood from the pile Boy left on the hearth. I hugged myself. Boy had always taken good care of me. Here was everything I needed for a good fire.

"Solace?" someone said gently at the door. "What's that I hear in there?" It sounded like Mother Magdalen. "Fire? Why do you need to build a fire in this heat, child?"

I rocked and stared into the growing fire and wondered why I couldn't have been born to people who would love me. Why did I have to come searching in this place of death for love? For belonging?

Loneliness.

A lifetime of loneliness, to finally be answered by a dead man. Or a beast man. Whatever Boy was.

If he was a beast, and not a living dead thing, like Rose Red, then maybe he wasn't so bad. Maybe loving him was still a part of life, a good thing.

There I went again. I should have known my hunger for Boy's love was stronger even than my resolution to die. *I'd better hurry this up.*

A body slammed my door. Again. Harder.

"Boy, don't." Was that Miss Rhea? "You going hurt yourself bad, now. If that gal want to die, let her. What she to you?"

My empty stomach squeezed with emotion. Would Boy tell her now? How much we had loved each other?

My love for him had been the truest and deepest feeling of my life. I would rather have had it and burned to escape it than never have had it.

And was he still too ashamed to admit to it?

I held my hand out over the fire. It singed the hairs on my hand. They smelled sickeningly after they burned.

I withdrew it. This would be difficult. How could I overcome the deep stinging pain and the fear enough to leap into the fire? And once in, how could I make myself stay?

The body slammed the door again. I thought I heard something crack.

I must do something. But what?

Sweat burst out on my forehead. It trickled from my armpits.

The body slammed the door again.

My dress would easily burn. And with all the buttons tightly buttoned, I could never get out of it in time to save myself.

I backed up from the fireplace and slowly pulled myself to my feet against the bedposts. At this distance from that stabbing heat, I could swallow down my fear of running into the fireplace.

I turned my back to the mirror on the chest of drawers so that I might check each button, from my hipline to my collar.

I swayed on my feet. I was so dizzy and weak. How long had I gone without water?

Maybe it took more than a few days to die of thirst. Or maybe time passed more slowly when one was waiting to die.

Lights burst from the fireplace. *No, don't faint,* I told myself. *Not yet. A few minutes more. Then you can faint in the fire.*

I pictured my body among the bricks, wrapped in flames. My face bunched in as if I would cry, but I had no water left for tears.

The room ran together before my eyes, as if it were melting. Lights like stars shimmered in the mirror on the dresser. I turned to look at it.

Thump went something on the door. The yelling voices faded.

I pushed myself from the bedpost and swayed in a circle, forward, side, back, side. Toward the fireplace and away.

Just throw yourself, I thought. *Stand. Brace yourself.*

Go! I leaned toward the fire.

"Solace."

I looked all around. Had someone broken in? Sneaked in?

Whose voice was it? A voice like starlight. Sharp and fine and very faint.

It sounded like all the comfort in a lonely world. Death must be like that voice. Death, final and forever, might be calling me with that voice.

Hands coated in silver like a million shining stars reached from the mirror toward me.

Hands. Arms followed the hands. Shimmering. Shivering with flickering firelight and a glow lit inside.

Was I seeing things? *Time to go. Now!*

I pushed myself from the post and crashed into the bricks behind the fire.

I was blinded by pain. I heard the hungry roar of the flames as they caught my wool dress. Then I could only hear myself scream.

Pain!

My eyes, my mind, my racing heart were consumed in roaring pain.

And now that I knew I didn't want to go this way, wanted to return to life and hope, I could only shriek.

Something pulled me from the fireplace.

I landed in the dankness of my room.

Through my closed eyes, I could see light that hovered over me and descended around me. I heard the heavy rush of air all around me as of beating wings.

The raging heat raced through my blood and sizzled as if smothered by ice. I pictured burning streams carrying chunks of breaking ice through my body. I felt snow fall and flow through my veins. My screams died to whimpers.

I clung to the cool being who held me.

Softness brushed my face again and again. The rhythmic brushing of cool wings calmed me. The starlit voice said, "Solace, you're safe. I have you now."

I opened my eyes. My vision cleared.

I lay on the carpeted floor of my bedroom, held in the arms of a shining winged woman.

It was her wings that brushed my face and stirred the cooling streams in me. Her radiance lit the room around us.

I opened my swollen mouth and tried to say, "I must be dead. You're an angel."

"Hush. Are the dead less a part of life than the living? How mistaken, Solace, to think so. Did you die in the forest, as your grandfather's widow wished you to? Were you brought here and revived, as had been Whip Man before you, and Rose Red after you? Before you answer in your heart that this is not so, ask yourself if you can ever really know."

Though her words brought dull shock, the angel's smile was bliss to see.

I stared into the depths of her unearthly calm.

"I love you, alive or dead. Won't you pass that love along? To comfort. To soothe. To encourage. This is all the meaning of life, Solace. To choose to die is to render life meaningless, when it *was not*."

She began singing my special lullaby. I lifted my arms to hold her.

Something cracked the door, and it fell forward onto the floor at the shimmering angel's feet. Boy fell on top of it.

Mother Magdalen stood behind him and flung her hands to her face. "Angel!" She rushed toward the being that held me but fell over Boy's crawling body. They reached us together.

I braced myself for the pain of having my burned body seized by Boy's frantic hands. But there was no pain.

Boy didn't say anything. He slid his arms around me where the angel's were not and tried to hold me to him, too. The smell of my singed dress and hair made him wrinkle his nose as he cried and clung.

I looked over his head. Beyond, in the hallway, huddled Whip Man and Miss Rhea. Angel Girl stared in at us, her shriveled arm wrapped in a long rag tightly tied to her chest. Large splotches of red bloomed on it, spreading. Rose Red stood near her and tried to hug Angel Girl on her good side. The silver wolf paced and whined.

They murmured things to each other that I couldn't make out over the lilt of the angel's lullaby.

Mother Magdalen moved aside the angel's wings to embrace her shining body. "My child, my child! You came back to me. I waited. I kept this place for you, and you came back!"

Miss Rhea began to weep.

After a while, Mother Magdalen's voice joined the angel's in the lullaby.

I listened drowsily and wondered if I was the only one who would ever notice what had become of the stained glass's pattern, shining past the people in the hallway, at their feet.

That wasn't a glaring sun above the burning beast. It was the brilliant halo of a radiant angel. And the burning beast looked up to it with tears on his face. I thought they must be tears of awe and joy.